"Imaginative, dyn[...] [...]arker

"Vampiric, post-punk, metal-fanged, dark-doomed romance at its best." — *Locus*

"Has style, energy, and black humor to spare."
— *The New York Review of Science Fiction*

Praise for the Novels of Golgotham

Left Hand Magic

"*Left Hand Magic* is rather like a Harry Potter book with some PG-13 sex thrown in. Along with the eye of newt and tongue of bat, there's plenty of action and some romance tossed into the recipe, along with a generous dash of humor.... Collins spins a workmanlike yarn, but the real attraction here is all the background detail and atmospherics wafting like a fog around Golgotham." —StarNews Online

"Nancy Collins builds skillfully upon the themes she established in *Right Hand Magic*.... Fans of the 'urban' in urban fantasy will love this new novel." —SFRevu

"*Left Hand Magic* was my most anticipated book of 2011. I became totally addicted with the first in the series and was blown away by Ms. Collins's fantastical subrealm of New York and its very multilayered inhabitants. The Golgotham series is urban fantasy on a whole new level of extraordinary. I literally feel like I'm a part of the story because it's so vividly created and narrated. The tension that grew throughout the pages of *Left Hand Magic* kept me on the edge of my seat and biting my nails.... I cannot wait for more Golgotham tales soon (hint, hint, Ms. Collins)."
— Manic Readers

"A great sequel to *Right Hand Magic*, revisiting the fantastical neighborhood with its remarkable denizens."
— Night Owl Reviews

continued ...

Also by Nancy A. Collins

The Novels of Golgotham
Right Hand Magic
Left Hand Magic

NANCY A. COLLINS

Magic and Loss

A Novel of
GOLGOTHAM

A ROC BOOK

ROC
Published by the Penguin Group
Penguin Group (USA) LLC, 375 Hudson Street,
New York, New York 10014

USA | Canada | UK | Ireland | Australia | New Zealand | India | South Africa | China
penguin.com
A Penguin Random House Company

First published by Roc, an imprint of New American Library,
a division of Penguin Group (USA) LLC

First Printing, November 2013

 REGISTERED TRADEMARK — MARCA REGISTRADA

ISBN 978-0-451-46492-7

Printed in the United States of America
10   9   8   7   6   5   4   3   2   1

For Judy Coppage, Golgotham's Fairy Godmother

As you pass through the fire
your right hand waving
there are things you have to throw out
That caustic dread inside your head
will never help you out
—"Magic and Loss," Lou Reed

Chapter 1

I awoke, as usual, to the sound of the alarm clock, the smell of bacon, and the sight of a winged hairless cat curled up beside me. I yawned and stretched as I swung my feet out of bed, glancing at the darkness outside my window. Still yawning, I made my way to the shower. Fifteen minutes later, I returned to find the previously mentioned butt-naked bat-winged feline sprawled full-length across the bed like a bolster.

"You don't waste any time, do you?" I chided the familiar as I put on my work clothes.

"You lose, I snooze," Scratch replied, eyes still shut.

As I headed downstairs, the aroma of breakfast grew stronger. I entered the kitchen and saw Hexe, my landlord and lover—and, oh yeah, heir to the Kymeran throne—standing in front of the antique stove, dressed in nothing but a pair of flannel pajama bottoms and an apron that said KISS THE COOK. He was frantically shaking a couple of cast-iron skillets, while our Boston terrier, Beanie, sat planted at his feet, intently watching every move, just in case an errant molecule of food might find its way to the floor.

I obeyed the apron and planted a big old sloppy smooch on my six-fingered cook. I glanced down at the stove top and saw that one pan contained yummy, yummy bacon and scrambled eggs, while the other held a grayish slice of what could charitably be described as pâté frying in a half-inch of grease.

"What's that?" I asked, cautiously eyeing the slab of mystery meat. One of the first things I had learned upon moving to Golgotham was that Kymerans had a far more, *ahem*, adventuresome palate than that of the average human, and exhibited a fondness for foods that would make even the most daring gastronome think twice. I took it as a testament of Hexe's love for me that he was willing to make a traditional "human" breakfast every morning and send me off to work with a neatly packed lunch pail that didn't contain such Kymeran staples as lutefisk sandwiches and white fungus soda.

"It's scrapple," he explained cheerfully, tossing a lock of purple hair out of his eyes with a practiced toss of his head. "It's made from hog offal—the heart, snouts, liver, that kind of stuff—mixed with cornmeal and seasonings. Want some? It's really good with maple syrup, ketchup, and horseradish."

"That's okay, honey," I replied, pushing aside the flutter in my stomach. "Some other time, perhaps. I think I'll stick to my usual this morning."

"You got it!" Hexe grinned as he snatched the other skillet off the burner and slid its contents onto a waiting plate. "Your coffee's already on the table."

"You really spoil me," I said with a laugh as I sat down. "None of my other boyfriends ever made breakfast for me, much less every day."

"That's because your other boyfriends sucked," he replied as he flipped over the square of scrapple.

"True, that," I agreed as I nibbled on my bacon—crisp as always, just the way I like it.

"Besides, it's only right that I make your breakfast and fix your lunch. After all, *you're* the one bringing home the steady paycheck."

"You lift curses and concoct potions for your clients," I pointed out.

"Yes, but I'm self-employed. I never know what I might make on any given day. You're the one putting in ten hours a day, six days a week, to support us."

"Speaking of which, I better get going," I said, washing down my last bite of scrambled eggs with a slug of French roast and chicory. "If I'm not punched in by seven, Canterbury will be champing at his bit."

"What time do you think you'll be home?" Hexe asked as he handed me my lunch pail.

"Hard to say," I replied with a sigh. "The deadline for that installation we've been working on is coming up fast, and we're nowhere near finished yet. What about you? Do you have any clients lined up for today?"

"Just some salves and ointments, that's all. Oh, that reminds me—here's that liniment Canterbury asked me to mix up for him," he said, handing me a bottle wrapped in twine and butcher paper. "Tell him to keep it below the waist, if he knows what's good for him."

As I stepped out onto the front stoop Hexe gave me my usual off-to-work kiss, a public display of affection guaranteed to scandalize the Blue Hairs, and I don't just mean old Madam Yaya, who lived across the street. The traditional Aristocrat class of Kymeran society, the same ones who were far from pleased by the fact Hexe's biological father was a member of the Servitor class, had made no secret that they disapproved of their Heir Apparent taking up with a—gasp!—human, even one with magical powers.

The dawn's first blush was lightening the morning sky as I made my way through Golgotham's winding cobblestone streets, passing shopkeepers cranking out the awnings above their stores in anticipation of another day of business. I shook my head, thinking about how many times I had witnessed such early-morning rituals while staggering home to bed after a night on the town. A year ago if anyone had told me that I would find myself romanced by a Kymeran warlock prince, disowned by my parents, and working a blue-collar job to pay the bills, I'd have laughed in his face. But here I am, knee-deep in love and gainfully employed—all for the very first time.

When I came to this ancient, exotic part of the city, all I was looking for was cheap rent and someplace where I could bang away on my metal sculptures without my neighbors trying to evict me. And, to be honest, I also sought out Golgotham because I knew my douche bag of an ex would be too chickenshit to follow me. At the time, I was on the verge of making a real name for myself, with an established gallery opening in my pocket....

But there's no point in dwelling on that. What's done is done, and I wouldn't change what happened, even if it were within my power to do so. My dreams of breaking onto the New York art scene might be delayed, but for the first time in my life I truly felt like I was where I belonged—although there are those who would argue that point.

There is no denying that my decision to move to Golgotham had repercussions. Many consider me responsible for establishing a beachhead for the recent influx of human artists and hipsters who have made the neighborhood the newest hot spot in the city. But then, Golgotham has changed me, as well—as evidenced by my recently acquired ability to bring the things I build to life. I don't know whether my relocating to Golgotham awakened a latent power within me, but there's no denying that I've got magic now. Who's to say where it came from? For all I know I caught it from a toilet seat.

My daily walk to work was just long enough to qualify as exercise, and helped me clear my mind and organize my thoughts for the day ahead. However, as I strolled past the local newsstand, I made the mistake of glancing at the headline of that morning's *Golgotham Gazette*: MACHEN ARMS SOLD TO CHECKMATE PROPERTIES.

Great. Just freaking wonderful. Things had finally calmed down after the race riots and the Sons of Adam panic, and now *this*. Golgothamites were worried enough about gentrification without Ronald Chess, the most rapacious real estate developer in the Triboroughs, snapping up an apartment building. This was exactly the kind of thing Hexe's race-baiting uncle, with his Kymeran Unification Party separatist group, used to whip up fear and resentment against humans.

The KUP had fallen idle since Esau's mysterious disappearance several months ago, which also coincided with the Sons of Adam's suddenly going to ground. It wasn't really *that* big a coinkydink that Esau and the SOA happened to fall off the face of the earth at the exact same time, since the necromancer was actually the one controlling the human supremacists from behind the scenes, having gone so far as to create them via alchemy. The last I saw of dear old Uncle Esau, he was being dragged to hell—or at least the Infernal Regions—by the very same demon he had summoned forth to kill me. And while the hateful old bastard was no longer around to stir up trouble, that didn't mean there still wasn't plenty of it to go around.

I sighed and tried to push my worries aside. Canterbury and I had a lot of work ahead of us, and fretting about something I had no control over or say in wasn't going to help us meet our deadline. Canterbury had been paid half the commission up front, and promised the rest upon delivery. Needless to say, the financial well-being of Canterbury Customs hinged on finishing the installation on time.

I would have to say that outside of falling in love and acquiring magical powers, joining the workforce has been the biggest change to my life since moving to Golgotham. After I refused to give up Hexe and move back in with my parents, I found myself cut off from my trust fund. No doubt my parents hoped I would wither up like a worm on a hot sidewalk. However, all it did was make me even more determined to stay put.

For the first time in my life I was living without a safety net, just like most Americans my age. Luckily I had a skilled trade to fall back on—in my case, welding and metalworking. I was also lucky that Hexe's childhood friend Kidron was willing to put in a good word for me at Chiron Livery.

I'm not going to lie—banging out horseshoes on an anvil is hard, dirty work. After my first week, my arms were so sore I could barely lift them over my head and my left thumb was the size and color of a plum. But, instead of quitting, I took my first pay voucher and settled that month's grocery bill. After six weeks, I was arm wrestling my coworkers on the line and no longer hitting my thumb on a regular basis. As much.

However, I will admit to being bored with the assembly line nature of the work and bummed there was no outlet for creative expression. But what bothered me the most was that by the time I got home, I was normally too tired to focus on my art.

Then, two months into my job as a blacksmith, I was approached by Canterbury and offered a job as a striker—essentially working as his apprentice. I jumped at the opportunity, as he was not only a well-regarded Master Smith but also a terromancer.

One of the biggest misconceptions humans have when it comes to magic is that it's like water from a tap, with the only difference being whether it's hot or cold. The truth is, there are as many different variants of magic as there are specialties in medicine. For example, weather witches summon storms; pyromancers control fire; necromancers work dark magic using the bodies of the dead; and ferromancers shape and control metal.

While centaurs normally are without magic, Canterbury was quite literally a horse of different color, courtesy of a Kymeran father. While he could be a bit of a taskmaster at times, we got along very well together and I had become quite fond of him. In many ways he reminded me of my old art instructor at Wellesley, Professor Stobaugh, who had been the first to suggest I focus on metalwork rather than on the more traditional clay and stone.

Unlike the other businesses along Horsecart Street, Canterbury Customs did not have a proper storefront. Instead, it was located in Fetlock Mews, a dead-end alleyway situated between Perdition Street and Shoemaker Lane. The mews was lined with two-story stables that served as both places of business and homes for various centaurian farriers, wainwrights, and saddlers. Although Chiron Livery churned out most of the horseshoes used by the centaur and ipotane communities, there was still plenty of commercial business for those who catered to Golgotham's carriage trade.

As I walked onto the shop floor, I saw my boss and mentor inspecting the armature for the wings of the clockwork dragon that took up half the workspace. The scale-model saurian was scattered about—a head here, a leg there, another leg somewhere else—like a classic car undergoing restoration. But in this case we were trying to rebuild a model that had not been seen on the road—or the skies—for over a thousand years.

Canterbury wore a leather blacksmith's apron over his upper torso, as well as safety goggles, and kept his chartreuse mane short and tail bobbed for fear of flying sparks from his forge. Although he had the power to shape metal without the use of tools, he also utilized traditional fabrication methods as well, in order to conserve energy. After all, magic can be exhausting work, even for someone with the constitution of a horse.

"Morning, boss. Here's that liniment you wanted," I said,

tossing him the bottle. "Hexe says to keep it off your Kymeran bits."

"Understood," Canterbury replied, catching the package with a six-fingered hand. "And don't forget to punch in."

I nodded my understanding and plucked my card from its slot on the "out" board of the antique time clock hanging on the wall and slipped it inside the slot in its face, accompanied by a loud "clunk," then dutifully placed it in a slot on the "in" side of the board. It seemed a lot of trouble for a single employee, but Canterbury was a stickler for punctuality.

"Do you think we'll make the deadline for the museum?" I asked as I opened my work locker and removed my safety gear.

"There's no 'thinking'—I *know* we'll make deadline," he replied. "We have to. I promised the Curator it would be ready in time for the Jubilee. I've got a lot riding on this piece."

"What part of it are we working on today?"

"The right foreleg," he replied, picking up the bar of steel sitting on the workbench in front of him as if it weighed no more than a two-by-four.

I watched in mute admiration as Canterbury stroked the metal as if it were a kitten, causing it to instantly soften beneath his touch. He then reworked it, like a potter at his wheel, with nothing more than his hands, teasing it into a new shape. Within minutes what had once been a simple steel bar was now the shin bone of a dragon.

Canterbury stepped aside, so I could pick up the piece with a pair of tongs and quench it in the nearby water bath. Although he had used his bare hands to shape the steel, the finished piece was as hot as if it had just been pulled from the heat of a forge. There was a mighty hiss and a plume of steam arose from the converted horse trough, as if the dragon we were assembling piecemeal was trying to communicate with us.

Once the tibia was properly tempered, I would then fit it into the articulated knee joint and weld it into place. After that we would construct the ankle and move on to the foot. In many ways, what I was doing with Canterbury was no different from what I had done creating my "action figures," save that instead of scrounging salvage yards for found metal, I was working with a living machine shop who could literally fabricate any necessary part by hand.

"What about the skin for this thing?" I asked, as I pulled on my welding gloves. "It doesn't seem right to send him out into the world with all his cogs and gears hanging out."

"I asked the Curator about that. She said the museum would be providing an actual shed."

I wasn't surprised that they had a dragon skin that had lasted so long. Hexe's mother had a suit of armor made from the same thing standing in her foyer. That shit's hard-core. We continued to labor over the clockwork dragon for the rest of the morning, until Canterbury signaled it was time for lunch.

As I retrieved my lunch pail from my locker, a tall, good-looking man with blond hair entered the workshop unannounced. He was dressed in a full-length mink pimp-coat, an open-necked velour shirt, and a pair of extremely tight pants cinched by a thick, buff-colored suede belt. It wasn't until the belt unknotted itself from about his waist and dropped to the floor, switching back and forth like the tail of a cat, that I recognized the visitor as Bjorn Cowpen, the leader of Golgotham's huldrefolk, a council member of the GoBOO, and owner of several adult entertainment establishments located on Duivel Street.

"Good afternoon, Councilman," Canterbury said, bobbing his head in ritual greeting. "To what do I owe the honor?"

"I'm in the market for a new carriage, Master Canterbury. Something suitably upscale, of course. Chiron tells me you're the best in Golgotham."

"Lord Chiron is most kind," the centaur replied, "but not inaccurate. There is nothing my apprentice and I can not fabricate."

The huldu turned to look at me as I sat at my workbench eating my lunch. "You have a female apprentice?" he asked, raising a dubious eyebrow. "And human, at that?"

My cheeks flushed as I bit into the sandwich, vigorously chewing in order to keep myself from saying something that might cost Canterbury Customs a sale.

"I assure you, Councilman, she is most adept, despite such shortcomings," Canterbury replied smoothly. "Come;

let us retire to my office. Perhaps you can elaborate on exactly what it is you're looking for? That will help me when I crunch the numbers for your quote." He then led Cowpen up the ramp that led to the second floor, which served as both his office and living space. When they came back down, a half hour later, I could tell by the way their tails were twitching that they'd struck a deal.

"Not to worry, Councilman," Canterbury assured him. "Your new carriage will be everything you desire, and more!" Upon closing the shop doors, the centaur sneezed violently, sending a shudder from the nape of his neck to his flanks. "Blood of Nessus! As much money as that huldu has, you'd think he could afford better cologne!"

"At least he was willing to overlook your hiring practices," I said sarcastically, pushing back the visor of my welding helmet.

"Don't take what I said about your 'shortcomings' seriously, my dear. And don't let what he said bother you. Bjorn Cowpen may be able to buy and sell me five times over, but he's far from the sharpest tool in the shed."

"Oh, he's a tool all right," I agreed.

"Well, if it's any consolation, he was more put off by you being a woman than a human. I'm afraid he doesn't see much use for females of *any* kind outside of his clubs."

"Great. He's a bigot *and* a sexist."

"When I first started out, I ran into a great deal of bigotry, as you might expect," Canterbury said, favoring me with a sad, wise smile. "After all, I am most certainly *not* Kymeran, but neither am I a true centaur. The herd tolerates me, but they've never fully *trusted* me. I was bullied a great deal as a colt. Although my father was never able to publicly acknowledge me, he *did* take responsibility for training me in the magical arts. 'Master your craft, and the fools will beat a path to your door,' he used to tell me. In time, the quality of my work made the ones who used to look down on me forget their prejudices—or at least rein them in while in my presence. You needn't worry about the likes of Bjorn, my dear," he said as he patted me on the shoulder. "Your talent will make them honor you, whether they like it or not."

*   *   *

It was past six in the evening by the time I finally punched out. I waved farewell to Canterbury, who wished me a good night and made sure to remind me, as always, that he expected me in bright and early the very next day.

Although Horsecart Street was largely the domain of the centaurs and their cousins, the horse-legged ipotanes, virtually every major paranormal ethnic group can be found hurrying in and out of its various storefronts. A pair of leprechauns, dressed in green designer clothes, stood on the street corner, handing out fliers for Seamus O'Fae's political campaign.

Seamus, leader of the Wee Folk Anti-Defamation League, had recently announced his candidacy for mayor of Golgotham. It was the first time in the pocket city-state's history that anyone besides a Kymeran had dared throw their hat into the ring. The incumbent, Mayor Lash, had every reason to sweat. His opponent was a well-spoken, politically savvy lawyer who, despite his diminutive size—or, perhaps, because of it—was as tenacious as a terrier.

"Best of the evenin' to ye, Miss Eresby," one of the leprechauns said as he slipped a leaflet into my hand.

"Same to you, Tullamore. How long before you finish probation?" I asked, motioning to the tiny monitoring bracelet strapped to his right ankle.

"I got another t'ree months to go," he replied solemnly. "Then I'm as free as a bird! I'm thankful for Mr. O'Fae pleadin' me charges down from Felony Enchantment to Mischief-Makin' and keepin' me out of lock-up. The Tombs is a miserable place for us Wee Folk."

"Well, Seamus has *my* support, for what it's worth," I said. "And try not to turn anyone into a pig again, no matter how much they might deserve it!"

"That I will, ma'am."

As I crossed to the other side of the street, I was suddenly aware that I was being watched. This, in and of itself, was not a new or unexpected sensation for me. As the human consort of the Heir Apparent, I was routinely gawked and glared at whenever I went out in public. But what I was feeling was decidedly more predatory than usual. The last time the hair on the back of my neck stood up like that, I found a demon staring in my window.

I abruptly spun on my heels, hoping to surprise whoever

it was tailing me, and saw a Kymeran woman with slate blue hair dart into a doorway. When she didn't reemerge, I shrugged and continued my walk home. I let the incident go and quickly put the woman out of my mind. After all, if I fixated on *everything* odd in Golgotham, I'd *never* get anything done.

Chapter 2

I arrived home that evening to find fellow artist, human, and recent citizen of Golgotham "Bartho" Bartholomew conferring with Hexe. They were drinking spiced chai and staring at a collection of cameras, both digital and old-school 35mm, which were sitting on the middle of the kitchen table like a paparazzi centerpiece.

"Where have you been keeping yourself?" I grinned as the photographer rose to hug me. "I haven't seen you since the morning after the riot!"

"Sorry I've been out of touch. I've been on the road with Talisman. I'm their official photographer, now," he explained.

"Well, I'm glad to see your eye no longer looks like an eggplant."

"You and me both!" he said with a humorless laugh. "I'm bringing a police brutality suit against the city, by the way. I'm not going to let those pigs get away with smashing my camera and trying to blind me! Seamus O'Fae is representing me, along with anyone else who got roughed up that night."

"Seamus is going up against City Hall?" I gave a low whistle of admiration. "Now *that* is going to be one hell of a courtroom battle! But what's with the cameras?"

"I think someone's put a curse on them," Bartho sighed. "The last couple of weeks I've been getting these crazy double exposures, even when I'm using the digital cameras. They were blurry at first, but now they're becoming more and more distinct."

"Who would want to curse your cameras?" I frowned.

"I don't know. Maybe someone jealous of the attention I'm getting? Or maybe the asshole cop I'm suing? That's usually who pays to have curses put on people, isn't it, Hexe—jealous bastards and assholes?"

"That has certainly been my experience," Hexe admitted as he turned one of the cameras over in his hands. "But, to be honest, I'm not so sure that's what is going on here. Usually curses have some sort of occult signature, if you know where to look—kind of like a poker player's tell. But I'm not seeing anything like that. Are you *sure* it isn't a manufacturing defect of some kind?"

"I've taken them to two certified repair shops—one here, and the other in London, when I was on the road. Each swears up and down there's nothing wrong with them. Besides, how could a manufacturing defect replicate itself identically in cameras made by three completely *different* companies?"

"You're right; that doesn't sound natural," Hexe conceded, his brow knitting even further. "Perhaps an individual component was cursed, instead of the entire mechanism? That would make it a lot harder to detect," he mused aloud. "I'll run a series of scrying stones over these so I can get a better idea of what I'm dealing with. I should be able to ascertain what's up within the next day or so."

"You're a lifesaver, Hexe." Bartho grinned. "Holy crap—is that the time? Sorry I can't hang around and chat, Tate, but I've got to go over depositions with Seamus."

As Hexe escorted Bartho to the front door, I headed upstairs to change out of my work clothes and take a shower. Twenty minutes later I returned to find Hexe sitting at the desk in his study, balancing the checkbook. I bent over and nuzzled his neck, savoring his unique scent of citrus, moss, and leather as I did so.

"So how was your day at work?" he asked, reaching up with one hand to stroke my hair.

"I made a dragon leg," I replied. "You know—same-old-same-old."

"Is that so?" He chuckled as I sat down in his lap.

"And how was *your* day?" I asked between kisses.

"Fairly." *Smooch.* "Uneventful." *Smack.* "I lifted a minor curse off a client." *Smooch.* "Someone afflicted him with crossed eyes." *Double smooch.*

I glanced down at the open checkbook and the stack of bills that sat beside it. "So—how are we doing?"

Hexe heaved a sigh, prodding the calculator as if it were a poisonous toad. "Well, between your day job, the rent from the boarders, and what I bring in from my steadier clients, we're making ends meet. But just barely."

"Why can't we use witchfire to light the house like they do at the Rookery?" I asked as I scowled at the most recent ConEd bill.

"Witchfire might not be metered, but it's not *free*," he replied. "Sorcerers can drain themselves pretty quickly, if they're not careful. The braziers at the Rookery are communal fires—each Kymeran who rents a booth there contributes a flame to the kitty. That's why they burn as brightly as they do. The GoBOO allowed gas lines and electricity into Golgotham because it frees up occult energy that normally would go toward 'public utilities.' Of course, there are those who claim that dependence on human inventions weakens us far more than lighting our homes with witchfire."

"So much for snapping your fingers and magically making the rent and keeping the lights on," I sighed.

"Hey, I'm just a wizard, not a miracle worker," Hexe said with a wry smile. "ConEd has no more qualms about shutting off a past-due warlock than they do a plumber in Queens."

"Is this a good time to talk, or would you guys rather be alone right now?"

I looked up to see our housemate and friend, Lukas, standing in the doorway of the study. The young shapeshifter had been living at the boardinghouse ever since he ended up in the backyard after escaping from Boss Marz's fighting pit, months ago. Despite the fact he was a boarder, I was actually surprised to see him, as he now spent most of his time working at Dr. Mao's apothecary and acupuncture parlor. Of course, the fact Lukas' girlfriend, Meikei, was also the boss's daughter might have had something to do with that.

"You're not interrupting anything—yet," Hexe replied. "What's on your mind, Lukas?"

The young were-cat frowned and lowered his gaze to his scuffed Vans. "I owe you guys everything," he said uneasily as he scratched at his sandy hair. "I mean, if it weren't for you, I'd either be pit-fighting or dead right now. You know I consider you guys more my family than the one I was born to. . . ."

Hexe quietly motioned for me to get out of his lap. "Lukas—what are you trying to say?" He frowned.

The young bastet's cheeks turned even redder. "I—I'm moving out."

"What?" I yelped. "You're not going back home, are you—?"

Lukas shook his head. "Of course not!" he said emphatically. "I'm not going back to the Preserve. It's just that— well, Dr. Mao has offered to make me his apprentice, and that means moving into the spare store room at the apothecary."

"Sounds to me like the old tiger wants to keep an eye on you and Meikei." Hexe chuckled, sending Lukas' blush all the way into his hairline.

"You don't hate me for leaving, do you?" The youth asked nervously.

"Oh, Lukas, you silly kitty cat!" I exclaimed as I threw my arms around him. "Of *course* not! You'll *always* be the little brother who shape-shifts into a cougar that I never had!"

"So you're not mad at me?" Lukas raised his shaggy unibrow in surprise. "You understand why I have to move out?"

"Of *course* we understand," Hexe said. "I wish you luck on your apprenticeship, my friend. That old were-tiger can be tough at times, but if you serve your master well, you'll learn more about herbs and acupuncture from him than you ever thought possible. Besides, it's not like you signed a lease with me."

"I'm moving out tomorrow, if that's okay with you," Lukas said excitedly. "It's been great living here. I'll miss you both—and Beanie, too."

"What about Scratch?" Hexe asked archly.

"Yeahhhh, him, too, I guess," Lukas replied. "Just don't tell him I said that, though."

As Lukas headed upstairs to pack his few belongings, Hexe let out a sigh and allowed the smile to drop from his face. "Well, *that* knocks next month's budget for a loop," he said sourly. He picked up the checkbook and studied it as if it were one of his grimoires. "I'll have to advertise for another lodger. It's time-consuming, but there's no getting around it. As long as Mr. Manto doesn't drop dead on us anytime soon, we'll squeak by."

I slipped my arms around him and kissed his cheek. "Don't look so stressed, sweetie. We'll manage to muddle through, just like we always do."

"I suppose you're right," he replied, returning my embrace. "But we're going to have to tighten our belts even further."

"I propose we loosen our belts," I smiled saucily.

"I don't know if that will help with the bills," he said, as his hands slipped under my blouse. "But it will *definitely* take our minds off them."

As we headed hand in hand up the stairs to our room, the opening bars of Screamin' Jay Hawkins' "I Put A Spell On You" suddenly came out of nowhere. Hexe fished his cell phone out of his pocket and grimaced at the caller ID. "It's a text from Captain Horn—I mean, my father."

There's an old saying about closing doors and opening windows. Four months ago my parents disinherited me. At the same time, Hexe finally learned the true identity of his biological father. I liked Hexe's dad, and Beanie positively *adored* him—every time Captain Horn came to visit, Beanie would bring him one of his favorite plush toys, so they could play tug-of-war. Hexe, on the other hand, seemed to be somewhat ambivalent about the whole thing.

"The Captain wants us to meet him at the Calf for dinner—his treat. I wonder what's up."

"Why does there have to be a reason for him to invite us to dinner?" I replied with a shrug. "He's not just 'The Captain'—he's your dad. That's reason enough to take you out to dinner for most people."

"I suppose you're right," he agreed grudgingly. "Besides, it might be some time before we can afford going out to eat again."

The Two-Headed Calf, Golgotham's oldest tavern, was busy as usual when we arrived. Upon entering the downstairs pub room, we were greeted by Bruno, the new bouncer. He was heavyset and stood seven feet tall, his unibrow marking him as a shape-shifter—in his case one of the *berskir*.

Ever since the Calf found itself with a four-star listing on

Yelp, more and more humans continued to make their way into Golgotham to sample its "authentic atmosphere" alongside the locals. It was this lucrative, potentially volatile mix of clientele that resulted in the now-famous Golgotham Race Riot. In the months since the initial conflict, the Calf's proprietor, Lafo, had hired the were-grizzly as a means of nipping another such clash in the bud. So far it seemed to be working.

"Good evening, Serenity," Bruno growled in welcome, running a pawlike hand through his unruly brown hair. "Good evening, Miss Eresby."

Chorea, the Calf's hostess, stepped forward to greet us. Although she had set aside her leopard skin and chiton in favor of AA and saving her marriage, she still wore the garland of ivy that marked her as a maenad. "Welcome, Serenity." She smiled. "Captain Horn is waiting for you in the dining room."

"Thanks, Chory," he said. "You needn't bother escorting us."

As we made our way across the crowded pub, I spotted the Calf's owner, head chef, and chief bottle washer balancing a serving platter loaded with bowls of flash-fried crickets and battered dragonflies. The towering restaurateur was almost as tall as his bouncer, with long, ketchup-red hair and a matching beard. He was dressed in a pair of bib overalls and a loud Hawaiian shirt nearly as colorful as the tattoos covering his forearms. Like all Kymerans, he exuded a unique scent that was part body odor and personal signifier, in his case a combination of corn dogs and bananas Foster.

"Welcome back, Serenity! Have you checked out our new merchandise yet?" Lafo nodded toward the small booth under the staircase that was stocked with T-shirts and beer mugs emblazoned with the Calf's double-headed logo. "Would you believe we're selling as many T shirts as we are drinks now? A couple of my old regulars got their noses out of joint over it, but you gotta make hay while the sun shines! Those renovations after the riot set me back quite a bit, even with the insurance. Now, if you'll excuse me, I've got to replenish the snack bowls at the bar."

I followed Hexe up the stairs, past the framed lithographs of his great-great-grandfather and the Founding Fathers signing the Treaty of Golgotham, to the dining area, with its dark wood floors and coffered ceiling. While I was no longer the only human to be seen in the dining room, the vast majority of the customers were still Kymeran. Despite the token addition of cheeseburgers to the menu, most of Lafo's newly acquired human clientele no doubt found it far easier to catch a buzz than enjoy a meal at the Calf.

Captain Horn rose from his seat as we approached. Although he had removed his hat to reveal his maroon crew cut, he was still wearing his PTU dress uniform. As he smiled down at me in welcome, I glimpsed a hint of his son's mouth and jawline.

"You're as lovely as ever, Tate," Horn said as he hugged me. I found myself enveloped by the sturdy and reassuring scent of oak leaves and musk. "Please, sit down. Feel free to order whatever you like—dinner and drinks courtesy of the Paranormal Threat Unit."

As we took our seats at the table, a waiter with mango-colored hair came forward and handed us menus. Hexe laughed and handed them back without looking. "That won't be necessary—I'll have the pork brains in gravy, and the lady would like the filet of herring."

"Very good, Serenity," the waiter said, bobbing his head in ritual obeisance as he jotted down our order. "Any drinks before dinner?"

"Yes, I'll have cod liver oil," Hexe replied. "What about you, Tate?"

"I've got to get up and go to work in the morning," I reminded him. "I'll have herbal tea, if you don't mind."

As our waiter hurried off, Hexe turned to his father. "So—what's the reason for inviting us to dinner?" he asked brusquely, ignoring my gentle kick to his shins. "And why is the PTU paying for it?"

The smile disappeared from Captain Horn's face. "I just wanted you to hear it from me, not the media, that's all," he sighed.

"Hear what?" A look of dismay crossed Hexe's face. "Heavens and hells—you and mother aren't getting *married*, are you?"

"No! It's nothing like that!" Horn assured him, only to fall silent as the waiter returned with a brandy snifter and a small pot of tea.

"What is it, then?" Hexe asked as he swirled his cod liver

oil in its glass like a fine cognac. "What else could you *possibly* tell us that would require cushioning the blow at company expense?"

"The charges against Boss Marz and his croggies have been dismissed."

I gasped, nearly dropping the teapot in midpour. It was as if the floor beneath my feet had suddenly disappeared, sending me into freefall. I looked over at Hexe, who was equally shocked. He reached out and took my hand and squeezed it. "How is that possible?" he asked.

"That fancy lawyer of his managed to spring him on a technicality," Captain Horn explained. "Come tomorrow morning, he'll be out of the Tombs and back on the streets. Son, I know what happened between you and the Maladanti, how they tried to force you to fight your friend Lukas the were-cougar to the death. I also know your biker friends were the ones who put the hurt on Marz before we arrived on the scene.

"I don't have to tell you that Boss Marz is not one to forgive and forget. You need to keep on your toes once he's back. If I know him, it won't be long before he's up to his old tricks again. If he or one of his croggies so much as looks cross-eyed at you, I want to know about it."

"I appreciate the concern," Hexe said stiffly, "but I'm *more* than capable of protecting both myself and Tate."

"I do not doubt your abilities," Horn replied. "There's no question that you've got the strongest right hand in Golgotham. But there's only *one* of you, while Marz has a squadron of spellslingers at his command. None of them are half the wizard you are, but add them all together . . . well, you can see what I mean."

"I can keep us safe," Hexe said firmly. "I was doing it long before I knew my father was the head of the Paranormal Threat Unit."

The corner of Captain Horn's mouth twitched slightly at the barb, but otherwise he remained impassive. "Boss Marz is not above relying on physical force as well as magic to get his way," he warned. "There's no glad eye amulet made that will protect you against a well-aimed knife or a cosh to the back of the head. All I'm asking is that you not take any unnecessary risks."

He fell silent once again when the waiter arrived with our

food. As I stared down at my filleted smoked herring on buttered rye, garnished with radishes, snipped chives and raw egg yolk, my stomach did an abrupt barrel roll. I jumped from my chair and ran to the ladies' room as fast as I could. My fellow diners shook their heads in reproach, smirking at the sight of yet another nump with a glass stomach.

Chapter 3

"I *knew* there had to be a reason why he invited us to dinner," Hexe said as he unlocked the front door. "There's no such thing as a free meal."

"Ugh! The thought of Boss Marz walking the streets again is making my guts flip-flop all over again," I exclaimed as I sat down at the kitchen table, holding my head in my hands.

"Stress will do that to you," he replied. "How about I fix you a nice cup of chamomile and skullcap?"

"Aren't you the least bit scared?" I asked as I watched him calmly tinker with the teapot. "Boss Marz tried to kill you last time, and he damn near succeeded."

"Of *course* I'm concerned," Hexe admitted. "But I *refuse* to be frightened by Marz and his croggies. Living in fear of someone like that lets them in your head and gives them control over you. And remember, you're *not* helpless anymore—you have the ability to protect yourself, even when I'm not around."

"I appreciate the vote of confidence, but I'm nowhere *near* ready to defend myself against the Maladanti!" I protested. "That's like expecting someone with a learner's permit to drive a getaway car."

"One of the most important things about magic—no matter what hand you use—is that you have to be as strong as, if not stronger than, the power you seek to control. That means possessing both will and vision. Anyone who could turn a car transmission into a fully articulated panther, even *before* it was brought to life, will rock out at being a wizard.

But if it makes you feel better, I'll put Scratch on night patrol for the time being. Now drink up," he said, pushing a steaming cup of tea into my hands. "This will ease your stomach and settle your nerves."

Just then Beanie scratched at the kitchen door and began to do his "gotta pee" dance. I opened the door and followed him out onto the back porch, hoping the night air would clear my mind. I wrapped my hands around the steaming cup of tea, savoring its warmth, as I looked out across the garden. My eye automatically strayed to the copper "maternal furnace" I had unwittingly built for Uncle Esau, which now sat in the far corner of the yard, its copper dragon's head pointed at the night sky, as if baying at the moon. Where once it hatched murderous, bird-footed homunculi, now it simply composted lawn clippings.

Beanie came bounding toward the door, ready to get out of the chill night air now that he'd relieved himself. I finished my tea and followed him inside. I peeked into the study and saw Hexe peering at one of Bartho's cameras through a teardrop-shaped scrying crystal, just like a jeweler studying the cleavage plane on a diamond.

"Don't stay up *too* late," I said, kissing him good night.

"Love you, too," he replied absently, not taking his eyes off his work.

Beanie ran up the stairs ahead of me, and upon reaching the second floor landing, he turned around and stared back down at me, his little Boston terrier head tilted to one side, as if to say "What's keeping you, Mom?"

As I crawled into bed, Beanie hopped in after me, burrowing under the covers like he was going after a vole. I heard the eaves outside the bedroom window groan ever-so-slightly, as Scratch, dressed in a far fiercer skin than the one he wore earlier that day, prowled about the rooftop, keeping watch for the things that go bump in the night.

One of the downsides of being an apprentice is that you do a lot of scut work. If a chore is trivial, tedious, or unpleasant, you can rely on your master to assign it to you. In this case, I was to pick up Canterbury's new suit from his tailor.

Before moving to Golgotham it had never occurred to me that centaurs were into couture. In fact, I had assumed what clothing they did wear was more for our modesty than theirs. Boy, did I get schooled. Turns out centaurs, male and female alike, are the biggest *fashionistas* this side of the Garment District.

While centaurs do tend toward minimal dressage while at work, once they're off the clock they like to dress to the nines in fancy jackets and vests, with matching ornamental caparisons that drape over their hindquarters. Oh, and they are absolutely *mental* for hats, the more elaborate the better. When they're not busy at work — and centaurs are easily the most industrious race to be found in Golgotham — they can be found swanning about the Hippodrome or the Clip-Clop Club, showing off their newest duds.

I guess the reason centaurs are so fashion-conscious is because *everything* they wear has to be either custom-made or retrofitted. There's no such thing as buying off-the-rack when your top half is a size six and your bottom half is a size horse. That means every centaur worth their oats has a personal tailor. Canterbury's happened to be Rienzi, who worked out of a stall in the oldest open-air market still operating in New York City.

The Fly Market, located inside an Industrial Gothic loggia with an iron-clad roof and brick porticos, is alive, in its way. And like all living things, it is constantly growing and changing. There are literally hundreds of stalls inside it, and just when I think I have a grip on who runs what, or what stall belongs where, everything seems to up and move about, if for no other reason than to be mischievous.

As I entered, the constant noise generated by the surrounding merchants as they haggled and argued with customers and suppliers made it sound as if I were walking into a gigantic beehive. I passed a mustard-haired Kymeran woman selling owl-faced tea sets, who sat across the aisle from an herbalist with plum-colored dreadlocks who was selling Arabian za'atar to housewives and warlocks alike, who was set up next to a confectioner selling lollipops coated in chili powder and hand-dipped chocolate centipedes. I scanned the labyrinth of stalls, finally spotting Rienzi's banner several aisles in.

As I walked up, the tailor was putting a hem in a length of fabric with a manual sewing machine especially designed to accommodate his lower body, working its treadle with a front hoof. Rienzi was a handsome bay centaur, with a reddish lower body, mane, and tail, dressed in a striking waistcoat fashioned from liquid satin and covered in embroidered silver roses.

"I'm here to pick up Canterbury's suit," I said, raising my voice to be heard over the noise of the sewing machine.

The tailor gave an equine snort and set aside his work. "Here it is," he said, handing me what looked like a folded satin quilt with a deep wine paisley pattern. "Will you be paying for it now, or should I add it to your master's bill?"

Before I could answer, the buzz and hubbub of the Fly Market stopped as if cut by a knife. Baffled, I looked around to see what could possibly make everyone fall silent all at once. I got my answer: Boss Marz was walking down one of the aisles, flanked on either side by strutting Maladanti spellslingers. The crime lord did not seem in the least diminished by his time in the Tombs, nor did he seem to be suffering any ill effects from taking a war-hammer to the solar plexus.

What made my blood run cold, however, was the sight of the tiny squirrel monkey, dressed in a red velvet fez and matching vest, perched on Marz's left shoulder. I had hoped I'd seen the last of his familiar when Bonzo disincorporated rather than risk being killed on the mortal plane by Scratch when they tangled one-on-one. But there he was, the little shit, accompanying his master on his rounds as if nothing had ever happened.

Boss Marz stood in the intersection of two wide aisles near the center of the loggia and smirked at the sea of fearful faces staring at him. His voice boomed out, echoing through the now-silent Fly Market like thunder from an approaching storm.

"It has come to my attention that many of you, over these last few months, have failed to pay your tribute to the Maladanti! In case you are suffering from the delusion that because I and my associates, here, have been detained elsewhere, that you are no longer under any obligation to provide us with a percentage of your profits in order to continue to do business in the Fly Market—please allow me to disabuse you of such wrong thinking!"

The crime lord pointed his left hand at a nearby magic candle booth, tended by an elderly Kymeran man with receding mint-green hair. "In Arum's name—please, no!" the candlemaker begged, lifting his hands in supplication.

But there was no point in pleading for mercy from Boss Marz—and none at all to be found from his familiar. With a squeal of delight, Bonzo leapt from his master's shoulder and scampered along his outstretched arm, jumping from Marz's hand like a swimmer off a diving board.

The moment the squirrel monkey hit the floor it took on its demonic aspect, transforming into what looked like the misbegotten result of a threesome between a mandrill baboon, a hyena, and a stegosaurus, while still dressed like an organ-grinder's monkey. With a bloodcurdling shriek, the familiar bounded over the counter and snatched up the hapless vendor, disappearing with his captive in a cloud of smoke that reeked of brimstone and monkey house.

A moment later, Bonzo, once more reduced in size, reappeared on his master's shoulder, licking his lips and picking at his teeth. Boss Marz chuckled and rewarded his familiar with a pistachio nut, which it greedily grabbed and devoured.

"I trust I have made myself perfectly clear," he said to his horror-struck audience. "Come the next tribute day, I expect each and every one of you to make good on *all* you owe me. Good day, citizens."

A gasp of horror rippled throughout the Fly Market, followed by a chorus of fearful murmurs as the merchants began frantically talking among themselves. As the lord of the Maladanti turned to leave, he looked about the Fly Market a final time. I desperately wanted to somehow duck out of sight, but I found myself rooted to the spot, too terrified to move. As his gaze fell on me, I saw a flicker of recognition in his eyes, and he raised his right hand to his brow, in a mock salute, accompanied by an unpleasant little smile.

The moment Marz turned his back on me, the fear that had kept me glued to the spot instantly dissolved. I snatched up the bundle I had been sent to retrieve and hurried in the opposite direction as fast as I could go.

Chapter 4

When I arrived at work, I told Canterbury what I'd seen at the Fly Market. He was visibly shocked and immediately told me to take the rest of the day off.

"But what about the exhibit for the museum?" I asked, pointing to the bits and pieces of clockwork dragon scattered about the workshop.

"Don't worry about that," he replied. "You'd be of no use to me, and a danger to yourself, if you tried to work right now. The last thing I need is for you to fire up a welding torch with shaky hands and a wandering mind. Just be here all the earlier tomorrow. And don't worry—I'm not going to dock you for the day."

"Thanks, Master," I said with a wan smile.

"No problem. Now beat it before I kick myself for my generosity."

Upon returning home, I heard voices conversing in the study. I peeked in and saw Hexe sitting at his desk, with Beanie cradled in his lap and Scratch perched atop the back of his chair while he talked to Bartho.

"What do you mean my cameras aren't jinxed?" The photographer frowned.

"I went over each of them several times with my finest scrying stones," Hexe replied, gesturing to the cameras arrayed before him. "They are definitely not cursed. However, I *did* discover that they have been exposed to magical energy."

"Can you tell who's responsible? Because I really want to put a boot up the ass of whoever did this."

"Then you better bend over. Because, according to my divinations, *you're* the source of the magic."

Bartho's jaw dropped open like a drawbridge. "You're kidding, right? I mean, *how* is that possible?"

"Because you're manifesting through your art form, just like I have," I interjected.

Hexe raised an eyebrow in surprise. "What are *you* doing home this time of day?"

"Canterbury gave me the day off," I said, brushing aside the question. "I'm more interested in hearing how Bartho got himself all magical."

"Well, I'm not exactly sure *what's* happening, but it's a well-known fact that the human psychics who live in Golgotham have considerably stronger abilities than those who live elsewhere," Hexe explained. "Perhaps artistic humans are affected in much the same way? I mean, artists routinely create something from nothing using only their craft and force of will—it's essentially the same thing a witch or warlock does when we work magic."

"If that's true, then why hasn't this phenomenon been documented before now?" Bartho asked, a dubious look on his face.

"For the simple reason that, despite a long history of artists being drawn to my people, up until recently 'normal' humans such as you and Tate have steered clear of Golgotham and similar enclaves," Hexe sighed. "Of course, Goya and Dali don't count, as they were Kymeran themselves. And then there was Toulouse-Lautrec, who was a member of the dwarven community. And while Picasso may have kept a Kymeran mistress, he did not live with her in the heart of the Pigalle, surrounded by her family. No, it has only been recently that the old prejudices against my people have finally begun to fade and humans like you and Tate have become brave enough to dwell amongst us."

The photographer scratched his head. "You mean any human who hangs out in Golgotham is going to end up with a case of the magics?"

"No, I suspect it will only affect artistic types, and only those that live here for several months. But, in any case, this is a *very* interesting development."

"But how does it explain why my mojo, or whatever you call it, is generating double exposures?"

"Oh, those aren't double exposures," Hexe replied matter-of-factly. "They're ghosts."

Bartho's eyes widened until it looked like they would launch themselves out of his skull. "You mean I see dead people?"

"No, you only take pictures of them," Hexe explained. "You've become a spirit photographer, just like the original Ouija. As your talent matures, and you learn to control it, the images will become more and more distinct and you'll be able to see them in the camera's viewfinder. In time, you may even learn to communicate with your subjects."

"Why the hell would I want to do *that*?" Bartho yelped.

"There's nothing to be worried about," Hexe said reassuringly. "The vast majority of ghosts are perfectly nice people. They just happen to be dead, that's all. However, should you see any with red eyes, run away as fast as you can."

"That doesn't sounds scary *at all*," Bartho groaned. "So what do I do about these ghosts popping up in my pictures?"

"Well, you can always Photoshop them out. . . ."

After a bewildered Bartho left with his collection of cameras, Hexe and I retired to the kitchen. "So why did Canterbury give you the day off?" he asked. "Was there an accident at work?"

Before I could answer, I heard an odd clattering sound from upstairs, as if someone were walking around in wooden shoes. "What's that noise?" I frowned.

"That's the new boarder," Hexe explained.

I raised an eyebrow in surprise as I glanced up at the ceiling. "That was quick! You didn't even have time to put up a flier at Strega Nona!"

"We were lucky. I got a call from Giles Gruff, right after you left this morning. He said a lady friend of his was in a tight spot. . . ."

"Why am I not surprised?" I said sarcastically. Giles was the leader of the satyr community and Golgotham's most notorious bon vivant and rarely seen without a comely nymph on both arms.

"Sorry about all the noise while I was traipsing about upstairs—I left my mufflers in my work locker."

I turned in the direction of the unfamiliar voice and saw an attractive young faun standing in the kitchen doorway. She had almond-shaped eyes with luxurious auburn curls that accented the small horn buds jutting from her forehead, and from the waist down she had the hind legs and tail of a goat. She was dressed in a long-sleeved red shirt with a black vest emblazoned with a stylized tongue of flame over her heart along with the initials GFD embroidered in gold thread—the traditional uniform of a Golgotham firefighter.

"You must be Tate; it's a pleasure to meet you," the faun said. "My uncle speaks very highly of you. I'm Octavia." She then flashed Hexe a heartfelt smile. "Thank you, Serenity. I appreciate you allowing me to move in on such short notice. It was something of a surprise, coming home after my shift to find an eviction notice tacked to my door."

"It's no problem at all," he replied. "Any friend of Giles is a friend of mine."

"I assure you both that you needn't worry about me partying to all hours," Octavia said solemnly. "We fauns are far more domesticated than our satyr brethren—save for Uncle Giles, of course."

"Let me guess—you had an apartment in the Machen Arms, didn't you?" I asked.

"You must have seen the headlines the other day," the faun said with a humorless laugh. "I had a one-bedroom apartment there for the last five years," she explained, her tone becoming bitter. "My lease came up for renewal yesterday, and suddenly my rent skyrocketed from seven hundred dollars to five thousand a month, literally overnight! Can you believe that minotaur shit?"

"I'm afraid I can," I sighed. "Ronald Chess has been playing the exact same game in the rest of Manhattan for over thirty years now. He buys up older, rent-controlled prewar apartment buildings and then, when the leases come up for renewal, he jacks the rent up through the roof. Once the previous tenants are evicted, he slaps granite countertops on everything and slops a new coat of paint on the walls and turns it condo."

"I can't believe a Golgothamite would agree to sell out to such a character," Hexe scowled. "Who was your old landlord?"

Octavia shrugged her shoulders. "Some company called Golden Egg Realty. All I did was drop off a rent check every month to the leasing agent who managed the property."

"When will you be settled in?" Hexe asked.

"I'll be moved in by tonight. I'm putting most of my belongings into storage until I can find a large enough place. As it is, you won't be seeing that much of me, anyway," she explained. "I work five days on, five days off, so I spend more time at the firehouse than I do at home. Speaking of which, I better fetch my spare set of mufflers from my work locker so I don't ruin these lovely hardwood floors of yours!" With that, the firefighter turned on her hooves and clattered away.

Once I was certain Octavia had left the house, I turned to face Hexe. "You asked me why Canterbury sent me home—it's because I saw Boss Marz at the Fly Market this morning. He was reminding everybody who runs the waterfront in Golgotham. He wanted to make an example to the others, so he sicced his familiar on some poor wretch. It was horrible."

Hexe's smile vanished like breath on a mirror. "Did he see you?"

"Yes," I said quietly, shuddering as I replayed the moment over in my head.

"Did he say anything to you?"

"No, he just smirked and gave me this little wave," I replied, unable to suppress a grimace of disgust. "I was so shook up, Canterbury sent me home for the day."

"I thought I heard something interesting going on," Scratch snarled, leaping from the kitchen floor to his usual perch atop the refrigerator. "I can't believe that asshole has the balls to show his face again in Golgotham!"

"You mean Marz?" I asked.

"*Phfft!* Screw Marz!" the familiar spat in disgust. "I'm talking about that jumped-up organ-grinder's monkey! I kicked Bonzo's baboon-butt so hard he teleported back home rather than risk getting killed in this dimension. Now *that's* what I call a wuss!"

Chapter 5

Whoever coined the term "absence makes the heart grow fonder" clearly had never met Boss Marz. Over the next few days the Maladanti quickly picked up from where they had left off, collecting "tribute" from the businesses along the waterfront and the brothels and cabarets of Duivel Street.

The return of the Maladanti was not felt just by the citizens of Golgotham; the twunts who had come to know the red-light district only during the crime cartel's eclipse were swiftly and roughly schooled as to what was considered proper decorum in the gentlemen's clubs under their "protection."

I kept waiting for the other shoe to drop, but it never did. After that creepy little smile he gave me at the Fly Market, I was convinced Marz had something villainous planned for us. But no one left a decapitated goat's head on our doorstep or attempted to curse me. I guess Boss Marz was simply too busy trying to reestablish his hold on Golgotham to waste time and energy on personal revenge.

Still, despite the Maladanti's apparent disinterest in us, Scratch continued his nightly patrols, and I never took off the protective glad eye amulet Hexe created for me. Better safe than sorry. I'll admit I was initially anxious, but after enduring jealous ex-girlfriends trying to curse me, being attacked by soulless homunculi, and having my arm broken by a demon, I had built up a pretty thick skin, and once several days had gone by and the crime lord had yet to make a move, I decided I had better things to do than worry about what Boss Marz's evil plan might be.

So I put on my welder's helmet and fired up my torch and threw myself headlong into my work. The Maladanti be damned, I had a project to finish and I wasn't going to let a bunch of spellslinging goons in bad suits screw with my deadline. For the next month, Canterbury and I put in long, arduous hours every day of the week. I came home so exhausted I could barely take off my clothes before crawling into bed.

We finished the installation at the end of March, less than a week before the Jubilee. Even replicated in reduced scale, it still took three brawny Clydesdale-sized centaurs and six ipotane drovers to load and haul the crates containing the clockwork dragon to its new home. On the day of the delivery Canterbury led the convoy from the shop, hitched to a cart containing our welding equipment and other tools, while I rode shotgun with Fabio, the head drover.

The Museum of Supernatural History, located on the corner of Nassau Street and Maiden Lane, towers ominously over the surrounding buildings like some ancient temple dedicated to a long-forgotten god. It is set atop a thirteen-hundred-foot-square granite-clad concrete platform that covers an entire city block. A fifty-foot-wide, three-hundred-step staircase leads to a pair of huge bronze doors embossed with scenes depicting such ancient heroes as Chiron, Pan, and Arum. To the right of the stairs are six forty-foot-tall marble statues of Kymerans, male and female, in historical dress, while on the left are arrayed six rampant jade battle-dragons.

However, as majestic and awe-inspiring as its public face may be, we were essentially tradesmen making a delivery, and the museum's loading dock, accessed via a subterranean deck, proved no different from that of any other skyscraper in New York.

"Stay put and keep an eye on the gear," Canterbury instructed as he unhitched himself from the equipment cart. "I'll go find the Curator."

"No need, Master Canterbury," said an elderly, but firm female voice. "I am already here." A Kymeran woman with long cornflower blue hair woven into an elaborate double-drape French braid emerged from the shadows at the far end of the receiving platform. She wore a floor-length satin jacket the color of celadon pottery, with wide, stiff sleeves and a Mandarin collar, and about her neck was hung the badge of her office: a jade dragon with its tail in its mouth.

"I take it this is the installation?" the Curator asked, pointing to the crates the drovers were loading onto the dock.

"Yes, milady," Canterbury replied, with a ritual bow of his head. "The larger box contains the body, while the others hold the wings, head and tail. It shouldn't take more than six hours for it to be assembled."

The Curator turned her pale gray gaze upon me. "I see your apprentice is human. That is most interesting. Please follow me to the exhibit hall." Without further explanation, she turned her back to us and began to walk away, forcing us to hurry after her as she headed into a warren of rooms filled with warehoused exhibits. Everywhere I looked the past and present seemed to be colliding in a jumble of dust, rust, and flaking paint, as a small army of restorers cleaned and rehabbed artifacts that dated back before the pyramids of Giza.

Eventually we came to a large freight elevator. As we drew near, a sloe-eyed sphinx stepped forward, blocking our path. Like most of her kind, the human-headed lioness wore a golden vulture cap atop her jet-black head and a bejeweled pectoral about her neck. When she spoke, her voice was deceptively beautiful.

"Wood, wire, iron or stone,
Inside of me are treasures sown.
Some say I'd be a seat on high
For those unable to decide.
I cannot be opened by lock or hinge,
And protect all things that lie within. What am I?"

"You're a garden fence," the Curator replied without pause.

The sphinx smiled, displaying a fearsome double row of very sharp teeth, and then bowed her head, moving aside. As we passed by, the Curator ran her hand down the length of the monster's spine, and in response the sphinx made a purring noise and arched her back like a house cat.

"Please forgive the extra security measures," the Curator said, "but we have recently suffered a theft."

Canterbury raised an eyebrow. "Was anything of value taken?"

"*All* our exhibits are of historical value," the Curator replied as the freight elevator's accordion gate opened on its own, revealing a car the size of a studio apartment. Upon entering, the gate trundled shut behind us, as if closed by spectral hands. "But, luckily, that which was taken is not completely irreplaceable."

A few moments later we arrived on the second floor of the museum, which was currently closed to the public. As we walked toward the main exhibit halls, Canterbury's hooves echoed loudly in the darkened hallway. The centaur grimaced and came to a halt.

"Give me a moment to muffle my shoes," he said, digging into the satchel he wore slung about his shoulder. "I'm making a hell of a racket and I don't want to scuff up your floors."

As we waited for my master to reshoe himself, I peered into a gallery off the main hall that bore a sign that read, in both Kymeran and English: THE LOST KINGDOM. The far wall was covered by a mural depicting a city of towering glass spires, about which flew brightly colored dragons bearing riders dressed in ornate suits of armor like the one I had seen at Lady Syra's penthouse, all of which was dwarfed by the terrifyingly huge tidal wave bearing down upon it. Scattered about the gallery were sealed display cases mounted on artfully lit plinths, inside of which were shards of pottery, bits of jewelry, and other tattered fragments that were all that remained of a civilization that drowned when mankind was picking its collective nits.

As I was studying the exhibits, I caught the scent of figs and dried roses and turned to find the Curator standing behind me. "There are artifacts in this section that date back fifty thousand years," she said, speaking in a hushed voice. "It's amazing anything was left at all, considering the survivors fled with nothing more than the clothes on their backs and what little they could gather in their arms."

"What's that?" I asked, pointing to an exhibit behind velvet ropes. Inside the display case was an opalescent vessel the size and shape of an amphora that contained a viscous pinkish-purple liquid that sluggishly churned to and fro, like a captive octopus hiding in a jar.

"*That* is our most precious exhibit," the Curator replied proudly. "It is the only living glass left in the world. Our ancestors used it to build their cities, much like the ancient Egyptians used mud and straw to build the pyramids."

"That stuff is glass?" I frowned. "It looks more like the goop inside a lava lamp."

"That's because living glass is, indeed, alive," she replied. "It's a boneless, amorphous creature, not unlike a jellyfish. It thrives on magic, much the same way plants feed on carbon dioxide. Although it possesses no intellect, living glass is highly sensitive to the thoughts of those around it. Once tamed and sculpted, it takes on the appearance of its namesake, but has the strength of tempered steel.

"Back when Kymera was in full flower, there was a class of wizards, known as artificēs, who specialized in domesticating and sculpting living glass. But when the tsunami struck, it wiped out the breeding tanks, along with those who tended them. The only artifex to escape the destruction of Kymera was the Lady Ursa, consort to the Witch King, Lord Arum. She brought this very same container of living glass with her when she fled Kymera. She planned to reestablish the species, but died before she could do so. There has not been another artifex since. It is considered a lost talent, drowned along with the shining spires it once raised."

At the far end of the gallery was an archway leading, according to the signage, to the Hall of Arum, which was twice the size of the first gallery, and included life-sized dioramas. I stared in fascination at a wax dummy with long hair as blue as a peacock's breast and golden eyes that seemed to possess an eerie luminosity. The mannequin was dressed in elaborately embroidered robes and seated on a golden throne shaped like a rampant dragon, its bejeweled wings spread wide to either side. On the wax figure's head sat a diadem resembling a pair of dragons, one jet black, the other gold, entwined from tail to snout so that they faced one another, holding a fire opal the size of an egg balanced between their gaping jaws.

Behind the throne was a detailed three-dimensional landscape showing the building of a great city high atop a mountain. Architects could be seen in the background, consulting their schematics as surveyors hovered overhead on winged dragons. Meanwhile, an armored guard sat astride a bearded, wingless dragon, keeping an eye on the brace of Cro-Magnons dragging a mammoth block of stone up the steep hillside.

I glanced down at the placard mounted at the foot of the diorama, which read, *Lord Arum, Savior of the Kymeran people and founder of the city-state of Dragon Arum, located in what is now known as the Carpathian Mountains, circa 50,000 B.C.E. (Before Common Era). The likeness of Lord Arum is modeled on his death mask.*

There came a dull thumping sound behind me, and I turned to see Canterbury enter the gallery, his hooves now safely muffled by rubber cuffs. "I see you're checking out your boyfriend's family tree," he commented dryly.

The Curator gave me a speculative look, as if sizing me up for a display case, then motioned for us to follow her. "Come this way, please."

As we entered yet another exhibition hall, this one called the Hall of Sufferance, we paused in front of yet another diorama, this one depicting a Kymeran with a forked cerulean beard holding a platinum scepter entwined by a golden and a black winged dragon. Arrayed before him were representatives of all the major supernatural races found in Golgotham, each of them wearing a crown. These royal figures were forever frozen in an attitude of ritual obeisance, with either their heads lowered or knees bent.

The plaque attached to the diorama read: *In the Year 1036 C.E. (Common Era), Lord Vexe accepted the fealty of King Chiron IX of the Centauri, King Omester XII of the Satyrisci, King Koukakala of the Leipreachán, Lord Tasson of the Dwarves, and Queen Tallemaja of the Huldrefolk, thereby granting their peoples eternal protection and asylum within his kingdom.*

A polite cough from the Curator drew my attention away from the tableaux. "This is where the exhibit will be installed," she said, motioning to a large alcove off the main gallery. "This section is dedicated specifically to the Dragon Rebellion and will feature a re-creation of the battle between Lord Bexe and his brother, General Vlad." She pointed toward the ceiling. "As you can see, Vlad's mount is already in place."

I looked up and gave an involuntary gasp at the sight of a fierce black dragon, its wings spread wide and claws extended, directly over my head. It was easily twenty feet long, from snout to tail, with a wingspan to match. Once my heart slowed back down, I was able to marvel at its workmanship. The attention to detail, from its glowing red eyes and razor-sharp teeth to the barb at the end of its tail, was amazing. The thought of the skies having once been filled with such glorious monsters was both awe inspiring and terrifying.

"Nice work," Canterbury admitted grudgingly. "Who fabricated it for you?"

"It's actually a piece of taxidermy," the Curator explained casually. "It's a juvenile, of course. There's no way we could display an adult battle-dragon indoors, much less two of them."

"Speaking of which—what's keeping those damned drovers?" Canterbury scowled as he fished his pocket watch from his waistcoat. "They should have been here by now!" He tapped the Bluetooth headset in his right ear. "Fabio! You better not be taking a break on my dime—and no, I *don't* care what the Union has to say about it. If you and your team want to get paid, get your horses' asses up here."

As Canterbury continued to argue into his headset, I returned to the main hall and sat down on a large marble bench. As I did so, a trio of monitors arranged in a semicircle flickered on and the fourth movement of Berlioz's *Symphonie Fantastique* swelled from hidden speakers. As I watched, a series of woodcuts and engravings of Witchfinders skinning werewolves, cutting off the extra digits of Kymerans, and burning nymphs and satyrs alive flashed across the flat screens.

"And so the war between the human and nonhuman populations of Europe and Eurasia raged for the better part of a century," intoned a deep, authoritative, and decidedly British voice, "until the sacred groves were dyed red and the skies grew black with the ashes from the autos-da-fé. Then, on the eleventh hour of the eleventh day of the eleventh month of the eleventh year of the twelfth century C.E., there came a sign from on high. . . ."

Suddenly images of the three holiest sites in Judeo-Christian-Islamic culture appeared, one to each screen: the Tomb of the Holy Sepulcher; the Wailing Wall; and the

Kaaba. Without warning, there came a thunderclap so loud it made me jump in my seat as fiery words written in Latin, Hebrew, and Arabic miraculously appeared on the walls of all three shrines at the very same moment.

"And so it was commanded by the God of the Christians, YHWH of the Hebrews, and Allah of the Muslims," the narrator intoned solemnly, "in words of fire, which still burn today, for all to see: 'Suffer the witches to live, and those who come unto them, for they, too, are precious in My sight. Judge them not, lest ye be judged accordingly; and with what measure ye mete, shall I return measure to you a hundredfold.'"

The photographs of modern-day Jerusalem and Mecca dissolved, to be replaced by Leonardo DaVinci's most famous painting: *The Divine Truce*. As I looked at Lord Bexe, surrounded by his former enemies, I was struck by how much Hexe resembled his ancestor. The only real difference between the two was the color of their hair—and the look of haunted sadness in the Witch King's golden eyes. But perhaps that was merely artistic license on Leonardo's part, since he re-created the famous meeting three hundred and eighty-seven years after the fact.

"Following what is now called the Divine Intervention, the Holy Roman Emperor Henry V, Pope Paschal II, Sultan Mehmed I, Patriarch John IX of Byzantium, Rabbi Ibn Megas, and Lord Bexe gathered in Constantinople, and with the signing of the Treaty of 1111, the Sufferance finally came to an end."

"I see you've found our new multimedia exhibit. We recently updated it in order to make it more immersive." The Curator had, once again, ghosted up behind me without my being aware of it. I had to hand it to the old girl—she had some mad ninja skills.

"Is that Sir Ian McKellen doing the narration?" I asked.

"Yes, it is," she said proudly. "Royal Shakespeare Company actors work best as the Voice of God, in my experience. The previous narration was by Sir Ralph Richardson, but we decided to record a new version when we upgraded from analog to digital sound."

As I turned away, a flash of bright yellow caught my attention. It was a length of police tape wrapped about a display case. "Is that the exhibit you mentioned earlier—?"

"Yes, it is," she sighed sadly. "We lost an entire collection of authentic Witchfinder devices: finger-cutters, witch-hammers, spell-gags—that sort of thing. The finger-cutter was particularly valuable, as it is rumored to be the same one Lord Bexe used to take his own magic upon surrendering the throne of Arum."

I grimaced in disgust. "Why on earth would anyone want to steal stuff like that?"

"There is a brisk business in antique witchbreaking devices, not unlike the underground trade in Nazi memorabilia," she replied. "Although it was part of the Treaty of 1111 that all such devices be destroyed, a few have managed to survive the centuries in private collections."

The Curator fell silent as the brace of horse-legged ipotanes came clattering into the hall, lugging the welding equipment and heavy crates as if they were made of balsa wood. The head drover, Fabio, set his burden down with a loud thud that resounded throughout the gallery.

"Here is your delivery, *Master* Canterbury," the ipotane announced sarcastically. "Please sign at the bottom, to verify that the items have been delivered in satisfactory condition. And I *will* be filing a complaint with my shop steward regarding your use of a racial slur."

"You go ahead and do that," the centaur grunted as he scribbled his initials on the paperwork.

Once Fabio and his team were out of the way, Canterbury and I opened the crates and set about connecting leg bones to hip bones, wing bones to shoulder bones, tailbone to butt bone. When I finished the final weld connecting the head bone to the neck bone, I stood back and gazed upon the fully assembled clockwork dragon.

It stood ten feet high and fifteen feet long, about a third of the size of an actual adult battle-dragon, or so I have been told, and was all gleaming gears and escapements. The body itself was eight feet long, with the remainder being its tail, which tapered down to a barbed point, like the cracker on a bullwhip. It had a long, wide snout, flaring nostrils, and antlerlike horns that grew from its forehead like antenna. Its powerful legs resembled those of a Komodo dragon, and the wings attached to its shoulder joints were tightly folded while grounded. Once activated, the clockwork mechanism inside it was designed to move the head and tail in a realistic fashion and trigger a bellows attached to a resonator in its chest, which simulated the creature's infamous war cry.

"You did amazing work, Canterbury," the Curator said with an appreciative nod. "She's a real beauty."

I raised an eyebrow in surprise. "You mean this thing is supposed to be female?"

"*All* battle-dragons were female; the males didn't have wings," the Curator replied. "The one Lord Bexe flew against General Vlad was called Skysplitter. She was the last dragon to die in the Disarmament. Immediately after Lord Bexe put her down, he severed his sixth fingers and went into exile."

"It seems like such a waste," I sighed.

"Indeed it does," the Curator agreed. "But Lord Bexe truly had no choice. I have studied this single moment in history my entire adult life, from every possible angle, and have found no other means of resolution. General Vlad's decision to attack human settlements following the signing of the Truce—knowing that mankind dare not retaliate for fear of divine punishment—forced the Witch King to take extreme action. There were already rumors circulating amongst the human powers that the Divine Intervention had been nothing more than Kymeran trickery. The Treaty of 1111 was in danger of being destroyed, and the Sufferance rekindled. Lord Bexe had no choice but to side with the human race against his own brother." The Curator shook her head, as if clearing it of visions only she could see. "Well, that's enough waltzing through history," she said with a wan smile. "It's time we put the finishing touches on our friend here and make her presentable so she can meet her public."

She briskly clapped her hands, like a schoolteacher summoning silence from her class, and a wooden trunk appeared before her. Reaching into the voluminous folds of her sleeves she retrieved a large ring of keys of various sizes and shapes, quickly flicking through them until she came to the one she sought. She opened the trunk, revealing what looked like folded cloth-of-gold. She gestured with her right hand, like an orchestra conductor calling four-four time, and the empty skin rose upward like a gilded ghost.

The fingers of the Curator's right hand moved like those of a puppeteer manipulating a marionette, guiding the shed so that it once more assumed the shape of the proud beast that had once worn it. The empty skin hovered above the clockwork dragon for a moment, then gently lowered itself so that it draped the automaton from the nape of its neck to an inch short of the barbed tail. Once the shed was in place, the Curator began tapping her fingertips together, as if she was playing a pair of invisible castanets, while at the same time miming a seamstress fitting a garment on a dressmaker's dummy, until the gleaming skin was securely bonded to the clockwork dragon.

"Look at you," Canterbury smiled, addressing his handiwork as if it were a beloved pet. "Aren't you gorgeous?" He then turned and nodded to me. "Okay, kid—time to do your stuff!"

Before I became Canterbury's apprentice, my talent for animating the sculptures I created was entirely unconscious, and invariably a response to "fight-or-flight" scenarios. But under his tutelage, I had since learned how to make deliberate contact with the spark that resides in my creations and activate it through the force of my will. All artists put a little of themselves into their work—but in my case it's literally true.

I took a deep breath and focused my attention on the clockwork dragon, rerunning how I had put it together, piece by piece, in my mind. As I slowed my heart rate and steadied my breathing, I felt the edges of my consciousness travel outward, like the ripples on a pond. Suddenly the clockwork dragon reared back onto its hind legs, its forelegs clawing at the air, and spread gold foil wings that shimmered like the sun. It opened its mighty jaws and a deep, reverberating growl, like that of a bull alligator, rumbled forth from its chest. For the briefest of moments it felt as if the thing was genuinely alive, and I was its master, holding it on the end of an invisible leash.

"Turn the head toward me a tad," Canterbury instructed. "Now lift the wings a little higher—spread them out farther—no! Too much! Pull it back a bit! Yes, that's it! *Perfect!* You can let go now, Tate."

I sighed and retracted my concentration, leaving the automaton posed to my master's specifications. As my will slipped free of the clockwork dragon, I felt the spark I had awakened within it retreat, as if the golden reptile had fallen into hibernation.

"*Most* impressive," the Curator said, regarding me like a potential exhibit. "I have never seen the inanimate made animate without the ritual of the Unspoken Word. Are you *certain* you're fully human?"

"Believe me, there is *nothing* magical about my parents," I assured her. "So how are we supposed to suspend this thing from the ceiling? I don't see any hooks or mounts up there...."

Before I could finish my sentence, the golden dragon floated upward like a Macy's parade balloon, positioning itself opposite its ebon foe.

"The remainder of your commission is waiting for you in the administrative office on the ground floor, Master Canterbury," the Curator said, returning her hands to her voluminous sleeves. "And don't forget the gift shop on your way out."

Chapter 6

Every year since 1778, there has been a parade and street fair on the first day of April to commemorate both the founding of Golgotham and the end of the Revolutionary War. Much like St. Patrick's Day and the Feast of San Gennaro, the Jubilee is a public celebration that attracts far more than the ethnic group that originally founded it. Just like you don't have to be Irish to dance a jig and swig green beer or Italian to knock back the vino and stuff your face with zeppole, you don't need six fingers or hooves to caper about Golgotham like a wine-soaked maenad.

The biggest crowd pleaser of the Jubilee celebration is the Procession, where all of Golgotham's major supernatural races, or ethnic groups, or whatever you want to call them, proudly strut their stuff. It's also the official kickoff ceremony for the rest of the festival, which goes on all day and well into the night. Getting a curbside view of the Procession is very important if you actually want to see the parade itself, and not the back of someone's head. So if you want to get a good spot you have to show up before the crowds do—say, around half-past the crack of dawn.

It was five thirty in the morning when my best friend, Vanessa, and her new hubby, Adrian, showed up on our doorstep, outfitted with matching backpacks and dragging a cooler-on-wheels.

"Thank God!" Vanessa groaned in relief upon seeing the pot of coffee waiting for her in the kitchen.

"Be careful with that stuff," I warned her. "It's a special

grind from the Devil's Brew. One cup is guaranteed to wire you for sound."

"Wow, you're not kidding." Adrian grimaced. "I've barely taken a sip and my eyelids feel like they're flapping behind my eyeballs. Where's Hexe?"

"He left about an hour ago to nail down a good spot," I explained. "Golgothamites take their Jubilee *very* seriously, so it pays to stake a claim as early as possible."

"Have you heard anything from your parents yet?" asked Vanessa.

"Not a peep," I replied. "Normally my dad would have tried an end run around my mother by now, but he's not going to risk crossing her when she's *this* mad. I don't need their money if the strings attached to it make me a puppet."

"Your cat just insulted me and flew upstairs," Adrian said, looking nonplussed.

"Don't mind Scratch," I laughed. "He's under strict orders not to eat friends and family."

Upon finishing our coffee, we grabbed up some collapsible camp chairs and headed out for the Procession, chatting among ourselves. Despite the early hour, there was already a steady stream of people, many of them outfitted with step-ladders, headed in the direction of Perdition, the widest and straightest street in Golgotham. Perdition stretched all the way from the Gate of Skulls, located on Broadway, to the wharves of the East River, and during the Jubilee, festive banners and bunting were hung from every window, doorway, and lamppost, and temporary archways of red, white, and blue had been erected along the Procession route.

As we arrived at the corner of Golden Hill and Perdition, I spotted Hexe standing on the curb, talking to his childhood friend Kidron. It was one of the few times I'd seen the centaur out-of-harness, and he was dressed to the nines in a blue silk caparison decorated with small diamond-shaped mirrors, with a matching doublet and a leather helmet crested by an ostrich feather dyed to match his clothes. I couldn't hear what they were discussing, but judging by the scowl on Hexe's face, it was something unpleasant.

"Jubilation, Tate, to you and your friends," Kidron said as we approached. "And I am glad to see you back on your feet, Miss Sullivan. I trust your ankle is no longer bothering you?"

"Thank you," Vanessa smiled. "And it's Mrs. Klein, now. But, yes, my sprain is fully healed, thanks to Hexe."

"That is good to hear. My people take such wounds very seriously," Kidron replied. "Now, if you'll excuse me, I must return to my herd." With that he clopped across the street to join a group of centaurs, all of them tricked out in equally fancy dress.

"So why the frowny face?" I asked as Hexe kissed me hello.

"The Maladanti are putting the bite on the livery drivers," he replied sotto voce. "They used to get ten percent. Now they're demanding thirty, and are threatening to kneecap anyone who balks." Upon seeing the look on my face, Hexe smiled and smoothed the hair away from my brow. "There will be other days on the calendar to worry about Boss Marz. I just want to enjoy the Jubilee with you before I end up being stuck judging who gets the blue ribbon for Best Potion for the rest of my life. Today is the Jubilee," he said, raising his voice so that the others could hear, "a time to celebrate our freedom and the unity of our peoples!"

"Damn straight!" Vanessa agreed as she set up her camp chair.

"You certainly have some interesting neighbors here in Golgotham," Adrian said, eyeing a clan of leprechauns as they clambered up a homemade reviewing stand constructed from a pair of ladders and a two-by-four.

"These are just the ones who come out during the day," Hexe said with a wink. "Wait until the sun goes down and the trolls, ghouls, and goblins take to the streets!"

Adrian laughed uneasily and then checked the app on his phone that told him what time the sun would set.

Within an hour of our arrival there were thousands of parade watchers, both looky-loos and native, thronging the length of Perdition Street. As the sun rose, the early morning chill quickly gave way to clear blue skies and pleasant spring temperatures. Children—human and otherwise—ran back and forth across the broad street in mindless, kinetic tribes, shouting and playing tag. A trio of centaur foals frisked about under the watchful eye of their dams, while a couple of young satyr kids amused themselves by butting heads. A vermilion-haired Kymeran street vendor carried a long pole covered in giant hand-twisted pretzels, hawking his wares to the hungry in the crowd, closely followed by a faun with a refrigerated pushcart selling ice-cold bottles of butterscotch root beer.

Suddenly, a red rubber ball bounced into the middle of the frolicking foals. A second later a five-year-old human child came running up to reclaim it, only to stare in amazement at the little centauride turning the toy over in her hands. Her upper portion resembled a four-year-old girl, her blond hair fixed in twin pigtails, and dressed in a My Little Pony T-shirt, while from the waist down she was a knobby-kneed palomino foal. Upon espying the little boy, she smiled and shyly held the ball out to him. He returned her smile and reached out to take it, all the while unable to take his eyes off her.

Hexe reached out and took my hand in his and gave it a squeeze. I grinned and kissed him on the cheek. "Maybe things aren't so hopeless, after all?" I said, resting my head on his shoulder.

"The problem isn't with the kids," he said as a woman hurried from the crowd and grabbed the young boy by the arm.

"*Jaxon!* What did I tell you about staying where I can keep an eye on you?"

"But I was just getting my ball back—!" the kid protested feebly.

A palomino centauress stepped out into the street, putting herself between the foal and the boy. "That's enough horseplay for now, Wynona!" she said sternly.

"See what I mean?" Hexe sighed.

The sound of distant, rhythmic drumbeats echoed throughout the neighborhood as a couple of centaurs in PTU helmets and crowd-control gear came trotting down Perdition, clearing away the vendors and pedestrians from the street. Upon espying these outliers, the crowds lining the curb began to cheer and clap.

A minute or two later the Procession itself hove into sight. At its head were six Kymerans marching abreast of one another, each one dressed in robes the color of their respective caste: blue, yellow, red, green, orange, and purple. Their billowing garments were covered with arcane symbols picked out in silver thread and they carried between them a long pole, three to each end, from which hung a heavy satin banner embellished with the seal of Golgotham: a six-fingered right hand within a pentagram.

Behind the walkers was the Motley Fool, a masked acrobat dressed in the trademark coat of many colors that was the symbol of Kymerans in exile, and who walked on his hands and performed backflips and somersaults. The crowd laughed and cheered, tossing coins into the street, which the Motley Fool scooped up and placed in a pouch cinched about his waist.

Following the costumed tumbler were three minotaurs with crimson loincloths knotted about their muscular waists and protective caps on their horns. Strapped across their backs were drums fashioned from the shells of gigantic tortoises. Marching immediately behind them were barrel-chested, horse-legged ipotanes wielding what looked like human leg bones in place of mallets. The rhythms the drummers summoned forth resonated like thunder and quickly invaded my pulse, making my scalp tighten and the hair on my arms stand erect.

After the drum line was the royal carriage containing Lady Syra, Witch Queen of the Kymerans. She rode in a phaeton wreathed in garlands of flowers, drawn by Illuminata, her private chauffeur. The albino centauride was dressed in a shimmering silver mail tunic and a helmet topped by a snow-white ostrich plume. The doors of the carriage were set with enameled panels bearing the Seal of Arum: a golden battle-dragon with its tail in its mouth. Lady Syra, wearing a tiara fashioned from a pair of intertwined dragons atop her peacock blue hair, waved to the cheering crowds with her right hand, while holding a scepter that resembled a caduceus in her left.

Directly behind the royal carriage was the Mayor's coach, which was as ornately carved and heavily gilded as a circus wagon, pulled by a team of four centaurs. Banners proclaiming REELECT MAYOR LASH were draped on either side while the Mayor enthusiastically hurled fists full of wrapped sweets at the crowds.

"Yay! Free candy!" Adrian exclaimed, eagerly scooping

up one of the treats. Before I could warn him, he opened it and popped it in his mouth. A second later he spat it back out, a horrified look on his face. "Holy hell! What *is* that shit? It tastes like black licorice mixed with salt and ammonia!"

"It's called salt licorice," I explained. "It's something of an acquired taste. Kymerans love it."

"*Agggh!* My tongue's gone numb!"

"Yeah, it'll do that," Hexe conceded.

As Adrian staggered off in search of something to wash the taste of free candy out of his mouth and restore sensation to his tongue, I returned my attention to the Procession. Directly behind the Mayor's coach was a phalanx of twelve centaur stallions outfitted in ceremonial barding, with elaborately detailed bronze pectorals protecting their lower equine chests, leather and brass croupiers shielding their haunches, and helmets with hinged cheek plates.

Suddenly there was a sound like a hundred beehives being overturned, and twenty-five leprechauns playing scaled-down Irish war pipes marched into view, followed by an equal number playing toy-sized hand drums. Both pipers and drummers alike wore the traditional leprechaun dress of bright green breeches, jackets, and broad-brimmed hats, with shiny golden buckles on their hatbands and shoes. All fifty were redheaded, though only the older ones had any facial hair, and none of them stood any taller than a three-year-old human child.

The Wee Folks Anti-Defamation League's float, drawn by a brace of centaur colts, was festooned with campaign banners that read: VOTE THE GREEN PARTY: SEAMUS O'FAE FOR MAYOR. Perched high atop a fake pot of gold at the end of an equally artificial rainbow was none other than Little Big Man himself. The tiny, charismatic lawyer and civic leader seemed to be enjoying himself immensely as he waved his shillelagh with one hand and tossed imitation gold doubloons to the crowd with the other.

While the leprechauns were the most numerous of the faeries that call Golgotham home, they were far from the only Wee Folk on the float. A quartet of foot-tall brownies, flat-faced with huge eyes and tufted ears, their bodies covered in short curly hair, scampered about like a litter of bipedal Pekingese puppies as they supplied necklaces, candy, and toy doubloons to a squadron of dragonfly-winged pixies, who zoomed in and out of the crowd like barnstormers.

There was a high-pitched buzzing sound and something suddenly swooped toward my head. I instinctively backed away, fearing a wasp or hornet had flown into my face, only to find myself staring at a pixie hovering inches in front of my nose. It was six inches long, with iridescent wings that beat so fast it seemed to hang in midair like a hummingbird. It was androgynous in appearance, with high-turned cheekbones and large eyes and a hairless, pale green body that resembled celadon pottery, clad in a simple, tuniclike garment woven from spider silk. It was carrying a doubloon in its tiny, yet surprisingly strong hands.

"Vote for Seamus!" the pixie said with its pennywhistle voice. Upon dropping its cargo in my outstretched hand, it promptly zipped back to the slowly moving float to rejoin its kin.

I looked down at the doubloon, which, despite its color, was made of anodized aluminum. On one side was stamped O'FAE FOR MAYOR; and on the other, GOOD FOR ONE FREE BEER @ BLARNEY'S BOOTH. I had to hand it to Seamus—he certainly knew his constituency.

After the faerie folk passed by there came a triple column of satyrs pulling rickshaws, who wove in and out like Shriners in midget parade cars. In the lead rickshaw was Giles Gruff, leader of the satyr community, monocle in one eye, dressed in a top hat and monogrammed waistcoat, waving his gold-topped walking stick like a drum major. Riding in the other rickshaws were a mixture of comely nymphs and fauns, who smiled and tossed strands of wine-colored beads to the onlookers thronging the street.

Next came Golgotham's merfolk contingent, fronted by ten strapping, green-haired mer-men, naked save for their seaweed skirts. Using conch shells to trumpet their arrival, they went into the ritual dance of their people, grimacing and chanting as they slapped their bare chests, thighs and upper arms with their wide, webbed hands. Upon finishing, a couple of juvenile mers sprayed them down with misting wands attached to tanks of salt water, so that they would not dehydrate and start to wither.

*   *   *

Given that Golgotham is an automobile-free zone, the throaty rumble of combustion engines, even at low throttle, seemed as out of place as the whinny of centaurs on Broadway. The Iron Maidens Motorcycle Club, composed of two dozen Amazon warriors and Valkyries, rolled their idling hogs down the cobblestone street, dressed in their club colors, longbows and spears slung across their backs.

At the head of the pack were Hildy and Lyta, the joint leaders of the merged gangs, sitting astride a chopped trike. Hildy, who stood over six feet tall and had long, blond Teutonic braids and a Harley-Davidson patch to hide her missing eye, was in the driver's seat. Behind her was Lyta, dressed in a leather bustier that proudly displayed her missing right breast. As Hildy gunned the throttle on the trike, Lyta stood upright, lifting her bow over her head, and cut loose with an ululating war cry. The other Amazons instantly did the same, shaking their bows at the sky. Hildy pulled her war-hammer from its holster on the side of the trike and held it on high as well, giving voice to the famous call of the Valkyries. Her sister Choosers of The Slain answered in kind, raising their spears while gunning their motors, until it sounded like Wagner at Sturgis: loud, proud, and fucking awesome.

The last float in the Procession was a flatbed pulled by a brace of Teamsters, on which a dozen hulders, fauns, and nymphs, wearing nothing but red-white-and-blue G-strings, star-shaped pasties, and tricorn hats writhed against stripper poles bolted to the floor of the trailer. Banners draped along either side of the float proudly proclaimed DUIVEL STREET WELCOMES YOU TO THE JUBILEE!

Bjorn Cowpen, dressed in a pair of form-fitting red velveteen bell-bottom pants and a bright blue silk shirt open to his navel, with a white cravat knotted about his throat, stood surrounded by his patriotically garbed, gyrating employees as he tossed out sealed star-spangled condoms and sampler packets of flavored personal lubrication. The parents in the crowd recoiled in horror, yanking their children away from the sight of near-naked exotic dancers hanging upside down by their thighs from mobile stripper poles, while the rest of the onlookers hooted and cheered.

"This'll come in handy later," Adrian quipped as he caught an All-American rubber.

"Better let *me* keep track of it," Vanessa said with a wink, plucking the patriotic prophylactic from his hand and sliding it into her cleavage.

Bringing up the Procession was the Paranormal Threat Unit, led by Captain Horn, who rode atop a police wagon pulled by a brawny centaur in PTU riot gear. Marching on foot alongside the wagon was his second-in-command, Lieutenant Viva, her long, copper-penny tresses tucked up under her helmet.

At first I thought they were merely participants in the parade until a drunken spectator, inflamed by lust and stupidity, clambered onto the Duivel Street float. Captain Horn pointed his right hand at the rowdy and an ectoplasmic cocoon instantly formed about the inebriated man, binding his arms to his side. Lieutenant Viva and another PTU officer quickly hurried forward and grabbed the subdued unruly, who now resembled a giant wad of cotton candy, and quickly tossed him in the back of the paddy wagon.

Now that the Procession had finally passed by, the crowds on either side of the street moved to fill the empty void, scavenging the gutters for missed throws and other treasures before experiencing the games of chance, carnival rides, and souvenir booths that lined the cross streets. Many of the local restaurants and pubs set up temporary stalls on the sidewalks as well, to take advantage of the festival-goers.

Blarney's booth, easily identifiable by its bright green awning, was already doing a brisk business selling corned beef sandwiches and baked potatoes to those eager to cash in their doubloons for free beer. I spotted Lafo, dressed in painstakingly accurate Colonial Era dress, right down to the powdered wig, manning a stall that flew the familiar two-headed calf logo.

"Jubilation to you and yours, Serenity!" the restaurateur said jovially, handing Hexe an enormous plastic novelty glass shaped like a revolutionary musket. "What can I get you and your friends?"

"What do you think I should try?" Vanessa whispered, eyeing the menu board warily.

"This is probably the closest you're going to get to 'typical' carnival food. Most of the other vendors are far more, uh, *ethnic* than this," I explained, pointing to another booth across the street advertising python kabobs and caramel apples dipped in deep-fried mealworms.

Vanessa and Adrian quickly agreed that I had a point, and decided to go with the roasted goat tamale and chili-cheese funnel cake, which they washed down with souvenir muskets of prickly pear margaritas.

Food in hand, we wandered deeper and deeper into Golgotham, past booths selling souvenir tricorn hats and red-white-and-blue papier-mâché skulls on sticks, leprechauns competing in clogging contests, and the occasional fire-eater. I decided not to drink anything harder than orchid cream soda, just in case a sober head might be needed, since Nessie and Adrian seemed determined to sample every wine, mead, and ale stall they saw. All in the name of epicurean curiosity, of course, not because they're lushes—or so they kept reassuring me.

The plaza that surrounds the Fly Market was temporarily transformed into a carnival midway, where Kymeran youngsters with Technicolor hair stood in line with their parents to ride the Ferris wheel, and the Flying Bobs. I watched in amusement as a pair of bleating satyr kids clattered excitedly up the metal steps of the Tilt-A-Whirl, while centaur foals rode a carousel outfitted with gaily colored moving stalls instead of merry-go-round horses.

At the far end was a large, raised wooden platform festooned in tricolor bunting, atop which could be seen the members of the GoBOO as well as Lady Syra and Mayor Lash. The assembled dignitaries were reviewing a collection of jars and bottles arrayed atop a long table, while down on the ground level, a nervous group of competing witches and warlocks watched their every movement, eager to find out who would claim the blue ribbon for best potion of the year.

While most of the booths sold concessions and souvenirs, there were more than a few manned by local merchants eager to advertise their businesses to potential customers. One such booth belonged to Dr. Mao, whose red awning boasted gold and black tigers and signage in Mandarin, Kymeran, and English. Behind the counter stood the proprietor himself, dressed in a traditional Chinese tunic and cap. His bushy gray eyebrow, which stretched across his forehead without a break, marked him as a shape-shifter, as did the extra-long ring fingers on either hand.

"Jubilation to you, Serenity," the old were-tiger said, bowing slightly.

"Jubilation to you and your family as well, my friend," Hexe replied. "I see you're putting my former lodger to good use." He pointed to Lukas, who was at the back of the stall, grinding roots and herbs with a mortar and pestle alongside Dr. Mao's only child, Meikei.

"Yes, if you call finding excuses to paw my daughter in public 'working,'" Dr. Mao said acerbically.

"*Daddy!*" Meikei protested. Lukas quickly let go of her hand, his ears suddenly bright pink.

"Don't 'daddy' me!" Mao said, wagging a long fingernail in her direction. "Don't forget I'm the boss of *both* of you! Now grind up some more fossilized dragon bone—we're almost out!"

As I chuckled at Lukas' expense, I felt Hexe suddenly grab my arm. I looked up to see Boss Marz walking through the crowd in our direction, flanked on either side by a pair of his croggies. His familiar, Bonzo, rode on his left shoulder, chattering excitedly.

"Get out of here, Lukas," Dr. Mao said in a quiet yet urgent voice. "I don't want him to see you."

"But, Master Mao—!" The youth protested, his eyes flashing like an angry cougar's.

"You heard me—go home!" Mao's drooping mustache suddenly became bristling whiskers as dark stripes swam to the surface of his skin. "Meikei and I can handle the booth."

The young were-cat bowed his head to his master and quickly slipped away, disappearing into the bustling street without a trace.

"I give Lukas a hard time," Mao said as he watched his apprentice leave, "but he is a good boy and I'll be skinned if Marz gets his hands on him again."

Speaking of the Maladanti, I stole another look in Boss Marz's direction and saw him stop at a Hit the Cats booth operated by a cyclops in a Knicks T-shirt. Although the carnie smiled as he handed the crime lord an envelope, it was clear from the glint in his solitary eye that he was nervous.

As Marz reached out to take the "tribute," Bonzo screeched and ran down the length of his master's arm and snatched up not only the payment, but a small plush teddy bear as well, before scampering back to his perch. Marz pocketed the money while Bonzo plucked the eyes off the toy before tearing its head off and gutting it of its stuffing. Chuckling, Boss Marz turned to stare directly at us.

Hexe stood his ground and looked at Marz and his men defiantly, his right hand at the ready, refusing to shrink from view or dodge detection. There was a gleam in his golden eyes, as if some hidden fire was being stoked deep within him, and for a heartbeat it was as if I was staring at Lord Bexe, the Last Witch King of Arum.

One of Marz's croggies started to raise his left hand, only to have his boss swat him like a parent correcting a child acting out at the supermarket. The Maladanti goon quickly stepped down, placing his left hand in the small of his back. The trio then turned away and proceeded down a nearby side street.

"*That* was a close one," I sighed in relief.

"Don't let him ruin the Jubilee for you," Hexe said, slipping his arm about my waist. "Marz isn't going to do anything that will bring the PTU down on him—not while he still has tribute to collect."

I smiled and nodded in agreement, but seeing Boss Marz wandering about the festival was like splashing about at the beach, only to have a shark brush your leg with its tail. Glimpsing the hesitation in my eyes, Hexe dragged me over to a nearby booth, where he spent the next fifteen minutes and twenty dollars throwing rubber rings at upright soda bottles in order to win a plush toy white gorilla wearing a plaid tam-o'-shanter.

You know how some women get excited over their men giving them jewelry? Well, in my case I get the exact same way when someone wins stuffed toys for me at carnivals. Needless to say, much kissing and squeezing followed.

As late afternoon turned into dusk, the Jubilee began to undergo a gradual sea change as Golgotham's darker denizens gradually joined in the celebration. Vanessa, Adrian, Hexe, and I were sitting in a beer garden when a group of trolls ambled past, muttering among themselves in their thick, unintelligible language, lashing their heavy, ropelike tails as they sniffed the air with big, bumpy noses the size of knockwursts.

"Gracious! Look at the time!" Adrian said, pretending

to look at a wrist watch. "Nessie and I must be getting back home! I need to be ready for work in the morning, you know."

Vanessa frowned. "I thought you said you had arranged with the head of your department to get tomorrow off—"

"Yeah, but he changed his mind," Adrian said quickly as he helped his wife up from the table. "Remember, I *told* you I got a text from him this afternoon—?"

"Huh?" Vanessa's frown deepened for a second; then her gaze fell on the gaggle of goblins, their bare, paddlelike feet slapping against the cobblestones like wet laundry. "Oh, yeah! *That's* right!" she said, gathering up her purse. "I was having such a good time I *totally* forgot!"

As a pride of sphinx moved through the street fair like lions on their way to a watering hole, Adrian and Vanessa hurried in the opposite direction, eager to return to the humdrum hazards of lower Manhattan.

"Well, *that* wasn't awkward at all, was it?" I sighed.

"Nessie and Adrian stayed a lot longer than I gave them credit for," Hexe said as he sipped his musket of barley wine. "Jubilee can be overwhelming even for Golgothamites—especially after dark. And it was good to see you enjoying yourself with your friends, especially after you've pushed yourself so hard at work. It's time you relaxed, kicked back, and had some fun."

"Sitting downwind from Ghastly's food stall is making me queasy," I said, pointing in the direction of the gaunt, bat-nosed ghouls lined up in front of the booth belonging to Golgotham's worst cook. Given the clientele, I really didn't want to know what was listed on the menu board.

As we wandered along Perdition Street, I realized what Hexe said about the Jubilee after dark was right—the feel of the festival had definitely changed with the setting of the sun. All the families—human and otherwise—had disappeared, surrendering the field to the more dedicated revelers and those citizens of Golgotham who normally shunned the sun's rays.

As the moon rose, a group of nymphs cast aside their flimsy chitons and began to run naked through the streets hand in hand, weaving in and out of the crowds like living daisy chains, giggling like mischievous schoolgirls. An amorous frat boy made a grab for one of them, only to have her slip free of his arms in the form of a cloud, her laughter tinkling like a silver bell.

It was not long before the nymphs were joined by maenads, who spun about, crying out in ecstasy, wineskins in one hand and drawn knives in the other, their eyes blazing like funeral pyres. A herd of satyrs quickly fell in among them, adding wild piping and the crashing of cymbals to the merrymaking. Suddenly one of the passing nymphs grabbed my hand and yanked me into the street, spinning me around and around like a child playing with a top. Her laughter was as clear as an Attic sky and sweet as honey fresh from the comb, and for a heartbeat I understood how handsome young shepherds could abandon their flocks in mad pursuit of such impossible, primal beauty.

After two or three spins, the nymph let go of me and hurried after her sisters as they continued to wind their way through the festival-goers. I staggered backward, shaking my head to try to clear the dizziness from it, then turned to where Hexe had been standing a moment before, only to find him gone.

I looked around, at first thinking he must have gone to one of the concession booths to freshen his drink, but there was still no sign of him. However, there was an unpleasant smell in the air, one that seemed familiar, yet which I could not immediately place. Just as I was beginning to get worried, I caught a glimpse of purple hair half a block away, headed in the direction of the riverfront. I hurried after him, shouting his name, but his back was to me and my voice was drowned out by the noise of the carnival. I pulled out my cell phone to try to call him, only to find my battery drained.

Just as I was closing in, he suddenly ducked into one of the nameless alleyways that thread their way through the neighborhood. Upon following him, I was surprised to find Hexe standing in the middle of the narrow passageway with his back to me, his limbs twitching and jerking as if afflicted with Saint Vitus' dance.

"Hey!" I shouted, more exasperated than angry. "What's the big idea ditching me back there?"

Upon hearing my voice, the thing I had mistaken for Hexe turned to face me. Although it possessed the exact physical build, with the same color hair, worn in the exact same style, and was dressed in identical clothing as Hexe, the face was a blank oval, save for a pair of gaping, empty holes where the eyes should be.

As I backed away from the decoy, I caught the distinct smell of scorched metal, as if someone had left a saucepan on the burner for too long. I turned to see Boss Marz looming behind me, blocking my escape.

"Foolish little nump." He grinned. "Don't you know better than to believe *anything* you see on Jubilee Night?"

Chapter 7

The next time I opened my eyes I was relieved to find myself looking across a table into the *real* Hexe's face, not that of the hideous simulacrum Marz had conjured forth to lure me away from the crowds. That relief was short lived as I realized I was tied to a chair and Hexe's arms were pinned down atop the table by what looked like croquet hoops fitted into holes drilled into its surface. The fingers of both his hands were kept splayed and rigid in metal splints, therefore preventing him from working magic.

"Did they hurt you?" he asked anxiously. Although his purple hair was hanging down into his face, I could see that his right eye was blackened and his lower lip was split.

"I'm okay," I replied, looking around as best I could at our surroundings. We seemed to be in a warehouse of some kind, and I could distinctly smell the river. "What is this place?"

"We're somewhere in the Stronghold—the Maladanti's private pier," Hexe replied.

"How did we get here?"

"Marz's familiar grabbed me the moment that nymph started spinning you around," he explained. "They must have been watching us the whole time, waiting to strike. He teleported in and out within the blink of an eye."

"I *thought* I caught a whiff of something hellish." I grimaced.

"This is all *my* fault," Hexe said bitterly. "We should have left the festival when I saw Marz, but I was unwilling to back down. Because of my pride, I've put both of us in danger."

"How gracious of you to take the blame, Serenity. But then, you've always been one for noblesse oblige," Boss Marz said as he emerged from the shadows, his familiar riding his shoulder, trailed by a pair of Maladanti goons. He smiled as he approached us, like a gracious host greeting welcome guests. "While I was away in the Tombs, I learned how little there is to do when one is in solitary confinement with steel mittens locked about your hands. They only allowed me the free use of my hands—and then, only the right one—for a few minutes each day to tend to meals, ablutions, and excretions. Having to rely on my weak hand to feed and groom myself proved quite eye-opening."

"Not enough to take you off the Left Hand path, it would seem," Hexe replied acidly.

"Ah, but it *did* provide me with a great deal of inspiration." Marz's smile became almost beatific as he stroked his familiar, Bonzo, who screeched and flashed his tiny fangs in my direction. "Gaza, show him the implements."

A Maladanti soldier with peach-colored Jheri curls stepped forward and placed a small bundle on the table next to Hexe. Without anyone touching it, it unrolled to reveal a collection of metal items that resembled a cross between surgical instruments and a handyman's tools. My blood ran cold as my mind suddenly flashed back to the display case wrapped in police tape at the museum.

"Those are witchbreaking devices," Hexe gasped.

"You're quite right, Serenity," Boss Marz replied. "Isn't it ironic that the Witchfinders, in order to rid the world of our kind, were forced to use magical weapons? But I can also appreciate the need to have the right tool for the job. Take this little beauty, for example," he said as he picked up what looked like a double-edged cigar cutter. "The last time it tasted Kymeran blood was when Lord Bexe scattered his people to the wind."

"You're *still* grinding that axe, Marz?"

"Aye, and it's quite sharp now," the crime boss replied as the finger-cutter's twin blades shut with an audible *click*.

Hexe's face went white and his cat-slit pupils expanded until they swallowed the gold in his eye. "You wouldn't dare," he croaked.

"I wouldn't be so certain as to what I *might* or might *not* do, if I were you, Serenity," Marz sneered. "After all, *you're* the one who didn't think I would make a move against you during the Jubilee. But you needn't worry—I'm not going to steal your magic so easily," he said, tossing the finger-cutter back onto the table. He then pulled open the cuffs of his shirt as if to invite inspection. "Please notice that there is nothing up my sleeves." He waved his left hand in an extravagant gesture, but instead of conjuring a bouquet of flowers from thin air he produced a metal mallet. *"Prest-o change-o!"*

Hexe tried to evade the blow, but there was no way to escape it. I closed my eyes, but could not block the sound of Hexe's scream as his metacarpals splintered. Although I didn't want to, I forced myself to look and saw that the color had drained from his face. He was hyperventilating and struggling to keep the pain from showing. Hexe raised his head to glare at Marz.

"Is that all you got?" he croaked.

Boss Marz brought the hammer down a second time, reducing the already-damaged fingers to kindling. Although he had to be in immense agony, Hexe gritted his teeth and remained silent, determined not to give the bastard the satisfaction of hearing him cry out.

However, I wasn't as strong. *"Stop it!"* I screamed as Marz lifted the hammer a third time. *"Please, don't hurt him any more!"*

"Very well, Ms. Eresby," Marz said, tossing aside the witchbreaking device. "Far be it from me to go against the wishes of a lady."

"You've gone too far, even for the Maladanti," Hexe rasped. His face was starting to go gray with shock and his pupils were distressingly large. "They'll throw you so deep into the Tombs you'll never see sunlight again."

"If I was frightened of your mother or the GoBOO, I never would have tossed you in that fighting pit in the first place," Marz snorted in derision. "Understand this, Serenity: *nobody* interferes with me and gets away with it—I don't care how blue their hair is! The fact you are the Heir Apparent means less than *nothing* to me. You are not, and never will be, *my* Witch King." He motioned for Gaza to remove the restraints pinning Hexe's arms to the table, and then ordered the other croggy to untie me from my chair. As I jumped to my feet and rushed to his side, Hexe instinctively reached out to me, only to grimace in agony. I sobbed as I saw the swollen mass of tortured flesh that was now his right hand.

"Don't cry, don't cry," he whispered hoarsely, clumsily wiping away my tears with his left hand. "It's going to be okay." Cradling his ruined hand to his chest, he turned to face his tormentor. "I don't care what you have planned for me, Marz—but leave her out of this. She's done you no harm."

"I would beg to differ," Boss Marz replied sourly. "That accursed mechanical cat of hers cost me an excellent lieutenant. But there's no need for you to plead for the nump's life. I don't want either of you dead, Serenity. Seeing you reduced to using your left hand to survive is *far* more satisfying to me than watching your blood dry on the floor. But I warn you: should you breathe a word of this to the authorities, I'll make sure your loved ones pay the price, starting with Her Majesty. And I won't stop there: the centaur Kidron and his mare; the kitchen-witch Lafo; that runaway bastet, Lukas, as well as the old were-tiger Mao and his cub—each and every one of them will die because of you. And do not think my reach is limited to Golgotham," he said, flashing me a nasty grin. "It would be quite gauche if your mother began to vomit venomous snakes in the middle of a garden party, don't you agree? And just imagine the headlines should your father and his yacht be attacked by a kraken! And it's always *so* sad when newlyweds like your nump friends come to an early, tragic end. And then there's the matter of your *dog. . . .*"

"That's enough! Stop threatening her!" Hexe growled, grimacing in pain. "You've made your point, Marz!"

"I'm glad we've reached an understanding. Bonzo, please show our guests out."

The squirrel-monkey jumped off its master's shoulder, transforming into its demonic aspect in midleap. As Bonzo reached for us, Hexe staggered to his feet, valiantly putting himself between me and the hell-ape. With a hideous shriek, the familiar swept us up in its shaggy arms as if we were dolls and disappeared in a cloud of brimstone.

Suddenly I was tumbling through darkness, my ears echoing with the distorted screams of an angry ape. Although I could see nothing in the void, I felt Hexe's arms wrapped about me. I returned his embrace, hanging on for dear life. Then the next thing I knew, I was dumped on the street outside the locked gates of one of the piers that jutted out into the East River. Hexe was lying on the pavement next to me, his face drawn and pale. He cradled his damaged hand close to his chest, as if protecting a small, wounded animal.

"We've got to get you to Golgotham General," I said as I helped him back onto his feet.

"No," he said with an emphatic shake of his head. "They'll ask questions. Take me to Dr. Mao."

Chapter 8

Dr. Mao's Apothecary and Acupuncture Parlor was located on the bleeding edge between Golgotham and Chinatown. By the time we arrived, Hexe was barely able to walk and I was genuinely terrified that he would collapse on the street and I wouldn't be able to get him back on his feet. I banged on the front door so hard that the SORRY, WE'RE CLOSED placard nearly flipped itself back over.

The door opened the length of its security chain and a feline eye peered out. "Can't you read?" Lukas growled, his face an intimidating admixture of puma and human. Upon recognizing us, he resumed his usual boyish appearance. "What are you two doing here?" he asked in surprise.

"Open up, Lukas," I said urgently. "Hexe has been hurt."

The young were-cougar threw open the door and helped me escort the near-unconscious warlock over the threshold. "Bast's eyes!" he gasped upon seeing Hexe's damaged hand. "What happened?"

"Never mind that," I said tersely. "Just fetch Dr. Mao."

"What's going on out there?" the old were-tiger asked sharply, stepping out from behind the curtain that separated his family's living quarters from the shop. He had shed his traditional black Mandarin jacket and was dressed in a damask robe covered with embroidered phoenixes. "Why did you open the door? You know I don't see patients after hours. . . ."

"There's been an accident, Doc," I explained. "Hexe told me to bring him here."

"Take him into the parlor," Dr. Mao said, pointing to an

alcove at the far end of the shop that was partially hidden by an elaborate lacquered screen.

Where the apothecary resembled a traditional Chinese herbalist shop, with jars and cases filled with dried caterpillars and sliced deer antler, the acupuncture parlor looked more like a doctor's examination room, complete with stainless-steel exam table. As Lukas and I lifted Hexe onto it, his eyelids fluttered and he groaned in pain.

Dr. Mao winced as he saw Hexe's hand. "Go fetch Meikei," he told Lukas. "I'm going to need her help."

Upon hearing his friend's voice, Hexe opened his eyes and attempted to sit up, only to have Dr. Mao push him back down. "Lie still, Serenity," he said gently. "I must assess your wounds." As the were-tiger attempted to examine Hexe's fingers, he gasped like a drowning man coming up for air and his golden eyes rolled back in their sockets.

"Where's Tate?" he rasped.

"I'm right here," I said as I grabbed his uninjured left hand and gave it a reassuring squeeze. His eyeballs abruptly dropped back down like the reels in a slot machine. "Don't worry, I'm not going anywhere."

He flashed me a wan smile before turning his attention to Dr. Mao. "How bad is it, Doc?"

"You need a boneknitter, not an acupuncturist," the old healer replied matter-of-factly.

Hexe shook his head. "A boneknitter would be worse than useless. It's a witch-hammer injury."

"Who did this?" Dr. Mao demanded, his head suddenly replaced by that of a snarling tiger. Although I knew he meant me no harm, I instinctively recoiled in fear at the sight of his razor-sharp teeth and flashing amber eyes. "It was Marz, wasn't it?" Mao growled, his stripes once more fading back into his skin. "I may be old, but I'm no fool."

"Yes, it was Boss Marz," Hexe replied grudgingly. "But you can't tell *anyone* what you know, Doc. Marz has threatened to kill our families and friends—including you and Meikei—if we talk."

"I understand," Mao sighed. "But how did the Maladanti get their hands on a witch-hammer?"

"They stole a collection of Witchfinder implements from the Museum of Supernatural History," I explained. "The

Curator was talking about the theft when I was there with Canterbury earlier this week."

"I'm not surprised that the Maladanti would stoop to such tactics," Mao grunted as he took out a black and red lacquer box from a nearby medicine cabinet. "Have no fear, you have my silence on the matter."

Meikei, dressed in a housecoat, entered the parlor. "What's going on? Lukas said something about an emergency—" She froze upon seeing Hexe lying on the exam table, her mouth hanging open in disbelief.

"Don't just stand there gawping at the patient, girl!" Mao snapped. "I need you to compound some *Chin Koo Tieh Shang Wan* while I block his nerves. You know the formulation?"

"Pseudoginseng, dragon's blood, Angelica root, myrrh, and safflower," Meikei replied, quickly regaining her composure under her father's quizzing.

"That's my girl," Mao said, with a proud smile. "Now go make pills."

Lukas moved to follow Meikei into the apothecary, but Dr. Mao shook his head. "You stay here, boy," he said sternly. "My daughter can run the pill mill by herself. I need you to hold him down when I insert the needles."

The young were-cat nodded his understanding and laid his arm across Hexe's shoulders, pinning him to the exam table.

The healer scowled down at his friend's hand, which now resembled an overfilled hot-water bottle, the fingers jutting from it at unnatural angles. "I wish I could lie and tell you this isn't going to hurt," he said apologetically.

"I understand," Hexe rasped, clenching his jaw. "Go ahead and do it."

Dr. Mao flipped open the lid of the lacquer box, revealing rows upon rows of golden acupuncture needles ranging from near-microscopic to something you could knit with. As he inserted the first of them into the fractured right hand, Hexe's body jerked and bowed, as if undergoing electroshock, and then suddenly went limp.

"Don't worry, he's still alive. He's just fainted, that's all. It is better he not be awake for this, anyway," the were-tiger explained. Seeing the worried look on my face, he gave me a reassuring smile. "You got him this far, Tate. Lukas and I will take him from here."

I nodded dumbly and stepped away from the exam table, leaving Dr. Mao and his apprentice to their work. It tore me up inside that the man I loved was in agony, and there was sweet FA I could do about it. As I entered the apothecary, I saw Meikei at the counter, wearing a half-mask respirator as she vigorously pounded the contents of a pharmacist's mortar with a pestle.

"If my father wants to know what's taking so long," she said in a muffled voice, "you can tell him that I'm working as fast as I can and to get off my back, Dad."

"Actually, I just came out here to keep from being underfoot," I admitted.

"You can help me make the pills, if you like," she said, gesturing to a machine that looked like a cross between an old-fashioned meat grinder and a die press. I joined her behind the counter and took my place at the compounding bench. "The *Chin Koo Tieh Shang Wan* will reduce the swelling and soft tissue damage, and dull the pain," she explained as she poured the powder from the mortar into the machine's hopper.

I turned the crank on the side of the press. There was a slight resistance, but not too much, and a second later the mechanism popped out a yellowish aspirin-sized tablet, which dropped down a narrow slide and fell into a small steel basin. Relieved to be of assistance, no matter how slight, I turned the handle faster and the solitary tablet was followed by several more. Suddenly, in midcrank, my vision abruptly dimmed and flared, like a malfunctioning video monitor, and the next thing I knew I was lying on the floor, staring up at a startled Meikei.

"Are you okay?" she gasped as she tore off her mask.

"Wh—what happened?" I muttered, blinking in surprise.

Meikei knelt beside me, checking my pulse and inspecting my pupils. "One moment you were cranking the pill press, the next you stopped and sat down—except there wasn't a chair."

"I'm sorry if I freaked you out," I said apologetically. "I guess everything just kind of caught up to me. . . ."

Meikei frowned and leaned in closer, sniffing me like a

cat checking out a mouse hole. "Have you been nauseous lately?" she asked.

"Well, I *have* been feeling a bit queasy, here and there," I admitted. "But I've been under a *lot* of stress at work. . . ."

"That's not why you fainted," she said with a shake of her head. "You are with child, Tate."

I sat there for a long moment, my brain vibrating like a struck gong. I tried to figure out what Meikei must have *really* meant to say, because there was *no way* it was what I just *thought* I'd heard. Maybe she said I'd been *beguiled*, and in my dazed state I heard something altogether different. Surely it *must* have been a simple misunderstanding on my part.

"Tate? Did you *hear* what I just said?" Meikei asked, snapping her fingers to get my attention. "I said that you're *pregnant*!"

"No, you're wrong." Even as I shook my head in denial, my mind was zipping around like a hummingbird on speed, finally making the connections I'd been steadfastly ignoring over the last month. "I mean, it's *impossible*! I've been on the pill for years!"

"Human contraception is all very well and good," Meikei said with a smile, "assuming your partner is *also* human."

"Oh, crap," I groaned as my last defense crumbled before me.

"Are you okay?" she asked gently, resting her hand on my shoulder.

"I'm not sure," I replied. "It's going to take a little while for this to *really* sink in. Right now, I've got to think about Hexe."

"Of course," she said as she helped me back onto my feet. "I won't say a thing."

"There you are!" Dr. Mao said as Meikei and I returned with the pills. "I was beginning to wonder if you had fallen into a black hole."

"There was a mechanical problem with the pill press," Meikei fibbed, glancing in my direction. "Tate was able to fix it, though."

"Ah, very good," her father replied, returning his attention to the last of the needles. Hexe's right hand bristled liked an angry golden porcupine.

"Where's Tate?" he moaned, drifting in and out of consciousness.

"It's okay, baby," I whispered as I brushed the hair from his face. "I'm here."

"Don't let them take it," Hexe rasped, his eyes rolling about in their sockets like greased ball bearings. "My hand—don't let them take it."

"Nobody's going to take away your hand, Hexe," Dr. Mao said in a loud, slow voice, as if speaking to a child on a bad phone line. "Take these—they will help with the pain."

Hexe clumsily tossed down the offered tablets with his left hand and chased them with a sip of water. Within a minute of taking them, the knot in his jaw unclenched and the muscles in his face relaxed. With a relieved sigh, he lay back down and closed his eyes.

"That should give him some relief for the time being. Safflower is similar to opioids for Kymerans," Mao explained. "Now that he's sedated, I can splint his hand properly."

"Is he going to be okay?" I asked anxiously.

Dr. Mao paused for a long moment before finally answering. "I've done everything in my power to help him, but there was a great deal of nerve damage. The hand, once splinted, should heal well enough. But I seriously doubt he will regain complete dexterity without the aid of magic."

My heart sank like a lead anchor, threatening to pull me downward into despair, but my brain told the rest of me that turning into a blubbering ball of boohoo was not going to help anything or solve any problems. I stared down at Hexe's unconscious face, still pale and drawn, and felt a surge of love so intense I almost forgot to breathe. We had been through more, in the relatively short time we'd been together, than most couples would ever face in a lifetime: escaping angry mobs, angrier demons, and crazed homunculi, all while saving one another's lives thrice over. If we could survive all that, then we would overcome this as well.

Despite Dr. Mao's grim diagnosis, I refused to give up hope. Golgotham was filled with wizards, witches, and miracle workers—somebody, somewhere, *had* to know how to fix that which could not be repaired.

Chapter 9

"Lukas will accompany you home," Doc Mao said as he helped me load an extremely groggy Hexe into the livery carriage. "You will require assistance getting him upstairs."

"That's okay, Doc," I replied. "I can handle him."

The old were-tiger raised his unibrow in surprise. "Are you sure of that? Given your condition?" Dr. Mao chuckled as my eyes darted suspiciously at Meikei. "No, my daughter has not betrayed your confidence, my dear. However, I did not get to the age I am now without knowing a pregnant woman when I smell one," he said, tapping the side of his nose.

As Lukas and I entered the front door, Hexe slung between us like a drunken sailor, we were greeted by Scratch, who was perched atop the newel post of the staircase like a living finial. "*Finally!* It's about *time* you two came home!" the familiar yowled indignantly. "Beanie is about to *explode*! And if you think that I'm going to clean up after him . . ." He trailed off as he watched us guide Hexe toward the stairs, his hairless brow furrowed into a feline frown. "What's wrong with the boss? Is he munted?"

"Yes, but not how you think," I replied as we dragged Hexe upstairs and steered him into his room. The carved owls atop the bedposts swiveled their heads about in concern as I propped a pillow under his splinted right hand. "Thanks for helping me, Lukas," I said as I unlaced and removed Hexe's high-tops before tucking him in. "I can handle it from here."

"Are you sure about that?" he asked worriedly.

"I'll be fine," I replied, trying to sound more confident than I felt. "Go home and get some sleep. It's been a long day for everybody."

"Call me if you need anything," he said as he gave me a farewell hug. "I'll bike right over."

Scratch jumped up onto the bed, nervously slapping his tail against the footboard as he watched me do my best to make Hexe comfortable. "What's going on?" he growled.

"There was an accident," I replied.

"What *kind* of accident?" Scratch scowled.

"It doesn't matter," I answered hastily, trying to dodge any further questioning. "It's none of your business. . . ."

"'None of my business'?" the familiar spat. "Hexe is my master! I have no business *but* him!" He cast back his head, sniffing the air as if on the trail of a rat hiding in the wainscoting. "What's that smell?" He hopped onto the mattress, slowly creeping forward. As his twitching whiskers brushed against Hexe's injured right hand, he recoiled in disgust. "Saint of the Pit!" he screeched. "*Malleus Maleficarum*—the witch-hammer!"

The familiar threw back his head and gave voice to a yowl that sounded like a band saw chewing its way through sheet metal. As he leapt off the bed he cast aside his domestic skin, revealing his demonic aspect—that of a hairless saber-toothed tiger with the wings of a dragon and the tail of a crocodile.

"Who has done this thing to my master?" Scratch roared, his outrage rattling the very walls and frightening poor Beanie so badly he peed himself in terror and dove under the bed skirt for protection.

"Calm down!" I shouted, clamping my hands over my ears.

"I'll 'calm down' once I've torn the throat from whoever's responsible for this affront!" the familiar snarled, his head nothing but blazing eyes and gleaming fang. The acerbic, wisecracking Scratch I thought I knew was nowhere to be seen, and in his place was a demon, born and bred in the pits of the Infernal Realm, transformed by anger into something truly terrifying. *"Tell me who did this!"* he thundered, slapping his tail against the floorboards so hard it shook the entire house.

"I *can't*!" I replied, my voice quavering with fear.

Scratch roared again, his monstrous, curving fangs flashing like scimitars. *"Tell me their name, nump!"* he growled as he took a menacing step in my direction.

I stood there, momentarily paralyzed, like a frightened gazelle, before breaking free of my fear. I snatched up one of Hexe's high-top Chucks and hurled it at Scratch's head, striking him between the eyes.

"*Bad* kitty!"

The familiar blinked in surprise, completely taken aback. "Did—did you just throw a *shoe* at me?" he asked indignantly.

"Scratch! Stand down!"

Hexe was awake and sitting up in the bed, fixing his familiar with a disapproving scowl. Although he looked to be in a lot of pain, he seemed in full control of himself.

Scratch lowered his head, literally shrinking before my eyes as he reassumed his domestic form. "Forgive me, boss," he said contritely. "I kinda lost it for a moment; you know how I get."

"Yes, I do—but I'm not the one you should be apologizing to," Hexe said sternly.

Scratch hopped back onto the foot of the mattress, staring down at his paws as he kneaded the bedclothes like a baker making biscuits. "Tate? I'm, uh, you know, uh, I'm, uh . . ."

"Sorry?" I suggested helpfully.

"Yeah! That's the word," he said, relieved that he hadn't been forced to actually utter the phrase. "We good?"

"Yeah, we good," I sighed, holding out my fist. The familiar bumped his forehead against it, his purr as loud as an idling tractor.

"Now that *that's* out of the way," Scratch said, turning to look at his master, "are you going to tell me who got medieval on your hand? It was Marz, wasn't it? He's the only cack-hander in this town, now that Esau's out of the picture, crazy enough to use Witchfinder implements. Just say the word, boss, and I'll get rid of that thug and his fancy-dress baboon once and for all!"

"Absolutely *not*," Hexe replied firmly.

"Look, I know you don't believe in offensive strikes, but you *can't* let Marz get away with this!"

"Even if I *was* prone to revenge, I still wouldn't permit it," Hexe said wearily. "I need you *here*, Scratch. You're the only defense I have left. I know you're powerful, but Marz has more than just his familiar backing him up. What if you attacked and lost?"

"Phfft!" Scratch snorted in derision. "Who? Me? Lose to that overgrown organ-grinder's monkey? Don't be ridiculous!"

"But what if you *did* lose, Scratch? What if you were slain? Not merely disincorporated—genuinely *killed*. Who would protect me then?"

"Your mother is no slouch in that arena," Scratch replied. "And your dad has an entire police force at his disposal. . . ."

"And Marz has promised to kill everyone we know if we go to them for help—he went so far as to threaten Beanie."

"Even he wouldn't do something like *that*—would he?" Scratch gasped, his eyes widening in alarm at the thought of "his" pet being harmed.

"Now that you understand the position I'm in, *please*, stop tempting me with revenge."

"But . . . but . . ." the familiar sputtered.

Hexe propped himself up a little straighter, fixing Scratch with a hard stare. "By whose blood are you bound?" he asked solemnly.

"Yours, my master," Scratch replied, lowering his gaze.

"Whose will is your will?"

"Yours, my master," the familiar said, bowing his head in ritual deference.

Hexe smiled and automatically reached out with his right hand to stroke the winged cat's back, only to grimace in pain.

"Are you okay?" I asked nervously as I readjusted his pillows.

"I'll be okay." He smiled wanly. "I'm just . . . tired, that's all. It's been a long day."

"Would you like some herbal tea?"

"Yes," he replied, the strength that had been in his voice mere moments before fading like breath on a windowpane. "That would be nice."

"Scratch, stay here with him, please."

"It'll take an exorcist to make me leave," the familiar said, his eyes glowing like stoplights.

I made my way downstairs, Beanie scampering along behind me as if his tail was on fire. Upon reaching the kitchen, I was surprised to find our reclusive housemate, Mr. Manto, dressed in a pair of flannel pajamas and an old bathrobe, pouring hot water from the tea kettle into the steeping pot sitting on the table. I knew all too well that the aged clairvoyant rarely left his cavernous basement apartment save for buying cat food, as he preferred the company of his crew of feline friends and his vast collection of books to dealing with people who lived in the here and now.

"Mr. Manto! What are you doing topside?" I exclaimed as I opened the back door to let out Beanie, who sped out into the garden as if propelled from a crossbow.

The old oracle looked up from his task, peering at me over the tops of his bifocals. "I am here because I saw that I must be here," he replied. "I am also making tea." He placed his wrinkled, liver-spotted hand on my elbow, steering me gently to one of the kitchen chairs. "Please sit down, my dear, for a few moments."

"But I need to bring Hexe his tea . . ." I protested feebly. I didn't realize how tired I was until Mr. Manto made me sit down. The moment I did I was overcome by a bout of lightheadedness identical to the one I'd experienced at Doc Mao's. Up until that moment I had been propelled by nothing more than nervous energy and the fear that if I didn't keep in constant motion, I would grind to a halt like an unwound clockwork.

"And that you shall," Mr. Manto said gently. "But first you must take care of yourself. You will do no one any good by fainting while carrying a loaded tray upstairs—especially your child."

"So, you know about me being pregnant, too," I sighed. "The way things are going, half of Golgotham is going to know about it before Hexe does."

"I know about a great deal more than the child you carry," the oracle replied. "Earlier this evening I decided to celebrate the Jubilee in my own way by imbibing a certain hallucinogen, which resulted in a vision. In it I saw Boss Marz maim Hexe with a witch-hammer. I assure you, had I known what the Maladanti planned prior to that, I would

have warned him—but you, more than anyone, know that
my prophecies are not the easiest to decipher, once spoken.
I also saw Boss Marz threaten your loved ones, should you
go for help—and I am honored to find myself amongst
those endangered."

"You said you're here because you 'must' be here. What
do you mean by that?" I asked.

"It is difficult to explain," Mr. Manto replied as he
poured a cup of tea from the steeping pot and pressed it
into my hand. "Drink this—it will help steady you."

"*What's* difficult to explain?" I asked, giving him a speculative look over the rim of the teacup.

"The means by which I see the future. Sometimes it points
straight as an arrow, but more often than not, the future is
more like a spider's web. Some threads are stronger than
others, while others are weaker than most. They all shine, in
their way, but those threads that are the strongest shine the
brightest, marking destiny's trail. But when all threads shine
equally—that indicates a Crossroads where *all* futures are
valid. No soothsayer can see beyond a Crossroads until the
fated one makes their decision. You stand now, my dear, at
one such Crossroads. Only your will, and no other, shall decide which thread will be cut, and which will be followed."

"But how will I know what decision is the right one to
make?"

"Do you recall the final portion of the prophecy I spoke
to you?" he inquired offhandedly, as if he was asking
whether I had remembered to pick up a carton of milk on
the way home from work.

"You know I can't remember any of that stuff until it's
damn near too late."

"It is true that the Fates do not surrender their mysteries
gladly," he admitted as he placed the teapot on the serving
tray. "When you stand on the Crossroads, the prophecy will
come to you and you will know what must be done. Just as
I know that the Fates have led me to this time and place, to
ensure you safely reach your destination."

As I finished my tea, the oracle took the cup from me
and, holding it in his left hand, swirled the contents about
three times clockwise.

"I didn't realize you read tea leaves," I said. "I thought
you foretold the future by tearing the pages out of books."

"Bibliomancy is my preferred means of divination," Mr. Manto replied as he placed the saucer on top of the cup and flipped it upside down, allowing what liquid remained to drain away. "But I have been known to dabble in tasseography, now and again."

Upon righting the cup, he removed the saucer and peered inside, his brow furrowed like a freshly tilled field. After studying the inner rim for a long moment, he smiled, apparently relieved by what he had read in the tea leaves.

"What did you see?" I asked.

"That you will not faint and fall down the stairs," he replied. "And that Hexe is waiting for his tea."

As I carried the tea service Mr. Manto had been kind enough to prepare for me upstairs, it occurred to me that perhaps instead of simply relying on trusting a were-tiger's sense of smell and a soothsayer's tripped-out prophecies, perhaps I should confirm things for myself with a nice, old-fashioned home pregnancy test. At least that would allow me to hold off on breaking the news to Hexe, who already had enough to worry about without my dumping this on top of him.

The last time I had to deal with something like this was back in college. My boyfriend at the time was a music major named Taylor. We had been seeing each other for eighteen months, and I thought what we had together was pretty real—up until the moment I told him I was late. Within seconds, the man I believed cared for me became a distant, stony-faced stranger. As emotionally devastating as the possibility of my being knocked up was, it was nothing compared to Taylor's rejection of me. A couple of days later I finally got my period, and we both heaved a sigh of relief, but the damage was done. There was no way our relationship could return to what it was after what I saw in his eyes. What disturbed me the most wasn't just Taylor's total disregard, but the sober realization that the love I believed we shared didn't truly exist. It was like walking far out onto what appeared to be solid ground, only to realize it was actually quicksand.

Although I knew my relationship with Hexe was completely different from the one with Taylor, part of me was still hesitant. The thought of his beautiful, golden eyes looking back at me with that same horrible, uncaring stare made my heart tighten with dread. I have withstood a lot of things in my life, but seeing that would completely destroy me. So I told myself it was best to put things off until I knew one hundred and ten percent for certain I was one hundred percent pregnant. Isn't rationalization grand?

As I reentered the bedroom, I was relieved to find Hexe looking far more collected than he had earlier. Scratch remained perched on the footboard, his wings folded against his sides.

"About time!" the familiar sniped as I placed the tray on the bedside table. "How long does it take humans to boil water?"

"I would have been back sooner," I said, ignoring the jibe, "but I ran into Mr. Manto in the kitchen."

Hexe sat up a little higher in the bed, a concerned look on his face. "Does he know—?"

"Of *course* he knows," I replied. "He's an oracle. But since he's in no hurry to end up on Boss Marz's hit list, we can trust him to keep quiet."

"It feels so strange, using my left hand," Hexe said as he reached for the cup I held out to him. "I'm so accustomed to doing everything with my right. . . ." He grimaced as he slopped nearly half its contents onto the floor and bed-clothes. "See what I mean?"

"You'll adjust to it, in time," I assured him. I turned to Scratch, who was still watching the bedroom door like it was a rat hole. "Would you mind giving us a little privacy, please?"

"If you can say it in front of them," the familiar said, gesturing with his wings to the owls atop the bedposts, "you can say it in front of me."

"Scratch: do as she says," Hexe said firmly. "Go make a perimeter check."

"As you wish, boss," he grumbled, hopping off the bed. He padded over to the fireplace and, in a single bound, disappeared up the chimney.

"How's the pain?" I asked.

"It's not as bad as it was," he replied. "But I can't move my fingers." He frowned at his splinted right hand, which lay motionless atop the pillow beside him. "I've been trying to make them twitch, but they won't respond."

"You shouldn't push yourself so soon. Even *with* magic, an injury like that takes time to recover from," I said, leaning in to deliver a reassuring kiss. "Remember the mauling you got in the pits? Even with your mother's regenerative salve, you were bed-bound for a week. Give yourself some time to recuperate, and take it easy for a little while, okay?"

Hexe's eyes abruptly darkened. "Where did you get that bruise on your check? Did Marz do that to you?"

Surprised, I reached up to touch my face, only to wince as my fingers came in contact with bruised flesh. "I must have gotten that when I passed out over at Doc Mao's," I explained.

"You fainted?" Hexe sat up even straighter, a look of concern on his face. "Are you okay?"

"Yes," I replied as I shrugged and dropped my gaze to the floor. "It was nothing, just . . ."

"Just what?" He frowned. "Tate, I can tell something is weighing on your mind." He reached out and took my hand, gently pulling me toward him, so that I was sitting next to him on the bed. "My right hand is broken, but that doesn't mean you have to treat me like I'm made out of spun glass." He touched my chin, lifting it so that he could look me in the eye. "If there's something you need to say, just tell me. Whatever it is, we can handle it together."

As I looked into his warm, golden eyes, all the rationalizations I had lined up for why I should keep my big trap shut melted away, and before I knew it the words came bubbling out. "I'm pregnant."

Hexe leaned back, his cat-slit pupils widening slightly as he absorbed the news. I held my breath, my mouth dry as cotton, as I waited for his reaction. I got it a second later when a wide, goofy smile spread across his face. I was so relieved, I promptly burst into tears.

"What are you grinning about?" I sobbed. "This couldn't happen at a worse time!"

"I know," he replied, clumsily dabbing at my tears with the corner of the bedsheet.

"It's going to change everything *forever*!"

"Everything has *already* changed," he pointed out gently. "But the one thing that is still the same is how I feel about you. I've loved you from the moment I first saw you, Tate. The Crown of Adon burns above your head—a sign from the ancient gods of Kymera that we are *meant* for one another." He picked up my hand and gently kissed its palm. "I am proud to be the father of your child, if that is what you wish."

Without warning, the hair on my arms stood up and my scalp prickled, and I heard Mr. Manto's voice, as if he was standing by my side, whispering in my ear, *"From two will be one turned three."* I realized that the future was upon me, and it was now time to leave the Crossroads. "And I'm proud to be its mother," I said, returning his kiss.

I shed my clothes and crawled into bed beside him, snuggling into the shelter of his left arm. As I rested my head on his chest, he kissed the nape of my neck and whispered something in Kymeran in my ear. "What did you just say?" I asked.

"'You are my forever.'"

"And you are mine," I smiled. As we embraced, there was suddenly a scrabbling sound from the direction of the fireplace, followed by a small explosion of tar-blackened brick dust. With a startled yowl, a sooty Scratch dropped out of the flue, landing on his butt in the hearth.

"Seven hells!" the winged cat spat in disgust. "What— wasn't the puppy enough? Now you idiots are going to have a *baby*? I guess I really shouldn't be surprised, since you two go at it like a pair of rabbits—!"

"You were eavesdropping on us!" I exclaimed.

"Technically, no, as I was in the chimney, not outside the window. . . ."

"Get out!" Hexe scowled, pointing to the door. "And this time *stay* out until I call you!"

Scratch trudged out of the bedroom, dragging his tail behind him like a length of wet rope. As the bedroom door closed itself behind him, I glanced up at the owls perched atop the four-poster bed. At least the furniture knew how to keep its mouth shut.

Chapter 10

Luckily, no one in Golgotham is expected to show up either to work or sober the day after Jubilee, so Hexe and I had a grace period to figure out a way to explain his broken hand that wouldn't result in our friends and family ending up dead. We decided to go with it being the result of a drunken accident, which at least sounded believable.

The first day I was expected back at work, I woke up to discover Hexe no longer in bed beside me. At first I assumed he had gotten up to use the bathroom, but a quick check revealed that he was not there, either. That's when I heard the sound of crashing crockery downstairs. I hurried down to the kitchen and found Hexe, dressed in only a pair of pajama bottoms, staring forlornly at the remains of what had been, moments before, a ceramic mixing bowl full of egg yolks. Beanie, who knew a bonanza when he saw it, was busily slurping away at the slimy goo as it spread across the linoleum.

"What are you doing down here?" I exclaimed as I scooped up the dog and deposited him on the back porch until I could clean up the mess. "You should still be in bed!"

"You've been waiting on me hand and foot, for two days," Hexe replied. "I just wanted to make breakfast, like I always do."

"I appreciate that you're eager to get back into the swing of things," I said, picking the larger pieces of broken crockery out of the rapidly congealing egg yolks. "But you're trying to do too much too soon."

"I need to get back to my old routine as soon as I can—I have it on very good authority that babies aren't cheap."

"Yes, but you're running the risk of making things even worse," I pointed out. "You've got to allow yourself to heal."

"But having my hand in a splint for several weeks seems so . . . wasteful. Normally I'd use a panacea to heal the soft tissue damage before going to a boneknitter. And if the nerve damage was *really* bad, I'd book a psychic surgeon to take care of it. My downtime would be three, maybe four days, tops."

"Granted, this way is slower, but it's a system that's worked for us humans for centuries," I pointed out. "After all, most of us don't have easy access to Golgotham General. And since these wounds are immune to magic, I'm afraid you're just going to have to be patient."

"But we healers are famous for being *awful* patients."

"So I've noticed." As I let the dog back in, Beanie ran straight to the spot on the floor I'd just cleaned, frantically sniffing at the linoleum in search of a stray atom of food that might have been missed. "I think it's really sweet that you want to still fix my breakfast for me, darling, but I can take care of myself. I'd rather you spend your time figuring out an easy way to break the news about the new addition to the Royal Family."

"Don't remind me." He grimaced. "If my renting a room to a human got the Blue Hairs worked into a lather, I can just imagine how *that* will go over."

As Hexe left the kitchen, I turned to look at Scratch, who was perched atop the refrigerator, licking his front paw. "Keep an eye on him while I'm at work, will you?" I said, keeping my voice low so as not to be overheard.

"I haven't been his babysitter in a very long time," the familiar replied. "But I'll do what I can. However, if he orders me to leave him alone, there's nothing I can do. He *is* my master."

As I walked to work, the reality of my situation settled onto my shoulders like a shawl made of lead. Until Hexe regained his dexterity—assuming he recovered it at all—I was *the* breadwinner for the household. But how much longer would that be? My job at Canterbury Customs was nowhere near as strenuous as banging out horseshoes for Chiron, but it was far from an office job. At some point I would have to take maternity leave, assuming Canterbury didn't simply fire me once he learned of my condition. As it was, telling my boss I was pregnant would have to wait until Hexe and I broke the news to his family. There *is* an etiquette to such things, after all.

Canterbury was working the forge as I entered the shop, his flanks shining with sweat. "I see you've finally come stumbling back from the Jubilee!" he chided. "And just in time! Bjorn Cowpen's carriage is ready. I need you to accompany the delivery and handle the paperwork and final payment."

As Canterbury's apprentice, I was used to being sent on errands, but this was the first one that went beyond merely being his gofer. The fact he trusted me to collect a payment for him spoke volumes, as he usually was the only one who handled the money from the clients. Since this was a major new step in our working relationship, I felt both proud and a bit nervous about my new responsibility.

About an hour later a centaur claiming to be Cowpen's chauffeur arrived and hitched himself to the awaiting carriage, which was about as subtle as a circus wagon. The carriage itself was a phaeton, the body of which was painted bright red, with overlarge wheels boasting gilded spokes and custom-designed hubs that bore the initials B.C. The calash top was made of faux–leopard skin, with matching plush velvet seat cushions, and had whirling mirrored discoballs in place of the usual carriage lights. It was so gloriously, unrepentantly vulgar that it was totally awesome.

After Canterbury made sure I had all the necessary paperwork, I hopped inside the carriage, and although it may have looked like something Liberace used to race harness, it rode like a dream. I barely felt a single jounce as we made our way to Golgotham's red-light district.

Although Duivel Street may be the shortest street in all of Golgotham, it is easily the busiest. Outside of Witches Alley, the Rookery, and the Fly Market, the flesh pits of Duivel Street are the biggest tourist attraction in the Strangest Neighbor in The Big Apple. If you can imagine a vice, there is guaranteed to be somebody or something catering to it somewhere along Duivel.

While Bjorn Cowpen owned several such adult entertainment operations, the Big Top Club was his flagship. The
front of the building was shaped to resemble an enormous,
leering clown's head, like the entrance of a funhouse. The
carnival decor was continued throughout the club, with vintage freak-show banners and circus posters covering the
walls. Red-and-white striped canvas bunting was draped
from the ceiling to give the illusion of a circus tent. Three
candy-striped "tent poles" were located along the elevated
runway that bisected the main room, providing the club's
entertainers the means to demonstrate their acrobatic skills.
As I entered the Big Top it was obvious from the dancers
strutting their considerable charms on the runway that the
club's name wasn't just an excuse for circus-related decor.

I walked over to the bar, which resembled a shooting
gallery you'd find at a carnival midway, complete with
bull's-eye targets and flying ducks. The bartender was a
young huldu dressed in the straw boater, striped shirt, and
red silk sleeve-garter of a sideshow barker.

"I'm from Canterbury Customs," I said. "Councilman
Cowpen is expecting me."

The bartender cut his eyes to the darkest corner of the
room. "The boss is, uh, in a meeting right now." Cowpen was
sitting in a red vinyl booth, talking to a shadowy figure
whose back was to me. "Take a seat. He'll be with you
shortly."

I glanced around the club. It was barely ten in the morning, but there were already a handful of patrons crowding
the tip rail. No matter the hour, there was always someone
ready to party on Duivel Street. The customers were watching a particularly pneumatic huldra in clear stripper heels
wrap herself around a pole while using her cow tail to pluck
the dollar bills from their hands. Back in their native Scan-
dinavia, the huldrefolk were famous for their physical beauty,
and the females of the species were especially notorious for
luring human men into the woods for sex. Now they simply
lured them into the champagne room.

As I sat down at one of the tables near the runway, a
topless waitress wearing greasepaint on her face and a pair
of red foam clown-nose pasties walked over to hand me a
box of popcorn and take my drink order. I smiled politely
and shook my head. She shrugged and went down to the

foot of the runway, where a couple of tourists were flashing platinum cards.

Suddenly there was a loud thudding noise that had nothing to do with the music pumping from the sound system. I looked up to see Cowpen's bull-tail thumping against the side of the booth he was sitting in as he talked to his guest.

"*Thirty percent?*" he exclaimed in angry disbelief. "Are you crazy? I'm already paying you guys fifteen for protection!"

"That's the deal, Councilman," the shadowy figure replied, his voice a throaty rumble.

"Look, your boss knows that I've always been amenable in the past. I'm sure we can negotiate a deal that's fair to both sides. . . ."

"Marz ain't lookin' to be fair," the other man said, cutting the strip club owner off before he could continue. "He's lookin' for thirty percent."

"That's *outrageous*!" the huldu exclaimed, this time slapping his tail onto the table for emphasis. "I *refuse* to pay it!"

"That's too bad," the Maladanti said as he slid out of the booth, tossing back his peach-colored Jheri curls. I recognized him as Gaza, the goon from the Stronghold who had shown Hexe the torture implements. My heart started to beat so fast it felt like it was standing still. "It was a nice place you had here." With a quick flourish of his left hand, the Maladanti sent a ball of hellfire flying toward the bar, and then casually strolled to the door, like a championship bowler turning his back on a strike roll. He didn't have to see the fireball land to know it was a direct hit.

The bartender leapt over the counter like a bullock jumping over a low fence as the hellfire struck the bull's-eye mounted over the top shelf stock. It splashed on contact like a water balloon full of napalm, sending flames in every direction. Tongues of fire raced up walls, setting the ceiling drapery ablaze within a heartbeat.

The huldra in the plastic heels was still twirling about, her back arched and head thrown back, her long honeyblond hair streaming behind her like a banner, when she saw the fire race across the ceiling. She gave a weird, decidedly nonhuman bleat of alarm and lost her grip, which sent her flying off the runway, landing with a loud crash on the table beside me. Jolted free of their lust by the fear of death, the Big Top Club's clientele cast aside their drinks and lap dancers and made a mad dash for the exits.

As the room rapidly filled with billows of acrid smoke and shouts of fear, I flashed back to the frantic chaos of the riot only a few months before. I knew it was important to stay as calm as possible and get out as soon as I could to avoid becoming lost in the choking fumes. I moved to help the dazed dancer back up onto her feet, even though she proved as wobbly on her six-inch plastic heels as a newborn calf.

As I guided the dancer toward the exit, I heard the bellow of an enraged bull, and saw Councilman Cowpen, his normally handsome features contorted into a masque of bestial fury, bound after the retreating Maladanti. The huldu grabbed Gaza, spinning the spellslinger around while wrapping his tail about his throat at the same time. Instead of struggling, Gaza merely made a gesture with his hand. As I exited the Big Top Club with my charge, I glanced over my shoulder in time to see Cowpen drop to the floor like a bag of wet cement.

Upon our escape from the burning building, a brace of huldren swarmed forward to claim their fellow dancer like a band of naked angels. I had to hand it to them—they did not seem the least bit embarrassed about standing in the middle of Duivel Street in nothing but their landing strips, surrounded by gawking tourists taking pictures with their cell phones.

"Where's Bjorn?" one of the dancers asked, casting about anxiously for some sign of the councilman.

"He's still inside," I said, turning to look at the entrance to the club. Smoke was billowing from the clown's mouth like the world's worst case of heartburn. "The spellslinger who torched the place pulled a sleeper on him."

Upon hearing this news, the bevy of huldren strippers started mooing like distraught cattle preparing to stampede. Although Councilman Cowpen was a sexist and a bigot, I could not find it in me to leave him to die in a fire. I stepped forward, waving at the strippers for silence.

"Calm down! I know where to find him, but I need someone to help me rescue him."

The young bartender stepped forward. "I'll go."

Together, we ran back inside club, holding our breath

against the curtain of smoke. Although fewer than three mere minutes had elapsed since Gaza first hurled the fireball, the interior of the club was almost unrecognizable, thanks to the flames and smoke. It seemed like an eternity as I sought for the place where I'd last seen Cowpen, but I finally spotted the huldu sprawled on the floor.

"Councilman Cowpen!" I shouted as I knelt beside him. "Wake up!"

"Pappa!" the bartender bellowed, grabbing what I now realized was his father by the shoulders. "You've got to get out of here!"

Cowpen managed to open one eye, which rolled about in its orbit like a greased ball bearing, but was otherwise unresponsive. To my surprise, the bartender lifted his father from the floor and tossed him over his shoulder in a fireman's carry as if he weighed no more than a bedroll. The moment we headed toward the dim glow of the fire exit sign, a huge chunk of burning canvas detached itself from the ceiling and crashed down on the spot we'd just vacated. We continued to push through the wall of smoke, and seconds later I was rewarded by a rush of fresh air into my aching lungs.

Upon seeing the bartender emerge from the burning building with the unconscious Bjorn thrown over his back, the dancer I had helped escape earlier gave voice to a strange, bovine cry and rushed forward to greet us. "Is he alive?" she asked, her tail switching anxiously back and forth.

"I think so, Mamma," the bartender replied as he lowered his father onto the sidewalk. Cowpen's limbs abruptly spasmed and he started to cough as Gaza's sleeper spell finally began to wear off.

"Tyr—go see to your sisters," the older dancer said, pointing to the gaggle of strippers staring worriedly in our direction. "The last thing we need right now is someone getting rustled."

The bartender nodded his understanding and went to put himself between his siblings and the leering throng of looky-loos that had gathered about them. Mrs. Cowpen knelt beside her husband, gently wiping the soot from his face with the end of her tail. She smiled up at me, tears shining in her cornflower blue eyes. Now that I was aware of the exact relationship between her and the rest of the club's employees, I suddenly found myself too embarrassed to look anywhere but directly at her face. I'd heard of family businesses before, but nothing like this.

"Thank you, young lady, for helping us. My name is Svenda."

"Well, we Golgothamites have to stick together, ma'am," I replied. "And you can call me Tate."

Suddenly there was the sound of a loudly clanging bell, and I looked up to see an old-fashioned pumper wagon, pulled by a brawny centaur wearing a fireman's helmet and a heavy canvas coat, arrive on the scene. There were identically dressed firefighters clinging to the sides of the wagon, one of whom was Octavia, our new boarder. As the pumper came to a halt, the faun leapt down and snatched up a four-foot-long metal tool that looked like a cross between a pry bar and a sledgehammer, wielding it like it weighed no more than a broom.

"It's a nasty one, Chief!" she shouted as she eyed the smoke and flames belching from the Big Top's entrance.

A Kymeran bearing the badge of fire chief on his helmet reached into the pocket of his canvas coat and removed a small glass bottle the size of a Christmas ornament. "There you go, my friend," he said as he removed the stopper. "Eat your fill!"

The jinn shot forth like a flash of lightning, and a second later the outline of a creature composed not of flesh and blood but from smokeless fire hovered in midair above Duivel Street. As the elemental turned its attention to the inferno before it, its eyes literally burned with hunger. It tossed back its blazing head and opened its fiery mouth and inhaled mightily, like a child preparing to blow out the candles on a birthday cake. A cascade of flame suddenly came pouring out of the building like the torrents of a flash flood. The gathered onlookers shouted in alarm and raised their arms to shield their faces and eyes from the blistering heat as the fire shot toward the hovering jinn. This seemed to amuse the elemental, whose laughter rang out like the peals from a great bell.

Within the space of a few heartbeats the conflagration was extinguished, and what had moments before been a raging inferno was now no more than a swelling in the jinn's belly. The elemental yawned and stretched its flickering limbs as it disappeared back into the safety of its bottle, where it could digest its meal in peace.

The moment the jinn was contained, the firefighters trained their hoses on the front of the building, dousing it in high-pressure streams of water. Once they finished with the exterior, Octavia entered the burned-out club through the clown's head, only now one side of it had melted from the extreme heat, causing the face to sag as if it had suffered a stroke. Using her metal fire tool as a walking stick, she made her way, sure-footed as a goat, through the charred ruins, searching for hidden hot spots to extinguish.

Bjorn Cowpen seemed woozy but otherwise unharmed. As his family gathered around him, he kissed each of his daughters on the forehead, muttering endearments in their native tongue, before warmly embracing the son who had carried him to safety. He slipped an arm around his wife and heir, using them as living crutches to hobble over to where I stood.

"I'm sorry about what happened to your club, Councilman," I said, and was surprised to realize that I actually meant it.

"I have others," he said with a weary shrug. "But this was the one I inherited from my father, when I was Tyr's age." As he looked me in the eye, I could tell he was truly seeing me for the first time. "You're Canterbury's apprentice, are you not?"

"Yes, I am," I replied. "He sent me to hand over the title to your new carriage and take the final payment. But I'm afraid I left the paperwork in the club. . . ."

"That old horse-wizard must *really* trust you," Cowpen said as he reached into the pocket of his skintight pants and pulled out a folded piece of paper, which he then handed to me.

I unfolded the paper and saw that it was a cashier's check drawn on Midas National Bank. I checked that the zeroes lined up before and after the comma and decimal were of the correct number, then nodded my head and carefully transferred it to my own pocket.

"I appreciate what you did, human," the councilman

continued, stepping in close to shake my hand. "But if anyone asks you what happened today, you didn't see *nothing*.
Understand?"

I stared down at the tightly bundled wad of hundred dollar
bills pressed into my palm. Part of me wanted to give the
money back and tell Cowpen that pretending nothing happened wasn't going to keep the Maladanti away. But then I
remembered my own delicate standing with Boss Marz, the
stack of bills on Hexe's desk, and the future cradled inside me.

"More than you realize," I replied.

Chapter 11

While my "tip" from Cowpen wasn't going to solve all our financial worries, it was enough to give us the first breathing room we'd known in months. For the first time since Jubilee Night, not only did there seem to be a glimmer of light at the end of the tunnel, for once it didn't appear to be a train barreling down on us. However, the moment I set foot in the door and saw a scowling Hexe waiting for me in the front parlor, my high spirits came crashing back down to earth.

"Octavia tells me that you ran into a burning building today. Is that true?"

"For crying out loud, Hexe!" I groaned, setting down my lunch pail on the coffee table. "I didn't do it for kicks! Did Octavia also mention I went in there to save Bjorn Cowpen?"

"What were you *thinking*?" Hexe exclaimed, coming out of his seat like a jack-in-the-box.

"I was thinking that I was the only person who saw him collapse and knew where to find him," I replied. "Are you actually *mad* at me for saving a man's life?"

"No, I'm more upset than anything else," he admitted, the scowl disappearing from his face. "You did a very brash thing. What if you'd been hurt? Did you give *any* thought at all to what might happen to you—or the baby?"

I blushed and dropped my gaze. He had me there. The fact I was now pregnant had not occurred to me in the heat of the moment. I simply knew what I had to do, and I just went ahead and did it, without taking anything else into consideration. "I guess you've got every right to be pissed off at me," I agreed. "It's not just me anymore, is it?"

"It hasn't been 'just you' since the day we met," he replied. "Were you in the club when the fire started?"

"Yes," I admitted grudgingly. "The Maladanti are raising their protection fees. Bjorn told them to get stuffed in no uncertain terms—so Marz's croggy Gaza hellfire-bombed the bar and put Cowpen under a sleeper spell. That's why I had to go back in and get him. I'm certain Cowpen's going to insist it was all an accident, though, and his family's going to back him up on it."

"What you did today was very courageous, Tate. But you've always been a brave woman—we would have never met if you didn't have the guts to move to Golgotham in the first place. Just promise me you won't do anything that dangerous again—at least not until *after* you have the baby."

"And here I was planning on juggling chainsaws to bring in extra money!" I laughed. "I'm just joking!" I added hastily, seeing the flash of alarm in his golden eyes, and planted a kiss on his cheek. "Oh—and speaking of putting off things until the baby arrives—have you told your parents the news yet?"

Now it was his turn to look at his shoes. "Not yet. I'll call them in a day or two."

"How about we put all this behind us and go out for dinner? After all, you were complaining about feeling cooped up earlier. . . ."

"That sounds great," he said with a rueful smile. "But there's no way we can afford it."

"Don't worry—I've got it covered," I said, taking out the money Cowpen had given me.

"Where did you get *that*?" Hexe asked, his eyes widening in surprise.

"Let's just say it was the councilman's way of saying 'thank you' for saving his life, as well as keeping my mouth shut."

"I don't feel good about this, Tate," Hexe said, frowning at the money.

"Uh-uh," I said, with a defiant shake of my head. "I *know* that look. You're getting ready to give me the big lecture about the Right Hand path and tell me to give the money back and report what happened to the PTU. I realize you

don't want to compromise your principles—but I am *not* returning this money, and I am definitely *not* talking to your father about what I saw.

"For one, I'm pretty sure giving back this money will offend Bjorn Cowpen only slightly less than setting fire to his club. And, secondly, since we're already playing our *own* little game of 'Don't Ask, Don't Tell' with Boss Marz, who are *we* to insist he go to the authorities? Hell, he's a chuffin' councilman; he *is* the authority in Golgotham! If Marz doesn't hesitate to physically strike out at members of the Royal Family and the GoBOO, then he must *really* have some badass mojo up his sleeve. And I, for one, have no desire to find out what it might be. I'll admit that running into a burning building in my current condition was reckless, but it's nowhere *near* as dangerous as what you're suggesting I do."

Hexe's shoulders dropped in resignation, as if all the weight in the world had suddenly settled upon them. "You're right," he sighed in agreement. "I can't blame Cowpen for keeping silent. He's doesn't want to do anything that will jeopardize his family." He gave a sad little smile as he rested his left hand on my belly. "It's like you said—it's not just me anymore."

As luck would have it, Talisman was playing at the Two-Headed Calf that night. Since the Kymeran punk band had become extremely popular with the younger humans intrepid enough to venture beyond Duivel Street and the Fly Market, the evenings they played the Calf were always guaranteed to be packed to the rafters.

As crowded as it was, I could still easily spot Lafo, standing head and shoulders over his patrons, his bright red hair spilling over the collar of a purple pinstripe zoot suit. Upon seeing us, the restaurateur elbowed his way across the packed room

"Good to see you again, Serenity!" he grinned, shouting over the amplified accordions and electric hurdy-gurdy.

As his friend moved to shake his hand, Hexe hastily recoiled. "No offense, Lafo," he said quickly, holding up his right hand by way of explanation, displaying the splint. "I had a little too much to drink Jubilee Night and lost my balance stepping off a curb. I tried to break my fall, and ended up breaking my hand instead."

Lafo's ketchup-red eyebrows shot up in surprise. "Nothing serious, I hope?"

"I'll be good as new within a week," he lied. "I just have to give the bones time to strengthen after being reknit, that's all. Tate and I were hoping to have dinner here this evening, but it looks like we picked the wrong night."

"No need to worry about that; most of the kids who show up for the band never set foot upstairs," Lafo snorted. "Luckily, they all drink like fish, though."

Upon reaching the upstairs dining room, we were unsurprised to discover only a handful of the tables and booths occupied, as the regular clientele had learned to steer clear of the Calf on those nights Talisman was scheduled to play. Not wanting to call attention to ourselves, we chose a booth toward the back of the dining area and placed our drink and dinner orders.

As we waited for our food, we chatted about work, friends, and our pet, trying hard to have a good time and not dwell on current problems. And, for a while, we actually succeeded in doing so. Then our meals arrived.

"Oh," Hexe said, his face collapsing as he stared at the roasted kangaroo tail draped across the platter. "I forgot you need two hands to eat this thing."

"You can have my parsnip casserole, if you like," I suggested.

"That's okay," he replied, as he unrolled the cutlery, fumbling with the steak knife. "I can cut it up into chunks." He studied his food for a long moment, trying to figure out the best way to attack the problem without it ending up in his lap.

"Darling, do you need some help?" I asked gently. "I can cut it up for you, if you like. . . ."

"No!" he replied sharply. "I'm fine. I do *not* need anyone to cut up my food for me!" He began to saw at the roo-tail, only to have the knife fly out his hand and land on the floor. His face flushed bright red as he bent to retrieve it, before our server appeared tableside with a fresh roll of cutlery.

"If you like, Serenity, I can take your entree back to the kitchen and have it replaced with a chopped version?" the waiter suggested politely as he retrieved the soiled knife.

"Yes, thank you," Hexe mumbled, his cheeks turning an even brighter shade of red.

After the waiter left with his plate, I learned forward, keenly aware that we were being watched by the other diners. "Maybe this wasn't such a good idea," I said sotto voce.

"I *said* I'm fine," Hexe insisted as he picked up his pint of barley wine, only to slosh a good portion of it onto his shirtfront. *"Heavens and hells!"* he snarled, slopping even more out of the glass as he slammed it back down.

I looked away as he attempted to blot the dark, sticky fluid from his clothes with his napkin, afraid of what he might see in my eyes. Hexe was the most graceful man I had ever known; watching him fumble with silverware and spill his drink was absolutely heartbreaking. All I wanted at that moment was to somehow find a way of taking his burden onto myself, so that he did not have to suffer alone. My frustration at being unable to do so was so great it threatened to push me into despair.

"Excuse me, Serenity. . . ."

An unfamiliar Kymeran woman in her early thirties with slate-blue hair and intense, gray eyes was standing beside our table. I had not seen her approach, nor had I noticed her earlier in the dining room, but she must have been there, all the same.

"I could not help but notice the . . . difficulty you are undergoing," she said with a discreet nod to Hexe's splinted hand. "Please allow me to introduce myself: I am Erys. I am a glover, by trade. And I believe I have an item in my inventory that would be of immense service to you."

"Thank you, but I'm not in the market for magic gloves, Madam Erys," Hexe said with a wan smile.

"Not even the Gauntlet of Nydd?" she countered, her pale gray eyes gleaming like pieces of tin in the muted light of the dining room.

Hexe paused for a long moment, like a fish contemplating the bait on the end of a hook, before shaking his head. "I appreciate your offer, but the splint is merely a temporary inconvenience," he explained. "I'll be as good as new in just a few days."

"Of course, Serenity," Erys replied, with a bow of her head. "But in case you should change your mind—feel free to come by my shop." She snapped her fingers, and a business card materialized from nowhere.

"Thank you for your concern, Madam Erys," Hexe said politely as he accepted the proffered card.

Erys nodded her head and turned to go, but not before flashing me a sidelong glance harsh enough to peel paint. Although I had become somewhat inured to the casual misanthropy of most Kymerans, I was momentarily shaken by the unalloyed revulsion in the other woman's pale eyes.

"Ugh!" I whispered, once she was out of earshot. "That woman gives me the creeps! And *magic gloves*? Is she for real?"

"There's always a market for enchanted clothing," Hexe replied with a shrug. "Seven league boots, cloaks of invisibility, ruby slippers, that sort of thing. Most of the shops are over on Shoemaker Lane."

"So who's this Nydd guy? And why would you want his gauntlet?"

"He was a lieutenant in the Dragon Calvary during the Sufferance," Hexe replied, staring down at his damaged hand. "He was also the son of General Vlad. When Nydd's right hand was badly maimed in a skirmish with Witchfinders, his father created a special gauntlet that enabled him to use his hand again."

"That sounds like something you could definitely use right now."

"Perhaps," he agreed. "But I seriously doubt she has the genuine article in her possession. The Gauntlet of Nydd disappeared during the Dragon War, and the spell that created it died with General Vlad."

"How does something like that get lost, anyway?"

"Vlad cut it off Nydd's hand when he refused to go to war against his uncle, the Witch King," he replied matter-of-factly.

We finished our dinner and returned home, although Hexe was far less talkative than usual. I could tell by the furrow in his brow that he was mulling over Madam Erys' words. The preoccupied look in his eyes was still there as we undressed for bed.

"You're so beautiful," Hexe said as I straddled him.

"I bet you say that to all the girls you knock up," I

grinned, removing my bra. I tossed it at the owl atop the nearest bedpost, covering its unblinking eyes with a C-cup.

"I have, so far," he chuckled. Out of reflex, he reached up to cup my breasts, only to have his face go white with pain.

"Do you need your pills?" I asked.

"Yeah," he grunted, cradling his wounded hand against his chest as he rode out the wave of agony.

I hopped off the bed and hurried to the bathroom, returning with a glass of water, which Hexe gratefully accepted as he choked down more of Dr. Mao's pills. After a minute or so the muscles in his face began to relax.

"I'm sorry, Tate," he said, his words already beginning to slur. "But I don't think I'm going to be of much use tonight."

"It's okay, baby," I said, lying down beside him. "We can cuddle; I don't mind."

But by the time I pulled the bedclothes over us, his eyes were already closed. I lay there for a long time, watching him sleep. He mumbled a couple of things under his breath, and from the way his body twitched against mine, I could tell his dreams were troubled. I glanced up at the bedposts. The owls looked worried.

"I'm so happy for you, Tate!" Vanessa was finally able to articulate, after an initial squeal of excitement so loud I had to hold the cell phone a foot from my ear. "You two are going to make *kick-ass* parents! I am going to throw you one *awesome* baby shower! Ooh! Can I be the godmother—assuming you don't already have an actual fairy lined up for the job?"

"Of *course* you're going to be the godmother, Nessie!" I laughed. "I wouldn't dream of appointing anyone else!"

"Speaking of mothers—have you told Mrs. E the big news yet?"

"You're the first person, outside of Hexe, I've notified. We haven't even talked to *his* mother, yet, much less mine."

"Yeah, but you really ought to let your folks know, Tate. I know they're horrible and everything, but becoming grandparents will turn their brains to mush," Vanessa pointed out helpfully. "You would not *believe* what my mother is willing to agree to just to have access to my brother's kid! And my dad! He actually stuffs twenty dollar bills in the brat's rompers! I swear, it's like someone stole my parents and replaced them with lobotomized doppelgangers."

"Yeah, but your brother didn't marry a witch," I replied.

"That's what *you* think!"

"I'm not going to lie—we could *really* use some outside financial help right now," I admitted as I dug the keys to the boardinghouse out of my pocket. "But I'm not breaking down and calling my parents. *They're* the ones who demanded that I give up Hexe, and then cut off my trust fund when I refused. If they want to be a part of their grandchild's life, it's up to *them* to make the first move, not me."

Before I could unlock the front door I heard a woman's voice from inside the house angrily shouting, "Look at me! *Look! At! Me!*"

"Uh, Nessie, I'm going to have to get back to you later," I said as I quickly cut off the call. Upon opening the door I saw Hexe desperately trying to block the path of a statuesque woman with auburn hair. I knew from her height, bone structure, and anorexia that she was a model of some sort, although it was difficult to tell if she was anyone famous or not, due to the luxurious full beard and mustache that covered the lower half of her face.

"I am *dreadfully* sorry, Ms. Pasternak," Hexe said in all earnestness. "I must have miscalculated one of the ingredients in the exfoliant I prepared for you. All I have to do is formulate a new batch, that's all. . . ."

"It's bad enough I woke up this morning with a handlebar mustache! I did *not* pay you good money so I could go to bed looking like the bearded lady at the freak show!" Ms. Pasternak exclaimed indignantly.

"Of *course* you didn't," Hexe said, using his best client-whisperer voice as he struggled to defuse the situation. "Now, if you would *just* give me some time, I'm sure I'll be able to reverse the condition. . . ."

"How *much* time?" Ms. Pasternak frowned as she stroked her bearded chin.

"An hour, perhaps—certainly no more than two . . ."

"I don't have that kind of time to waste hanging around waiting to see if you might be able to reverse this . . . this . . ."

"Hypertrichosis," Hexe supplied helpfully.

"I don't care *what* you call it. I want it gone!" she snapped, grabbing a handful of beard in illustration. "And I want it gone *now*! I came here because I was told you were the *best* curse-lifter in Golgotham! I've got an *important* fashion shoot tomorrow; I can't show up looking like I belong on a box of cough drops!"

"As I said, I simply need to reformulate the lotion and reapply it to your face. . . ."

"If you think I'm going to let you put *more* of that stuff on me again, you're out of your mind!" the hirsute Ms. Pasternak exclaimed. "I'm getting out of here before I end up like Rip Van Winkle! Now give me back my money!"

"But Ms. Pasternak, if you would *just* give me another chance—!"

"I'd rather take my chances in the Rookery, if it's all the same to you," the bearded fashion model said sternly, thrusting forth a perfectly manicured hand. "I demand a refund, or do I have to call the cops—or whatever the hell you people call them in this godforsaken ghetto of yours?"

"That won't be necessary," he said glumly. Hexe stuck his left hand in his pocket, reluctantly withdrawing five crisp hundred dollar bills. "Here's your money."

Ms. Pasternak snatched the cash back, tucking it into whatever cleavage lurked behind her whiskers. "Just be glad I didn't ask for damages as well!" she snapped. As she headed for the door, she paused to give me a warning glance. "I wouldn't waste your money on him if I were you, sister. The guy's a charlatan!"

After the front door slammed behind his disgruntled former client, Hexe silently strode out of the parlor and headed for his office. A second later he returned with Madam Erys' business card.

"C'mon," he said in a clipped voice. "Let's go try on some gloves."

Chapter 12

Shoemaker Lane had, at one time, been the home of the leprechaun cobblers who make footwear for Kymerans and other hard-to-fit customers. They also had a thriving side business selling charmed boots and shoes to humans. Although there were still quite a few signs shaped like oversized boots visible along the street, most of the Wee Folk had relocated eastward to Ferry Street, allowing other tradesmen to take their place.

I paused outside one of the remaining enchanted cobbler shops and stared at a dazzling array of gleaming glass slippers. Each pair had a little sign with a brief description of its particular charm to potential buyers, such as "makes you irresistible," "world-class ballroom dancer," or "beautiful until midnight." Of course, you might have to cut off a toe or two to get them to fit, but then, all fashion has its price.

"Come on," Hexe said, giving my arm a tug. "You can window-shop later." He continued down the street, checking the address on the business card with the house numbers over the shops. After passing a tailor specializing in cloaks of invisibility and a millinery selling thinking caps, he came to a stop in front of a wooden trade sign in the shape of a six-fingered hand. Perched atop it was a large raven, preening its shiny black feathers with its ebon beak. As we approached the storefront, it cawed noisily and took to the air.

In the window of the shop were a number of mannequin hands posed in a variety of spell configurations, both left-and-right handed, each sheathed in a glove of some kind.

Some of the gloves looked fairly ordinary, but the display also included one made from spiderwebs and another that looked like it was fashioned from pieced together bits of a broken mirror.

The bell over the shop door tinkled discreetly as we entered. The atmosphere inside the shop was strangely close and smelled faintly of dust, like a rarely used storage locker. The back of the shop was curtained off from the sales floor, which featured a long glass display counter, behind which stood a cabinet full of small, narrow drawers that took up the entire wall. An antique cash register, the kind with elaborate scrollwork and amount flags instead of digital readouts, sat unattended on the counter. A pair of white, full length silk opera gloves were casually draped over the edge of the counter like the shed skins of twin albino pythons.

Hexe stepped forward, looking about the otherwise empty store. "Hello? Is anyone there?"

The curtain at the back of the shop twitched aside and Erys emerged, moving with slightly overly deliberate movements, like an actress playing a part onstage. "Ah! Serenity! Welcome to my humble establishment! You honor me greatly!" She smiled. "I take it you've changed your mind since last we spoke?"

"Let's just say you've piqued my interest," Hexe replied. "How long have you been keeping shop on Shoemaker Lane, Madam Erys?"

"I am a relative newcomer to Golgotham," she explained. "I only recently relocated my business from the Faubourg Cauchemar."

"Is there *that* much of a demand for magic gloves nowadays?" I asked, staring at the wall-sized cabinets in disbelief.

Madam Erys' pale gray eyes flickered toward me in thinly veiled distaste. Away from the aromas of the Calf's dining room, I was finally able to get a good whiff of her scent. She smelled strongly of dill and sulfured molasses—two scents that were, in and of themselves, pleasant enough, but, when combined, seemed unnatural.

"Should a customer wish to be a classical pianist, or a virtuoso violinist, I can make them the next Rachmaninoff or Isaac Stern with a pair of silk concert gloves," she replied stiffly. "Or should they desire to win at the crap tables, I have a pair of special kid gloves that will ensure they'll never roll snake eyes again. I also have an outfielder's mitt guaranteed to attract baseballs like a magnet. Anything that can be done by hand, can be enhanced by my merchandise." She turned to Hexe, flashing him an obsequious smile. "Allow me to show you the gauntlet. Once you inspect it, you'll see it is, indeed, the genuine article." Madam Erys pulled one of the drawers from its cubby hole, like a banker removing a safety deposit box, and placed it atop the counter. The interior of the drawer was lined in velvet and contained a solitary chain-mail glove that shimmered in the dusty light of the shop like a jeweled fish still wet from the sea.

It didn't look forged as much as *woven* from silver filigree. The palm and knuckle-bridge were protected by a metal cuff of white gold and engraved with the sinuous form of a dragon, while the tips of each digit—all six of them—were capped in platinum and inset with pieces of polished jade to give the semblance of fingernails. It was, without a doubt, the most breathtakingly beautiful item of clothing I'd ever seen in my life.

Hexe removed a small scrying stone from his pocket and passed it back and forth over the gauntlet like a magnifying glass. "It *does* appear to be Vlad's spellwork," he mused aloud. "I recognize his signature from the family archives." He studied it for a long moment, the glittering silver skin reflected in his golden eyes. "How much do you want?" he asked.

"Are you *nuts*?" I whispered. "There's no way we can *afford* that thing, even if I *wasn't* cut off from the family fortune!"

Hexe gave me a tiny shake of the head and put a finger to his lips, his signal for *let me handle this.* I grudgingly fell silent.

"I would rather not bring something so vulgar as money into this," Madam Erys replied carefully. "As a loyal Kymeran, it is my honor, nay, my *duty* to offer such an artifact to you, Serenity."

"You humble me with your generosity, Madam Erys," Hexe said, with a ritual bow of his head. "But surely there is *something* I can offer in return?"

"A royal warrant of appointment would be most appreciated, Serenity. As you can see, my business is not what it could be," she said, gesturing to the dust gathering in the corners of the shop. "There are still those in Golgotham, and elsewhere, who put great stock in where members of the Royal Family receive their goods, especially the Heir Apparent."

"Consider it done, Madam Erys," Hexe replied. "But I only accept your kind offer on condition that it is merely a *loan*. As soon as I no longer require the use of the gauntlet, I will return it to you, with my sincerest thanks."

"Of course, Serenity," Erys smiled, bowing her head. "However, I must warn you that in order for you to wield the Gauntlet of Nydd, it must be bonded to your nervous system."

"Ah. I see," Hexe said, the smile falling away from his face. He pushed the gauntlet's display case back toward the glover. "I'm afraid I'll have to leave it in your care until I can afford such elective surgery."

"That won't be necessary, Serenity," Madam Erys said quickly. "I know a psychic surgeon who owes me a favor. I'm certain he'll quote you a reasonable price."

"How soon would he be able to do the work?"

Madam Erys reached into her décolletage and removed a heart-shaped locket-watch on a golden chain. "If we hurry, he should be able to squeeze you in today."

"I thought you said we were going to your doctor-friend's office?" Hexe frowned.

"I didn't say he was my friend," Erys replied a bit sharply. "Just that he owed me a favor. Besides, he conducts most of his business from here."

As it turned out, "here," as Madam Erys so put it, was none other than the Stagger Inn, one of the lowest of Golgotham's low taverns. It was not the kind of establishment one would expect a respectable psychic surgeon to be hanging out in during office hours. However, if you were looking for cheap intoxicants and a knife fight, you'd *definitely* come to the right place.

"I don't like this at all." I whispered. "And I *really* don't like her. Something's screwy about all this. Can't we just forget about this gauntlet thing and go back home, please?"

"Normally, I'd agree with you," Hexe replied. "But these aren't normal times, Tate. I *have* to regain the use of my right hand. If that means becoming involved with a dodgy sorceress . . . well, it won't be the first time."

"Dori was different, and you know that," I protested. "And I can't *believe* I just defended someone who tried to turn me into a toad."

"Is there a problem, Serenity?" Madam Erys asked, turning back to give me a disapproving look as she opened the door to the Stagger Inn.

"No, everything's fine," he assured her.

Against my better judgment, I followed them into the bar. The moment I set foot inside, my eyes began to water and I started to cough. Kymerans tend to smoke like clogged chimneys when they're sober, and even more so when they're drunk. The interior of the Stagger Inn was filled with a blue-tinged pall that hung in the air as thick as fog. Judging from its smell, the miasma was a mixture of tobacco, hashish, and opium smoke from a variety of cigars, hookahs, and pipes.

We continued through a low-slung archway into a public room with ponderous beams overhead and worm-shot planking underfoot. The main room had neither electric nor gaslight fixtures, and was instead lit by stray balls of witch-fire, which bumped against the low ceiling like wandering toy balloons. The Stagger Inn's clientele was composed of the hardest drinkers in Golgotham, mostly satyrs, ipotanes, maenads, and leprechauns, and it was reflected in the pub's atmosphere. This was not the kind of place you go to in order to celebrate a birthday or commemorate an anniversary; this was the kind of place you go to in order to drink as much as possible, for as cheaply as possible, for as long as possible before either throwing up, losing consciousness, or being thrown out, if not all three.

At the back of the room was what passed for the bar, behind which stood an older maenad, her leopard-skin cloak askew and one boob hanging out. As I watched, she poured absinthe into a greasy-looking cocktail glass and handed it to a blowzy nymph, who transported it to a booth in one of the shadowier corners of the main room.

"That's our contact," Madam Erys said, pointing to the older Kymeran the waitress had just served.

Although I had never personally met the tall, thin man with the receding sage-colored hair and long, tapering fingers before, I instantly recognized him as Dr. Moot, who occasionally worked for the Maladanti. This was because, months ago, I had seen him reflected within a scrying stone, mutilating the feet of my friend Lukas with a silver scalpel.

Hexe recoiled, his mouth twisted into a grimace of distaste. "You can keep the gauntlet, Madam Erys. I know this man, and I *refuse* to have anything to do with him."

As Hexe turned to leave, Dr. Moot raised his glass of absinthe in a mock salute. "Have it your way, Serenity," he said in a slightly slurred, overloud voice. "But good luck finding anyone else willing to work as cheap as me. Or, perhaps, you'll find a boneknitter somewhere who can turn a *Malleus Maleficarum* fracture widdershins."

Hexe spun back around to glare at Moot, his face gray as old porridge. "How do you know about that?"

"How do you *think* I know?" the psychic surgeon sneered. "Now sit down before you call any more attention to yourself." He gestured to the seat opposite him with a long-fingered hand. "The tosspots around here aren't so soused they won't eventually notice the Heir Apparent slumming it amongst them. And if Marz finds out I'm talking to you, he won't hesitate to clip my wings, so to speak," he said, miming cutting off one of his fingers with a pair of scissors.

Hexe hesitated for a moment and then grudgingly sat down in the booth opposite the disgraced surgeon. I slid in after him, leaving Erys to drag over a chair from a nearby table. The smell of wormwood radiated from Moot so strongly I at first assumed he'd accidently spilled his absinthe onto himself.

"When Madam here told me she had someone interested in the Gauntlet of Nydd, I knew it had to be you. I've agreed to do the surgery—but only because I owe her a debt. After which, we're done; is that understood?" Moot said, shooting a meaningful look in the glover's direction.

"Of course," Madam Erys replied stiffly.

"I used to be friends with your Uncle Esau, you know," Dr. Moot said as he studied Hexe over the rim of his glass. "I worked with him on those clockwork limbs of his. He first learned how to construct them from the Royal Surgeon, Dr. Tork, but Esau later went on to refine the technique. He crafted the limbs, and I handled the surgery. That was a long, long time ago, though."

"Did you know his wife back then?" Hexe asked.

The question seemed to catch Moot off guard. He glanced over at Madam Erys and then dropped his gaze into the green depths of the absinthe. "Of course, I knew Nina," he said solemnly. "I'm the one who introduced them."

"What was she like?" Hexe asked, a quizzical look on his face. "No one in my family is willing to talk about her. In fact, I never even knew she existed until recently."

Before Dr. Moot could reply, Madam Erys abruptly stood up as if an unseen puppeteer had yanked her upright by invisible strings. "Please excuse me; I need a drink," she said in a cold, clipped voice. As the glover headed toward the bar, a look of relief flickered across Dr. Moot's eyes.

"Nina was a wonderful, wonderful woman," he said, speaking in a conspiratorial whisper, as if afraid of being overheard. "I met her at the same place I met your uncle— at Thamaturgical College. She and I were both studying the Healing Arts, and happened to take the same potions class under Professor Kohl. I later went into psychic surgery, while she developed into one of the best potion-makers I've ever known. One day I invited her over to the workshop I shared with your uncle, to see what we were working on. The moment she and Esau saw one another, any chance I had with her went out the window." He gave a wry, sad laugh at that point, and suddenly, despite myself, I felt a twinge of pity for the butchering bastard. "Nina was a very kind and caring woman—and that's what made her such a marvelous healer. She could not look at a person in pain and not be moved to alleviate their suffering."

"I'm having a hard time imagining my uncle being married to someone like that," Hexe said skeptically.

"Esau was . . . *different* back then," Dr. Moot said with a heavy sigh. "He was always possessed of a strong personality, and he was never *that* fond of humans to begin with, but he didn't become a devotee of the Left Hand Path and radical misanthrope until after he lost Nina. She was the one who kept his darker nature in check, I guess."

"What, exactly, happened to her?"

"About thirty-five years ago, Nina got a call from one of

her steady clients who lived outside Golgotham. The client had originally been cursed with dropsy, which Nina succeeded in reversing. However, the client later suffered an unexpected relapse, swelling up like a parade balloon. Although she was uncomfortable with leaving Golgotham at that time of night, Nina agreed to personally deliver the necessary potion. On her way back from the client's apartment, she ran afoul of a group of human street toughs, who, once they realized she was Kymeran, starting chasing her.

"Nina wasn't a strong spellcaster—like I said, her specialty was potions—and didn't believe in using offensive magic, even for defensive purposes. She was so desperate to avoid conflict, she ran out into Broadway without looking, and was hit by a Yellow Cab. She was already in a coma when they wheeled her into the ER at Golgotham General. As it happened, I was working the surgery rotation when she came in. I tried my best to revive her, but the trauma was too great. I was forced to declare her brain-dead. Esau never forgave me for not saving her. And neither did I." Moot fell silent for a long moment, his eyes unfocused, as if watching something far away and long ago, before taking a deep breath and shaking himself free. "Let me see your hand."

Hexe shifted about uncomfortably, but did as he was asked, presenting his splinted hand for inspection. Dr. Moot pursed his lips and gently probed the damaged appendage, his own hand climbing about it like a spider checking its web. To my horror, the psychic surgeon's fingertips dipped beneath Hexe's skin as easily as if they were breaking the surface of a pool of water.

"The injuries to the metacarpals are quite severe," Moot said with a frown. "But the nerve damage isn't as bad as I would have thought. I should be able to bond the gauntlet relatively easily."

"How soon can you do the work?" Hexe asked, excitement starting to seep into his voice.

"I've got a surgery set up in Pickman's Slip," Moot replied. "I can do it now, if that's what you want."

"Are you *certain* you want to go through with this, Hexe?" I asked worriedly. Everything seemed to be moving way too fast and way too weird, even for Golgotham.

"What I 'want' has nothing to do with it," he replied

grimly. "I have *no* choice in this matter. I *have* to regain dexterity in my right hand. Without it, I can't provide for myself, much less our child."

There was a sudden gasp, and I looked up to find Madam Erys had returned from the bar. She stood there with a snifter of Cynar in one hand, staring at me with a barely concealed looked of disgust and horror. So much for inviting *her* to the baby shower.

Chapter 13

It was not surprising Moot worked out of Pickman's Slip. Golgotham's riverfront neighborhood was notorious for its rows of ancient warehouses, flops, and taverns that catered to longshoremen, and had long been considered the kind of place where dirty deeds could be done dirt cheap.

Save for the tacky, over-the-top splendor of Lorelei's tiki restaurant, Pickman's Slip can be best described as low-rent, although "depressing" and "unsafe" also come to mind. The neighborhood's general gloominess is due to its close proximity to the Ferry Street Terminus, which houses the elaborate barques that transport Golgotham's dead to their final resting place on Scylla Point. As for the Slip's reputation for being dangerous, that was largely due to the troll community that dwelt beneath the nearby Brooklyn Bridge.

Dr. Moot's place of business was located in the basement below a dilapidated meat pie shop, next door to a hookah bar. The so-called "surgery" was one huge room that smelled of rising damp, with thick, square-cut posts supporting the ceiling, which was so low it was impossible to wear a hat indoors. There was an antique surgery table, the type raised and lowered by a huge, wheellike crank, in the middle of the room, above which dangled a mechanic's lamp suspended by a bright orange extension cord. One corner was sectioned off with old blankets strung from clothesline, behind which was what passed for Moot's living quarters.

"Roll up your sleeve and make yourself comfortable, Serenity," Moot said, patting the surgical table's stainless-steel top.

"Hexe, I don't think this is a good idea," I whispered as he hopped up onto the table. "I mean, *look* at this place! It couldn't pass inspection as a tattoo parlor! I wouldn't let this guy neuter Beanie, much less try to fix your hand!"

"Tate, I know you're concerned," he replied wearily. "But, please, I beg of you, stop trying to talk me out of this."

"I know, I know," I sighed. "It's a Kymeran thing; I wouldn't understand."

Dr. Moot opened a cupboard and removed a dark green bottle without a label. He poured a finger of thick, bright yellow liquid into a greasy-looking shot glass and handed it to Hexe.

"What is that?" I asked, intercepting the glass and giving it a suspicious sniff.

"Safflower oil, if you *must* know," Dr. Moot replied sharply, snatching it back from my hand. "It's for his safety. Psychic surgery itself is relatively painless, but I can't have him wriggling around while I'm working, can I?"

"I'll be okay, Tate," Hexe said as he accepted the shot glass, "just as long as you promise to hold my left hand."

"Believe me, I'm not going anywhere," I assured him.

Hexe knocked back the safflower oil like it was a shot of tequila and stretched out on the surgical table. I stood next to him, holding his left hand in both of my own. Within seconds his facial muscles began to relax and his golden eyes rolled back in his head.

Moot slipped on a headband that resembled an antique doctor's reflector, save that it was fashioned from a flat scrying stone and set on a swivel, so that it could be rotated in front of his eyes. After removing the splint from Hexe's right hand, he turned to Madam Erys, who was holding what looked like a clamshell jewelry case. She flipped open the lid, revealing the Gauntlet of Nydd. Even in the miserable light of Moot's dingy surgery, the artifact glittered and gleamed like frost at sunrise.

"Heavens and hells!" Moot exclaimed hoarsely, shaking his head in admiration. "Such exquisite workmanship! It makes Esau's prosthetic arms look like clockwork toys!" Once he removed the gauntlet, Erys closed the case with a snap that would have done a crocodile proud.

Dr. Moot removed the splint on Hexe's wounded hand and carefully slipped the gauntlet onto Hexe's hand. As he did so, I was finally able to get my first unobstructed view of the damage inflicted by the witch-hammer since the night of the attack. Although I was relieved to see the swelling and bruising had been greatly reduced, I was shocked to discover that Hexe's fingers looked as if they were trying to avoid one another.

Once the gauntlet was secured in place, Moot strode over to a nearby table and plunged his hands into a jar of that blue stuff barbers keep their combs in. Flicking the excess disinfectant from his hands, he took a deep breath and flipped the scrying stone attached to his headband into place over his right eye and began to gently stroke Hexe's wrist and forearm with his long, delicate fingers.

At first I could not tell what he was doing. Then I saw the psychic surgeon's fingertips dip past the gauntlet covering Hexe's mangled hand. Moot's spidery digits moved like those of a skilled lace maker as he spliced nerve endings, grafted muscle, and shaved away bone without shedding a drop of blood. After an hour, he stepped away from the table and swung the scrying stone back into place, his face drawn and covered in sweat.

"The bonding is completed," he said, his voice shaking ever so slightly. He walked back over to the prep table and took a swig from the jar of blue stuff. "There. That's better."

"How long before he wakes up?" I asked anxiously, staring at Hexe's silver-clad hand.

"He should come out of it in five minutes or so," Dr. Moot said. "Now, if you'll excuse me, there are some matters that require discussion with Madam Erys." With that, he and the glover retired behind the curtains at the back of the surgery.

I looked down at my own hands, which were still clasping Hexe's motionless left one. His breathing was that of a man in a deep sleep, and I could tell that his eyeballs were twitching behind their lids, keeping track of whatever was gamboling through his drug-fueled dreams. It was the most peaceful I'd seen him since the Jubilee.

"Everything's going to be all right," I murmured aloud, more for my benefit than his, as I brushed the purple hair away from his face.

Suddenly Dr. Moot's voice announced heatedly from behind the curtain: "I've done what you asked of me! Whatever debt I owed is now paid in full! Never contact me again—is that understood? I can't bear the sight of you. Wasn't it enough that you lured her away? Must you torment me in such a ghastly manner as well?"

"She was not 'lured,'" Erys replied dryly. "She chose of her own free will. When will you get that through that liquor-soaked sponge you call your brain? But I am more than happy to agree to your conditions. Far be it from me to prevent you from continuing to wallow in self-pity and whatever intoxicant might be closest to hand."

Before I could wonder what the two could be possibly squabbling about, Hexe's eyelids fluttered and he began to stir.

"He's coming around!" I shouted.

The arguing voices fell silent. Dr. Moot threw back the blankets that served as his privacy curtain and returned to the table. He took Hexe's pulse and inspected his pupils. "How do you feel, Serenity?" he asked.

"Did it work?" Hexe rasped in reply.

"There's only one way to find out," Moot said as he helped his patient sit up. As Hexe swung his legs over the side of the table, the psychic surgeon picked up the shot glass he had used to serve the sedative and tossed it at him. "Catch!"

Hexe snatched the flying glass in midair with his right hand without a moment's hesitation. He then stared in amazement at his appendage, now encased from wrist to fingertips in shimmering silver and white gold.

"Is there any pain?" Moot asked.

"There's no pain," Hexe replied with a shake of his head. "I can tell that the glass I'm holding has weight and is hard and smooth, but the sensations themselves are . . . distant, like I'm picking something up while wearing a silk glove."

"That disconnected feeling should fade, in time," Moot assured him. "Eventually the gauntlet will completely merge with the sensory receptors in your brain, and it'll be just like the hand you were born with."

"I owe you my life, Dr. Moot," Hexe said solemnly.

Moot flinched and dropped his gaze. "You owe me nothing, Serenity. This was done to discharge a debt, not out of any desire to curry favor."

"Regardless of the reason, you have still done me a great service I will not soon forget."

"You are too kind, Serenity," the psychic surgeon muttered, his cheeks flushing red.

"Can I take him home now?" I asked, not bothering to hide my eagerness to get the hell away from Moot and Madam Erys.

"Of course," Moot replied, quickly regathering himself. "There may be the occasional 'hiccup' over the next few days as his nervous system becomes accustomed to the gauntlet, but otherwise, he's good to go."

"I thank you for the loan of the gauntlet, Madam Erys," Hexe said as he put his jacket back on, this time without my help.

"The honor is all mine, Serenity," the glover replied, her pale gray eyes shining like pieces of polished tin. "May you wear it in good health."

As we exited Dr. Moot's surgery, we were greeted by a wall of fog from the nearby river, which turned the surrounding buildings into smeared outlines and hid us from any nosy neighbors. Although the streets seemed deserted, Hexe kept his hands stuffed deep into his pockets, just to be on the safe side.

As we headed back to the boardinghouse, I noticed that his shoulders were no longer stooped and that he now walked with a far more confident stride. I wasn't sure how much of it was directly due to the gauntlet, or simply a placebo effect, but I was glad to see him more like his old self.

Upon our return to the boardinghouse Beanie came scampering out of the kitchen. He was so eager to tell us "hello," he leapt up in the air like a two-tone springbok.

"I'm glad to see you, too!" Hexe laughed, reaching out to pet Beanie, only to have the dog suddenly yelp in alarm.

"What's wrong, boy?" Hexe frowned as Beanie dropped his ears and drew away, shivering as if he was freezing.

"He's freaked out because your hand doesn't have the same scent as the rest of you," Scratch explained as he entered the front parlor.

Hexe lifted the gauntlet to his nose and gave it a sniff. "I hadn't really noticed it before, but now that you mention it, it *does* smell like Erys. I guess that's to be expected—it was in her possession for some time. No doubt it'll eventually acquire my scent once I've worn it for a while."

"A little heavy on the bling, don't you think?" Scratch asked, eyeing his master's silver-clad hand.

"It can glow in the dark, for all I care, just as long as it enables me to use my right hand."

Later, as we prepared for bed, I found myself watching Hexe as he undressed, marveling at how the silver filigree mesh of the gauntlet gleamed like crushed ice on a hot summer day. Hexe caught me staring and halted his disrobing.

"Does the sight of it bother you?" he asked.

"No, I think it's quite beautiful," I replied truthfully. "But I'm uneasy about Madam Erys' motivation for giving it to you. I don't like that woman, Hexe, and I don't trust her. Whenever she looks in my direction, I can feel hatred oozing out of her."

"Granted, Madam Erys is a misanthrope," Hexe agreed. "But there's no reason to suspect her of anything more than calculated self-interest. It's fairly common for tradesmen to curry favor from the Royal Family by presenting us with elaborate gifts in hopes of winning a royal warrant. Why do you think Lafo and Lorelei are always so glad to see me at their establishments? It's not *just* because they're my friends. Being able to claim a member of the Royal Family as a regular client still means something in Golgotham, even in this day and age. Sometimes it's *good* to be the Witch King—or at least the Heir Apparent. And tonight was one of those times."

"Does it *feel* like your hand?" I asked.

"Why don't *you* tell me?" he smiled, sliding it along my naked body until it finally came to rest on my hip.

The silver chain mail was so tightly woven it was more like the skin of a snake than something forged from metal. Although his right hand felt slightly cool and distant against my flesh, it didn't keep me from noticing how warm and close the rest of him was.

A couple of hours later, after thoroughly testing how his gauntleted hand held up under pressure (which turned out to be "pretty well"), I woke up from a sound sleep. I lay in the bed for a long moment, my thoughts still muzzy, trying to figure out what had jettisoned me back into the waking world. Did I have to pee? Was I thirsty? Was I tangled up in the bedclothes? Was Beanie snoring? Was Scratch kicking me in his sleep again?

As I ran down the checklist, answering "no" to each question, I became aware of a rhythmic tapping sound. I rose up on one elbow and looked down at Hexe, who was asleep on his back, his left arm carelessly thrown across his forehead and his right hand resting on his naked chest. The tapping noise—which I now realized was what had awakened me—was that of the fingers of his gauntleted hand drumming against his sternum, as if patiently biding their time.

Chapter 14

Now that he had regained the use of his right hand, Hexe was his old self once again. I was relieved to see the gleam back in his golden eyes and hear the confidence return to his voice. Since that very next day was my day off, Hexe had planned a leisurely, romantic breakfast for the two of us. However, those plans were quickly dashed by an unexpected knock.

Upon opening the door, Hexe was surprised to find his mother, Lady Syra, standing on the stoop. Before he could say hello, she breezed past him and into the front room.

"So, exactly *when* were you going to tell me I'm going to be a grandmother?" she asked, fixing him with a withering glare. "*Before* the baby arrived, or *after*?"

"How did you know—?" Hexe sputtered in surprise.

"Besides being your mother, I am *also* a professional astrologer," she reminded him sharply. "And it so happens, while I was drawing up your father's horoscope, as a present for his birthday—and don't you *dare* tell him that's what he's getting—I saw in the stars that he was going to be a *grandfather*! Imagine my surprise! Especially since I was finding out from the orientation of Orion's Belt and *not my own son*! I might as well have read it in the gossip column of the *Gazette*!"

"I'm sorry, Mom," Hexe apologized. "I've been meaning to tell you, but Tate and I just wanted a little private time as a couple before everything goes crazy and the Blue Hairs start calling for my head on a pike."

"Granted, the hard-line aristos are *not* going to be

thrilled when they hear the news," she sighed. "But that's no reason to keep *me* out of the loop!"

"So—you're not upset that we're having a baby?" I asked anxiously.

"Heavens and hells, no!" Lady Syra exclaimed, throwing her arms around me. "I can't *wait* to be a grandmamma!"

I blinked in surprise. "You mean you don't have any problems with the new Heir Apparent being half human?"

An odd look crossed the Witch Queen's face, which she quickly tried to camouflage by smiling. "Why don't we deal with that problem when it arises, shall we? *Whatever* happens, I won't love my grandchild any less."

"What do you mean by 'whatever happens'?" I asked suspiciously.

"You think our child is going to be a norlock, don't you?" Hexe said flatly.

"A what-lock?" I frowned.

"It's slang for Kymerans born incapable of working magic," he explained grimly. "Their 'extra' fingers end at the second knuckle. My grandfather used to employ a norlock named Jake when I was a boy. He lived in a little cottage at the foot of the garden."

"Please don't take what I'm about to say the wrong way, my dear," Syra said apologetically. "But very few half-castes are born fully functional in the magic department. Understand I'm not trying to be negative, my dear; I'm just being *practical*. There is also a very good chance your child might not even be of Royal blood. . . ."

"Are you suggesting that Hexe isn't the father?" I gasped.

"Of course not!" Lady Syra replied quickly. "It's just that . . ."

"Just *what*, exactly?" I retorted, trying to keep hold of my temper.

"If the baby doesn't have gold eyes, it can't be recognized as heir to the Throne of Arum," she replied, shifting about uncomfortably. "It can never be a member of the Royal Family."

"Why are you so certain this will be the case with our child?" Hexe scowled.

"Because you're not the *first* Heir Apparent to take a fancy to a human," Lady Syra explained. "Great Uncle

Jack, the one who built this house, had a child by a human mistress shortly before he disappeared. His son was born a norlock. Your great-grandfather, Lord Jynx, refused to acknowledge him as one of us because he had his mother's eyes."

"This norlock child of Uncle Jack's—what happened to him?" Hexe asked.

"After Lord Jynx died, my father took pity on the boy and made him his gardener."

"You mean Jake was—?"

"Your first cousin, once removed," Syra said with a sad nod of her head. "But you must remember that was another time. Things are *different* now." She reached out to touch her son's arm, only to have the ivory bracelet wrapped about her wrist abruptly rise up, revealing itself to be a tiny albino serpent. The familiar hissed loudly and flared its hood, which popped open like the miniature parasol in a Mai Tai. "*Trinket—!*" Lady Syra scolded, delivering a light tap to the top of its milk-white head with the tip of her finger. "By the Outer Dark! What has come over you?"

The micro-cobra flinched at the reprimand, but did not resume its previous, passive stance, and continued to keep its ruby-red eyes focused on Hexe.

"Perhaps this is what has her upset," he said, holding up the glittering glove that now covered his right hand.

"By the sunken spires!" Lady Syra exclaimed in surprise. "What *is* that thing?"

"The Gauntlet of Nydd."

"Well, no wonder Trinket became alarmed!" His mother frowned. "She's *very* sensitive to charmed objects. But I thought the Gauntlet of Nydd was lost during the Dragon War. Where on earth did you find it—and how could you possibly *afford* it once you did?"

"I know what you're thinking, Mother—it's not a forgery," Hexe assured her. "I checked the enchantment—the signature on the spell is General Vlad's. And as to how I ended up in possession of it—it was a gift from a tradeswoman seeking a royal warrant. It's really no different from that time Bulgari sent you that cocktail necklace. . . ."

"Yes, yes, that's all very well and good," Lady Syra said impatiently. "But *why* are you wearing it?"

"I find it helps focus and enhance my Right Hand magic. I need all the help I can get if I want to bring in even more paying business. After all, I'm going to be a father soon."

Although it was obvious that Lady Syra did not completely believe what her son had just told her, she did not push the issue. "In any case, you should be careful. The Gauntlet of Nydd was neither truly Left or Right Hand magic. Since it is ambidextrous it can easily go either way, depending on the user."

"Well, I don't think you have to worry about me using a right-handed glove to work Left Hand magic," Hexe reassured her.

"*I'm* not the one who's concerned," Lady Syra replied, gesturing to Trinket, who was still weaving about atop her wrist. "There, there, little one," she said soothingly, planting a kiss atop the familiar's wedge-shaped head. "No need to be upset." This seemed to placate the albino serpent, which once more resumed its role as living jewelry. "Now go get dressed, dear," Lady Syra exclaimed gaily, turning to address me. "I'm taking you shopping!"

During the course of my life, my mother has dragged me through every upscale department store in the city at least once. But where my mother entered Bergdorf's or Barney's like an arctic explorer intent on driving a flag into the North Pole, Lady Syra was far more laid back. The moment she set foot on the sales floor, the personal shoppers seemed to appear as if summoned by a spell, greeting her with eager smiles, without any sign of the nervous trepidation usually displayed by whatever sales staff was unlucky enough to wait on my mother.

However, while the floorwalkers and clerks were pleased to see Lady Syra, the same could not be said for our fellow shoppers, many of whom scowled in disapproval. But if Syra noticed them, she showed no sign of it as she moved through the stalking grounds of Manhattan's elite with unflappable calm, as elegant and gracious as any crowned head of Europe stooping to visit a department store. No wonder Warhol had been so fascinated by her.

After spending an hour trying on clothes, I found myself staring at a daunting array of flowing tops and frilly, Empire-waisted dresses, any one of which cost more than my take-home pay for a month.

"Syra, I can't let you pay for all of this!" I exclaimed.

"Tosh! Of *course* you can!" She laughed as she handed the saleslady a platinum credit card. "I can't allow the mother of my grandchild to go about dressed in nothing but a pair of overalls, can I? Besides, you've done a marvelous job of living lean and making ends meet. A lot of young ladies from your background would have chucked it all by now and returned home with their tails between their legs. You must love my son very, *very* much."

"Yes, I do," I replied. "He's the only man I've ever known who has looked at me and really seen *me* instead of what he *expected* to see, or *wanted* to be there. It's like I don't have to explain things to him—he just instinctively *knows* what's important to me. Do you understand what I mean?"

"Yes, I do. That's how I felt about Hexe's father, when I first fell in love with him. And I *still* feel the same way, all these years and hardships later."

"I like Captain Horn a lot. He reminds me of Hexe, sometimes."

"I suspect he inherited his sense of justice from his father," Lady Syra said, nodding her head in agreement. "I just wish Hexe would be a little warmer toward him. I realize that it was difficult for him, growing up the way he did—but it wasn't Horn's decision to leave him without a father."

"I'm certain once he starts seeing things through the eyes of a parent, he'll come to understand his dad a little better," I assured her.

"I'm sure you're right," Lady Syra conceded. "And perhaps the same will hold true for you as well."

"You're not seriously suggesting I reconcile with my mother and father, are you?" I scoffed.

"I'm well aware that your mother has cultivated a layer of bitch you can break a shovel on," Syra said with a rueful smile. "However, in her defense, the mistakes we parents make trying to protect our children are often the hardest for us to admit."

The sun was beginning to set by the time I returned home, laden with maternity swag. Since neither Hexe nor Beanie

were there to greet me, I assumed he had elected to take the
dog for a walk. I went upstairs and was hanging my three new
maternity tops in the wardrobe when I heard a rustling sound
behind me. As I turned around to see what was making the
noise, one of the shopping bags from Barney's abruptly tilted
over, spilling Scratch out onto the floor. Although he may be
a demon, in many ways the familiar was no different from the
typical housecat—right down to the mad passion for investigating paper bags.

"There you are!" I laughed. "Where's Hexe?"

"He's out in the garden with Beanie," the familiar replied as he rubbed the side of his face along the outer edge
of a Neiman-Marcus bag.

I walked over to the window and peered out into the
backyard, which was incredibly huge, thanks to the Kymeran talent of folding physical space like origami. Hexe
was at the bottom of the garden, beyond the living hedge
maze, playing with Beanie, who was eagerly chasing a red
rubber ball around like a star soccer player.

"I see you survived your shopping expedition with my
mother," Hexe said by way of greeting as I made my way
across the garden. "How many stores did she drag you to?"

"I stopped counting at five," I replied. "It wasn't that bad.
In fact, I actually kind of enjoyed myself. Your mom is a
helluva lot more fun to go shopping with than anyone in *my*
family."

"I'm glad you had a nice time. You *deserve* to treat yourself," he said. "Now that I've got my hand back, maybe next
time *I'll* be the one buying you nice things." He gave the
ball another kick and Beanie leapt up as if he was spring-
loaded, bumping it with his truncated snout like a trained
seal. The ball flew into the dense tangle of ivy in the corner
of the garden where the two walls joined, followed by the
sound of breaking window glass. As I looked closer, I realized there was a small wooden structure, slightly larger than
a potting shed, hidden deep in the dark green foliage.

Hexe walked up to the overgrown door and tried the
knob, but it was rusted shut and refused to turn in his hand.
I glanced through the broken window, as the other remaining pane was heavily covered by dirt, and saw a small pot-
bellied stove, a table with a solitary, overturned chair, and
the rotting remains of a narrow cot, all of it covered in dust.

I looked over at Hexe, who had plucked the ball from the ivy and was turning it in his hands like one of his scrying stones.

"I had almost forgotten this was still here," he muttered. "This was where Jake lived. I was very young at the time, but I remember how he and my grandfather used to sit over there"—he pointed to a pair of weathered Adirondack chairs positioned under a decorative wisteria bower—"and chat while sharing a hookah—not at all like servant and master. When Jake died, it was the only time I ever saw my grandfather cry.

"I wonder what it was like for him, living out his life in the garden, serving those who lived in the house his father built. To be denied his birthright, yet have it constantly dangled in his face—how cruel is that?" He shook his head in disgust. "My family has a long tradition of getting too caught up in *what* we are, instead of *who* we are. The gods and devils know it's hard enough being a half-caste in the Royal Family . . . but a norlock?"

"Are you worried about what your mother said about the baby—?" I asked gently, slipping an arm about his waist.

Hexe grimaced as if he'd bitten into a lemon. "Astrologer or not, my mother doesn't know *everything*. I don't care how many fingers our kid has or what color his or her eyes might be—*no one* is going to make him ashamed of who and what he is. Or her."

"You're going to make a hell of a dad, you know that?" I grinned.

"I still can't help thinking about how if Uncle Jack hadn't disappeared, all those years ago, both Jake and I would have grown up knowing our fathers," he said wistfully.

"How so?"

"Jack was the true Heir Apparent, not my grandfather. But when Jack was swallowed up by the dimensional rift on the third floor, the mantle was automatically passed to Eben. Had Jack taken his rightful place as Witch King, my grandfather would have simply become yet another member of the aristocracy. He would have no reason to disown Esau in favor of my mother. Indeed, Esau would have had no expectations of inheriting the Throne of Arum at all. And maybe, just maybe, my uncle wouldn't have become such a twisted, bitter creature. As a minor noble without any claims to the throne, my mother wouldn't have had a reason to hide her love away, and she could have married whoever she wished without anyone raising an eyebrow...."

"You might as well worry about what would have happened if President Kennedy had been assassinated in Dallas, instead of San Francisco," I countered. "Or what if Christianity and Islam had gone to war with one another, instead of uniting to fight the Unholy War? What's the point of brooding about things that never happened? All you get is a bunch of what-ifs that don't add up to anything real. You can't change the fact your father wasn't around when you were a kid. But you can take advantage of the fact he's around *now*. Just like you can't change what happened to Jake, but you *can* make sure our child will never be treated in such a manner."

Hexe laughed and pulled me into his arms. "You're as smart as you are sexy, you know that? Why don't you put on your cutest new maternity clothes? I might not be able to take you out on a shopping spree at Bergdorf's, but I think I can swing a night out at the Calf. Hey, maybe if we tell Lafo we're expecting, he'll throw in dessert!"

The clientele at the Calf that night was what Hexe called "the new normal": a sixty-forty mix of Golgothamites and humans, both sides skewing young, as most of the older, more conservative clientele had decamped to far less human-friendly establishments, such as Blarney's and Steppenwolf's, or stopped by only for lunch.

As we made our way through the crowded pub toward the dining room, I spotted an all-too-familiar figure with curly, peach-colored hair ahead of us. I instinctively grabbed Hexe's arm in fear.

"That's Marz's croggy, Gaza," I whispered.

"I recognize him," he said darkly.

"He's the one who fireballed the Big Top Club. What's he doing here?"

"I don't know," Hexe replied as he watched the Maladanti disappear into the ground-floor kitchen. "But I intend to find out."

We changed course and made a beeline toward the swinging double doors. Hexe pushed one of them open just enough to peer inside without being noticed. I had expected the kitchen of the Two-Headed Calf to be a large, noisy place full of sizzling flattops, flaming grills, rack ovens, and stainless-steel prep stations, crammed full of loudly cursing sous chefs, cooks, sauciers, and dishwashers. However, to my surprise, the only person in the entire kitchen was Lafo, who stood before a huge antique stove dressed in his cook's apron, stirring one of a dozen simmering copper vessels shaped like cornucopia arrayed atop the numerous burners. I had always assumed he was joking whenever he called himself chief cook, bartender, and head bottle washer, but apparently he was simply telling the truth.

Outside of the total absence of other cooks, the kitchen seemed otherwise normal, with coils of handmade sausage and hams hanging from racks suspended from the ceiling, and a wheel of cheese large enough to roll a wagon sitting on one of the counters.

Gaza strolled up behind Lafo as if he had every right to be there and announced himself by saying, "I gotta admit, this joint has the best owl soup in Golgotham."

"What are *you* doing in my kitchen, Gaza?" Lafo growled, turning away from his pots to glower at the intruder.

"You're in arrears on your protection money, Lafo," the Maladanti replied tersely. "Boss Marz told me to come collect what's due him."

"Did he also tell you to pull my foot out of your ass?" Lafo snarled. "Because that's totally happening next if you don't get out of here! And you can tell Marz I'm not coughing up another cent."

"I'd watch what I say if I were you, kitchen-witch," Gaza glowered, raising his left hand in a menacing gesture. "It'd be a *real* shame if this place suddenly caught fire so soon after being renovated. . . ."

"That's all I'm taking from you!" Lafo exclaimed, tossing aside his apron. "I'm not going to stand here and be threatened by a jackal in a bad suit!"

Before Lafo could make another move, Gaza made a snapping motion with his hand, freezing the business owner in his tracks. "Oh, but you *are* going to stand there, kitchen-witch," Marz's croggy sneered as he stepped forward. He reached into his pocket and withdrew the Witchfinder

finger-cutter and held it up before Lafo's temporarily paralyzed face, so that he could see it. He then slid it onto the
magic finger of his victim's right hand in a grotesque parody
of a wedding vow. "Let's find out how your customers like
eating here once you're no longer able to charm the pots
and pans. . . ."

"Get away from him!" Hexe shouted, pushing open the
kitchen doors hard enough to make them bang into the
walls.

The fireball was already in Gaza's left hand as he spun
around, hurling the deadly missile like a southpaw pitcher
tossing a knuckleball. Instead of moving his right hand in a
defensive counterspell, Hexe caught the roiling ball of hellfire and held it in the palm of the gauntlet. He looked down
at the mass of supernatural flame then back up at his at-
tacker, and then, with the tiniest of smiles, he closed his
mailed hand into a fist, snuffing out the fireball as if it were
nothing more than a candlewick.

Hexe gestured again with his right hand and one of the
coils of sausage hanging from the kitchen racks over Gaza's
head suddenly wrapped itself around the Maladanti's throat
like a python and yanked him off his feet. I hurried past the
struggling goon and snatched the finger-cutter from Lafo's
hand, as the restaurateur was still trapped by Gaza's paral-
ysis spell.

"I've got it!" I exclaimed, holding up the torture instru-
ment so Hexe could see it. But if he heard me, he showed
no sign of it; the look on his face was both angry and distant
at the same time. He moved his right hand a quarter turn,
and the meaty garrote about Gaza's neck tightened even
further. The Maladanti's eyes started from his head and his
tongue protruded from his mouth as he fought to suck air
into his constricted windpipe.

I grabbed Hexe by the shoulder and shook him as hard
as I could. "Stop it!" I shouted. "You're killing him!"

The look of horror on Hexe's face as he emerged from
his weird trance was identical to that of a sleepwalker who
has awakened to find himself standing on a precipice. The
noose about the Maladanti's neck went slack, dropping him
onto the floor. Gaza staggered to his feet, massaging his
bruised trachea.

"I'd get out of here if I was you, buddy," I told the dazed

goon, who promptly dashed out the swinging doors, but not before casting a scalding parting glance in Hexe's direction. Normally, I would have put a call in to the PTU, but fear of Boss Marz making good on his threat against our friends and families kept me from doing so.

A couple of seconds later Lafo snapped back to life, freed from the Maladanti's spell. The first thing out of the restaurateur's mouth was a stream of Kymeran which, even to my ignorant ears, was clearly profanity.

"Heavens and hells!" Lafo bellowed angrily, once he finally switched over to English. "That was the most horrible feeling I've experienced in my life—being completely conscious of what was going on around me, but utterly unable to move or speak! That chuffer was going to take my magic!" He threw his arms around Hexe, yanking him into a brotherly embrace. "Praise Arum you showed up when you did, Serenity!"

"I'm glad you're not hurt, but really, I just did what anyone else would have done in the same situation," Hexe said humbly.

"That's manticore bollocks and you know it!" Lafo replied. "Most Golgothamites are scared shitless of the Maladanti and won't lift a hand against them. I can never thank you two enough!" He reached out and grabbed me with a long, heavily tattooed arm, dragging me into his impromptu group hug. "You guys are *awesome*! You're both eating and drinking on the house for the rest of the year!" Once he let us go, Lafo finally seemed to notice the silver gauntlet covering Hexe's hand for the first time. "Hey, what's with the shiny glove?"

"It's a . . . family relic," Hexe replied vaguely.

"Is that how you were able to field Gaza's fireball? I've never seen anyone actually *catch* hellfire before, much less snuff it out like that!"

Just then a nymph with a pencil tucked in her laurel wreath crown barged into the kitchen. "Lafo! Where's that order for the four-top at table twelve? Two more minutes and I'll have to comp them their drinks!"

Lafo snatched up his discarded apron and put it back on. "Excuse me, folks—I've still got a restaurant to run!" He returned his attention to the collection of bottomless pots still bubbling on the stove. "Go make yourself comfortable in the dining room. If there's anything in particular you'd like that's not on the menu, tell your server and I'll whip it up special!"

Despite the rocky start, it turned out to be a wonderful evening, with good food and excellent company. And even though we didn't need to tell Lafo I was pregnant to get a free meal, we went ahead and told him anyway.

Upon hearing the news, he grinned and belted out yet another one of his "awesomes" and returned momentarily with a towering meringue concoction atop a devil's food cake that, when doused in absinthe and set alight, burned an eerily beautiful blue. As we watched, the outline of a young man took form within the sapphire-colored flames, then just as quickly disappeared.

"The dessert never lies!" Lafo crowed. "Congratulations! It's a boy!"

I looked across the table at Hexe, who had the same loopy grin on his face as when I told him I was pregnant. He reached across the table and took my hand in his own, the silver mail of the magic gauntlet shimmering like the scales of a bejeweled fish. I had never felt more loved and in love than I did at that moment. And yet, despite my happiness, the image of Hexe strangling Gaza by proxy continued to nag at the back of my mind.

Chapter 15

For the next couple of weeks Hexe dedicated himself to making up for lost time, cranking out potions and charms for all his regular clients who relied on him, as well as working hard to bring in new ones. For the first time in months it seemed as if we were finally starting to dig our way out of the financial hole we had found ourselves in. With both of us bringing in money on a regular basis, I was able to start setting aside part of my pay for the baby and other maternity-related expenses in a decorative cookie tin I kept on the dresser.

One evening, as I returned home from work, I spotted a woman standing on the sidewalk outside the boarding-house, frowning at a piece of paper she held in her hand. She had red-gold shoulder-length hair that shone like a bur-nished shield. As I headed up the front steps, she stepped forward, casting her brilliant green eyes about nervously. She looked to be slightly older than myself and was easily one of the most beautiful women I'd ever seen outside of a movie theater, although the Aéropostale dress she was wearing was way too young for her.

"Excuse me, ma'am?" she asked. "Can I ask you a question?"

"Of course," I replied, trying to hide my bemusement at being addressed as "ma'am" by someone at least four years older than myself. Although I was three months pregnant, I wasn't in *that* big a hurry to be mistaken for someone's mom.

"Does someone called Hexy live here?" she asked anxiously, gesturing to the boardinghouse.

"Why, yes, *Hex* lives here," I answered politely. "He's my boyfriend. Are you looking to become a client?"

"I dunno," the beautiful redhead said. "I guess so. This guy with a green mustache in Witches Alley said he's the person I needed to talk to if I wanted to get a curse lifted. All I know is that I'm in a *lot* of trouble and I'm scared."

Her lower lip suddenly began to quiver and she started to cry. And not the way a grown woman breaks down, either, by choking back tears and trying to keep it together—she was just straight-up boohooing. Maybe it was my hormones kicking in, but I felt instantly protective of her. I put my arm around her shoulders, trying my best to comfort her as I escorted her up the front stairs and into the house.

"Don't worry; it's going to be okay," I said soothingly. "By the way—what's your name?"

"Ashley," the redhead snuffled, wiping at her eyes.

"Hello, Ashley. My name's Tate, and I can tell you that you've come to the right place. Hexe is one of the best lifters in all of Golgotham. And I'm not saying that simply because he's my boyfriend," I assured her as I unlocked the front door.

Once we were inside, I ushered her into the front parlor and had her take a seat while I went in search of Hexe. He was in the kitchen, dressed in an apron and a half-mask respirator, decanting a freshly brewed potion into a row of smaller bottles.

"Honey—you've got a new client! I found her on the front steps, trying to work up the nerve to knock on the door. Her name's Ashley and she thinks she's been cursed."

"Good! I haven't had a chance to do any real spell-lifting yet. I'm curious to find out just what the gauntlet can do," he exclaimed as he stripped off the respirator. "Welcome to my home." Hexe smiled as he entered the room. "Tate informs me that you are in need of my services, Ms. Ashley. What exactly is the problem?"

"Ashley's my first name," she said with a nervous giggle. "My last name is Lattimer."

"I see. How may I be of assistance, Ms. Lattimer—or is it Mrs.?"

Again with the nervous giggle. "Mrs. Lattimer's my mom." Ashley's eyes suddenly widened upon catching sight of Scratch as he emerged, yawning, from under the skirt of the couch and hopped onto the back of one of the chairs. "Hello, kitty cat!" she said with a laugh, reaching out to stroke the familiar's sleek skull. "What happened to your hair?"

Scratch recoiled from her touch, fanning out his batlike wings in warning. "Are you *drunk* or are you just stupid?"

Ashley's eyes widened even further. "You can talk—*and* you've got wings!" she exclaimed in delight. "That is *so* cool!"

"Glad you approve," Scratch grunted, his ego mollified by her display of awe.

"Do you mind? I have business to conduct," Hexe scolded, shooing the familiar off the furniture. "Where were we? Ah, yes! Tate informed me that you believe you have been cursed. May I ask the nature of the infliction, Ms. Lattimer?"

"Can't you see? Just *look* at me!" she said in exasperation, gesturing to her outwardly perfect body. If there was anything physically wrong with Ashley Lattimer, I certainly couldn't see it.

"Could you perhaps be a bit more *specific*?" Hexe suggested.

Ashley sighed and opened her purse, fishing out an official-looking piece of paper bearing the seal of the state of New York, which she then handed to him. "This is a New York State learner's permit," Hexe said, still baffled. "Wait a minute—!" His golden eyes widened in surprise. "You're *sixteen*?"

"I was when I went to bed last night," Ashley replied, her voice beginning to tremble again. "But when I got up this morning I was like—*this*!"

"I see," Hexe said sympathetically, handing her back her learner's permit. "Please step into my office, Miss Lattimer."

Now that I was fully aware of the situation, it wasn't hard to see the teenaged girl trapped within the body of the grown woman standing before me. As she entered Hexe's office she stared in openmouthed amazement at the taxidermied crocodile hanging suspended from the ceiling. Hexe took one of his scrying stones from his rolltop desk and passed it over her body like it was a magnifying glass.

"It's as I suspected—you've been inflicted with progeria, a supernatural form of accelerated aging."

"Am I going to keep getting older?" she asked nervously.

"No," he assured her. "It doesn't appear to be an ongoing curse. Do you have any idea why anyone would have done something like this to you?"

Ashley nodded, an unhappy look on her face. "I go to this fancy prep school called Pridehurst. My parents aren't rich or anything like that—I got in on an academic scholarship. I really like it there, and I've made a lot of friends. Then last week I found out I'm on the Homecoming Queen ballot."

"I get it," I said knowingly. "So someone decided to cut down on the competition by turning you from prom queen to chaperone. Sounds like a really lovely school."

"Not everyone at Pridehurst is like that," Ashley insisted. "But the ones that *are* like that are really rich, and they're very mean."

"They'd *have* to be rich; progeria is a pricey curse," Hexe said in a serious voice. "It's considered a petit mal infliction—straddling the line between Greater and Lesser curses."

"Can you help me, Mr. Hexe?" Ashley asked plaintively.

"Yes, but I need the permission of one of your parents to go forward," he explained. "Despite your current physical condition, you're still legally underage."

"*Please* don't make me call my mom and dad!" Ashley pleaded, sounding very much like the sixteen-year-old she truly was. "I don't want them knowing about this! I snuck out of the house before they could see me this morning. If they find out what happened, they'll yank me out of Pridehurst and sue the school! I really like it there—I don't want the school and the rest of the student body to get a bad name, because it's not really their fault."

"I understand your position, Ashley. Truly, I do. And it's commendable that you don't want to drag anyone else into this. But, like I said, progeria curses are pricey. That also holds true for lifting them. It's going to cost a thousand dollars to reverse the spell cast over you."

"I've got my own money!" she exclaimed, frantically scrambling inside her purse. "I've been babysitting to save up for an iPad. I've got almost five hundred dollars—I'm good for the rest. My neighbor, Mrs. Moretti, has twins. . . ." She pulled out an envelope filled with five, ten, and twenty dollar bills and handed it to him.

"Very well," Hexe sighed. "I'll do it. But only because I'm going to be in the market for a babysitter pretty soon."

"Oh, thank you, thank you, thank you, Mr. Hexe! And you, too, Mrs. Hexe."

I opened my mouth to correct her, then shrugged my shoulders. What the hell. I was having his baby—might as well get used to it.

Hexe walked over to one of the glass-fronted barrister cases that lined the walls of his office and removed what looked like an old-fashioned windup alarm clock, save that it was made of brass and the face was set with Kymeran numerals. He spoke an incantation in his native tongue under his breath while winding the clock with his right hand, then handed it to Ashley.

"Miss Lattimer, I need you to sit on that sofa over there," he said, pointing to the fainting couch, "and hold this clock in your hands while pointing its face *away* from you. Is that understood?"

Ashley nodded her head and took her place on the couch, tightly clutching the magic clock as if it might leap from her hands and go running out the door. Although she looked like a woman in her early thirties, her face was as open as that of the young girl she really was.

Hexe raised his silver-clad hand over his head and began to chant in a loud voice. As he did so, the Gauntlet of Nydd became bathed in witchfire, the spiritual luminescence all Kymerans possess. The phosphorescent glow grew in intensity until, with an earsplitting crackle, a jagged finger of supernatural energy shot from his palm like the spark from a Tesla coil and struck the face of the clock. Ashley flinched and gave voice to a mouse-sized squeal but, to her credit, she did not let go.

As I watched in amazement, the hands on the clock began to turn backward, and Ashley's adult features began to soften and grow younger. Then, all of a sudden, there was a weird noise, as if the gears of some great, invisible machine had been thrown into reverse, causing the entire room to vibrate, as the color of the witchfire shrouding Hexe's hand changed from bluish white to purple-black. At the same time, the hands on the clock began turning *forward*, and I gasped in horror as Ashley's reclaimed youth melted away

and her brilliant red hair rapidly faded as traceries of white
sprouted from her temples.

Hexe shouted something in Kymeran and grabbed his
upraised right hand by the wrist with his left, abruptly forcing it against his side, severing the feed to the magic clock.
His face was drawn and pale, and his golden eyes shone
with barely controlled panic as he stared at his handiwork.
Instead of reversing the progeria, his spell had aged Ashley
twenty years further. Crows feet and laugh lines—evidence
of a life yet to be lived—marked the corner of her eyes and
mouth, and her throat and cleavage both had sagging skin.

"What's wrong?" she asked, her voice sounding huskier
than before. She let go of the clock and reached up to touch
her face, only to freeze upon seeing the wrinkled skin and
bulging veins on the backs of her hands. *Oh my God—
what did you do?"*

"I'm dreadfully sorry, Ashley," Hexe said. "Whoever cast
the progeria spell over you protected it with a stinger—a
magical booby trap. That means anyone who tries to reverse
it will, instead, age you even further. I had no way of knowing the stinger was there until it was too late."

"What can we do?" Ashley asked, her voice wavering on
the verge of tears.

"There's nothing I *can* do," Hexe replied solemnly.
"However, most progeria spells will reverse themselves after a month or two."

"But what about Homecoming? I can't show up looking
like my Aunt Lorraine! Please, can't you try something else
to fix this?"

"I'm not willing to take that risk, no matter how much
I'm paid," Hexe replied. "I could accidentally kill you, Ashley. Here, take your money," he said, handing back the stack
of bills. "I've done nothing to deserve it."

My heart went out to Ashley as the poor girl began to
weep in despair. High school is bad enough already without
adding menopause on top of it. I slipped an arm about her
shoulders as she sobbed, doing my best to comfort her.
"Don't worry, we'll figure something out—isn't that *right*,
honey?" I said, overloudly.

"Of course! I just need time to consult my spell books.
Leave your contact information with Tate, and the moment

I find the proper counterspell, I'll remove the curse free of charge—it's the least I can do, given the, um, circumstances."

"Thank you, Mr. Hexe," Ashley sniffled.

"Thank me once the curse is lifted, not before."

"I don't know *how* I'm going to explain this when I get home," Ashley groaned as I walked her to the front door.

"Just tell your mom and dad you've been cursed," I said gently. "I'm sure they'll understand."

"No, not my parents," she sighed. "I mean my *boyfriend*, Justin. I love him, and he *says* he loves me. But the last time he saw me I was *me*. What if he doesn't love me anymore now that I'm like, you know—?" She hesitated, afraid to speak the word aloud.

I turned her by her shoulders so that we were facing each other. Despite the crow's feet, her eyes were still those of a young girl. "Ashley, if your boyfriend doesn't love you *now*, he didn't love you *then*," I said in a kind but firm voice. "Because you're still the same person, no matter how different you appear to be. And if this Justin kid won't stand by you, simply because of how you look—? Well, I may have only just met you, but I think you deserve something better than that."

"You sound just like my mom," Ashley said, smiling with her fifty-year-old mouth.

"Good. I need the practice."

Once I had seen Ashley safely to the door, I returned to Hexe's office to find him seated at his desk, peering intently at his gauntleted hand through one of his many scrying stones. He looked like a scientist trying to identify a particularly malignant strain of bacteria.

"Something's wrong with the gauntlet," he announced in a worried voice. "There was no 'stinger' on that child's progeria curse. When I was in the middle of lifting it, the spell I was working began to reverse itself without me willing it. It was as if my Right Hand was being used to work Left Hand magic."

"You mean *you're* the one responsible for aging that poor girl even further?"

Hexe nodded his head, a heartsick look on his face. "I'm

sorry I lied, Tate, but things are bad enough already without being sued by her parents!"

"Are you *sure* the problem is with the gauntlet?"

"There's no doubt in my mind," he replied, returning his attention to the scrying stone. "The spell-signature has mutated. There seems to be a second signature emerging from beneath the original—like a message written in invisible ink that's finally becoming detectable."

"You mean this isn't the real Gauntlet of Nydd?"

"No, it's authentic all right. But it appears that the original charm has been used as a Trojan horse for another spell—not unlike a computer virus."

"What do we do?"

"The same thing you do whenever a microwave or television starts malfunctioning: take it back to the store it came from."

The first thing I noticed as we approached Madam Erys' shop was the FOR LEASE sign posted in the front window. Hexe rattled the door, but it was tightly locked. Although the interior of the shop was dim and dusty, there was still enough light to see that the pair of silk opera gloves still lay draped over the counter, apparently untouched since the last time I'd seen them, more than two weeks ago.

"Excuse me, sir," Hexe said, addressing an older Kymeran with thinning, puce-colored hair, who was sweeping the stoop in front of the millinery next door. "Do you know when Madam Erys closed her shop?"

"I couldn't give you an exact date, Serenity," the hatter replied, pausing to lean on his broom. "It's been at least a couple weeks since I last saw her. Not that she was one for 'how-you-dos'. I thought it passing strange when I saw the FOR LET sign in the window, since she had just opened for business a day or two before."

"How could I be such a fool?" Hexe groaned as we headed back down the street. "I was so desperate to reclaim my magic, I waltzed right into a trap!" He banged his gauntleted fist against his thigh in frustration. "I was stupid! Stupid! Stupid! *Stupid!*"

"Don't be so hard on yourself," I said, placing a hand on his arm. "You had no way of knowing what she was up to."

"Yes, but part of me knew it was all too good to be true, *even* for magic!" he replied bitterly. "But I was so desperate to make myself whole, I ignored my instincts! And that bitch Erys played me like a hurdy-gurdy."

"What now?"

"We go find Moot," Hexe said grimly. "It was obvious from the way they talked there's plenty of history between those two. If anyone might know where to find Madam Erys, it'll be the good doctor. And even if he doesn't have a clue as to where she is, he's the one who bonded the gauntlet to my hand. If he can put it on, the bastard can sure as hell take it off again."

The Stagger Inn was little changed from the first time I saw it, except maybe even smokier and more vomit-drenched, if possible. The odor was sickening, and I had to clench my jaw in order to keep from adding to the establishment's already impressive collection of puke puddles.

Dr. Moot was seated in the same booth as last time, although, like the rest of the Stagger Inn, considerably worse for wear, with his chin resting on his breastbone and his hands curled limply about a glass of absinthe.

"Where is she, Moot?" Hexe barked, causing the more alert patrons of the bar to turn and stare in his direction. "Where's Erys?" When the disgraced psychic surgeon did not even twitch in reply, Hexe grabbed him by the shoulder and gave him a rough shake. "Wake up, you miserable old tosspot! Tell me where I can find Erys!"

As if in response, Dr. Moot toppled out of the booth and onto the sawdust-strewn floor, staring up at us with the cold, cloudy eyes of the dead.

Chapter 16

"Was he like that when you found him?" Lieutenant Viva asked, gesturing to the body, now hidden under a soiled tablecloth acting as a makeshift shroud.

"Yes. I mean, no," Hexe replied with a shake of his head. "He was sitting upright when we arrived. He only fell onto the floor after I touched him. I just thought he was dead drunk not, you know, actually *dead*."

"I see," the PTU officer muttered as she jotted down notes, her badge dangling about her neck from a lanyard. Her long, vivid-red hair was worked into a French braid that hung all the way down to the base of her spine, and her scent—that of pink peppercorns and fresh cranberry—was a welcome respite from the sour reek of the Stagger Inn.

Once news that the PTU was on its way percolated through the tavern's clientele, most of them had vacated the premises, leaving behind half-finished drinks and upended chairs, save for those too stupefied to either notice or care.

"Do you think it was murder?" I asked as I eyed a slightly built Kymeran with tangerine-colored hair inspecting what was left of Moot's last drink.

"We'll know for sure once our potion-master finishes his tests," Viva replied. "Personally, I wouldn't be surprised if it turns out the old tosser simply rode the dragon one time too many—you know, mixing safflower oil capsules with absinthe," she explained, upon seeing the look of confusion on my face. "Addicts claim it gives them the sensation of riding on the back of a battle-dragon—not that anyone really knows what *that* feels like anymore."

"Lieutenant—? The absinthe tests positive for Green Death," the potion-master announced grimly. "It's a paly-toxin made from a highly venomous form of coral. There was enough in his glass to kill him three times over."

"Green Death was considered a relatively quick means of execution and an honorable death in ancient Kymera—there's no known antidote," Hexe explained. "The condemned were given a choice of either death in the arena or drinking it mixed with wine."

"Is that bastet friend of yours still working for Dr. Mao?" Viva asked pointedly.

"Surely you don't think Lukas had anything to do with this?" I gasped.

"I have to start my inquiries *somewhere*," Viva replied with a shrug. "Your friend certainly had a reason to hate Moot—after all, he worked as Boss Marz's hambler, mutilating the feet of the weres who fought in the pits, including his own. I'm sure it pissed him off that Marz's case getting chucked out meant Moot would be back at work, sooner or later."

"The same could be said of most of the half beasts and werefolk who were liberated from the Maladanti's gladiator pens—including my mother's footman, Elmer," Hexe countered. "Moot had plenty of enemies in Golgotham."

"True, but even a Stagger Inn regular would have noticed a minotaur in their midst. No, whoever did this had to be able to pass for Kymeran—or at least human. And doesn't Lukas work in an apothecary—with access to all sorts of drugs and poisons? That gives him a lot of motive and plenty of means in my book."

"You're assuming this was murder and not suicide?"

"Green Death might be preferable to dying in the arena, but it's not a pleasant way to go. You basically suffocate, while remaining conscious to the very end. As a psychic surgeon, Moot would have known that. And I never pegged him as one to suffer unduly," Viva said wryly. "Now, Serenity, if you don't mind telling me—what, exactly, was your reason for seeking out this man?"

Hexe shifted about uncomfortably, sliding his gauntleted hand into his coat pocket. "He was my surgeon."

Lieutenant Viva raised a bright red eyebrow but said nothing.

"Yes, I know what you're thinking." Hexe sighed. "But being the Heir Apparent and two dollars won't get me a tall latte at the Devil's Brew."

"You let that *butcher* work on you?"

I turned to see Captain Horn, frowning in disgust, striding toward us.

"He was all I could afford," Hexe replied stonily. "Beside, when he was sober—or close enough to it—Moot was still a skilled psychic surgeon. It was his indiscretion, not a lack of ability, that got his license to practice revoked."

"The man sold organs to the black magic market!" Horn exclaimed, barely able to restrain his revulsion. "Hearts, livers, fetuses—!"

"I am well aware of that," Hexe sighed. "However, I have come to believe Dr. Moot may have taken the rap in that case out of a sense of misplaced guilt."

"He's the one who stitched the Gauntlet of Nydd onto you? No need to look surprised—your mother told me all about it."

"Yes," Hexe replied hesitantly. "I sought him out today because I felt the gauntlet was in need of a slight . . . adjustment. When we arrived, we found him dead."

"Son, I realize you have your pride," Horn sighed wearily, "but if you needed money for something like that, you could have asked me. I would have fronted you the funds, no questions asked."

"I don't go to my mother for financial help," Hexe replied stiffly, getting to his feet. "So why would I come to you? Now, if you'll excuse me, I have business elsewhere. Good evening, Captain."

Once we were back on the street, I grabbed Hexe by the arm, forcing him to turn and face me. I was alarmed to see the same strange, cold cast to his eyes I first glimpsed when he tried to kill Gaza. "How can you speak to your own father like that?" I exclaimed. "He's just worried about you, that's all!"

"I've gone my entire life without his help," Hexe replied stonily, yanking his arm free of my grasp. "And I don't need him butting in now. Now, if you don't mind, I'm going to try to track down Erys. I'll see you at home." With that he stalked off, hands shoved deep into his pockets.

I stared after him for a long moment, feeling as if I'd just walked into someone else's life. I kept telling myself that Hexe was under an immense amount of stress. He had already undergone a life-altering event that would have shattered a lesser man, and was extremely worried about being able to not only provide for, but also protect, both me and our unborn child. Hexe's entire professional life, not to mention his personal identity and sense of purpose, was tied up in his ability to work Right Hand magic. And now he had discovered, in the worst way possible, that not only was his talent corrupted, but that he had been tricked into going along with it. I realized I could never fully understand the turmoil he must be going through, no more than he could truly know what it was like to be pregnant—so perhaps the best I could hope to do was be there for him while he wrestled with the question of what to do next.

As I arrived at the house, I found Captain Horn sitting on the front stoop. "I handled that badly back there, didn't I?" The PTU chief smiled sadly. "I always had this fantasy in my head about how it would be between us, once the truth was known—but the reality is that I don't know how to be his father, and he doesn't know how to be my son." He sighed as he stood up. "It may be too late for me to be the father I always wanted to be, but it's not too late to be a proper *grandfather*. Here, I want you to have this," he said, pressing money into my hand. "It's not much—but it's the least I can do."

"Cap, I can't accept this. You know how Hexe feels about parental charity."

"And I respect him for it. But the money isn't for him *or* you—it's for my grandchild."

"Then you should put it in a college fund," I said as I handed the cash back to him. "That'll do more good in the long run."

"Very well," Horn sighed. "If that's what you think is best. But I want you to promise me that you'll call next time my son is desperate enough to resort to someone like Moot."

"I promise, Cap," I smiled, standing on tiptoes to kiss his cheek.

"That's a good girl," he said, favoring me with a wink as he left. "And maybe, some day, you'll get around to telling me what *really* happened to his hand."

As I reached into my jacket for the keys to the door, my fingers brushed against something else. I pulled it from my pocket to see what it might be, and discovered a wad of cash suspiciously similar to the one I'd just handed back to Captain Horn. As I smiled and shook my head, I was reminded of how, back in college, my dad would surreptitiously slip money into my pocket whenever he and mom came to visit me at the dorm. And suddenly, just like that, I found myself missing my parents.

A knot bloomed in my throat and my eyes grew damp. However, before I could open the front door and escape into the privacy of the house for a good cry, an unwelcome voice called my name. I turned to see Boss Marz—nattily dressed as ever—standing on the sidewalk, with his familiar Bonzo riding his left shoulder and Gaza standing at his right.

"Good evening, Ms. Eresby!" the crime lord smiled, gesturing floridly with his ring-covered hand. "Lovely night for a stroll, isn't it?"

"What do you want, Marz?" I snarled, trying to hide my discomfort at discovering the Maladanti at my doorstep.

"That's *Boss* Marz to you, nump!" Gaza snapped, flexing his left hand as he spoke.

"Now, now!" Marz said as if chastising his lieutenant for using the wrong fork at table. "There'll be time enough for that, later on. But to answer your question, Ms. Eresby, all I want to know is what you and Captain Horn were discussing so intently?"

"I wasn't chatting about you kidnapping us and breaking Hexe's hand, if that's what you're afraid of," I said acidly.

"See? Was that so hard?" Marz's lips pulled into a nasty smile. "As long as we understand one another, you have nothing to fear from me, Ms. Eresby. Such stress isn't good for the baby, after all."

"How do you know about that—?"

"A little bird told me," Boss Marz replied, with an unpleasant glint in his eye. "Enjoy the rest of your evening, Ms. Eresby. If you can."

Chapter 17

I woke up and reached for his side of the bed, only to find cold sheets. Again.

In the weeks since the murder of Dr. Moot and the disappearance of Madam Erys, Hexe rarely came to bed anymore. Instead, he spent most of his nights either haunting Golgotham's numerous nooks and crannies for some trace of the mysterious glover or locked away in his study, poring over his collection of grimoires in hope of finding a counterspell that would remove the curse on the gauntlet.

I went downstairs to a dark kitchen. There were no breakfast smells to greet me, no coffee percolating. If I wanted java, I would have to grab something at the Devil's Brew on the way to work. I poured cold cereal into a bowl and splashed some milk on top of it and shoveled it down as fast as I could. I flipped open the lid of my lunch pail, only to find it empty. I came home so tired from work the night before, I'd neglected to make myself a sandwich and fill the thermos before going to bed. That meant buying lunch from one of the pushcarts on the street—money we really couldn't afford to spare. Now that Hexe was no longer taking on new clients, and had parceled his regulars out to a couple of associates, our budget was tighter than a drumhead. Luckily, I still had a few more months before I had to worry about taking maternity leave.

I tried the door to Hexe's office before I left for the day, only to find it locked. Pressing my ear to one of the panels I could hear the muffled sound of his snoring on the other side.

When I arrived at work I found Canterbury in talks with his real estate agent. He had recently decided to buy the property next door to the shop in order to expand his business, perhaps even set up a genuine showroom. I knew better than to bother him, so I quietly set to work on Canterbury Customs' newest commission: a swanky custom rickshaw for Giles Gruff, who had been very impressed by his friend Bjorn Cowpen's new ride. I must have lost track of time, because the next thing I knew, Canterbury was looming over me.

"It's noon," he announced. "Where's your lunch pail?"

"I left it at home," I replied. "I'll just grab something from Nyko's pushcart."

Canterbury wrinkled his nose in disgust. "You shouldn't eat crap like that even when you *aren't* pregnant," he said with a depreciative snort. "How about I take you to lunch? My treat?"

"You don't have to do that, Master," I protested.

"Hey, I feel like celebrating," he smiled. "I just closed on the space next door. Besides, I have a business proposition for you—so we might as well discuss it over a nosh."

"Okay—if you insist." I grinned. "After all, you're the boss of me."

"Indeed I am," he whinnied.

The Feed Bag, located on the corner of Maiden Lane and Horsecart Street, was a restaurant that catered exclusively to Golgotham's centaur population. Upon entering the barnlike doorway, I was greeted by the flavorful aroma of fresh bread.

"It smells marvelous in here!" I exclaimed.

"Yes, they bake all their own bread here on the premises," Canterbury explained as he led me up a wide ramp that took the place of a staircase. "It's all organic—plenty of whole grains, oatmeal, that sort of thing. They also prepare marvelous salads and have an extensive vegetarian menu, both raw and cooked. A centaur's diet is very healthy, you know, even though we eat like horses!"

Upon arriving at the second floor dining room, we were greeted by a handsome young sorrel centaur dressed from the waist up in a waiter's jacket. "Good afternoon, Master

Canterbury," he said with a polite bob of his head. "Your stall is ready."

"Thank you, River," Canterbury replied, bobbing his head in kind.

The dining room was a huge, loftlike space, the walls of which were lined with box stalls of various sizes. I walked past a group of centaurs dining in one of the larger ones; they were seated on their haunches around a circular, pedestal-style table, the middle of which rotated like a lazy Susan and was loaded down with humongous loaves of homemade bread and heaping plates of turnips, apples, and alfalfa. They were all impeccably dressed from the waist up, with the males sporting elegantly tailored brocaded waistcoats and the females wearing elaborate Edwardian hats you'd expect to see on Derby Day. As we passed, one of the centaurs paused in his meal to stare at Canterbury and then shuddered from head to tail, as if trying to rid himself of a horsefly.

We were escorted to a cozy stall in the corner, where I found what looked like an adult-sized version of a baby's high chair waiting for me. Upon clambering into the seat, I suddenly realized this was the first time I'd ever actually been face-to-face with my boss.

An ipotane dressed in a waiter's jacket appeared, carrying a tray heavily laden with loaves of bread and raw vegetables. Without preamble, he set a salad bowl the size of a hubcap in front of me, along with a bucket of beer.

"Take that away and bring the lady some spring water!" Canterbury said sternly. Our server nodded his understanding and whisked away the offending pail.

"Don't I even get to see a menu?" I asked.

"Since we centaurs all eat the same foodstuffs, there's no need to waste time ordering different items," he explained as the ipotane waiter returned, this time lugging a gallon jug of water and a plastic straw. "The moment you arrive at a table, they start bringing out food and don't stop until they're told otherwise."

"Well, I certainly can't complain about the portions," I laughed. "This isn't just a salad—it's the whole garden!"

"Have you given any thought as to what you'll do after you've foaled?" Canterbury asked pointedly.

"I was planning on coming back to work—assuming you still want me there," I replied.

"I'm *very* pleased to hear that," he smiled, a look of relief in his eyes. "You are the best apprentice I've ever trained, Tate."

"That means a lot coming from you, Master Canterbury," I said, bowing my head in a show of respect.

"It won't be long before you will be making the transition to journeyman," he said. "You could set up your own shop, if that's what you want. And I won't stand in your way, should you make that decision."

"But I don't *want* to leave. I *like* working with you. You're the only person, besides Hexe, who ever really seemed to understand why working with my hands is so important to me."

His smile grew even wider. "I can not tell you how it gladdens my heart to hear you say such things, my dear. How do feel about joining me as my business partner?"

My jaw dropped open and the salad fork fell from my hand, hitting the floor with a loud clatter. It seemed like an eternity before I was finally able to find my words. "Master—I don't know what to say!"

"Just say yes," he said with a laugh. "We'll hammer out the partnership agreement before you take your maternity leave. I would be a fool to let a talent like yours walk away from me."

"I'm sorry about getting emotional," I said, dabbing at the sudden tears welling in my eyes with a napkin. "It must be the damn hormones!"

"At least you don't kick like our women do!" Canterbury smiled. "You can even nurse your foal at the workshop. If it's anything like you, it'll have acetylene in its veins, anyway."

We had finished lunch and were heading back to the workshop when we ran into traffic congestion on Maiden Lane. I didn't really think anything of it, at first—despite the lack of automobiles, traffic jams were all too common in Golgotham. But then I heard several voices chanting in unison, as if at a sporting event.

"What's going on?" I asked, standing up in the horse trap into order to peer over Canterbury's withers.

"Looks like some kind of protest in front of the Machen Arms," he replied.

As I scanned the crowded sidewalks, I spotted a familiar face. "Could you wait here for a second?" I asked as I hopped down.

"I don't think I have much choice in the matter," Canterbury said acerbically. "There's no way I can back out of this snarl."

As I moved through the outer ring of onlookers, I discovered the source of the chanting was a group of protestors, most of them Kymeran, standing behind traffic barricades. To my dismay several of them were wearing Kymeran Unification Party pins, and one of them was even waving an ESAU WAS RIGHT sign.

Directly across the street from the protestor stood the Machen Arms, a ten story apartment building with a central block and two flanking wings. The recessed courtyard that served as the approach to the main building was normally kept empty, save for a couple of decorative potted shrubs on either side of the entryway, but that afternoon it was filled with haphazard piles of furniture, stacks of books, and mounds of clothes. An elderly Kymeran woman, her faded scarlet tresses bound into lengthy braids coiled about her head like a pretzel, flitted back and forth among the bedsteads, armoires, and steamer trunks like a hummingbird in a summer garden. From where I stood I couldn't tell if she was trying to cast protection spells over the items in hopes of keeping them from being stolen or simply babbling to herself in despair.

The familiar face I had glimpsed belonged to Octavia, who was talking to an elderly Kymeran gentleman with receding maroon hair liberally laced with threads of silver. I pushed my way through the throng to join them.

"Octavia—! What's going on?"

As the firefighter turned to face me, I saw she was wearing a T-shirt bearing the message STALEMATE CHESS. "That chuffer Ronnie Chess is throwing my old next-door neighbor, Torn, and his wife out of their apartment today! I came here as soon as I heard to try to help."

"Thank you, my dear," Torn said humbly. "You were always a good neighbor." He turned back to stare up at the building that until that day had been his home. "The old landlord promised we would be 'grandfathered' in. But the new owner raised our rent from seven hundred and fifty dollars to six thousand a month! Arum's blood, there's no way we could possibly afford that! Hana! Look who has come to help us! And she's brought a friend!"

Torn's wife paused in her frantic checking and double checking of their belongings to peer over the top of her Ben Franklin glasses at us. "Adon bless you both," she said, fighting to keep the waver from her voice. "I don't know what we're going to do. . . ."

Before Hana could finish her sentence, an ipotane emerged from the entryway, carrying a rolled-up carpet under one arm and balancing a steamer trunk like a boom box on his opposite shoulder, and unceremoniously dumped his cargo with the rest of the couple's property. Unable to take yet another blow to her dignity, the old woman sank down onto a mound of casually discarded clothes and began to weep into her apron.

Torn hurried to his wife's side, slipping a protective arm about her trembling shoulders. "Now, now, Hana, darling—don't cry," he said, trying his best to console her.

"I can't help it, Torn," she sobbed. "What are we to do? We've lived in the same apartment for twenty years! Where do we go now?"

"Don't you have a son who can help you?" Octavia asked hopefully.

"We *had* a son," Torn replied tersely, all but spitting the words. "We haven't spoken to him since he disgraced the family, thirty years ago!"

I looked up to see real estate developer Ronald Chess, the new landlord of the Machen Arms and the author of Hana and Torn's misery, step out of the front door of the apartment building. An errant gust of wind caught his trademark comb-over, setting it momentarily on end, like the fin of a shark, before slamming it back down onto his head.

His pale eyes always seemed to be narrowed in permanent suspicion and were too small for his face, which resembled that of an overfed, slightly lumpy baby. As he scanned his surroundings, his cheeks abruptly turned bright red and his face grew even lumpier.

"What are *they* doing here?" he bellowed, pointing to Octavia and myself. He turned to the blue-haired Kymeran standing beside him who carried a five-foot-tall brass staff topped by the seal of the GoBOO. "Lash promised me all protestors would be kept five hundred feet away!"

"Who's the dude with the big stick?" I asked.

"That's Elok, the GoBOO's beadle," Torn replied forlornly. "He's here to oversee the evictions."

"I thought the PTU were the police in Golgotham."

"They only deal with criminal cases," Octavia explained. "Beadle Elok handles all the civil stuff, like collecting fines, seizing property, and evictions—that kind of thing."

"You there!" Elok said imperiously, gesturing with his staff as if to shoo us away. "What are you doing on this side of the street? I expressly stated no protestors beyond the barricades!"

"We're not protesters!" Octavia snapped, flashing the Golgotham Fire Department credentials she wore on a lanyard about her neck. "We're friends of Hana and Torn's and we're here to help them relocate."

Elok's pinched features visibly relaxed. "Very well," he sighed. "I'll leave you to it, then. Believe me, I don't like evictions any more than you do. But I swore an oath to do as the GoBOO commands. . . ."

"Hey! You—! Beadle!" Chess shouted, refusing to come any closer to us than he had to. "What do you think you're doing? Why aren't you arresting those hippies like I told you to? And get these geezers out of here!" he added, pointing to Hana and Torn. "I've got photographers coming in from the *Herald* to take pictures for the Sunday Living section, and I don't need them seeing this kind of shit! It looks like a goddamned yard sale out here!"

"I *know* what my duties are, Mr. Chess," Elok replied frostily. "And must I remind you that I answer to the Golgotham Business Owners' Organization, *not* to you?"

"Is that a fact, huh?" Chess scowled as he tapped the screen of his smartphone. "Hey, it's me. Your boy here is giving me some lip. Says he only answers to the GoBOO. You going to set him straight or what? Here—your boss wants to talk to you," Chess smirked as he handed the phone to Elok.

The beadle grudgingly accepted the phone as if it was a

poisonous reptile. "Hello? Yes, sir," he said, his cheeks suddenly turning beet red. "I'm sorry, I didn't *realize* . . . yes, of *course*, Mayor Lash! Whatever you say!"

"I'm glad we've gotten *that* cleared up," Chess said as he reclaimed his phone. "Now bust these hippies and get them out of here."

As the sigil atop Elok's beadle-staff suddenly began to glow, I took a step toward Chess, who drew back as if I might spit on him.

"I don't think that's a smart idea, Ronnie."

The real estate tycoon gave me the same look he would something he'd scraped off the bottom of his shoe. "That's *Mr. Chess* to you, toots."

"And that's *Ms. Eresby* to you, fella," I replied.

"You're not related to Timothy Eresby, are you?" he asked, unease flickering in his too-small eyes.

"He's my dad." I said, taking a perverse pleasure as I watched the color drain from his overstuffed face.

Back when my father had harbored political aspirations, he and Chess had butted heads more than once. What was it my old man used to call him? Ah, yes "that short-fingered vulgarian." Ronald Chess might not respect the arts, Golgotham, women, or people he called "hippies," but he most certainly respected money, which meant at that moment he respected *me*.

Of course, he had no idea that my parents had cut me off without a dime and we hadn't spoken in months, but there was no way I was going to tell *him* that. . . .

"Perhaps I was a little *too* rash," he said to Elok. "There's no need to get rough. If these young, um, ladies are here to help the old couple move their things, I've got no beef with that. Just be quick about it."

"You heard Mr. Chess," the beadle grunted. "Get the old man and his wife packed up, if that's what you're here for. You've got two hours, or I'll have the lot of you in the Tombs for obstruction. . . . " Suddenly a snowball came sailing through the midsummer air, striking Elok square in the face. "Who conjured that?" the beadle sputtered as he wiped the ice crystals from his eyes.

"*Traitor!*" one of the protestors from across the street shouted. *"Why is the GoBOO sucking up to numps?"*

"Here now! I'm just doing my job!" Elok protested angrily. The sigil atop his staff of office flickered back to life, this time even stronger than before.

"The GoBOO is selling us out!" A second voice shouted as another snowball came arcing toward the beadle.

As Elok slammed the butt of the staff against the pavement there was a ringing sound, like that of a gigantic gong. Fingers of blue-white electricity shot forth from the seal of office, vaporizing the icy projectile in midflight while scorching a zigzag pattern into the cobblestones, scant millimeters from where the protestors were gathered. There was so much electricity in the air it made my hair fluff out like an angry cat and Chess' comb-over stand up like a cockatoo's crest.

For a horrible moment I thought I was going to be caught in yet another race riot, like the one at the Calf. But instead of retaliating, the protestors lowered their signs and gradually dispersed. Although there was a good deal of mumbling and resentful looks thrown in the beadle's direction, none of them were willing to go against the GoBOO's authority.

Elok pulled a handkerchief from his pocket and mopped his forehead, a look of open relief on his face. "Praise the Sunken Spires *that's* over with," he grunted. "That could have been far uglier. At least they were only throwing snowballs. Now get the old couple out of here, while you still can."

"I'm sorry, Tate," Octavia sighed. "I didn't mean for you to get mixed up in this."

"That's okay. Any friend of yours is a friend of mine. I don't mind helping Torn and Hana move."

"Move to where?" Hana said tearfully. "We have nowhere to go."

"Perhaps I can be of some assistance?" Now that the roadblock had been removed, Canterbury had freed himself from the traffic jam and was now standing at the curb in front of the apartment building. "I have just purchased the stable adjoining my shop. There is an apartment loft on its second floor. Granted, it's designed for centaurs, but it can be easily retrofitted to accommodate bipeds. It's yours if you want it."

"That is most kind of you, friend centaur," Torn said. "But we do not expect charity. My wife and I insist on paying our way."

"Of course," Canterbury replied with a nod of his head. "I'm sure we can reach a satisfactory agreement."

"You have saved us, just as Arum delivered our people!" Hana exclaimed, lifting her glasses to wipe the tears from her eyes.

"Are we not *all* Golgothamites here?" Canterbury smiled.

"Okay, let 'er drop!"

There was a sound from high above, like the sail of a tall ship being unfurled, and a huge canvas banner fell from the roof of the center structure of the Machen Arms. It was so big it covered every window on the apartment building from the tenth to the fifth floor.

GOLGOTHAMVUE CONDOS
VINTAGE LUXURY STARTING AT EIGHT HUNDRED THOUSAND.

A CHECKMATE PROPERTY.

Chapter 18

After carting Hana and Torn's belongings back to Fetlock Mews, Canterbury, Octavia, and I immediately set to work retrofitting the loft next door.

The second floor apartment was a huge open space with no interior walls save for a stable-box in one corner large enough to accommodate a pair of centaurs, which was fairly easy to convert into a traditional bedroom. However, upon laying eyes on the bathroom—with its tiled surfaces, reticulated shower-hoses, and scrubbing wands—I coaxed Canterbury into bringing in a licensed plumber to tackle the task of making it truly biped-friendly. Some things, I have learned, are best left to the professionals.

Since it was going to be a couple of days before the loft would be truly habitable, Octavia volunteered her room at the boardinghouse to her former neighbors. At first the old couple refused, claiming they didn't want to impose any more than they already had, but finally relented once she explained she was scheduled for a week's rotation at the firehouse anyway. Octavia and I helped the elderly couple pack a couple of changes of clothes and a few other essentials into a carpetbag and left Canterbury to deal with the plumber.

"Is this where you live now?" Torn asked in surprise, peering out the window of the brougham at the boardinghouse.

"Yes," Octavia replied. "I'm renting from Tate's boyfriend."

"This boyfriend of yours—he's Kymeran?" Torn asked warily.

"Yes," I replied. "Is that a problem?"

He opened his mouth, as if to launch into a tirade, only to be silenced by a glare from his wife. The old man shook his head and dropped his gaze to the floor. "Things were *different* when we were coming up, that's all," he muttered, by way of explanation.

As we entered, we were greeted, as usual, by Beanie, who came scampering from the back of the house, eyes agog and tongue flapping.

"That's an unusual-looking familiar," Torn said as he studied the Boston terrier. "What kind of demon is it?"

"It's a pedigreed frog-bat. Can't you tell?" Scratch sneered as he sauntered into the room. "Now that I've answered your question, it's your turn to answer mine: what are you two doing here?"

Torn gave a dry, humorless laugh. "I see the cat still has a tongue."

"You two know each other?" I frowned.

"We *three* know each other," the familiar purred as he brushed up against Hana's leg. "Now *you* I'm glad to see. You're the one who made those *scrumptious* mouse-meat pies. . . "

"You mean mincemeat, don't you?" Octavia corrected.

"I *know* what I said."

"It's good to see you, *too*, Scratch," Hana smiled. As she reached down to stroke the familiar's chamoislike skin, Scratch rose onto his hind legs and pressed the flat of his head into the palm of her hand, a public show of fondness I'd never seen him bestow on anyone besides Hexe.

I turned and gave Torn a quizzical look. "Do you mind telling me how it is you're so, uh, familiar with my boy-friend's familiar?"

"My wife and I served the late Witch King, Lord Eben and his consort, Lady Lyra, for forty years," Torn explained with a melancholy smile. "I was the butler; she was the cook. My own father had served the previous Witch King in the same capacity, as had his father before him, and *his* father before *him*—going back to the drowning of Kymera.

"In fact, I was born in the servants' quarters on the third floor, back before it became unstable," he said, gesturing to the stairs that led to the upper stories of the house. "Hana and I began our service as children, and we saw to the Royal

Family until the day Lord Eben breathed his last. After that, Lady Syra pensioned us off and we moved into the Machen Arms. Today is the first time we've set foot in this house in twenty years."

"Is Hexe, I mean, His Serenity at home?" Hana asked hopefully.

"He left just before you arrived. I'm afraid he had pressing business elsewhere," Scratch replied.

"Let me show you and Hana where you'll be staying," Octavia said as she reached to take the carpetbag from Torn. "It's the second bedroom off the stairs. . . ."

"That would be Lady Syra's old room," the old butler grunted, refusing to relinquish his grip on his luggage. "I know it well."

As Octavia made sure her friends were settled in, I retreated to my room to change out of my work clothes. I tried to call Hexe on his cell, to let him know about our new houseguests, but it rolled straight to voice mail. I left a brief message, asking him to call me back ASAP, and then stripped down to my undies.

I turned sideways to inspect my silhouette in the mirror. I was just over three months along, and my lower abdomen was already swelling like a ripening fruit. I rested a hand on my stomach and gave it a little pat. I was still conflicted about advertising my pregnancy to the world at large, given the recent racial tensions in Golgotham, but there was only so much camouflage I could expect from my welder's jumpsuit. Pretty soon everyone and his familiar was going to know I was carrying the Heir Apparent's child simply by looking at me.

I found myself suddenly overwhelmed by a feeling of dizziness and decided to stretch out on the bed for a couple of minutes. I must have been more tired than I realized, because the next thing I knew I was awakened by the smell of cooking.

My initial thought was that it was morning and that Hexe was once more making breakfast in the kitchen. Then I glanced at the bedside clock and realized it was still evening, albeit an hour or so later than when I first lay down. Feeling slightly disoriented, I put on a pair of jeans and a loose T-shirt and headed downstairs.

Hana was in the kitchen, tending boiling pots and a sizzling skillet, while her husband busied himself setting the table in the dining room, each moving about their tasks as easily as if they were in their own home. The old woman smiled upon spotting me standing in the doorway.

"Did you have a nice nap, dear?" she asked pleasantly. "I checked in on you earlier and saw you were asleep—you must be exhausted after today, given your situation." She glanced meaningfully at my shrouded midriff.

"Yes, thank you," I replied. "But you didn't have to do all this. . . ."

"It's the least Torn and I can do," she said as she retrieved a roasting pan from the oven. "You have been extremely good to us—I daresay you have shown far more kindness to us than any human ever has."

"We're not *all* like Chess," I said with a wry smile. "Although I should point out that you don't have to be a Kymeran for him to treat you shabbily."

"Such an *awful* man!" Hana clucked her tongue in reproach. "Truly dreadful!"

"You should have let me curse him."

Hana cast a disapproving glance at Torn, who was standing in the doorway of the dining room. "Things were bad enough already without us making it worse. Besides, he was probably wearing protective talismans strong enough to turn back every spell in the book. His type never set foot in Golgotham without loading themselves down with countercharms."

"I still should have *tried*," Torn grunted. "It's the principle of the thing."

"You've never cursed anyone in your life." Hana laughed as she kissed his cheek. "You're not that kind of man; that's why I married you."

Torn's normally taciturn demeanor melted away as he took his wife's hand and gave it a gentle squeeze. "And all this time I thought it was my good looks and chiseled abs."

We took dinner that night in the formal dining room. Hana had whipped up an impressive four course meal from items I'd forgotten were even in the kitchen: creamed parsnips, butterscotch yams, braised kale, and roast caribou in blackberry sauce. Torn insisted on serving me, neatly depositing portions of each entrée onto my plate with the precision of a brain surgeon.

As I watched him at work, I was suddenly reminded of
Clarence, my family's butler. Clarence had been my friend
and confidante throughout childhood, and the only adult in
my young life that actively encouraged my artistic streak. I
found myself wondering how he was doing, as he was getting on in years, and felt a surge of shame that I had not
called him to tell him about the baby. I silently scolded myself for holding the fact my parents were his employers
against him.

"You know, this is the first time I've ever taken a meal at
this table," Torn said as he sat down. "Back when Hana and
I were in service, we normally ate in the kitchen."

"It's the first time I've eaten in here, as well," I admitted,
glancing up at the twin crystal chandeliers that dangled
from the claws of a wrought-iron dragon mounted to the
ceiling. "It always seemed a little bit much for just Hexe
and me."

"In the old days, Lord Eben and Lady Lyra took every
meal in here," Hana said wistfully. "Even toward the end,
with Lord Eben bedridden, Lady Lyra still dined in this
room."

"Perhaps you could tell me what Hexe's grandparents
were like? He doesn't really talk about them that much."

"Lord Eben was what you would call Old School, nowadays," Torn replied. "He believed in keeping faith with the
traditions of our ancestors, and was often very stern in that
regard when it came to his children. However, he was far
more . . . progressive than his own father. Lord Jynx would
have had Hexe smothered at birth and taken Lady Syra's
magic as punishment for daring to bring a half-caste child
into the Royal Family.

"As for myself, I found Lord Eben to be a just man —
strict at times, but fair-minded when it came to his rulings
as justicar. He was particularly well regarded by the dwarven Thanes. As for Lady Lyra, she was a gracious, kind-
hearted woman. She's the one who made sure Hana and I
were properly pensioned off by the GoBOO. In the old
days, retainers were paid out of the Royal Treasury — now
we're considered civil servants."

"Did they love him?"

"Who? Hexe? They positively *adored* the boy!" Hana
said with a laugh.

"Almost as much as they were ashamed of him," Torn added sourly.

After dinner, Torn and Hana insisted on clearing the tables and doing the dishes. The two of them moved like a well-oiled machine, whisking away the plates without having to ask one another a single question. Not that there wasn't plenty of communication going on between them—but it was done in the shorthand of the exchanged glance, which is unique to the deeply married.

At one point I announced that I was headed down to the basement to fetch a load of fresh towels and bed linens from the dryer. On my way back, I noticed that the kitchen was empty and all the dinner dishes washed and returned to their cabinets. As I reached the second floor landing, I saw that the door to Octavia's room was shut, although I could hear the muted murmur of voices on the other side.

"She's *what*?" Torn's shout was enough to make me drop the folded blankets I was carrying.

"Must you be so *loud*?" Hana responded in a hushed voice. "What if she hears you?"

"It's Syra all over again!" Torn fumed. "He's just like his father! No respect for tradition!"

"After all this time, can't you let that go? Tradition has already cost us a son, as well as a grandson. Isn't that enough? And frankly, he could do a great deal worse, if you ask me."

"I'm glad to hear it," I said as I opened the door to Octavia's room.

Torn and Hana spun about in guilty surprise, like children caught raiding the cookie jar. "I *told* you to mind your voice!" Hana hissed.

"You're Hexe's *other* set of grandparents, aren't you?"

"So you're *finally* figuring that out," Scratch sneered as he strolled into the room. "Will wonders never cease?"

"Yes, it's true," Hana admitted. "Horn is our son."

"*Was* our son," Torn interjected stiffly. "I disowned him when I discovered what he'd done. Our family has served the heirs of Adon for countless generations—but he disobeyed the one rule *all* Servitors must obey: no fraternization. Of course, Lord Eben had to let him go when they discovered the truth, severing a tradition of service that stretched back to the sinking of the spires! He dishonored his family, disgraced his lineage . . . he's brought nothing but shame on us."

"But Horn's the captain of the PTU!" I interjected. "He's one of the most important people in Golgotham!"

"His place was to *serve*!" Torn shot back angrily. "Just as I served, and my father before me, and *his* father before *him*!"

"But he *does* serve—except now his duty is to *all* of Golgotham, not just the Royal Family," I pointed out.

"The girl's right, you old grump," Hana said, folding her arms over her sagging breasts. "I've tolerated this grudge against our son long enough! Besides, it's not like you don't have a scrapbook of newspaper clippings detailing every arrest he's ever made and promotion he's received."

"Why didn't you tell me the truth about who you are?" I asked.

"Force of habit, I suppose," Torn sighed. "The only way we were allowed to be a part of Hexe's life was if we never revealed the true nature of our relationship to him. Lord Eben made us swear an oath of secrecy. Should we break it, we would be banished from Golgotham."

"Ugh. How awful! That must have been difficult for you."

"Yes, but we got used to it," Hana said as she took her husband's hand in hers. "At least we had access to our grandson when he was young, even if we couldn't tell him who we were. That all changed when Lord Eben died and Lady Syra became the Witch Queen. Once we were pensioned off, we were no longer able to see Hexe on a regular basis. Oh, Lady Syra would send us snapshots now and then, but that's not the same. The last time we actually laid eyes on him was at Lady Lyra's funeral, fifteen years ago. He was already growing into a fine young man."

"I don't understand—why have you kept your distance for so long? Lord Eben was the one who swore you to secrecy, not Lady Syra. Why not come forward once the old Witch King was dead?"

"The boy had enough trouble being accepted by the Aristocracy without his calling the family butler and cook grandpa and grandma," Torn replied sourly. "A lot of things have changed in Golgotham since I was a lad—but not *everything*."

*   *   *

After bidding Torn and Hana good night, I checked my cell phone to see if I had missed any messages from Hexe. Zilch. I tried calling him again, only to be informed by a polite, if robotic voice, that "this phone's subscriber was currently unavailable" after the first ring. It occurred to me that if I wanted to talk to Hexe, I was going to have to wait up for him.

I took a spare blanket and made myself a nest on the sofa in the front parlor. Beanie promptly joined me, snuggling in tight between my hip and the sofa cushions as I read the copy of *What to Expect When You're Expecting* Nessie had given me. Despite my best intentions, I must have dozed off, because the next thing I knew the sound of the front door closing startled me awake.

"What are you doing down here?" Hexe asked, sounding more surprised than pleased to see me. The smell of barley wine and cigarette smoke clung to him like perfume. No doubt he had rounded off the evening by stopping in at the Calf and claiming his fair share of free drinks.

"Waiting for you." I yawned. "I've got some big news. I tried calling you earlier, but you didn't pick up. Why didn't you call me back?"

"My phone lost its charge," he replied with a shrug.

As I got off the couch to greet him, I noticed for the first time that his right eye sported a nice new shiner. "Heavens and hells! What happened?"

"I got jumped by a couple of unrulies," he replied bitterly.

"What for?"

"Because I'm walking around wearing the equivalent of five solid gold Rolexes," he explained, holding up his gauntleted right hand.

"You need to get an ice pack on that," I said, steering him toward the back of the house. As Hexe took his place at the kitchen table, I removed a bag of frozen vegetables from the freezer and wrapped it in a dish towel. "Here—put that over your eye," I said, holding it out to him. Hexe did as he was instructed, wincing slightly as the ice-cold compress touched his face. "It's not magic, but it'll work."

"So—what did you have to tell me that was so important?" Hexe asked.

"Canterbury offered to make me a partner in his business today."

Hexe perked up upon hearing this news. "Does that mean you're getting a raise?"

"I suppose so," I replied. "We haven't really hammered out the details yet. But it does mean my job is secure. He took me to lunch to talk it over, and on the way back we passed the Machen Arms—except now it's GolgothamVue—just as Ronnie Chess was evicting this old couple. I saw Octavia trying to help them and stopped to see what was going on—well, long story short, they're staying here until their new apartment is ready. It shouldn't be more than a few days."

"How much are you charging them?"

My smile suddenly faltered. "Huh?"

"We're in no position to hand out charity right now. We've got bills to pay. Anyone who stays under my roof is using electricity and water, and they're eating our food. You *are* charging them rent, aren't you?"

"It never even crossed my mind," I admitted. "I mean, Octavia's already paying for her room. I just assumed—"

"Of *course* it didn't cross your mind," he snapped, tossing aside the makeshift ice pack. "Why should you care, after all? It's not *your* name on the utility bills, is it?"

"Are you serious?" I asked, suddenly feeling as disoriented and off-balance as a sleepwalker who has awakened to find herself standing in the middle of someone else's house. Within a heartbeat everything I had imagined safe and familiar had turned hostile and alien, and I was at a loss at how to change it back.

"Do I *look* like I'm having a laugh?" he replied in the kind of deliberate, overloud voice reserved for particularly slow children.

"But these aren't just two random nobodies who came in off the street," I said, trying my best to explain the situation. "Hana and Torn used to work for your grandparents! They're really looking forward to seeing you again. . . ."

He gave an incredulous laugh, as if I'd just said the stupidest thing he'd ever heard. "Why would I want to interact with my grandfather's old servants? Perhaps you'd like me to spend time with a discarded coat and a bent paper clip as well?"

"I—I just thought you might want to say hello—" I stammered.

"You just 'thought'; is that it?" he jeered mockingly. "See, that's the *problem* with you, Tate—you're human. You *can't* think like me, and you *never* will." Hexe lurched to his feet, swaying unsteadily. I knew he had been drinking, but up until that point I had no idea just how drunk he truly was. "Either you get some money out of them or I show them the door—it's as simple as that. I don't need another pair of mouths to feed under my roof. And I certainly don't need a couple of doddering antiques getting in my way, yammering on about the 'good old days.' I don't care *who* they are—they could be my chuffing *grandparents* for all it means to me! Either they pony up some rent, or they're out on the curb!" With that, he staggered into his office, slamming the door behind him loud enough for it to be heard throughout the house.

I stood in the kitchen, trembling like a tuning fork, my cheeks burning with shame, as I struggled to try to understand what I had done to trigger such a flood of venom. He had never spoken to me in such an insulting, dismissive tone before, even when I'd done things to deserve it. I kept telling myself he was drunk and upset about being mugged, but that didn't keep the words from hurting any less. I wiped the tears from my eyes and then went to the sink and threw some water on my face before going upstairs to bed.

As I crested the second floor landing, I was startled to see Hana and Torn standing in the doorway of their room. I could tell from the looks on their faces that they had heard more than enough of Hexe's harangue. I opened my mouth to try to apologize, but before I could say anything they closed the door.

When I got up the next morning to go to work, they were already gone.

Chapter 19

To be honest, it would not have surprised me if I never saw Hana and Torn again. But, to my relief, they showed back up at Fetlock Mews later that day. Torn explained that they had decided it would be better "for everyone involved" if they stayed elsewhere until the loft space was ready, and had taken a room at the Sabbat Inn, the only hotel located within Golgotham. A couple of days later, they moved into the refurbished loft and set about making it their new home. Neither of them ever said a word to me about what had transpired that night, but I could see the shadow of it in their eyes whenever they stopped by the shop, which was quite often, as Hana seemed determined to stuff both Canterbury and myself as if we were taxidermy with a seemingly never-ending supply of freshly baked breads, pastries, and cookies.

A couple of weeks after they moved in, Canterbury's attorney came by with a sheaf of legal documents requiring my signature. While my salary as junior partner wasn't large enough to completely offset the loss of Hexe's income, it did provide me with the stability and peace of mind that comes with job security. And for the first time since learning I was pregnant, I was finally able to focus on truly getting things ready for the baby.

Outside of the boneknitters and psychic surgeons found at Golgotham General, the majority of health care in Golgotham was provided by hedgewitches such as Hexe. Although I knew from personal experience their healing arts were effective, I still wasn't completely comfortable with the idea of trusting the health of my unborn child to someone dangling a crystal pendulum over my rapidly swelling belly. Magic was all well and good for Kymerans in my situation, but I was human and I needed the comfort afforded by my people's own unique arts—science and technology.

There was a clinic just across the river, in Brooklyn, just off the F, that offered a low-cost prenatal service. It was eight hundred dollars up front, which was a hefty chunk of change for our household, but it would pay for monthly office visits for the first twenty-four weeks, as well as blood tests and one ultrasound. I'd been squirreling away a percentage of my paycheck, plus whatever money was left over after paying the bills, in the cookie tin. So far I had just over six hundred dollars saved up.

Upon finding myself with a spare thirty dollars after settling the grocer's bill, I opened the lid on the tin, only to find the kitty considerably lighter than before. My heart somehow managed to both sink and speed up as I counted out the bills, then tallied them up twice more, telling myself I must have miscounted. But each time it came up short the exact same amount: one hundred and fifty dollars.

Surely some nefarious burglar had managed to sneak into the house, somehow managed to make it past Scratch, and then made a beeline to the cookie tin on my dresser without touching anything else at all. I really, really wanted to believe that was the case, because, otherwise, I would have to suspect the only other person in the world—well, the only one with thumbs, anyway—who knew where I was stashing money.

"Do you know anything about this?" I asked, shaking the cookie tin at Scratch.

"I ain't no snitch," the familiar replied and quickly ran out of the room.

I glanced in the direction of the four-poster, only to find the carved owls perched atop the bedposts had turned their backs to me.

Maybe it was the hormones, but that's when I lost it. I had put up with his increasing moodiness and going out drinking every night because I felt bad about him losing his magic, but I had finally had enough of being treated like a clueless fool simply because I had five fingers instead of six.

"Where are you going?" Scratch asked as I yanked my peacoat out of the downstairs closet.

"I'm going to go and get my money back," I snapped. It didn't help my mood that I now discovered my coat would no longer button thanks to my baby bump.

"Don't get your knickers in a twist! So he took some money without telling you . . ."

"You don't understand, Scratch!" I snapped. "He didn't do this to *me*; he did it to the *baby*!"

I managed to keep a pretty good mad-on all the way to the Two-Headed Calf. Over the last month or so, Hexe had put Lafo's promise of free eats and drink to the test. Up until recently we had been eating at the Calf twice a week, but now that I had stopped drinking because of the baby, Hexe had been hitting the pub every night on his own, coming back later and later each time. I was usually asleep by the time he would stagger home, reeking of artichoke schnapps. Half the time he didn't even bother to come to bed, passing out instead on the couch in his office.

Since it was a weeknight, the Calf was relatively quiet when I arrived. Bruno nodded in welcome as I entered, but I brushed by without responding. I was too busy scanning the booths and tables for some sign of Hexe. I then hurried upstairs, but he wasn't among the diners, either.

As I went back downstairs, I caught sight of Lafo, who was manning the taps behind the bar. He smiled in welcome as I approached. "Evening, Tate. Looking for someone?"

"Has Hexe been here tonight?" I asked.

"No, he hasn't," he replied as he pulled a pint for one of his customers. "In fact, I don't think I've seen him in a couple of weeks."

"What? But he's been coming here almost every night . . ."

Lafo shook his head, a grim look on his face. "I don't know where he's going, Tate—but it ain't here. In fact, I had to cut him off. He was coming in here every night, drinking on the cuff. You know I don't grudge him that, don't you? After all, the man saved my life and livelihood. But then he started getting stroppy with the paying customers. It wasn't too bad, at first—just some snide remarks, here and there.

But the last time he came in here, it got ugly. He picked a fight with this human—only Arum knows what about—and next thing I know they're getting into it, throwing punches left and right! Bruno put a stop to it, quick enough—but not before the nump, uh, I mean, human punched Hexe in the eye. After it was over, I told him he'd had his last drink on the house. I haven't seen him since."

My mind flashed back to the night Hexe came home looking like he'd been in a fight. Although I could not believe what I was hearing, I had to admit that a lot of things were suddenly starting to make sense.

"He told me he got that black eye from fighting off a mugger."

Lafo glanced about, as if on the lookout for spies, then leaned forward, his voice dropping down into a husky whisper. "You know I consider Hexe to be a true friend, not just another one of my customers. So I've got to ask, what's going on with him? I know Hexe enjoys his drink, but he's always known when to stop. I've *never* seen him drink like that before. He seemed like a totally different person. I hated having to cut him off like that, but he gave me no choice."

"I'm really sorry, Lafo. Hexe has been under a lot of stress lately, what with money being tight and the baby on the way. . . ."

"The buzz I've been hearing is that he's shut down his practice and handed his clients over to Madam Kuka. Why would he do that?"

"You'll have to ask him yourself. That's Hexe's business, not mine," I replied, perhaps a little too tersely. As much as I so wanted to tell Lafo the truth, I didn't dare say anything more. It's not that I didn't trust the restaurateur, but if news of Hexe's hand being broken managed to reach the Maladanti, Boss Marz could very well jump to the wrong conclusion and decide to take action.

"I didn't mean to butt in, Tate," Lafo said gently. "I'm just concerned about the guy, that's all."

"I know," I sighed. "So—if he hasn't been coming here every night—where *is* he going?"

Lafo shrugged. "I wish I could tell you, Tate—but I honestly don't know."

As I turned to leave, I felt a hand on my arm. It belonged

to Chorea, the hostess for the Two-Headed Calf. I could tell she was still on the wagon since she was wearing a low-cut cocktail dress in place of the traditional diaphanous gown and leopard skin of her sisterhood. The maenad had joined Alcoholics Anonymous in an attempt to save her marriage to the Kymeran mover, Faro. Something about consuming raw flesh while in a Dionysian frenzy—it's complicated.

"I heard you asking about Hexe," she whispered. "I'd look across the street if I were you."

"You mean the Highlander?" I frowned. "Are you sure, Chory?"

"I saw him go inside a couple of hours ago," she replied.

I thanked the teetotaling bacchante and left the pub, setting my sites on the hookah lounge across the street. On the sliding scale of Golgotham nightspots, with the Golden Bough at the very top and the Stagger Inn at the bottom, the Highlander hovered somewhere in the lower middle. Unlike similar establishments elsewhere in the city, the Highlander's customers weren't there to smoke exotic tobaccos—they were there for the hashish. While there were plenty of hookah joints near Duivel Street that served human stoners looking for a hassle-free high, the Highlander's clientele tended more toward the locals.

The wooden sign outside of the lounge depicted a hookah with a sinuous dragon in place of the hose, smoke pouring from its nostrils. Although I don't have any issues with the idea of a hash café, I had never had occasion to step foot in the Highlander before because, well, I don't smoke. Hell, the average Kymeran place of business was smoky enough to cure meat—I could just imagine what one of their hookah lounges was like. I paused for a moment to steel myself, taking a final breath of clean air, and then opened the door.

The interior of the Highlander was dark and surprisingly elegant, with low couches and ottomans scattered about a rambling layout. There were also curtained booths, where smokers could retire to enjoy their pipes in privacy. Everywhere I looked there was a bluish haze that smelled strongly of musk and hash-oil. I couldn't keep from wondering how much my dry-cleaning bill was going to be once they finally got the reek out of my jacket.

There was a kiosk just inside the door, manned by a young Kymeran with green dreadlocks. Inside the booth were rows upon rows of water pipes of different sizes, including one with so many hoses radiating from its vase it was positively octopedal. "Rent a pipe, lady?" he asked helpfully.

I shook my head. "I just stepped in to see if a friend of mine was in here."

"We've got a special tonight on Dragon Balm," he said, pointing to a nearby service counter, where various blends of hashish wrapped in brightly colored foil were offered for sale alongside pot brownies and demitasses of espresso.

"That's okay," I said, sidestepping the suggested selling. "I'll just go look for my friend. . . ."

I moved past the kiosk into the open social room, but did not spot Hexe among the groups of smokers lounging about, talking to one another as they listened to the acoustic hurdy-gurdy player in the corner. Trying not to look *too* nosy, I pulled back the curtain on the privacy booth next to me to find Giles Gruff reclining on a pillow-strewn bench, his behorned head resting in the lap of one well-endowed, naked nymph while she dutifully massaged his temples, while a second, equally busty and unclothed nymph fed him grapes. Although he was missing his vest, his monocle and ascot were still in place.

"Hello, my dear," the satyr said, between puffs on his hookah. "Good to see you again—if somewhat unexpectedly."

"I'm sorry, Councilman," I apologized. "I didn't mean to intrude."

"That's quite all right. I'm simply unwinding after another day of butting heads with Mayor Lash. He's so desperate to outspend O'Fae in his reelection campaign, he's willing to court a scheming cormorant like Ronald Chess. It's bad enough I have to combat such recklessness amongst my own people—but to have to deal with the same trait in others is most tiresome. I *am* the lord of the satyrs, after all, not a congressman from Delaware. But on to a more pleasant subject: I trust my niece Octavia has settled into her new digs?"

"I suppose so, although we don't see that much of her. She spends most of her time at the fire station."

"Such is the life of a dedicated civil servant, I fear," Giles said, pausing to sample another grape. "But then, the fe-

males of our species have *always* been industrious and
civic-minded, and for that I am truly thankful, or else the
satyrisci would have gone the same route as the woodwoses
and ogres during the Sufferance."

"You wouldn't have happened to have seen Hexe?" I
asked. "I was told he was here."

"Indeed he is. You should find him in his usual spot—the
far corner booth. Now, if you don't mind, my lady friends
and I have some business to attend to," he said, gesturing to
his tumescent goat-pizzle.

I quickly dropped the privacy curtain. I was going to
need a lot of brain bleach to erase *that* particular image
from my mental catalog.

I found Hexe exactly where Giles said he would be—
sitting by himself in the farthest booth, in the deepest corner of the room, where the shadows were so thick there was
no need to draw a curtain for privacy. Judging from the
empty wrapper crumpled beside the brass hookah at his
elbow, he was smoking Dragon Balm.

"What are you doing here?" He scowled, looking up at
me with the same cold, distant eyes I'd seen the night he'd
supposedly been mugged.

The last of the anger that had spurred me on my quest
disappeared, to be replaced by unease. Although his features and voice were still the same, there was something
imperceptibly "off" about the way he spoke and moved—as
if I wasn't talking to Hexe himself, but rather a clever simulacrum.

"I want you to come home, Hexe." I cringed at the sound
of my own voice. It sounded so weak—almost wheedling;
like a mother trying to coerce an unruly child to go to bed.

"What for?" he grunted.

"It's *really* important that we talk," I said, shifting about
uneasily, aware that the hurdy-gurdy player had halted and
our conversation was now perfectly audible to everyone
seated nearby.

"Why? You can talk to me here," he retorted.

I stepped inside the booth and sat down opposite him,
pulling the privacy curtain shut as I did so. "Look, I *know*
you took money from the baby stash."

Instead of looking surprised or ashamed, Hexe merely
shrugged his shoulders, his face as unreadable as a mask,

while his silver-gloved fingers drummed against the table-top, as if waiting for me to say something interesting. I wasn't really sure what his reaction would be when I confronted him with the truth, but I certainly hadn't expected it to boil down to *"So?"*

"Hexe, *please*—this is serious. We need to talk about what's going on with you, and I'd rather do it at home."

"What's going on with *me*, huh?" he sneered. As he took another hit, the water pipe gurgled as if it was laughing. "I'll come home when I damn well feel like it, and not because you *nagged* me into doing it."

There it was. The "why do you have to be such a bitch?" card. The one that every other boyfriend had played— usually just before the end of the relationship. I felt my heart sink as if it had been filled with lead. I didn't dare say anything for fear I would lose what little control I had and start to cry. That's all I needed at that moment—to be dismissed as an overemotional pregnant woman. And I definitely didn't want to freak out in public, only to find it splashed all over YouTube by the time I got home. Fighting back my tears, I yanked back the privacy curtain and angrily strode toward the door, hoping with every step that Hexe would come to his senses.

I was halfway down the block when I realized he wasn't going to follow. *That's* when I started to cry.

I'd never felt so overwhelmed in my life. The framework on which I had chosen to build my new life was suddenly crumbling underneath me, in a way that was all too familiar. I had committed myself to Hexe to a degree I had never done before. Until now, the trust I had in him was as pure and strong as that of a child. Even on those occasions where I had been leery of the choices he made, I still knew that his decisions were born from genuine concern for both me and the baby. But now—?

I remembered how Lady Syra and Dr. Moot spoke about Esau—about how he had once been a good friend and loving brother—a healer, just like Hexe. But then he lost his wife, and anger and bitterness dragged him down the Left Hand path until he became a misanthropic, racist, homicidal zealot who wouldn't think twice about killing his own flesh and blood. Was that what was occurring with Hexe now that he had lost his Right Hand magic—?

Just then the image of Hexe's silver-clad hand drumming its fingers against the table, as if waiting for something to happen, flooded my mind's eye. Hexe may have been depressed and frustrated after Boss Marz maimed him, but the cold, distant look in his eyes didn't appear until Madam Erys tricked him into donning the Gauntlet of Nydd. If the Trojan spell on the gauntlet could somehow turn Right Hand spells into Left Hand magic, maybe it was also capable of doing the same thing to the wearer as well.

Upon reaching the house I was greeted at the door by Beanie, who licked the drying tears from my face as I hugged him. It was way past my normal bedtime, and I had to be at work the next day. I changed out of my clothes and crawled into the big, empty bed, feeling both emotionally and physically exhausted. Over the last few weeks my pregnancy had really started to affect my body—my feet and ankles had started to swell, along with my breasts, and my lower back felt like it had been whacked with the flat of a cricket bat. But my physical discomfort was nothing compared to the gnawing fear that I was losing Hexe—not to another woman, but to something dark within himself.

I fell asleep with the sound of his silver fingers drumming, drumming, drumming in my ears.

Suddenly the lights were on, rendering me as blind as the owls standing guard atop the four-poster. Hexe was standing by the bed, looming over me like a vengeful ghost, his face contorted in munted rage, smelling of tobacco, hashish, and safflower. His gauntleted hand flashed like the scales of a fish as he snatched away the bedclothes, leaving me exposed, wearing nothing but a pair of panties and a camisole.

"How *dare* you come hunting me down like a nagging fishwife, embarrassing me in front of my subjects?" he thundered.

I clambered out of bed moments before he grabbed the edge of the mattress and upended it onto the floor. Beanie, who had been sleeping at the foot of the bed, gave a frightened yelp and quickly scurried for cover under the nightstand.

"Why *shouldn't* I take that money?" he bellowed. "You're living rent free, aren't you? I'm just taking what's owed me!"

"Hexe, please, calm down! Just *listen* to what you're saying!" I pleaded as I moved away from him, trying my best to stay beyond arm's reach. "Something's *wrong* with you!"

"Of *course* something was wrong with me, you stupid nump! But it's all *better* now, see?" he said with a nasty laugh, holding up his gauntleted right hand and wiggling the fingers in parody of a wave.

"No, Hexe—that's what's making you act this way! The gauntlet is cursed! It's perverted your magic and now it's trying to do the same thing to you! You've *got* to get rid of it, Hexe!"

"*You're* the one who's crazy if you think I'm going to surrender my hand!" he snapped. "You've got no idea what you're asking me to do!" Suddenly he lunged forward, his right hand moving with the speed of a striking cobra, grabbing my upper arm. For the first time since we first met, his golden eyes with their cat-slit pupils seemed genuinely inhuman. "You're always yammering about how much you 'belong' in Golgotham—but the truth is you'll *never* know what it *really* means to be Kymeran. It doesn't rub off, no matter how hard you try."

"Hexe, please, let go! You're *hurting* me!"

"So what are you going to do about it?" He smirked, his gloved fingertips digging deeper into the flesh of my upper arm.

I don't know who was more surprised when I punched him. My months of working as a blacksmith came in good stead as I landed a hard enough blow to his jaw to stagger him. The moment he let go of my arm I darted past him and ran out of the bedroom and headed down the hall to my studio. I closed the door behind me and I felt it shudder as he threw his weight against it, trying to force it open.

"Let me in, Tate!" he barked, rattling the doorknob like a tambourine.

"Go away!" I sobbed as I hastily secured the locks. "Just leave me alone, Hexe!"

"You can't tell me to leave! This is *my* house!"

I cried out in alarm as he struck the door with his gauntleted fist, causing one of the upper panels to split. I backed away as the second blow shattered the panel entirely, allowing him to reach the lock and kick open the ruined door. I realize this might sound deluded, considering the situation

I found myself in, but although I was surrounded by power tools and other equipment, I did not move to arm myself because I knew the man that I loved was still in there somewhere. If I could just say the right word or do the right thing to trigger his reemergence, to replace this angry stranger with the man I loved and who loved me in return, then everything would go back to the way it should be. . . .

As he moved to cross the threshold, there came a clattering sound from up the hall. Hexe frowned and turned his head to look in the direction of the noise, only to be sent flying beyond my field of vision.

"Leave her alone!" Octavia bleated.

I stepped out of the studio to see Hexe lying sprawled on the second floor landing. The cruel, distant look had disappeared from his eyes, to be replaced by one of dazed confusion. "What in seven hells is going on—?" he groaned.

As I moved to go to his side, Octavia blocked my way with her arm and shook her head. She then turned back to address Hexe in a stern voice. "Get out of here—go take a walk."

"Tate—what's going on—?" Hexe's eyes widened and his voice trailed off as he caught sight of the livid hand-shaped bruise that now adorned my upper arm.

"I mean it," Octavia said, stamping one of her cloven hooves in emphasis. "Or do you want me to knock some more sense into you?"

With that the look in Hexe's eyes abruptly changed again, reverting to the previous cold, hard stare. I automatically took a step backward as he glared at me. "I could *use* some fresh air," he sneered. "It smells like a barnyard in here." He turned and headed down the stairs and, a few seconds later, we were rewarded by the sound of the front door slamming.

Octavia heaved a sigh of relief and then turned to look at me. "Good thing I switched shifts with a friend of mine, or I wouldn't have been home for that. Did he hurt you?"

"Not really," I replied. "The door got the worst of it. But thank you for stopping it before it could get really ugly."

"It's nothing I haven't had to do for my sisters, time and again. *All* men are alike, at some point. It's just that satyrs are at their worst *all* the time."

"The thing is, Hexe *isn't* like that. No, I mean it—truly

he's *not.* Something's happening to him—I just don't know how to explain it, but he's genuinely not himself anymore."

"Is it drugs?"

"Not exactly," I replied.

"Do you have someplace where you can go?" Octavia asked gently. "Somewhere outside of Golgotham?"

I blinked in surprise, taken aback by the question. "Do you think that's really necessary?"

"Do you trust him not to do it again?" the faun countered.

Up until that moment, the thought of leaving Hexe had not crossed my mind. But now that the subject had been broached, there was no banishing it. I went into my studio and stared out the window that overlooked the street. I could see Hexe trudging away from the house, fists jammed deep into the pockets of his coat. At this time of night there was only one place he could be headed: the Stagger Inn.

Chapter 20

As I stepped out of the elevator, the only things I noticed about the hallway were that it was very long and that there was no way to tell one doorway from another. The entire apartment building was also very quiet, which was to be expected at a quarter to four in the morning, and the sound of my footsteps and the clickity-click of Beanie's toenails seemed incredibly loud in comparison. After a few moments' search, I finally found the apartment I was looking for—marked by an adhesive sticker shaped like the Loch Ness Monster pasted just below the peephole drilled in the door. I set down my suitcase, tightened my hold on Beanie's leash, and pushed the doorbell. A minute or two later a decidedly disgruntled male voice, still thick from sleep, spoke from the other side.

"Who is it? Don't you know what goddamned time it is?"

"It's me, Adrian—Tate," I said, standing back so that he could see for himself through the peephole.

"Who is it?" asked an equally sleepy female voice.

"It's Tate."

There was a sudden rattle of locks and deadbolts being turned, followed by the door opening. Vanessa stood in the tiny foyer of her apartment dressed in a faux leopard-skin bathrobe, with her bright red hair sticking out in every direction. Standing behind her was her husband, Adrian, dressed in a pair of pajama bottoms and armed with a T-ball bat.

"What's wrong?" she asked, already reaching out to pull me inside the apartment. "Has something happened?"

"I left Hexe."

The control I'd held over my emotions from the moment I packed my bags and allowed Octavia to escort me to the taxi stand opposite the Gate of Skulls finally dissolved into a torrent of tears.

"Oh, sweetie—I'm *so* sorry!" Vanessa said as she slipped her arm about my shaking shoulders and steered me from the front door and into the living room.

As I let go of the leash, Beanie trotted ahead of me and jumped up onto their couch, making himself immediately at home by burrowing under the throw pillows and falling sound asleep. "I'm sorry. I should have called first, but I wasn't thinking straight," I managed to apologize between sobs. "Oh, God, Nessie, what am I going to do?"

"You're going to sit down and tell me all about it," she said solicitously.

"Oh, Nessie, it was so horrible—Hexe came home munted and we got into this *terrible* fight about money—"

"He was *whated*?" Adrian frowned. He had set aside the T-ball bat and was standing off to the side with the same awkwardly consternated look on his face that all men get when the women around them begin to weep.

"He was messed up on some kind of Kymeran drug," I explained. "The next thing I know he's screaming at me about money, and then things got out of hand. . . ."

"Did he hit you?" Vanessa asked, her voice suddenly hard as flint. With her bright red hair and her flashing emerald green eyes, she reminded me of one of Golgotham's leprechauns rolling up his sleeves in anticipation of a fight.

"It got bad, but not *that* bad," I replied quickly. I reflexively touched my upper arm as I spoke, but since I had changed into a long-sleeved shirt, neither Vanessa nor Adrian could see the bruises. Although I had made up my mind to walk out on Hexe, part of me was still trying to protect him.

"It would *have* to be drugs, wouldn't it?" Vanessa replied, with a shake of her head. "I mean, Hexe *worships* the ground you walk on! I can tell it by the way he looks at you, how he talks about you to others when you're not around." She leaned forward and took one of my hands and gave it a squeeze. "Look, I know this looks like it's the end, but it doesn't *have* to be. Before Adrian and I got married, we had a couple of big fights; I mean, *real* doozies. I almost called the engagement off over one of them. But after we gave each other a little space, and cooled down, we realized even though we drive each other crazy now and again, we couldn't live without one another. Sometimes you've got to get shit out in the open for a relationship to grow, even if it hurts."

"I know that, Nessie." I sniffled, wiping my eyes with one of the tissues Adrian handed me in an attempt to be supportive while staying out of the way. "I love Hexe so much it hurts to think about him not being in my life. But this isn't about just about *me*, and what *I* want, anymore," I said, placing a protective hand atop my belly. "It's like I'm watching him fade away while being replaced by someone I don't know. I can't stay in that house while he's like that. And I certainly can't bring a baby into that kind of craziness."

Adrian shuffled into the living room, carrying a blanket and a bed pillow in his arms. "I'm going to crash on the sofa, and you can share the bed with Nessie," he announced, stifling a yawn. "It's a queen—you should have plenty of room."

"I'll do no such thing!" I replied, taking the bedclothes from him. "I'll sleep on the sofa—you go back to bed with your wife. I'm pregnant, not made out of glass. Besides, I wouldn't subject Beanie's snoring and gas to anyone unprepared for it. I think it's actually against the Geneva Convention."

Since both Adrian and Vanessa had to get up to go to work in the morning, neither was in the mood to argue the situation, so they retired to their bedroom and left me to make a bed for myself on the sofa. As I went to the bathroom before turning in, I could hear their voices conversing in low tones. Although I could not make out the words, I knew they were talking about what to do about me.

I stretched out as best I could on the couch and Beanie snuggled in close against me, pressing his sleek little body against my swollen belly. Even though it had been weeks since the last time Hexe had slept alongside me, I still missed the heat of his body and the sound of his breathing. The thought of never waking up to find him in bed beside me again made my heart ache as if it were being torn apart with hooks. I remembered the cold, distant look in Hexe's eyes and the sneering, ugly tone of his voice as he spoke barbed words full of venom, and how he seemed to take a perverse delight in saying things that shredded my self-confidence and self-worth. I tried to think of the last time I was genuinely happy, and my mind went back to the Jubilee, when he won a stuffed monkey wearing a plaid tam-o'-shanter for me at the Hit the Cats booth.

As the sights and sounds of that moment flooded my memory, I experienced what felt like a small, sharp kick in my midriff, followed by a second, slightly less enthusiastic bump. Beanie snorted in disgust and moved toward the foot of the couch, clearly resentful of having his beauty rest interrupted by a rumbaing fetus. I closed my eyes and pretended that Hexe had his arms wrapped about me, and that it was his hands, not mine, clasped across my belly, feeling our wondrous, nameless child-to-be tapping on the walls of his world, as if in search of a secret passage. The tears built until they turned my vision into a watery blur and spilled from the corners of my eyes.

The sound of movement in the room started me awake. I opened my eyes and frowned at the unfamiliar bookcases and coffee table before remembering where I was. I could hear Adrian and Vanessa moving around in their galley-style kitchen as they prepared breakfast before leaving for the day. Adrian taught Art History at NYU, and Vanessa worked for a pet cremation service, both designing and throwing custom pottery urns for dearly departed four-legged friends. Beanie hopped off the sofa and went trotting off to investigate upon hearing the toaster pop. I guess he missed the old breakfast routine as much as I did.

Stifling a yawn, I shuffled into the kitchen, to find Beanie standing on his hind legs in front of Adrian, eyes focused on his strawberry toaster pastry as if it were the Holy Grail. "Good morning, li'l guy!" Adrian laughed. "Do you want a Pop-Tart?"

"Damn it, dog!" I exclaimed, with a clap of my hands. "Get out from underfoot."

"Sorry," Vanessa said as she poured a dollop of soymilk into her morning coffee. "We didn't mean to wake you up."

"That's okay," I replied. "Normally I'm up and out of the house even earlier than this. I guess I was more exhausted than I realized. I almost feel hungover."

"Once Adrian and I leave for work, you're welcome to crash in the bedroom," Vanessa said. "Feel free to make yourself at home while we're gone."

"Thanks, Nessie, Adrian—you two are really great for putting me up at such short notice."

"Are you kidding?" she grinned. "It's going to be *awesome*! I'll buy some ice cream and microwave a bag of popcorn, and we'll stream a cheesy horror movie on Netflix—it'll be just like college!"

"Sounds wonderful," I agreed.

"See you after work!" Vanessa promised as she and Adrian hustled out the door and into the world beyond.

The moment the door closed behind them, I sprinted to the bathroom, barely making it in time before vomiting what was left of the previous evening's meal. I wasn't sure if my nausea was just another bout of morning sickness or a delayed reaction to everything I'd gone through over the last ten hours. Once I felt better, I walked back into the living room and stared at the rumpled sofa. Vanessa and Adrian lived in a newish tower block, and by New York standards their seven-hundred-square-foot apartment was fairly spacious, but after living in the boardinghouse I couldn't help but feel claustrophobic.

I unplugged my phone from its charger and called Canterbury to tell him I was taking a couple of sick days.

"Morning sickness, eh?" the centaur chuckled. "Well, that's to be expected. Just tell that man of yours to look after you. It's the least he can do for getting you pregnant."

I laughed and assured him I would do just that. I didn't like lying to Canterbury, but I wasn't comfortable airing my dirty laundry just yet. Nessie was one thing—she was the closest thing I had to a sister, and we had seen one another through more than one Bad Breakup in the past—but unburdening myself on my boss and business partner was something else entirely. As it was, the logistics of commuting to work while trying to find a new place to live, on my salary, whether in or out of Golgotham, was enough to make me lie down on the floor and stare at the ceiling in surrender.

I started as my phone began to play the opening guitar lick to Heart's "Magic Man." That was Hexe's ringtone. I stared at the caller ID for a long moment before finally hitting the accept button. He sounded hungover. "Tate—? I can't find Beanie. I've called and called, but he won't answer . . . and I found this weird note from Octavia, saying she's moving out, like, immediately."

"Beanie's with me, Hexe," I replied, trying to sound calmer than I actually felt.

"What's he doing at Canterbury's?" he asked, genuinely baffled.

"I'm not at work."

"Then where are you?"

"I'd rather not say."

"Tate, what's going? Does this have something to do with the door to your studio?"

Now it was my turn to sound confused. "You don't remember?"

"Remember what?"

"You came home munted on Dragon's Balm last night. You were mad at me because I confronted you at the Highlander about stealing money from the baby stash to get smoked up. Then you went mental when I said you needed to get rid of the gauntlet. If Octavia hadn't stopped you, I don't know *what* would have happened after that."

"Wait—what are you talking about?" he asked in a perplexed voice. "I've *never* set foot in the Highlander."

"Heavens and hells, Hexe!" I shot back angrily, no longer able to hide my frustration. "I was *there*! I *saw* you smoking Dragon Balm! Lying about it is not going to make me change my mind."

"But I'm *not* lying!" he said with a plaintive wail. "I honestly *don't know* what you're talking about!"

"Oh? And I guess you don't know anything about Lafo cutting you off at the Calf because you were picking fights with his customers, either?"

"Lafo said *that*?"

"Stop it, Hexe!" I snapped. "Whatever game you think you're playing—just *stop it*! I've *tried* to be understanding about everything. I know you're going through hell, but I just can't stay under the same roof with you after last night. If it was just me, maybe things could be different . . . but it's *not* just me anymore. . . ."

"What are you trying to say—?"

"I'm telling you that *you're* what happened to the door, Hexe. That's why I left and took Beanie with me."

"I . . . I . . . did *that*?" He gasped.

"Hexe, I don't know exactly what's going on, but I *do* know it has something to do with that damned thing Moot put on your hand. You need help, baby—you need to get rid of the gauntlet before the curse on it turns you inside out."

"Please, Tate—whatever I did, I'm *sorry*. I won't do it again—I *promise*. Just come back home. *Please*, don't do this to me. I l*ove* you, Tate."

At that moment he sounded so much like the Hexe I used to know, the one I fell in love with and came to trust, I was afraid my heart was going to split in two from the pain it was enduring. "And I love *you*, Hexe; more than I've loved anyone in my life." As I spoke those words, my throat grew tight and tears fell with every bat of my eyelashes. "You once made me promise you I wouldn't run into any more burning buildings while I was pregnant—well, that's exactly what you're asking me to do right now. I *want* to come home, but I *can't*, not as long as you're still wearing the gauntlet."

"Please, Tate. Don't do this to me," he begged, his voice wavering. "I don't want to lose you and the baby!"

"I don't want to lose *you*, either—believe me, walking out of that house was the hardest thing I've ever done. But I *can't* live with you while you've still got that thing fused to your right hand. I just can't take the risk."

"Please, Tate. You don't know what you're asking of me. . . ."

"I'm hanging up now, Hexe."

I hit the END button and set the phone aside so I could wipe my eyes and collect myself. Within seconds "Magic Man" started playing. I stabbed at the REJECT CALL, only to have it start to play again. I snatched up the phone and powered it down. I needed time to think, to decide what to do. As I stared at the cramped confines of Vanessa and Adrian's apartment—barely big enough for a newlywed couple, much less an indefinite houseguest, a bothersome dog, and eventual newborn—I realized I should not impose any further on their lives. Although I might eventually be able to find a place in Golgotham, that meant placing me in dangerously close proximity to Hexe. I wasn't afraid of him stalking or intimidating me as much as I was worried that my resolve might weaken and I would move back in. Like it or not, I found myself with only one viable choice. But it would mean swallowing my pride and putting on my big girl panties and doing the one thing I had promised myself I would not do.

Beanie all but dragged me out of the elevator, his paws scrabbling frantically on the polished marble floor of the penthouse's foyer. It had been months since the last time I had been there, but nothing much had changed. Save for the life-sized portrait of an old robber baron hanging on the wall, it still looked more like the antechamber of a four-star hotel's presidential suite than the entrance to a private residence.

I took a deep breath to steady my nerves and then pressed the doorbell. Although it seemed to make no sound, I knew that somewhere deep within the penthouse, where the servants spent most of their time, a buzzer was going off. A few seconds later the door opened, revealing a very proper-looking older man in his early sixties, neatly dressed in the formal wear of a butler. The moment he saw me, his reserve disappeared and he grinned from ear to ear.

"Miss Timmy! Welcome home!"

Chapter 21

The water from the multiple-head shower felt good on my body. I could have stood there for another hour, without worrying about the hot water running out, but I knew I was just postponing the inevitable. And, besides, I was starting to prune. As I toweled myself dry in my old bedroom, Beanie patrolled the perimeter, diligently sniffing the baseboards, his eyes bugging even farther out of his skull than usual. There was a polite knock on the door just as I finished slipping into some fresh clothes. It was Clarence, of course.

"Your parents are awaiting you in the Grand Salon, Miss Timmy," he announced.

"Can't they just sit around the kitchen table like normal people?" I sighed.

"Then they wouldn't be Eresbies, would they?" Clarence replied, with the same small, conspiratorial smile we used to share when I was in junior high and chafing under my parents' rules.

"No, they wouldn't," I agreed. "Well, no point in putting it off any longer, I suppose. Come along, Beanie."

Beanie stopped his sniffing and obediently trotted at my heels as I led him down the pristine marble staircase that was the only access to the Grand Salon, a cavernous room with ceilings, paneling, and mantelpieces looted from only the finest Venetian palaces by the family's founder.

My parents were there, seated before the massive fireplace in antique club chairs. My father looked like he had just come back from yachting, his face still ruddy from the wind, while my mother was dressed in her after-luncheon ensemble and working on what I hoped was her first high-ball of the day. I was surprised to find myself actually glad to see them.

My father's weathered face split into a wide grin as I descended the stairs. "There's my girl!" he exclaimed, as he rose to hug me. "I've missed you, Princess!"

"I missed you, too, Dad," I said around the lump in my throat.

"I *told* you she'd come back once she got tired of playing haunted house," my mother said as she rattled the ice in her glass. "What on earth has that Kymie been feeding you? Look at that pot belly – oh my God, you're pregnant." As my mother realized what she was looking at, her usual sense of decorum disappeared and her jaw dropped in disbelief.

"Thanks for noticing," I said proudly.

"You hear that, Millie?" my father asked with an excited laugh. "We're going to be grandparents!"

"Yes. I heard," my mother replied curtly, reaching for her decanter of bourbon. "How far along are you?"

"Eighteen weeks."

She glanced at my stomach again. "Are you *sure* about that?"

Before I could ask her what she meant by that, my dog walked over to one of the statues that decorated the salon—in this case, a Bernini—and pissed all over its base.

"Beanie—! No—!" I yelped. Instead of stopping, he merely turned to look at me as he continued to urinate.

My father seemed more amused than irritated as he gestured to the butler. "Clarence, it would appear my daughter's dog needs to be walked."

"I'll see to it personally, sir," Clarence said. Once Beanie finished emptying his bladder, Clarence picked him up and, tucking him under his arm like a football, carried him out of the room.

"So—I take it *that* is the reason you've come back," my mother said, gesturing vaguely toward my midsection with her glass. "Slumming it isn't nearly as much fun when you actually have to *live* in the slums, is it?"

"I'll admit, living without a trust fund to fall back on is hard," I replied. "But working at a steady job has taught me a lot about life, especially what is and isn't necessary for me to be happy."

"So what is it that you do?" my father asked.

"I'm employed at Canterbury Customs as a fabricator and apprentice blacksmith."

"You're working as a common *laborer*?" This information seemed to shock my mother even more than the news I was pregnant.

"It's a *skilled* trade, Mother," I pointed out sharply. "And my Master has recently taken me on as his partner."

"It sounds positively pornographic," she replied with a grimace. "So, what does your magic man—what's his name? Vex?—think about becoming a father?"

"His name is *Hexe* and he's very excited about the whole thing and is looking forward to being a dad. . . ."

"There *has* to be a 'but' after that sentence," my mother said, fixing me with one of her patented glares. "You wouldn't be here if there wasn't."

"Things have been a little . . . tense . . . between us lately," I admitted grudgingly. "Hexe and I are both going through some changes right now, and I decided it would be better if we gave each other some . . . space."

To my surprise, my mother abruptly set aside her drink, a concerned look on her face. "Has he laid hands on you, Timmy?"

"No!" I replied, although not as quickly or as forcefully as I would have liked.

Her eyes narrowed, and I could tell she was trying to figure out if I was telling the truth or not by parsing out my response in her head. If ever there was a human lie detector, it was my mother. However, her calculations were interrupted by the downstairs maid who arrived armed with a bucket and mop. For some reason, my mother had an aversion—if not an actual phobia—when it came to watching others engage in manual labor of any sort, and would invariably leave the room.

"We'll discuss this later, at dinner," she said, hastily rising from her club chair. "Seven o'clock, sharp."

After the reunion with my parents—which did not go nearly as horribly as I had dreaded—I returned upstairs to see Clarence closing the door to my room behind him. He smiled upon espying me. "I just finished taking your Beanie for a brief stroll in the park. I must say, he is a very friendly little chap—although he appears to have a decided dislike of squirrels."

"Yes, he does seem to take their existence as a personal affront," I agreed with a chuckle.

"It's good to have you back, Miss Timmy. You have been missed."

"I've missed you, too, Clarence," I said, giving him a warm hug.

"Oh—and Madam requests that you dress for dinner."

"Of course she does," I sighed.

Upon entering the bedroom, I saw that Beanie had made himself at home by hopping up onto the king-sized bed and falling asleep at its very center, his legs stretched out as far as they would go, as if it was the world's biggest dog bed. As I set about searching my suitcase for something my mother would consider "dressing" for dinner, I heard a scrabbling sound outside the window, which I assumed was just pigeons from the nearby park perching on the ledge. Suddenly Beanie snapped out of his snooze and leapt off the bed and began frantically jumping up and down like a kangaroo, all while yapping excitedly. I drew back the curtain to see what could possibly trigger such a reaction from him, only to find Scratch squatting outside the window.

"Nice digs," the familiar purred as I slid open the window, allowing him to drop down onto the carpet. "Really swank."

"What are *you* doing here?"

"Since you're refusing to answer your phone, I've been turned into a message delivery service. Yes, yes, I've missed you, too," Scratch said, bumping his head against Beanie as he continued to hop about excitedly.

"How did you find me?" I asked cautiously.

"I sniffed out Beanie," he replied. "I knew you wouldn't be far away."

"So what does Hexe have to say?"

In reply, the familiar leapt up onto the dresser and opened his mouth. To my surprise Hexe's voice issued forth, sounding eerily like the playback on an answering machine. "Tate, whatever it is I've done, I'm sorry, and I swear it won't happen again. I'll get help, I'll go to couples counseling—whatever it is you need me to do, I'll do it. Just please come back home. It's not the same without you—the house is so empty without you here. I love you, Tate. And I love our baby. Just say you'll come back."

"Stop it!" I said with a shudder. "You're giving me the creeps."

"So—what do I tell him?" Scratch asked. "Are you coming back or what?"

"I won't come home until he agrees to get rid of the gauntlet," I said firmly. "Once he's willing to do that, I'll come back, but not before."

"He's not going to want to hear that. But I'll deliver the message just the same." Scratch then sighed and I saw true concern in his bloodred eyes and the furrow of his hairless brow. "I am a familiar, and I am bound to my master. I must obey him, regardless of the order, and I am powerless to thwart his will. That is the nature of the bargain we have made, he and I. But, for what it's worth—you were right to leave. I have never seen him like this before. And it scares me. Oh—and for what it's worth—the house really *isn't* the same without you."

And with that, the familiar jumped from the dresser and dove through the open window, leaving a heartbroken Beanie standing propped against the sill, whining inconsolably as he watched his best friend wing his way back downtown.

Chapter 22

When most people sit down for dinner with their folks, it's a time for casual banter about school, friends, and weekend plans. In my family it's far more . . . complicated than that. I have never once seen my mother take a meal without diamonds in her ears and haute couture on her back. And instead of reaching for the bowl of mashed potatoes or passing around a basket of rolls on our own, either Clarence or Langston, his deputy, always does it for us.

"So . . . what are your plans?" my mother asked as Clarence carefully deposited three spears of white asparagus onto her plate.

"You mean for my child?" I replied. "I intend on keeping it, of course."

My mother raised an elegantly sculpted eyebrow. "Have you truly thought this out?"

"Yes, but clearly not the same way *you* have," I replied, already feeling my hackles rise.

"I'm just saying you have your whole life ahead of you. Are you *sure* you want to lumber yourself with a constant, living reminder of a bad decision you once made?"

"Despite what you may think, my being with Hexe was *not* a bad decision," I snapped. "Once things get worked out between us, I'm planning on going back home."

"But, darling, you *are* home."

"No," I said, with a shake of my head. "This is where I grew up. My *home* is in Golgotham. With Hexe."

"Golgotham's a haven for freaks and monstrosities," my mother sniffed. "Decent humans have no place there."

"I belong in that world far more than I ever have in yours," I said flatly. "In fact—I'm a full-fledged Golgotham-ite now."

My mother's eyes narrowed. "What do you mean by that?"

I turned to Clarence, who was in the process of sliding a nice, juicy slice of prime rib onto my father's plate. "Clarence, could you bring me a pair of paper clips?"

"Of course, Miss Timmy," he replied. Clarence nodded to Langston, who nimbly stepped in and took over the carving knife and fork, and then disappeared into the kitchen.

"What on earth do *paper clips* have to do with this?" my mother asked with a frown.

A few moments later, Clarence returned to the dining room, brandishing a pair of jumbo gold-colored paper clips. "Will these do, Miss Timmy?"

"Just what I need," I smiled. "Thank you, Clarence."

I quickly unbent the metal wires and used them to construct an impromptu sculpture utilizing the welter of table-ware on either side of my plate. The "body" was fashioned from my coffee spoon, while its four "legs," joined by the repurposed paper clips, were made from the salad and dessert fork, the seafood fork, and the butter knife. I decided it looked like a horse. Granted, a spindly, somewhat lopsided horse, but a horse nonetheless.

"What *are* you doing?" my mother sighed. "And couldn't this have waited until after we've had dinner?"

"Your mother *does* have a point, Princess," my father agreed as he munched on his prime rib.

"You asked me what I meant when I said I was a Gol-gothamite," I replied, as I placed my handiwork down in the middle of the table. "It's far easier for me to show you."

I reached out to my creation, just as I had with the clock-work dragon, and felt the familiar spark of connection. Suddenly my ungainly little tableware horse began moving forward under its own steam across the tabletop, although the cocktail fork did result in giving it a pronounced limp.

My father dropped the roll he was buttering onto the floor, along with the knife he was using. To his credit, Clarence promptly retrieved the fallen utensil without batting an eye. My mother squealed in horror and threw her napkin at the thing stumping toward her, knocking it over. The "horse" lay on its side, its mismatched legs still moving, like those of a tipped turtle trying to regain purchase. Although I will admit to taking a certain satisfaction in freaking my mother out, I was genuinely surprised when she suddenly burst into tears and leapt up from the table, fleeing the room. I jumped up and hurried after her, leaving my father to poke at the now-lifeless construct with his own fork.

I found my mother in the conservatory. As unlikely as it seems, she has always had a green thumb. But where other "ladies who lunch" make a hobby out of cultivating orchids or tending bonsai gardens, her passion was container gardening—tomatoes, zucchini, squash, various peppers, cucumbers, even watermelons. Indeed, most of the vegetables that graced the family table were grown on the premises. But not only was her penthouse vegetable garden her hobby; it also served as my mother's private refuge.

She was sitting in a wicker plantation chair, between the beefsteak tomatoes and the snap peas, daubing at the tears in her eyes with a tissue as she struggled to regain her composure.

"Mom—are you all right?" I asked gently. "I really didn't mean to scare you like that."

"I'm okay," she said between sniffles. "I guess I should have known this day would come. After all, magic has its price. But I never thought the price would be *you*."

I frowned in confusion. "What are you talking about?"

She heaved a deep sigh that seemed almost to deflate her. "All of this is my fault. I brought it upon myself and on you."

"Mom, you're not making any sense. . . ."

"I'm a complete fraud, you know," she announced matter-of-factly. "A complete and utter fraud. Have been from the start." She looked at me appraisingly. "Do you know where I was born?"

"Sure; in Philadelphia."

"Oh, I was born in Pennsylvania, all right!" she said with a humorless laugh. "But not in Philly. I was actually born in rural Lancaster County, deep in Pennsylvania Dutch country, on a Mennonite farm."

I blinked in surprise. Although my maternal grandparents had died long before I was born, I was fairly familiar with their family history. "I thought Grandfather Bieler owned a textile company."

My mother smiled ruefully. "The closest my father came to textiles was the wool on the sheep he raised. I was the fourth of their seven children—yes, that's right. I'm not an only child, either. You have aunts and uncles and rafts of cousins I've never told you about, most of them still in Lancaster County, I suppose.

"The farm I grew up on wasn't big, but it wasn't that small, either. The boys helped Father work the fields, while the girls kept the house and tended the livestock. Every morning before school I had to milk the goat and feed the chickens and then, when I got home, I had to muck out the horse stalls. And I *hated* every minute of it. The goats would try to butt me, the chickens would peck at me, and the horses were always trying to step on my feet. I promised myself that when I grew up, I would make sure I never had to look at the wrong end of a mule for the rest of my life."

"Your parents—my grandparents—are they still alive?" I asked hopefully.

"I'm afraid not," she replied, with a shake of her head. "My father died a couple years after I ran away when a tractor rolled over on him. My mother died of cancer, not long before you were born.

"They were good people, I suppose—but uneducated. Neither of them had graduated from high school. My mother was fifteen when she married my father and sixteen when she started popping out kids. I never really knew her that well—she was always either pregnant or tired. I wasn't particularly close to any of my siblings, either—I was the only one of the litter who had dreams of doing something besides working on a farm or marrying a farmer. I wanted bigger, better things than that, and was determined to escape the first chance I got. So I ran away from home when I was seventeen. I wanted to go to New York City and become a dancer on Broadway. It took some doing, but I eventually got there."

My jaw dropped in surprise. "You were a *showgirl*?"

"I realize I'm your mother, but you don't have to look *that* incredulous," she chided. "Yes, I was a showgirl—and a damn good one, too. I could line-kick with the best of 'em, and in high heels, no less." She paused to study me for a moment. "Did I ever tell you how your father and I first met?"

"Sure," I replied automatically. "It was at the after-party for the Met's staging of Rossini's *Cinderella*. . . ."

"It was at an after-party—but for *A Chorus Line*, not the opera. It was being held out in the Hamptons, and one of the producers of the show I was in asked me to be his 'date.' He was queer as a three-dollar bill, of course, but he would bring me along as arm candy, for appearances' sake. When we got there, I realized the mansion was full of younger society types—the ones who went to Elaine's and Studio 54. Everywhere I looked there were glamorous women with pedigrees as long as my arm, dressed in the latest from Paris, and literally dripping with diamonds. I felt like a hick farm girl with hayseeds in my hair and pig shit on my shoes.

"The minute we arrived my producer friend dumped me to go fool around with some pretty boy in the pool house. The minute he leaves me alone, this creepy swinger type gloms on to me, trying to chat me up. I must have looked pretty nervous, because the next thing I know, your father walks over and hands me a drink and says, 'Sorry that took so long. Is this guy bothering you?' After the creep hurried off, Timothy apologized for butting in, but said he could tell I needed some help. Then he introduced himself to me and we started talking.

"I didn't know who he was—not at first, anyway—but I could tell he came from money. When he asked me about myself, I panicked and the next thing I know I'm telling him my family owns a textile company and that I'm visiting from Philadelphia." She shook her head in disbelief at the actions of her younger self. "Before I know it, your father is asking me if I wanted to go out to dinner the next time I'm 'in town.' I said yes because he was such a gentleman—not like all the other men I knew, who were all hands and tongue."

"Mom!"

"Don't give me that look!" she sniffed. "You're not a five-year-old anymore, Timmy. Everyone knows what you have to do to make it onto a Broadway stage.

"Once my producer friend was finished amusing himself, he came and gathered me up. On the way back into the city, he asked me if I'd made any new friends. And he winked when he said it. When I told him I'd met a nice young man named Tim Eresby, he nearly drove off the road! That's when I realized I'd lucked into something *really* big. But I'd also managed to screw myself at the same time.

"If I was going to make any headway with him, I was going to have to 'live' the part I'd created for myself. But how could I possibly fill my closet with designer clothes and cover myself in jewelry? I was just the third girl from the left in a mediocre revival of a mediocre musical. If I wanted to dress for success, it meant resorting to magic.

"I had grown up in a religious family, and the idea of turning to a witch for help was . . . troublesome for me. But I also knew several other people who worked in the theater that had used magic to further their careers, most of whom seemed to have suffered no ill effects from doing it. So I went ahead and picked up the *Village Voice* and looked through the listings in the back for magical services. I found an ad for a Mistress Syra—that's what she called herself back then; none of that "Lady" nonsense—who specialized in glamours and enchantments, especially the appearance of wealth and social status. Best of all, she made house calls, because, back then, decent people didn't travel to Golgotham unless they couldn't avoid it.

"I called the number in the ad, and she showed up at my apartment the very next day. I will admit that I was very impressed when I saw her. She arrived carrying a squarish valise that looked like a salesman's sample case. I told her what my problem was, and she said what I needed was a No-Knickers spell, which would guarantee me the outward appearance of wealth without actually providing me with riches.

"She opened up her case and a pair of legs popped out of it, so that she could use it like a table. I could see that it was full of different little vials and canisters. She mixed up a sampler batch of the potion, which she poured into a perfume atomizer, and told me to spray it all over myself, from head to toe, and then count to ten before looking at myself in a mirror.

"I did as I was directed, and when I opened my eyes I was amazed by what I saw. I was no longer wearing an off-the-rack dress, but the latest design from Halston, complete with a diamond necklace and matching diamond stud ear-rings. I made Audrey Hepburn look like a bag lady.

"She then instructed me to take my coat out of the closet and put it on. When I did, it turned into a glorious mink stole! I was ecstatic! It was like I was staring at a totally new woman, one who had never gathered eggs and milked goats, and didn't know which end of a shovel was used to muck out a horse stable—in fact, she didn't know what 'muck' meant.

"Syra told me that while all of this might look real—even feel and smell real—it was nothing but an illusion. Once its potency wore off, the glamour would evaporate, leaving me revealed as a pauper. Hence the saying: 'fur coat and no knickers.'

"She told me the more I used it, the weaker the spell would become. I was young and desperate, so I went ahead and paid for the spell, and it wasn't long before I was on my way to being a faux heiress.

"On my first date with your father, I lied and told him I was staying at the Plaza, because I didn't want him to see the apartment building I was living in. It was definitely not the kind of place where one would expect an heiress—even one from Philly—to be staying. An hour before he was supposed to pick me up, I took a cab to the Plaza and hung around in the lobby, waiting for your father to come collect me. I must have looked like I belonged, because no one asked me what I was doing there."

"So how was your first date?" I asked, intrigued by this secret history of my parents' meeting and courtship.

"It was *wonderful*—your father took me to this charming little Italian place called Mama Rosa's, and then we went to Xenon over on Forty-third and danced for *hours*. Why are you gaping at me like that, child?"

"I'm just having a hard time picturing you and Dad boogieing down at a disco, that's all," I admitted.

"What did you *think* we were doing back then—dancing minuets? It was the *seventies*, darling! Now, where was I? Ah, yes! We ended by going for coffee at an all-night diner, and then your father dropped me back off at the Plaza. He was gentleman enough not to expect an invitation to my room—which was a good thing, considering. Once he left, I came back out of the hotel and caught a cab downtown.

"The very next day your father called and asked me out again. Soon we were seeing each other twice a week, then three. It wasn't long before I ran out of the No-Knickers spray. I called Mistress Syra for a refill. She returned and made a new batch for me, but this time it cost twice as much as before! She said it was because she had to increase the glamour's potency, since I was using it so often. I wasn't thrilled by the price hike, but what else could I do?

"However, I started noticing something different about the spell. When I first started using it, a single application would last for six to eight hours. But now it was wearing off after only four. One night, when we were at the Russian Tea Room, I left the table wearing Diane von Furstenberg and an emerald necklace, only to arrive in the ladies' room dressed in J. C. Penney and costume jewelry. Luckily, I was carrying the atomizer in my purse, so I was able to reapply the glamour in one of the stalls. Your father and I had been seeing one another for three months by the time the second atomizer ran dry. When I called Mistress Syra about a refill, the price was even higher than before. The musical I'd been dancing in had closed by that point, and I was living off crackers and tomato soup made from hot water and ketchup. The only thing I owned I could use as payment was a platinum and ruby tennis bracelet Timothy gave me as a token of his affection. It was the first *real* jewelry I'd ever owned. But I had no choice—if I didn't pay what she asked, Timothy would discover I was worse than a fraud. So I gave the bracelet to Syra.

"The third bottle of No-Knickers spray was twice as strong as the previous one, but its staying power was eroding even faster. Where once a single spritz had been good for most of the evening, now I was forced to keep ducking into the ladies' room to reapply my glamour, for fear of the illusion dissolving in the middle of nightclubbing.

"Your father and I had been dating for nearly six months—and I will admit, when we first started seeing one another, I had dollar signs in my eyes. But as I got to know him, I found myself falling in love with him. He was far kinder and sweeter than *any* man I'd ever known, and not just because he was looking to get in my pants. He was considerate to *everyone* he met, from nightclub impresarios to the hatcheck girl. He was also smart, funny, a good dancer, and an *excellent* lover. . . ."

"Mom! *Ick!* Too much information!"

"Honestly, Timmy," she said, patting her hair to make sure it was still in place, something she did whenever she was embarrassed. "You know damn well your generation didn't invent premarital sex! Anyway, one evening your father and I went to a charity gala for some museum or hospital, I suppose. Anyway, we were ballroom dancing and I was enjoying myself so much, I completely lost track of time. Then I looked down and realized I was no longer wearing Chanel, but an off-the-rack shift from Filene's Basement, and my matching pearl necklace and earrings had turned back into cheap paste knockoffs!

"I looked into Timothy's eyes and I saw surprise, then confusion. The couples closest to us were openly snickering. Although I was fully clothed, I'd never been any more naked than I was at that moment. I had been revealed as a No-Knickers, and now they knew I wasn't one of them. I bolted from the dance floor and fled the building. Timothy and I had arrived at the ball in a chauffeured limousine, but there I was, running off into the night on foot all by myself. I ended up taking the subway back to my neighborhood.

"I was so devastated; I was crying so hard I couldn't see. The man I loved now knew the woman he thought he had been courting for the last six months didn't truly exist, and that I had lied to him about who and what I was. I'd had a chance at landing my very own Prince Charming, only to fail in the most spectacularly humiliating way imaginable. I returned to my dismal little studio apartment and didn't go outside for two days.

"Then, on the third day, there was a knock on my door. I was sure it was the landlord, wanting to know where his rent was. But when I opened the door, instead of the landlord, I saw your father standing there, holding a huge bouquet of flowers! He'd tracked me down by talking to the producer who had taken me to the after-party. He told me he didn't care if I was rich or poor—as long as I was me. But once he returned home, my insecurity got the better of me again. I began to worry that his parents might pressure him into marrying someone with more social standing.

"So I made one last call to Mistress Syra. I didn't have much in the way of money, but I figured since I had grossly overpaid her with the tennis bracelet, I might have a little leeway. I told her I wanted a love potion; one that would make me the unquestioned queen of Timothy's heart. The love potion she crafted was odorless and colorless, perfect for being slipped into food or drink, and I put it in his champagne while he wasn't looking.

"I am not proud of what I did—in fact, I regretted doing it within moments of pouring it in his glass. But there was no going back, and I was genuinely terrified of losing him. Not so much to another woman, mind you, but to his sense of responsibility to his family. If your father is anything, he's a dutiful Eresby. That very night he proposed to me. It should have been the happiest moment of my life, but it seemed so terribly hollow. It was like I had won a long distance marathon by cheating at the last mile.

"But what really worried me was the fact the love potion, like all magic, would eventually wear off. Of course I could always buy *another* vial and dose him again, but I had learned my lesson from the No-Knickers spell. I knew I'd end up paying a fortune every other week for potions of ever-decreasing strength.

"I decided the best plan would be for me to steer clear of any more magic and simply make myself indispensable to your father. I thought that if I became the perfect high-society wife, he might stay married to me once the potion wore off, or even fall in love with me for real. So I threw myself into doing all the things expected of me: organizing charity balls, lunching with the right ladies, and keeping myself a size two—and I haven't stopped since."

"And did it? Wear off, that is?" I asked, although I wasn't sure I wanted to know the answer.

"I don't know," she admitted. "In the thirty-five years we've been married, your father's feelings for me have not changed in the least. That just means every morning I wake up wondering if this is the day I'll find him looking at me as if I was a stranger."

She paused for a moment and when she looked at me her face softened and lost its usual reserve, which I had come to view as its default expression. Up until a half hour ago, I thought my mother was just another socialite with a drinking problem who spent her life doing nothing but shopping, gossiping, and dieting, but now I was seeing a whole different person I had never dreamed existed.

"I'm sorry I haven't been the mother I should have been to you, Timmy. I was so busy imitating the high-society women around me in order to fit in, I copied all their failings, too. Part of me has always been ... distant toward you, through no fault of your own. Perhaps it's because I was never close to my own mother, or because I'm unsure whether you were conceived in love—or something else. Whatever the reason, it's no excuse for me handing you over to others to raise." She suddenly leaned forward and grasped my forearm, clutching it tightly, like a drowning woman grabbing the hand of a rescuer. It was the closest she had come to hugging me in years. "I know I don't show it the way I should, but never, ever doubt for a moment that I love you, Timmy. I have everything I ever dreamed of when I was candling eggs and milking goats on my parents' farm: a rich husband, a wonderful home, fast cars and fashionable clothes, and a beautiful and talented daughter. But I got it through trickery, and now I'm paying the price through my child."

"Mom—I don't know what to say," I said, shaking my head in amazement. "I had no idea. . . ."

"Of course you didn't. What mother wants to admit that she cheated her way into marriage? Or that she let her own insecurity get in the way of raising her child? Much less that her dabbling in magic has turned her only daughter into a ... a ..."

"'Weirdo'?" I suggested helpfully. "Mom, you've got to stop beating yourself up over this. My magic powers have *nothing* to do with whatever potions you swallowed or spritzed on yourself, decades ago. I know for a fact that I'm not the only human in Golgotham who has been affected. I'm not a hundred percent sure *why* I'm able to do magic now, but I *do* know that none of this is your fault."

My mother smiled and gave a half laugh and half sob as she daubed at the tears returning to her eyes.

"And, Mom? I like this story of how you and Dad met a lot better than the old one."

"Thank you for saying that, sweetheart. Your father and I will always love you, no matter what, but, I beg you, *never* bring the silverware to life again. We have to eat with those things."

*   *   *

As I headed back to my room, I kept thinking about every-thing my mother had said. It was the first time in our shared lives that she had spoken to me as a fellow adult, instead of a child. The mythology of my childhood had been blown apart, but, to my surprise, I was cool with it. So my textile tycoon grandfather didn't really exist—big deal. I never met him in the first place. But now I know where my artistic streak came from—my ex-showgirl mother! It almost made up for the news that the only reason my father asked her to marry him was because she slipped him a love potion.

As I prepared to go to bed, there was a knock on the door, and a second later my father stuck his head into the room. "Are you decent?"

"About as much as I'll ever be," I replied with a laugh.

He stepped into the room and sat down on the corner of the bed beside Beanie, who was sound asleep and snoring like a buzz saw. "Does he always sound like that?" He frowned.

"If you think *that's* bad, just wait until he starts breaking wind," I chuckled. "Is something wrong, Dad?"

"Can't a father check in on his daughter and see how she's doing?" he protested.

"I'm okay, I guess. I'm just feeling a bit dazed and glazed right now," I admitted. "It's been a long, stressful twenty-four hours."

"I'm pleased that you and your mother were able to talk—and without any shouting, I might add."

I studied him for a long moment, uncertain whether to say anything. Growing up, I had wondered why he always allowed my mother to have her way, no matter what it might be. Now it all seemed to make sense.

"Dad—how would you feel if everything you thought was real turned out to be an illusion—?"

"So I take it your mother finally got around to telling you about how we met," he said with a laugh. "Did she also tell you about how she slipped a love potion into my cham-pagne?"

"You *know* about that?"

"Of course!" he replied. "I'm one of the richest men in the world! And back then I was one of the most eligible bachelors in this, or any, country! I was *always* getting dosed with love potions and having Come Hithers cast over me by gold diggers. That's why I always wore counter-charms and carried antidotes on my person at all times."

"You mean Mom didn't bewitch you?"

"Oh, I'm under her spell—but it has *nothing* to do with magic!" he laughed. "I was enchanted by your mother the first time I laid eyes on her. She's an amazing woman, you know that? She's a real firecracker, and isn't afraid to speak her mind and stand up for what she believes in. You and she are a *lot* alike. I suspect that's why you two are always butting heads. Unfortunately, I fear she's reliving some unresolved issues she had with her parents through you, especially in regard to your decision to become an artist. I know she hated quitting the stage to marry me—but my parents insisted on it. That's why she's such a passionate fund-raiser for the ballet, you know."

"If you're not spellbound, why haven't you told her yet? She's spent years waiting for you to come to your senses and replace her with some bimbo who looks like a pool toy."

"And lose what little leverage I have in the relationship?" he exclaimed. "Are you *nuts*?"

After my father bid good night and kissed me on the forehead, I changed into my nightclothes and climbed into bed. It was far bigger and much more comfortable than Nessie's living room couch, but it was also just as cold and lonely. My only consolation, as I drifted off into a troubled sleep, was knowing I, like my child, had been conceived in love. Granted, a weird, fucked-up kind of love—but love nonetheless.

Chapter 23

"How did you sleep, dear?" my mother asked, as she spread marmalade on her English muffin.

"Okay, I guess," I replied, as I eyed the plate of bacon and eggs Clarence set before me. "I'm afraid I'm not used to the sound of traffic in the streets anymore. It's going to take some readjusting."

"Have you seen an obstetrician? Or were you simply relying on witch doctors for your prenatal care?"

Despite my mother's recent decision to treat me as an adult, I didn't see any point in testing her resolution by revealing that I'd left Golgotham because Hexe had stolen money I needed for a prenatal exam. "Well, I have a friend who practices traditional Chinese medicine. . . ."

"I suspected as much," she said, setting down her knife. "So I took the liberty of booking you an appointment with my gyno, Dr. Blumlein—he's also an obstetrician. You'll love him—he warms his hands before he does his exam."

"That's very thoughtful of you," I said, the image of my mother with her feet in gyno stirrups now seared into my mind's eye. So much for breakfast . . .

Dr. Blumlein's practice was in a state-of-the-art office building on East Seventy-second Street, within easy reach of Prada, Frédéric Malle, and Swifty's. When my mother and I arrived, we entered a tastefully appointed reception room with nicer furniture than most people have in their homes and were greeted by a pleasantly smiling woman who only glanced at my tattoos and eyebrow piercing once as she entered my information into a computer. After that was taken care of, I was handed over to a second, equally pleasant woman dressed in nurse's whites, who escorted me to an examination room, leaving my mother to her own devices.

I changed out of my street clothes into a smocklike garment, and the nurse took my medical history and drew a blood sample. She then handed me a little plastic cup with a screw-on lid and pointed me to the bathroom at the end of the hall. Once that was taken care of, I was returned to the examination room, where I sat on the paper-wrapped exam table, staring at a laminated poster depicting cutaway views of a gestating womb during the various stages of pregnancy.

There was a polite rap on the door as the nurse reappeared, this time in the company of a dapper middle-aged man dressed in a white lab coat with a stethoscope looped about his neck. He had a nice smile and kind eyes, and seemed exactly the sort of man my mother and her high-society friends would trust to look at their hoo-has on a regular basis.

"Good afternoon, Ms. Eresby," he said, flashing me a welcoming smile. "My name is Dr. Blumlein. I'll be looking after you and your baby from here on." As the nurse busied herself with preparing the room for my pelvic exam, he glanced down at the clipboard he was carrying. "It says here that you are in your eighteenth week."

"That's correct."

He gave me a dubious look. "Are you certain?"

"I might be off a week in either direction," I admitted. "But I'm in the general ballpark."

"I see," he grunted, jotting something down on the clipboard. "I understand that this is your first prenatal exam? I realize you're young, but there are risk factors in all pregnancies. You don't want to gamble with your baby's health, do you?" he chided. "I see that you're twenty-six. And the father? He's ?"

"Kymeran."

The gynecologist's smile abruptly blinked off. "I was asking his age."

"Sorry, my mistake. He's thirty," I replied.

The pelvic exam and pap smear proved to be as awkward, uncomfortable, and tedious as all such exams tend to be, landing somewhere between a getting-my-teeth-cleaned and changing-the-oil-in-my-car on the Necessary Evil scale.

"I'm going to leave you with Nurse Riggins here," Dr. Blumlein announced as he shed his gloves. "She'll conduct the ultrasound, so we can check on the development of your baby and triangulate your due date. Once that's finished, I'll be conferring with you in my office."

"Just stay on your back and uncover your tummy, Ms. Eresby," Nurse Riggins said as she rolled over the portable ultrasound machine. Once my abdomen was exposed, she slathered it with a clear gel and then turned on the machine.

"What, exactly, are you looking for when you do this?" I asked as she placed the transducer against my swollen belly.

"Right now I'm monitoring the baby's heartbeat and seeing if your placenta is in the right place," the nurse replied, keeping one eye on the monitor as she slowly moved the transducer across the expanse of my bared belly. "I'm also looking for fetal abnormalities. So far everything is checking out just fine." She turned the computer screen about so that it was facing me. "Do you want to say hello?"

I stared at the black-and-white image on the screen—although it looked like a cross between a smudged Xerox and an X-ray, there was no mistaking what I held within me was a very well-developed fetus, with its legs folded up like landing gear and its tiny hands held before its face like a boxer. The first thing I did was laugh in delight at the sight of my child—so close, and yet so far from me. And then I began to cry.

"I'm sorry," I said as the nurse paused in her duties long enough to hand me a tissue. "I didn't mean to lose control like that."

"It happens all the time." She smiled. "I'm used to it."

"I just wish my boyfriend was here to see it," I said as I blew my nose. "Can you tell if it's a boy or a girl?"

"Oh, yes," Nurse Riggins replied, nodding her head. "He's definitely a boy."

I nodded my head. So Lafo's dessert was right, after all.

"And is he—is he—?" I couldn't bring myself to finish the sentence for fear of saying what I dreaded would somehow make it so.

"There's nothing to worry about, Ms. Eresby," the nurse said reassuringly. "Your little boy is perfectly normal. . . ."

A big, stupid smile split my face as I heaved a sigh of relief upon hearing the news.

"He's got all ten fingers and toes."

Dr. Blumlein's private office was every bit as tastefully appointed as his waiting room, with diplomas from a prestigious university and medical school hanging on the walls, alongside framed photographs of famous women whose vaginas he had looked at over the years—including my own mother.

"Nice to see you, again, Millicent," the doctor said, motioning for my mother and me to take a seat. "I must say it's a good thing you brought your daughter in when you did."

"Is there a problem?" I frowned, protectively crossing my arms over my stomach.

"Although your general health is excellent, Ms. Eresby, and the baby's fetal heartbeat is very strong, it appears there has been a *gross* miscalculation somewhere along the line. According to the ultrasound and my own physical examination, I'd say you are closer to thirty weeks."

"That's impossible!" I exclaimed in disbelief. "There is no way I'm almost eight months pregnant!"

"I don't know how else to explain it, Ms. Eresby, save that it might have something to do with the baby's mixed parentage. I admit I know practically nothing about Kymeran biology, save that their gestation period is *far* shorter than ours. To be frank, I don't feel comfortable taking you on as a patient, as this falls way outside my area of expertise. However, I *can* give you a referral to a colleague who specializes in high-risk pregnancies. . . ." He scribbled down a name and address on a piece of notepaper and handed it to me. "He's in a much better position to handle a case as . . . unique as yours."

"I see," my mother said stiffly, gathering up her purse. "Why don't you just come out and say that your malpractice insurance doesn't cover hybrid pregnancies, Daniel?"

"Now, Millicent, you're not being fair—!" he objected.

"Perhaps I'm not," she conceded. "But that can be said for a *lot* of things in life. Come along, dear." As we left the doctor's office, she paused to give him a final, withering look. "Oh, and by the way, I'll be stopping by your receptionist on the way out in order to cancel my next appointment."

"I can't believe he would try to fob you off on another doctor like that!" my mother fumed as we exited the penthouse elevator.

"He *did* have a point, Mom."

"So does a pencil," she sniffed. "That doesn't mean I should sit there and let someone jab it in my eye."

Clarence opened the door before my mother had a chance to retrieve her keys from her purse. "Welcome back, Madam," he said, then turned to address me. "Miss Timmy— you have a lady caller in the Grand Salon."

My mother frowned and glanced at me. "Who could that possibly be?"

"Perhaps it's Nessie," I suggested.

Upon entering the Grand Salon, I instantly recognized the regal figure with the peacock blue hair standing before the fireplace, staring at the museum-quality Dürer hung over the mantel.

"Lady Syra!" I exclaimed, unable to refrain from smiling in welcome.

"What are *you* doing here?" My mother asked frostily. She was standing on the staircase behind me, glaring down at the Witch Queen with unconcealed hostility.

"Hello to you, too, Millicent," Syra replied graciously.

"Why on Earth did you allow this woman into my house?" my mother snapped, turning her withering glare on Clarence.

"The lady said she wished to speak to Miss Timmy, and refused to leave until she did so," the butler explained apologetically. "I deemed it best not to aggravate the situation, given her . . . abilities."

My mother snorted in disgust and returned her attention to Lady Syra. "What do you want with my daughter, sorceress?"

"That is between Tate and me," the Witch Queen replied politely but firmly.

"Her name is *Timothea*!" My mother's shout was loud enough to make the pendants on the crystal chandelier jingle.

"Mom, please! Let me handle this," I said, doing my best to try to soothe her. "Do you trust me to do that?" For a moment it looked like she was going to fight me on it, but then she grudgingly sighed and nodded her head. "So," I said, turning to face Lady Syra, "why *are* you here?"

"It's about Hexe. Is there someplace where we can speak in private?" she asked, glancing about the ballroom-sized salon.

"We can talk in the library," I said, motioning for her to follow me. My mother glared at Lady Syra as she passed her on the stairs, but remained silent.

Compared to the Grand Salon, the library seemed relatively cozy. Once I closed the door behind us, Lady Syra heaved a sigh of relief and allowed her shoulders to drop.

"If Hexe sent you here to try to talk me into coming back," I warned her, "I'm going to tell you the same thing I told Scratch: I'm not setting foot in that house until he agrees to give up the gauntlet."

"While I am here on Hexe's behalf," she admitted, "he didn't send me. Something is horribly wrong with my son, and I need your help. I stopped by the house last night for a visit, but no one answered the door. I was about to leave when Scratch called out to me from the rooftop and said Hexe had locked himself inside his office and was refusing to come out. So I used my passkey to let myself in. It took some cajoling, but I finally got Hexe to open the door to his office. I don't know what he was doing in there, but he positively reeked of Dragon Balm. I asked him what was going on, but all he would say was that you'd left him because you were tired of being poor, and then slammed the door in my face." She shook her head as she spoke, as if she could not believe her own words. "This has something to do with the Gauntlet of Nydd, doesn't it?"

"I'm convinced that's what's wrong," I replied grimly. "There's a curse on the gauntlet that's keeping Hexe from using his Right Hand magic."

"I should have known that thing was trouble the moment Trinket hissed at it!" Lady Syra said ruefully, reaching up to pet the familiar looped about her neck. "Is it true Dr. Moot was the one who bonded that thing to Hexe's hand?"

"I'm afraid so."

She frowned in consternation. "But *why* would he go to that old tosser? Was it just a question of money? I would have paid to have it done properly, you know. Curse that foolish pride of his. He's just like his father!"

"He had his reasons. They seemed to make sense, at the time," I replied, leery of going into detail for fear of saying too much. Things were bad enough already without dragging the Maladanti into it. "I've tried to talk him into getting the thing removed, but he's convinced that if he can find Madam Erys, he can get the curse lifted without having to remove the gauntlet itself. He won't listen to reason."

"It's the damned Dragon Balm," Lady Syra said with a grimace. "Esau used to smoke that crap to try to forget the man he used to be. There was always a touch of darkness to my brother—the same that exists in all Kymerans—but once Nina was no longer in his life, it spread like a cancer throughout his soul, until it drew him down the spiral of the Left Hand path."

"Is that what you think Hexe is trying to do—forget?"

"If my son has indeed lost his Right Hand magic to a curse, he is suffering a fate most Kymerans would rather die than endure. No wonder he seemed a shadow of himself. Tate—I don't know what happened between you and Hexe, but if you *truly* love my son, you will come back with me to Golgotham."

"Please don't ask me to do that, Syra."

"I'm not asking, Tate; I'm *begging*," she said, taking my hand and clasping it tightly. "I could have cast a Come Hither and dragged you back downtown against your will, but I *didn't*, because I know that's not what Hexe would have wanted. You wear the Crown of Adon, which marks you as his true love, just as it marked his father as *my* true love. When my father forced me to send Horn away, I became bitter and angry, and I could feel the darkness rise in me, whispering in my ear in a shadow's voice. The only thing that kept me centered, that drew me back to the light was my child. When I looked into Hexe's eyes for the first time, I was filled with hope and strength. If not for my son, I would have joined my brother on his downward spiral. Of that I have no doubt.

"*That* is why you must go back to Golgotham—Hexe needs you and his child to fight the darkness gathering within him. I have already lost my brother to the Left Hand path—I will not stand by and allow it to claim my son as well. If you can get Hexe to agree to it, I will pay to have the Gauntlet of Nydd removed. Once it's off, I'll have it destroyed. I don't care if it's a historical artifact—it has meant nothing but sorrow to the Royal Family."

I fully intended to tell her no. The word was resting on my tongue, waiting to be spoken. Going back to Golgotham was risky for me, not to mention the baby. But when I looked into Syra's eyes, I saw a mother terrified for the sake of her son—a son who had the same golden eyes.

When I told my mother I would be returning to Golgotham with Lady Syra, she was so taken aback she actually set aside her bourbon. "What do you *mean* you're going back?" I could almost see the steam shooting out her ears.

"Hexe needs my help," I explained. "We might be having problems right now, but I still love him."

This did not mollify my mother in the least. "I know what you're up to, witch!" she snapped, pointing at Lady Syra. "You're trying to steal my daughter away from me! You've cast some kind of spell over her so you can drag her back to your good-for-nothing son!"

"Mother, *please*! You make it sound like I've pricked my finger on a spinning wheel!"

She turned to glare at me in disapproval. "This was all an elaborate trick, wasn't it?" she fumed. "You just wanted to get back into my good graces long enough for your father and me to unfreeze your trust fund. Is that why you got pregnant in the first place—to get Grandma and Grandpa on the hook?"

"I don't *want* your money if it means turning back into a kid you can push around and tell what to do!" I replied. "I've been there and done that, Mom. I didn't like it the first time, so why should I sign up for it again, and bring my kid along for the ride? And speaking of which, as far as I'm concerned, my baby only has *one* grandmother . . . and it's not *you*." I knew I drew blood with that last remark because

I saw her flinch, and I realized that I would regret saying it later on, but at that moment I couldn't have cared less that I said something so cruel to someone I loved. I was my mother's child, after all. I turned to Lady Syra and motioned for her to follow me. "Come on—I need to pack."

"No need, Miss Timmy," Clarence announced. He was standing at the head of the stairs that led to the Grand Salon, holding my suitcase in one hand and Beanie's leash in the other. "I trust I wasn't being too presumptuous?"

"Honestly, Clarence!" my mother spat. "First you let that witch in the door; now you're helping Timmy pack her bags! Have you no sense of loyalty?"

"Ah! That reminds me," the butler said, taking an envelope from his breast pocket as he stepped forward. "Here is my letter of resignation, effective immediately. Normally, I would have given substantially more notice than this, but the circumstances are unique. I will be accompanying Miss Timmy, as she is in greater need of my services than either yourself or the master."

She opened the envelope, scowling at the contents. "This letter isn't dated."

"I wrote it some time ago," Clarence replied. "I've just been waiting for the right opportunity to deliver it."

"You're leaving us to go work for *her*?" she scoffed. "How do you expect to get paid? In magic beans?"

"While I may have served the Eresbies, from boy to man, with my mouth shut and my thoughts to myself, I have also kept my eyes and ears open and have used information I have overheard at table to make certain investments in the stock market," Clarence replied. "I have managed to accumulate something of a nest egg. Granted, it's nothing compared to the Eresby fortune, but, to be blunt, I don't need your stinking money, ma'am. I've got plenty of my own; more than enough to retire anywhere in the world. And as it so happens, I've chosen to retire in Golgotham—at least until the baby comes."

"*You're* behind this as well, aren't you?" my mother snarled at Lady Syra, her eyes narrowing into suspicious slits. "You weren't happy with taking away my daughter, so now you've cast a spell over Clarence and turned him against me as well!"

"You still don't get it, even after all this time, do you,

Millicent?" Lady Syra said sadly. "A true heart is stronger than *any* magic I can cast."

And with that, I walked back out of my parents' penthouse, leaving my mother sputtering to herself, alone and untended, in the echoing expanse of the Grand Salon.

Chapter 24

"This is most certainly a . . . *change* from the Upper East Side," Clarence said as he looked up at the looming boardinghouse. He was trying to remain positive, although I could tell he was somewhat intimidated by his surroundings. "Most . . . quaint. In a peculiar way."

"Don't worry, Clarence," I smiled reassuringly. "It'll grow on you. I promise."

As I unlocked the front door, Beanie was so excited he slipped his leash and dashed headlong into the house. He was greeted by Scratch, who rubbed himself along the length of the Boston terrier, a look of feline delight on his hairless, wrinkled face.

"You've come back!" Scratch exclaimed, his voice barely audible above his purrs. "I was afraid you were gone for good! Thank you-thank you-*thank you* for bringing back my dog!"

"Oh. My." Clarence gasped, staring in astonishment at the hairless winged cat rubbing itself against my shins.

Scratch froze in midpurr. "Who's the nump in the suit?" he growled.

"Clarence is an old friend of mine. Please don't call him a nump. He's going to be living here now. Clarence, this is Scratch."

"Pleased to make your acquaintance . . . sir?" Clarence said, with his usual aplomb.

"Great, another num—I mean, human underfoot," the familiar sniffed, fixing the butler with a bloodred glare. "But if Tate and Beanie say you're cool, then I guess I'm okay with it."

"Where's Hexe?" I asked.

"He's still locked in his office," the familiar replied in a worried voice. "He won't talk to me anymore. I've never seen him like this—it scares me."

"Hexe—it's me, Tate," I called out, tapping on the closed door. "Can you hear me?" The dead bolt abruptly unlocked itself, although I had not heard any movement inside the room. I glanced down at Scratch, who nodded his head, before pushing open the door.

The office looked like it had been ransacked. The floor was covered with books and scattered papers pulled from Hexe's sizable collection of grimoires, as if someone had been frantically searching for something. The shadows thrown by the Tiffany lamp with the armadillo-shell shade made the taxidermied crocodile hanging from the ceiling seem far less dead than usual. Hexe was slumped across his desk, surrounded by empty bottles of absinthe, Cynar, and barley wine, with a hookah sitting by his silver-clad right hand.

As I stepped into the office, I was struck by the peculiar odor that permeated the room. At first I was at a loss to identify it; then, with a start, I realized it was Hexe. He normally had a warm, pleasantly chypre-like smell that reminded me of citrus and oakmoss with just a hint of leather, but now he seemed to be exuding something closer to bitter lime with a touch of mildew. I knew then I had made the right decision coming back.

He stirred as I drew closer, raising his head to squint at me. "Tate—? Is that really you?" he asked in a ragged voice. Although his hair was uncombed and he was wearing a couple of days' worth of beard, there was no sign of the sneering, cold-eyed stranger in his weary face.

"Yes, it's really me." I smiled gently as I knelt beside him. "I've come back to help you, baby."

"I never meant to say and do those things to you," he said in an earnest whisper. "It makes me sick to my stomach to even think about it. I never wanted to harm you, Tate—you've got to believe me."

"I know," I said as I caressed his stubbled chin. "The gauntlet is doing something to you, poisoning you, somehow. Your mother says she knows a psychic surgeon who can help you."

Hexe drew back and a flicker of fear crossed his face. "But—but—I *need* the gauntlet."

"Do you need it more than you need me? More than you need our baby?"

"But that means I'll no longer be able to work Right Hand magic."

"You can't work Right Hand magic now, anyway. So why fight getting rid of the damned thing?"

Hexe dropped his gaze to his gauntleted hand, which he had yet to move or try to touch me with. "I was going to cast a Come Hither to summon you back and hold you to me. I even looked up the spell. But I couldn't bring myself to do it. Does that make me weak?"

"No," I said as I put my arms around him. "You're the strongest man I know."

It took a pot of coffee and a couple of Vegemite sandwiches, but I eventually coaxed Hexe out of his office and into the kitchen. As he sobered up he became more and more like his old self, even though he still smelled a bit "off." Throughout it all, Scratch sat on his favorite perch atop the refrigerator and watched his master intently, as if afraid Hexe might disappear if he looked away.

"What did you say to my mother about the gauntlet?"

"Just that it's cursed and turning your Right Hand magic widdershins. I didn't tell her about Boss Marz smashing your hand with a witch-hammer. She's scheduled a meeting with the psychic surgeon for tomorrow."

Hexe froze in midchew. "That soon?"

"The quicker we can get that thing off you, the better," I replied.

"I suppose you're right." He set down his half-eaten sandwich and stood up from the table. "I'm going to go take a shower. Care to join me?"

"I'll be there shortly," I said. "I just want to check in on Clarence and see how he's settling in. This has been a big day for all of us."

After tidying up the kitchen, I headed upstairs and stopped by what, until recently, had been Octavia's room and knocked on the door.

"It's unlocked, Miss Timmy."

I opened the door to find Beanie sitting on the bed, patiently watching Clarence as he unpacked a collection of loud Hawaiian shirts from his luggage and placed them in the wardrobe.

"I see you've got a fan." I laughed.

"He seems to find everything I do fascinating and of the utmost importance," Clarence replied. "It's certainly a boost to my self-confidence."

"What's with all the Hawaiian shirts?"

"All my adult life, I have dressed like a butler. Years ago, I promised myself, once I retired, I would never wear a suit and tie again. I have been collecting Hawaiian shirts for exactly this occasion. I can't wait to start trying them out."

I tried to picture Clarence in something besides the tidy three-piece suits he had worn for as long as I could remember, but my mind just wouldn't go there. It was like trying to imagine my grandparents naked.

"I trust your young man is feeling better?" he asked solicitously.

"He's not out of the woods yet, but he's doing a lot better," I replied. "He's more like his old self than he's been in a while."

"I'm glad to hear it. I know you love him very much. I can see it in your eyes whenever you talk about him."

"I was never able to sneak much past you when I was a kid."

"No, you couldn't," he agreed as he unpacked the clay ashtray I made for him at summer camp twenty years ago, and carefully placed it on the bed stand. "But, then, you were always a very loving child."

"Clarence—are you *sure* about all this?" I asked gently. "I appreciate you wanting to help me, but if this places any hardship on you at all . . ."

"Ever since I was a boy I've wanted to see exotic places and unusual people," he smiled wryly. "However, I am not much for travelling. I have a deathly fear of flying, I turn green the moment I set foot on a boat, and I have an unfortunate tendency to become carsick after a couple of hours

For someone like me, Golgotham is the answer to my prayers ... provided the cat doesn't eat me.

"And as for hardships ... what I said to your mother wasn't hot air, Miss Timmy. You don't have to worry about money for the time being. I would be honored to handle the household finances until you and your young gentleman get back on your feet."

I jumped off the bed and threw my arms around the old butler—or at least tried to, since my belly was now in the way. "Clarence, you're my very own fairy godfather!" I exclaimed. "And you've *really* got to stop calling me 'Miss Timmy.'"

"Whatever you say, Miss Timmy."

As I entered the bedroom, Hexe strolled out of the bathroom, fresh from his shower. As he toweled his hair dry I realized it was the first time in weeks I'd seen him naked, and was startled to see how thin he had become.

"I went to see an obstetrician today," I said.

Hexe lowered the towel to stare at me apprehensively. "Is the baby—?"

"He's perfectly healthy," I replied. "But we're going to be parents a little sooner than we thought."

He laughed joyously as he grabbed me up in his arms, twirling about as if we were on a dance floor. For a few glorious moments everything we'd gone through seemed to disappear, and we were happy again, just like we used to be. We were still laughing as he pulled me down onto the bed.

"When you went away, I was afraid I'd never get the chance to be a father to my child," he said, placing his hand over my gravid belly. "I know what it's like, growing up without a father. I don't want to perpetuate that kind of a family tradition."

"You're not being fair to your dad, Hexe. Your mother sent Horn away to keep your grandfather from banishing him."

"I realize it's stupid and childish," he sighed, "but part of me is still mad at him for not being around when I was a kid. There's so much I needed to learn that only he could teach me—like how to be a father and a husband. This is all new territory for me, and I'm afraid I'm going to fail at it."

"The fact that you're worried about being a good dad is

a good sign," I reassured him. "I attended some of the most exclusive private schools in the city and, believe me, *truly* bad fathers fuck up their kids without giving what they're doing a single thought."

Hexe held up his right hand, turning it from side to side as he studied the Gauntlet of Nydd. "The funny thing is, I just wanted to be able to support you and the baby. You would think I, of all people, would know that magic has its price. The gauntlet may have given me back the use of my right hand, but it's come at the cost of nearly driving away those I care most for in life."

"Well, it'll be gone for good in a couple of days," I said firmly.

"Still, even though it perverts my magic, at least it allows me to use my hand for more wholesome purposes, such as brushing my hair . . . and other things," he said as he slipped his hands underneath my blouse. The gauntlet's finely-crafted chain mail felt as smooth and organic as snakeskin sliding against my flesh. "It's been a long time . . ." he whispered.

"Too long," I agreed, as I pulled his hungry mouth toward mine. We made love for the first time in weeks, fumbling and giggling until we found the best position to accommodate the changes to my anatomy. And once it was done, we drifted off to sleep, with Hexe cradling me in his arms as if I might disappear. The bitter lime smell that clung to him was almost entirely gone, save for a faint, lingering trace.

I am walking up a long, winding staircase of living glass, its colors forever shifting and pulsing. The staircase twines about a towering pillar, and as I climb I look out across a vast cityscape made of living glass, its spires shining and strobing in the sunlight. I raise my eyes to the skies and see massive dragons wheeling far above my head, their long, narrow tails fluttering in the wind like the tails of a kite.

At the top of the staircase is a temple. Although it, too, is made of living glass, its doorway is fashioned from the skull of a massive dragon, its fleshless maw yawning wide to accept the faithful. I enter the temple, the interior of which is one vast room, in the center of which is a huge cauldron filled with multicolored flames. Kneeling before the holy fire is a figure dressed in a hooded robe, its head lowered in prayer. Although I have never seen this place or this person before, I know that I stand in the Temple of Adon and that this is the Dragon Oracle.

The robed figure rises and turns to face me. In one hand he holds a tall staff made from the shin of a battle-dragon. I start with surprise, for the face of the Dragon Oracle is that of Mr. Manto. The only difference is the white sash that binds the blind prophet's eyes. The Dragon Oracle points to the multicolored fire dancing in the cauldron, causing it to flare and jump even higher. When he speaks, his voice echoes like a struck gong.

"The hand is in the heart."

As the Dragon Oracle intones the words, I recognize them as the final portion of the prophecy pieced together by Mr. Manto, a world and countless millennia away. But before I can unravel the meaning of his words, I am overwhelmed by the smell of rotting limes. Suddenly a disembodied six-fingered right hand emerges from the sacred fire and strikes with the speed of a cobra, grabbing me by the neck. I try to pry the phantom hand from about my throat, only to have it tighten its grip. I struggle to free myself as the life is throttled from my body. . . .

And I awoke from my dream to find Hexe leaning over me, his eyes rolled back in his head, as his gauntlet-clad hand squeezed my windpipe.

Chapter 25

I tried to call out his name, but all that came out was a strangled groan. I kicked and flailed at him, but he did not let go. Just as my vision started to turn gray around the edges, there was a horrific screeching noise and Scratch launched himself at Hexe, beating his master about the head and shoulders with his batlike wings while raking him with his claws.

Hexe let go of me and jumped off the bed, cursing in Kymeran as he grappled with Scratch. Blood poured down his face and neck and onto his naked chest and arms from the dozens of deep scratches that the familiar had dealt him. His eyes had dropped back down, but were as glassy and unfocused as those of a sleepwalker.

"You dare attack your master, hellspawn!" Hexe shouted indignantly as he tore the madly clawing winged cat off his head and hurled it to the floor.

"I don't know who *you* are, buddy," the familiar hissed, his eyes glowing like live coals, "but you're *not* my master!"

As Hexe lifted his left hand, I saw the flicker of hellfire ignite in his palm. Scratch flattened his ears against his skull and growled in preparation of a second attack.

I tried to shout, but the best I could do was a hoarse croak that made me grimace in pain. "Hexe! Don't do it!" To my relief, his eyes regained their focus and his left hand dropped to his side, extinguishing the flame.

"You did it, Tate!" Scratch said. "You woke him up!"

"What—what happened?" Hexe winced as he touched his face, staring in bafflement at the blood staining his left hand. His eyes jerked in my direction, only to widen at the sight of the bruises that now ringed my neck. He then looked down at his right hand, to find its fingers still moving of their own accord, as if trying to strangle an unseen throat. With a shout of wordless horror, Hexe dashed from the bedroom.

"What's wrong with him, Scratch?" I rasped.

"The boss is possessed," the familiar replied. "But not by a demon; I'd recognize the smell if he was. It's some kind of evil spirit—" Whatever else Scratch had to say after that was abruptly drowned out by the bansheelike screech of a power tool.

"He's in my studio!" I exclaimed. I leapt from the bed and hurried down the hall without bothering to throw on my housecoat, Scratch following at my heels.

As I entered the room, I saw Hexe standing naked at my workbench, brandishing one of the cordless power saws. He held his right hand away from his body, staring in disgust at its wildly writhing fingers as if they were venomous snakes.

"Hexe! Put that down!" I croaked, my voice still rough from being throttled. "What are you doing?"

"I *have* to do this, Tate! Don't stop me!" he replied, gesturing with the power tool. "The darkness is in my hand—I can feel it—it's crawling up my arm, creeping into my brain, and spreading through my heart. I can hear it inside my head—it's whispering to me—it's telling me things—promising me things—it wants me to hurt you and the baby—I can't let that happen—I *won't* let that happen—!"

As if in response, the gauntleted hand suddenly lunged at his left forearm, as if to knock the saw away. Hexe responded by menacing his right hand with the spinning blade, and it promptly recoiled.

"You were right, Tate!" Hexe exclaimed, his eyes filled with a terrible determination. "I have to get rid of the gauntlet—before it takes me over completely and makes me hurt you and the baby again!"

"Hexe! No! Don't do it!" I pleaded.

"There's no other way!" he replied. "The voice is too strong—if I don't do it now, it'll be too late!"

"Miss Timmy—? What on earth is going on? Oh. My."

I turned to see Clarence standing in the open doorway of the studio, dressed in his pajamas and bedroom slippers, his eyes agog at the sight of a naked, crazed Hexe wielding a live power tool. Hexe used the distraction to bring the saw down on his right forearm, just above the Gauntlet of Nydd's white-gold cuff. There was a sickening crunching sound, followed by an agonized scream as blood sprayed across the floor. I added my screams to Hexe's own and covered my eyes, unable to bear the sight of the saw blade ripping through unresisting flesh and bone.

The gauntleted hand dropped to the floor with a heavy thud, only to promptly right itself and scuttle away like a silver-clad spider. Scratch gave an angry yowl and pounced on the amputated limb, sinking his fangs deep into the back of the hand, just like a house cat attacking a rat. The fingers of the severed hand wriggled frantically for a few seconds, like the legs of a crab, before finally going limp.

The power saw slipped from Hexe's grip mere seconds before he collapsed. I knelt beside him, desperately trying to stem the lifeblood spurting from the stump of his right wrist. I felt something drape across my shoulders, and I realized that I had just been covered with a blanket. Suddenly Clarence was there, kneeling beside me with a first-aid kit.

"It'll be all right, Miss Timmy," he said reassuringly as he placed a tourniquet fashioned from one of his ties about Hexe's forearm. "I was an Eagle Scout, in my day—always be prepared."

"I had to do it. . . . There was no other way . . ." Hexe mumbled, his golden eyes seeming to grow paler with each spurt of blood.

"Hold on, Hexe," I said, squeezing his remaining hand as hard as I could. "Don't you *dare* die on me."

"Boss—are you in there?" Scratch mewed, butting his head against his master's bloodied chin. "Can you hear me?"

"I'm still here, old friend," Hexe replied with a faint smile as he squeezed my hand, his voice sounding frighteningly weak. "I'm not going anywhere."

"You better not," I said through the tears streaming down my cheeks. "You've got a son to raise, you know." Suddenly Hexe's eyelids flickered and his eyes once again rolled back, exposing their whites. "He's going into shock, Clarence," I said anxiously.

"You *both* are," he replied quietly.

With a start, I realized he was right. The initial burst of

adrenaline that had first spurred me to fight, and then kept me on my feet, was finally starting to disappear. I felt like Alice tumbling down the rabbit hole, watching helplessly as the light from the world above dwindled into nothingness. As my vision telescoped down from gray into black, I thought I could hear the Queen of Hearts shouting somewhere off in the distance: *Off with his hand! Off with his hand!*

Chapter 26

I woke up to find myself in one of the recovery rooms at Golgotham General, the community hospital that served the city-state's diverse population. I had been there, once before, when a demon broke my arm. I sat up straight, gasping like a swimmer coming up for air. "The baby . . . ? Hexe . . . ? Are they—?"

"Your baby is fine, Miss Timmy," Clarence said reassuringly from his post at my bedside. "As for your young gentleman, I would say he's in amazing spirits for someone who has just chopped off his own hand."

I looked to where Clarence was pointing and saw Hexe sitting propped up in the hospital bed beside me, talking to his parents. His face was still pale but no longer bloody and the bites and claw marks Scratch dealt him had already disappeared, as if nothing had happened. The same could not be said for his right wrist, which now ended in a gauze-wrapped stump. Upon seeing I was awake, Hexe tossed aside his blankets with his remaining hand and swung his legs out of the bed. He took a couple of steps, only to have his knees buckle. Captain Horn stepped forward, helping to steady him. Hexe flashed his father a brief but grateful smile.

"Thank God you're alive; I was so afraid I'd lost you," I sobbed as he wrapped his arms about me.

"Don't cry, Tate," he said soothingly, wiping at my tears with his left hand. "Everything's going to be better now."

"But your hand—!"

"What's done is done," he replied. "Ever since I put on the Gauntlet of Nydd, my mind has been filled with a thick fog. Sometimes I was aware of what was going on, but most of the time it was like I was watching myself in a dream. I could hear horrible, ugly words coming out of my mouth, and at the same time I was wondering 'why am I saying this to her?' It broke my heart to see the hurt look on your face, but I still couldn't stop the words from spilling out. I realize my saying 'I'm sorry' doesn't begin to cover everything I've done and what I've put you through—"

"Of course I forgive you," I said, cutting him off in mid-apology. "I knew something was wrong. *You* would never hurt me or our baby."

"I had my forensics team go over the gauntlet," Captain Horn interjected. "Turns out there was a puppetry spell woven into the original enchantment that allowed the spell-caster to exert control over whoever wore the gauntlet. I've never seen such an insidious bit of spellwork in all my years of investigation. Do you think this Madam Erys is the person responsible?"

"It *has* to be her," Hexe replied. "She's the one who approached me about the Gauntlet of Nydd and arranged for Moot to do the surgery."

"I looked into this woman—there's no evidence of her living either here or the Faubourg, at least under that name. It's like she simply walked, full grown, from the Outer Dark. The landlord who actually owns the glover's shop on Shoemaker Lane says she only paid him to rent the storefront for a month or two, and used cash to do it with. As soon as the two of you are clearheaded enough, I'll send our picture-maker around to do an automatic drawing of the suspect, so my people will have an idea of who to look for."

"First things first, though," Lady Syra said firmly. "Once news of Hexe losing his hand begins to spread, both of you are going to need charms and spells for protection. You have plenty of enemies—not all of them Maladanti—who will no doubt make a move against you when they realize you are defenseless."

"What do you propose we do?" Hexe asked.

"Just leave it to me. I *am* the Witch Queen, after all."

After being released from Golgotham General, Hexe and I rode back to Lady Syra's apartment building in her private

coach, driven by the albino centauride Illuminata. The panacea I'd been given at the hospital had healed me, inside
and out, but left me feeling like I'd just finished fifty laps in
a swimming pool. Suddenly I felt the baby kick. I automatically reached out to place Hexe's hand on my belly, only to
have my fingers close upon thin air.

Lady Syra lived on Beke Street in a fifteen story neo-
Gothic apartment building. Like my parents, her home was
the penthouse, which was crowned by a copper-sheathed
observatory that she used in order to draw up astrology
charts for her clients. As we entered the ground floor lobby,
the elevator doors began to open, prompting Hexe to hide
his missing hand in his jacket pocket.

A second later Syra's fellow tenant, Giles Gruff, accompanied by Mayor Lash, stepped out into the lobby. While Giles
was dapper as ever, monocle in place and monogrammed cane
in hand, Lash was nervously working the five-foot-long peri-
winkle blue braided ponytail he wore about his shoulders like
a rosary. The two politicians were so heavily engaged in their
conversation they did not seem to notice our little contingent.

"But I've *always* been able to count on you delivering the
satyr and faun vote in the past, Giles—!" The mayor protested.

"Well, you should have thought about *that* before you
decided to get into bed with Ronald Chess!" Giles replied
sharply. "Because of *you*, my niece was kicked out of her
apartment!"

"How else could I afford to campaign against O'Fae?"
Lash snapped. "Do you have any idea how many pots of
gold that sawed-off shyster has in his war coffer?"

Lady Syra scowled and mock-coughed into her fist.
Mayor Lash started at the sound, his face losing all color as
he realized who was standing before him. Giles, on the
other hand, merely smirked as his companion quickly scurried across the lobby and out the front door.

"Your Majesty," the satyr said, touching the brim of his
top hat with his cane.

The first thing I noticed upon reaching Lady Syra's penthouse was that there was no minotaur stationed outside the
front door.

"What happened to Elmer?" I asked.

"I had to let the poor dear go," she explained. "He was the proverbial bull in a china shop—always getting his horns caught in the chandeliers. He's now working as a longshoreman down on the docks. I think he's much happier there, to tell you the truth."

As we entered the apartment, we were greeted by Lady Syra's manservant, Amos, whose welcoming smile quickly dissolved as he caught sight of the beige-colored arm sock that covered the stump of Hexe's right hand.

"My son's condition is not to be discussed. Is that understood?" Lady Syra stated firmly.

"Of course, Your Majesty," Amos replied with a bow of his maroon buzz cut.

"Come with me," Lady Syra said, motioning for us to follow her up the spiral staircase that led to her workshop.

The inside of the observatory reminded me of an inverted copper bowl and was dominated by an antique sixteen-inch refracting telescope measuring twenty feet in length. The gleaming brass eyepiece was positioned six feet off the floor and was accessible only by a wrought-iron gangway. The retractable roof was decorated with murals depicting the zodiac and other astrological signs, and the walls were lined with bookcases, pigeonhole bins full of rolled-up charts, and a glass display case containing a taxidermied crocodile—the hallmark of the Kymeran archmage. Lady Syra made a beeline to a large horseshoe-shaped table at the foot of the telescope.

"Perhaps I could have prevented you losing your hand if I'd cast your chart as a boy," she said as she rifled through the collection of alchemical equipment, magical ingredients, and astrological charts before her. "But I have learned it isn't wise to know too much of the future, especially of those you love. The temptation to muck about with that which has yet to be can be very strong, and often quite futile. If Greek tragedy has proven anything, it's that attempting to evade the inevitable is what brings it about."

"But didn't you cast a horoscope for my father?" Hexe countered.

"There are different types of charts," she replied. "The

one I cast for your father was little more than a toy. And I certainly wouldn't have given it to him as a birthday present if it revealed his death, or that of a loved one. In any case, blaming myself for not foreseeing what has happened does not change the fact it *has* occurred. This Erys woman, who-ever she may be, seems determined to destroy you, and I'm not going to allow her to do any more damage than she al-ready has." After a few more moments spent rummaging about, she produced a small brass bowl, a large bottle of rosewater, an organic sponge, and a box of henna pens. "Okay—I need you two to strip down."

"Down to what?" I asked uneasily.

"As far as you're willing to go," she replied. "I'll need access to your entire torso. But first use the sponge to cleanse yourself with the rosewater."

A few minutes later both Hexe and I were down to our skivvies and smelling like a rose garden.

"Are you ready?" Lady Syra asked.

"Take care of Tate first," Hexe said firmly. "I can wait."

His mother nodded her understanding and motioned for me to step forward. "Okay—let's get started." She un-capped the first henna pen and started to chant in Kymeran. As the tip of the applicator made contact with my skin, I felt an electric prickling that made the hair on my arms rise. For the next hour Lady Syra drew a series of interlocking symbols and patterns over my breasts, belly, and back, never once halting her sonorous incantation. By the time she was finished I was covered with an elaborate henna tattoo from my shoulder blades to my hips, with specific attention paid to my heart, spine, lungs, and belly.

"That should protect you from the majority of curses for the next thirty days, or when the temporary tattoos wear off, whichever comes first," Lady Syra said, looking consider-ably drained from when we'd first started. "Your turn," she said, motioning for Hexe to take my place.

As I waited for the protective wards inked onto my body to finish drying—it wouldn't do to have the symbols smudged—I noticed a jumble of old photographs mixed in with the arcana littering Lady Syra's workbench. The one on the top of the pile showed a five-year-old boy with pur-ple hair and gold eyes, dressed in a *Star Wars* T-shirt, sitting on the lap of a dignified older Kymeran with dark blue hair, golden eyes, and a closely manicured German goatee. With a start, I realized I was looking at Hexe and his grandfather, Lord Eben.

The next photograph was in black-and-white and showed a much younger Syra seated at a table in a restaurant, enjoying a cocktail and the company of Lou Reed and Andy Warhol. I flipped the picture over and read the notation: *Elaine's*. Reed, resplendent in black leather, had one arm about Syra, and the two seemed to be sharing a laugh while Warhol stared directly into the camera, looking far more otherworldly than the teenaged witch seated at his elbow.

The third photograph was also in black-and-white and showed three Kymerans—two men and a woman—gathered about one end of the formal dining table in the boardinghouse. It was strange to see Esau as a young man, as he was almost unrecognizable from the person I had come to know. It was not so much his youth that made the difference, but the fact the Esau in the photograph was . . . happy. Seated opposite him was a young man with a Beatles haircut and pair of tinted Ben Franklin glasses. It wasn't until I saw his long, elegant fingers that I recognized him as the drug-addled, alcoholic Dr. Moot. However, the real shock came when I looked at the woman, seated between them. Although she was a little younger in the photo, I had no problems identifying her. I flipped the photo over and saw it was dated forty-five years earlier.

I turned to look at Lady Syra, who had just finished inscribing the last protective sigil on her son's body. "Who is this woman in this picture?" I asked.

"That's Nina," she replied with a sad little sigh. "She was my brother's wife."

"But that's impossible," I said as I handed the snapshot to Hexe. "That's Madam Erys."

"Tate's right," he said excitedly. "This is the woman who gave me the Gauntlet of Nydd. But how can it possibly be the same woman—? She's dead—isn't she?"

"Oh—Nina's not dead," Lady Syra replied. "Well, not *exactly*, anyway."

Chapter 27

The Golden Years was located on the corner of Pearl and Hag, and, from the outside, resembled a Gilded Age hotel more than a nursing home. A twenty-foot-tall marble statue of a hooded and berobed figure leaning on a staff in its left hand while holding aloft an hourglass in its right stood in the center of the spacious lobby. At its foot was a reception station, manned by various Golgothamites in nurse's whites.

I glanced around the handsomely appointed lobby and noticed that most of the older people seemed to be Kymeran, their once-vibrantly colored hair now faded to pastel. A large knot of them where gathered about the flat-screen TV hanging over the fireplace, watching *Wheel of Fortune*, while smaller clusters were scattered about reading books, talking among themselves, or playing board games like Parcheesi and the Game of Thirty. As we approached the front desk, several of them stopped what they were doing to watch us, with expectant looks on their faces, only to return to their pastimes once they realized we weren't family members. But I also saw flickers of confusion, fear, and mistrust in some eyes as well, and I wondered if a human had ever set foot inside the facility before.

"Yes, may I help you?" the cyclopean receptionist asked, rising from her seat to greet us. Like most of the cyclopes living in Golgotham, she stood nearly seven feet tall and was built like a linebacker. A name tag affixed to her blouse identified her as Polyphema.

"We're looking for a certain patient who's supposed to be here—"

"We don't have patients here at Golden Years, Serenity," she replied. "We have residents. But I should be able to help you locate who you're looking for. May I have the resident's name and your relation to them?"

"Her name is Nina, and she's my aunt," Hexe explained. "She was placed here by her husband, my uncle, thirty-five years ago."

The receptionist blinked her solitary eye, revealing a preference for dusky purple eye shadow, and typed the information into her desktop computer. "Ah, yes. She's one of our Perpetual Care residents in the Eternal Rest ward. Please follow me, Serenity."

As we followed Polyphema through the lobby toward the elevators, we were approached by a Kymeran nurse pushing a very old warlock in a wheelchair. Although he was bald as an egg, he had a long, flowing pale green beard and bristling brows to match. His hands were encased in what looked like a cross between children's snow mittens and boxing gloves that were laced tightly shut. As the old warlock was rolled past us, he turned his head to stare at Hexe with glaucoma-clouded eyes the color of mutton jade and said something in Kymeran, his voice a rasping croak.

"This place reminds me of my grandfather's last days," Hexe muttered to me under his breath as we waited for an elevator to arrive. "He succumbed to the gazing sickness toward the end—it's not unlike what your people call Alzheimer's. He became unstuck in time, unaware of when and where he was—we had to bind his hands to keep him from casting spells against threats that didn't exist. His mind was gone, but the magic was still there. . . ."

"The old man—what did he say to you?" I asked.

"'My king,'" he replied grimly.

The Eternal Rest ward was located on the sublevel of the facility. As the elevator doors opened we were greeted by the sight of a scarlet-haired Kymeran dressed in orderly's whites with his feet up on his desk, reading a Louis L'Amour paperback. Around his neck hung a large, old-fashioned key, like the ones used to unlock treasure chests.

"Sorry, Nurse Polyphema," he said as he awkwardly righted himself.

"As well you should be, Hark," she replied frostily. "I have two visitors for the Eternal Rest ward. I need the manifest."

"Yes, ma'am," the orderly said meekly as he removed the key from about his neck and handed her the clipboard from his desk.

At the end of the hallway was a large, featureless metal door. Upon the orderly unlocking it, the door swung open with a squeal of rusty hinges, revealing absolute darkness beyond its threshold. The orderly then flipped the light switch next to the door and rows of fluorescent lights flickered to life, illuminating a vast chamber filled with row upon row of glass caskets, all of them occupied.

I stared in stunned horror at the various figures in repose. There were men, women, and even children from all the various races that comprised the citizenry of Golgotham, as well as humans, dressed in everything from pantaloons and knee-hose to the latest in modern fashion. I noticed that while some of them had long beards, hair, and fingernails, others were neatly coifed and manicured. Seeing the look on my face, Hexe took my hand and gave it a reassuring squeeze.

"A-are they dead?" I whispered.

"Yes—and no," Nurse Polyphema replied. "All the residents in the Eternal Rest ward have been placed under a sleeping spell, balanced forever between life and death. They neither age nor decay, but instead exist in a perpetual state of suspended animation. However, their hair and nails *do* continue to grow. Those whose loved ones have paid for perpetual care are groomed by our staff every six weeks, as you can see. While most of the residents in this ward were cursed, the others were dying, and put to sleep by their loved ones in order to keep them from breathing their last breath."

"Why would someone want to do that to someone they loved?" I frowned.

"Some simply have a hard time letting go, especially if the sleeper was taken from them too soon," the cyclops replied, gesturing to a nearby casket that contained the sleeping form of a small Kymeran boy still dressed in knee socks and a sailor suit. "Many lift the spell when they, themselves, are close to death, so that they and their loved one will pass on at the same time."

"That's the saddest and sweetest thing I've ever heard," I said, forcing down the lump rising in my throat.

Nurse Polyphema glanced down at the clipboard she was carrying. "According to the manifest, Madam Nina should be on this aisle. Number two forty-seven . . ."

Hexe stepped forward and peered down through the glass lid of the casket at the sleeping form of a middle-aged Kymeran woman dressed in clothes from the late seventies.

"That's not Nina," he said, pointing to the sleeper's green hair.

Polyphema's single eye widened in surprise. "That's Dyad! She's one of our staff—or, rather, she *was*. She was the groomer for the perpetual care residents. She walked off the job without giving notice a couple months ago. Never even came to pick up her last check."

"Is it possible Nina somehow revived while Dyad was grooming her?" I asked.

Hexe shook his head. "From all accounts, Nina was brain-dead. She was nothing more than an empty husk. My uncle put her under a sleeping spell before her heart stopped beating. Besides, even if she *did* somehow manage to revive, why would she place the groomer under a spell and exchange places with her?"

"Well, *someone* managed to revive her," I replied. "The question is *who* and *why*?"

Upon arriving back home, we were greeted at the door by Clarence, adorned in one of his Hawaiian shirts. "Welcome back home, Master Hexe, Miss Timmy. I trust you both are feeling better?"

"You don't *have* to be a butler anymore, Clarence," I pointed out. "You're retired, remember?"

"Yes, but I feel somewhat at a loss, otherwise. It's going to take me some time to get used to the idea. Please indulge an old man while he adjusts, if you will."

"Whatever floats your boat," I said as I gave him a peck on the cheek.

"Thank you, Miss Timmy."

" 'Miss Timmy'?" Hexe chuckled, raising his eyebrow.

"It's a long story," I sighed.

"By the way, Master Hexe," Clarence said, "a young gen-

tleman by the name of Bartho stopped by earlier with a
package for you. I placed it on your desk. Now, if you don't
mind, I'm going to finish polishing the silver."

"You know, I could get really used to having a butler,"
Hexe said with a laugh. "Clarence is nowhere near as snarky
as Scratch."

"I heard that," the familiar announced as he emerged
from the shadows. "How are you doing, boss?"

"You tell me," Hexe said, taking the stump of his right
wrist from its hiding place in his pocket.

"Don't take this the wrong way, boss—but you're better
off without it," Scratch said matter-of-factly.

"I realize that now, old friend," Hexe sighed. "All my life
I've favored my right hand; but, in the end, it was my left
hand that remained loyal to me. But the question is—what
do I do *now*?"

Suddenly my dream from the night before flashed before
my mind's eye and I remembered the words spoken by Mr.
Manto's dream avatar. "Last night—before everything went
nuts—I had a dream. Except it was more like a vision. I
should have mentioned it earlier, but with all the crazy shit
that's been going on, I pushed it to the back burner.

"In my dream I was in a temple overlooking a strange
city—I think it was in Kymera, because I could see dragons
flying overhead. Mr. Manto was there, except he *wasn't* Mr.
Manto, but something called a Dragon Oracle. . . ."

"Did he say anything to you in your dream?" Hexe
asked intently.

"Yes. He said 'the hand is in the heart.' I don't know what
it means, but it must mean *something* because I can remember it. Mr. Manto says that prophecy can only truly be heard
and understood when the time is right."

A pensive look crossed Hexe's face. "*The hand is in the
heart . . .*" I couldn't tell if he was speaking to me or simply
talking out loud. Suddenly he broke into a smile and hurried down the hallway. His office was pretty much as he'd
left it the night before. "Now that the gauntlet is gone, I'm
thinking faster and clearer than I have in weeks," he said
excitedly as he bent to gather up the books strewn across
the floor. "It's as if scales have fallen from my eyes. 'The
hand is in the heart.' Of *course* it is!"

As he plopped the stack of books down onto his desk, he

accidentally knocked a thick manila envelope onto the floor, spilling forth a number of full-color eight by ten photographs.

"This must be the package Bartho dropped off earlier," I said as I bent to retrieve the pictures. What at first looked like nothing but photos of people going about their daily business on the streets of Manhattan, on closer inspection revealed semitransparent, phantomlike figures, sometimes in the background, or occasionally in the foreground. Some of the wraiths were little more than blurs, but others were easily identifiable. There were Lenape Indians walking unseen among the stockbrokers of Wall Street; Colonial-era knickerbockers in tricorn hats and square-buckled shoes smoking long-stemmed clay pipes in the shadow of City Hall; women in hoopskirts, men in Victorian top hats and muttonchops, and flappers in cloche hats rubbing intangible elbows with the oblivious bike messengers, aspiring rap stars, and harried office workers thronging West Broadway. However, of all the ghostly images, there was only one that made my blood run cold.

"Look at this!" I said, holding out the picture to Hexe with a trembling hand. "Do you see anyone you know?"

He scowled at the photograph of Perdition Street, with its usual hectic mix of looky-loos and native Golgothamites going about their day-to-day business. His eyes widened as he spotted the image of Erys threading her way through the crowds. But, more important, was the spectral passenger she carried piggyback, his arms and legs wrapped tightly about her torso. Even when as substantial as morning fog, there was no mistaking the identity of Erys' phantom rider.

"*Esau*," Hexe whispered.

Chapter 28

After finding the snapshot among Bartho's prints, Hexe and I lost no time returning to his mother's apartment. Amos ushered us into the sunken living room, where we found Lady Syra sipping a demitasse of civet coffee and listening to *Aladdin Sane* on the stereo.

"There can be no doubting it—that is my brother," Lady Syra said grimly as she studied the photograph. "And that is, most definitely, his wife, Nina."

"But isn't he trapped in the Infernal Region?" I asked.

"Physically, yes," she replied. "But his spirit is another matter entirely. It appears he has regained access to this world by taking possession of the perfect empty vessel."

"I always thought Erys' mannerisms were a bit stiff, but I just thought that was because she had a stick up her ass," I said with a humorless laugh. "Now I realize she's another one of Esau's mindless meat puppets, like the Sons of Adam. It also explains why she kept giving me the stink eye. But why did he come back—? It can't be easy for him to cross dimensions, even in spirit form."

"Tate's got a point," Hexe agreed. "I know Uncle Esau despises me, but expending that kind of energy just to try to drive me to the Left Hand path seems kind of crazy, even for *him*. There's *got* to be something *else* he's trying to accomplish. But what?"

"If I know my brother, whatever it is will be operatic and apocalyptic." Lady Syra scowled. "Not to mention extremely inconvenient."

*   *   *

Upon leaving Lady Syra's apartment, Hexe and I hailed a hansom. Normally, we would have walked home, but my back and feet were killing me and the idea of waddling six city blocks, the last two uphill, did not tantalize me in the least. However, as we reached Perdition, we were forced to come to a halt as the broad street was jammed with people waving picket signs.

"What's the holdup?" Hexe asked the cabbie.

"There's some kind of protest going on outside the bank," the centaur replied. "It looks like Seamus O'Fae is involved."

"We'll get out here," Hexe said, handing our driver a ten-dollar bill.

As I climbed down from the hansom, I could see Seamus, dressed in an impeccable emerald-green Armani suit, standing on the marble steps that led to the doors of First Midas, Golgotham's only bank. The leprechaun chieftain was carrying a bullhorn, which he used to address the throng of angry protestors that now spilled out onto the street. One of the faces I recognized among the picketers belonged to Octavia.

"Good people of Golgotham!" Seamus shouted, his amplified voice ringing out over the noise of the crowd. "Are ye goin' to stand by and let Mayor Lash sell ye out? Golden Egg Realty—a shell corporation owned by Hizzoner—is the company that sold Machen Arms to Ronald Chess, for over three million dollars! Chess then turned around and raised rent a *thousand* percent and threw hardworkin' Golgothamites out of their homes and into the streets! I ask ye, my friends, does it sound like Mayor Lash has Golgotham's best interests at heart—or his own?"

As the crowd waved their signs and shouted in angry agreement, the leprechaun strutted back and forth, nodding his coppery head in approval, like a banty rooster on patrol. He might come up only to my knee, but Seamus O'Fae radiated the kind of charisma you'd expect from a born politician and lived up to the nickname Little Big Man.

Just then the door to the bank opened and its president, Mayor Lash, stormed out onto the front steps, his face livid. "Damn you, O'Fae!" he shouted. "Take your rabble to Blarney's!"

"What's the matter, Mr. Mayor?" Seamus replied in a taunting voice. "Yer not afraid of answerin' to yer constituents, are ye?"

Before Lash could respond, the crowd suddenly parted itself to allow Beadle Elok to approach. "Here now! What's going on here?" he growled, calling for order by holding his staff of office aloft.

"It's about time you got here!" Mayor Lash snapped disdainfully. "I demand that you arrest Seamus O'Fae for disturbing the peace and unlawful assembly!"

"It's only unlawful if there's no permit, Your Honor," Elok reminded the mayor. The beadle then turned to address Seamus. "*Do* you have an assembly permit, Councilman?"

"As a matter of fact, I do," O'Fae replied as he handed the beadle a folded piece of parchment.

Elok unfolded the document and stared at it for a long moment while nodding his head.

"Well? Don't just stand there—arrest him!" Mayor Lash demanded petulantly.

"I'm afraid I can't do that, Your Honor," Elok replied. "The GoBOO has granted Councilman O'Fae the right to assemble in protest against you."

"That's impossible!" Lash sputtered. "I never signed off on such a thing!"

"It didn't require your signature to make it official, Your Honor, only the acting justicar's—and there's Lady Syra's signature and seal on the bottom," Elok explained, handing the parchment over to Lash for inspection.

"This is an outrage!" The mayor was by this point trembling like a furious tuning fork. "If you won't clear this mob from my place of business, I'll call in the PTU and have *them* handle the situation!"

"I wouldn't do that if I were you, Mayor," said an all-too-familiar voice from the crowd.

The picketers began to murmur among themselves as Boss Marz stepped forward, flanked by his lieutenant, Gaza. His familiar, riding astride his shoulder, turned and flashed its fangs at the assembled protestors in an angry grin.

"What are *you* doing here, Marz?" Mayor Lash asked stonily.

"I merely wish to add my voice to those asking why you would betray your own kind to the numps—and in an election year, no less," the crime lord replied with an unpleasant smile.

Lash's face went from bright red to white as paper as he turned on his heel and hurried back up the stairs into the bank, his braided ponytail flapping along behind him like the tail on a kite.

"I commend your stance on gentrification, Councilman," Boss Marz said, turning to address Seamus. "You can count on the Maladanti in the coming election."

"I don't need the likes of you stumpin' for me, Marz," Seamus replied sharply, scowling at the Maladanti like he was something he'd just scraped off the bottom of his shoe.

"I wouldn't be so sure of that, if I was you, Councilman," Marz warned. "The Maladanti can be a powerful ally at the voting booths—or a dreadful enemy."

"And with an ally like ye, who needs a foe, eh?" the leprechaun said, spitting on the ground for emphasis. "Go on with ye, Marz. I'll sink or swim on me own."

"Have it your way, little man," the Maladanti snarled. "But don't let it be said you weren't given your chance."

With that Boss Marz turned and headed back through the crowd, which recoiled en masse, as if he were a deadly serpent. As he scanned the picketers, his gaze fell upon Hexe and me, and a nasty grin spread across his face. Marz raised his right hand, as if in greeting, then slowly drew his left index finger across the wrist in a mock amputation.

Needless to say, neither one of us was in the best of moods after our latest brush with the Maladanti. In fact, we argued the entire way back to the house.

"I want you to go back uptown to your parents," Hexe said insistently. "It's not safe in Golgotham right now."

"And what makes you think I'd be any safer up there?" I countered. "If Esau can make it all the way from the Infernal Region, crosstown traffic isn't going to be much of a deterrent to him."

"I just don't want you and the baby to get mixed up in whatever batshit evil scheme my uncle has up his sleeve. And that doesn't even factor in the Maladanti."

"I get a funny feeling I'm on the hit list, no matter *what* we do. Your uncle seems to have a really creepy thing for me," I said with a shudder. "I'm also pretty sure that part of Esau's plan is to split us up."

"I think the old chuffer can't stand to see anyone happy," he said sourly.

"Besides, I can't find anyone either willing or qualified to deliver our baby outside Golgotham," I pointed out.

"I still say it's too dangerous," Hexe insisted.

"You're probably right. But I'm *still* not packing up and heading home to Mother. I might not be able to sling spells like you used to, but I do have *some* magic I can bring to the table."

We were still arguing the matter as we entered the house, only to fall silent at the sound of laughter coming from the kitchen. Upon investigating, we found Mr. Manto sitting at the table next to Clarence, drinking tea.

"Aloysius!" Hexe exclaimed in surprise. "What are *you* doing upstairs?"

"I came to bear witness," Mr. Manto replied. As he turned to smile at us, I could tell the old soothsayer was flying high on diviner's sage again. "And also to spend some time in the company of this charming young fellow," Mr. Manto leaned over and patted Clarence on the leg. Clarence's cheeks turned pink, but he did not offer to remove the older man's hand from his thigh, "as he is an excellent conversationalist and makes a damn fine cup of tea."

"Bear witness to what?" I frowned.

Just as I finished the sentence I was gripped by a strong cramp in the middle of my back and upper abdomen that seemed to come out of nowhere. I gave a sudden gasp of pain and grabbed at the kitchen counter to steady myself. Suddenly Hexe was there, slipping his arm around me as he helped me to a chair.

"To that," the oracle replied simply. "The dawn of the coming age."

"Tate—are you all right?" Hexe asked anxiously.

"I'm scared the baby's coming," I groaned. "The doctor said I was farther along than I realized, but it's *still* too soon. . . ."

"Not by Kymeran standards—our women normally carry a child for six months."

"*Now* you tell me!" I grunted.

"Stay right here and let Aloysius and Clarence look after

you—I'll go upstairs and pack your overnight case, and then I'm taking you to the Temple of Nana."

"The Temple of who—?"

"The Kymeran goddess of childbirth," he explained as he hurried out of the kitchen. "Her priestesses are trained as midwives. Nearly every Kymeran child in Golgotham is born in her temple."

"Is there anything I can do for you, Miss Timmy?" Clarence asked solicitously.

"Yes, you can call my parents and let them know what's going on."

"Are you sure you want me to do that?"

"My mother may be a massively insecure, social-climbing racist, but she *is* my mother and she *does* care about me, in her own weird, fucked-up way. Besides, you're probably still advising my father over the phone as to which tie he should wear."

"You know me too well, Miss Timmy." Clarence's smile disappeared as I grimaced in discomfort as yet another wave of pain radiated through my body. "There, there," he said as he patted my hand. "Everything's going to be all right."

I looked past him to where Mr. Manto sat, still sipping his tea. "Is it?" I asked anxiously. The oracle did not answer, but instead simply smiled, his pupils so dilated they eclipsed the whites of his eyes.

Chapter 29

"There's nothing to be afraid of, Tate," Hexe said as he helped me into the hansom. "The Daughters will see to everything—it'll all be over soon."

"Where to, Serenity?" Kidron asked.

"The Temple of Nana—and watch the potholes!"

The centaur snorted his understanding, breaking into a brisk canter.

"How do you feel?" Hexe asked, eyeing me cautiously.

"Like I'm trying to lay an egg," I grunted. "Honey, I should have said something before now—but I thought we had more time than this. There's something I need to tell you about the baby. When I had an ultrasound . . . I found out our baby is human. He only has ten fingers and toes. I'm sorry. I should have told you sooner . . . but I was afraid. . . ."

Hexe merely laughed and wrapped his arms around me. "It doesn't matter to me if our child is human or Kymeran. I don't even care if he's born a norlock. The only thing that really matters to me is that he arrives in this world safe and sound. That's it. I surrendered my right hand because trying to keep it would rob me of the woman I love; you gave up your inheritance because keeping it meant giving up everything that makes you happy. So what if our child doesn't have magic? He's not going to have a million dollars, either. That just means he'll be like every other kid that comes into this world. And you know what? I'm good with that."

"You know why I love you?" I managed to smile, despite the contractions. "Because you can make chopping off your

hand and getting disinherited sound like the best decisions
we've ever made."

The Temple of Nana was located, appropriately enough, on
Maiden Lane, home to Golgotham's self-segregated female
communities, such as the Amazons, Valkyries, and fauns. It
was a neoclassical rotunda, its façade of brick covered in
stucco, with a roof of slate and lead. The central rotunda
stood a hundred feet high, with a domed and balustraded
roof. The main entrance was an oval-shaped door that was
so narrow Hexe and I had to enter single file. The foyer of
the temple was long and equally claustrophobic, its walls
barely three feet apart. There was no light at all in the cor-
ridor, save for the glimmer at its farthest point.

Upon reaching the end of the hallway, we found ourselves in the rotunda of the temple, which had ten separate
interior stories that opened onto a central atrium capped
by a rose-quartz skylight that tinged everything slightly
pink.

At the heart of the temple stood a fifty-foot statue of a
triple-visaged, four-armed woman. The far right face was
that of a young girl, the middle face that of an adult woman,
while the far left face belonged to an old woman. Both her
breasts were bared, the right full and pert, while the left teat
hung withered and flat. The goddess' first hand wielded a
pair of shears, her second cradled an infant, the third held a
length of umbilical cord, while the fourth and final hand
held a jug from which water eternally poured forth into the
fountain pool in which the idol stood.

At the foot of Nana was a receptionist desk you'd expect
to see in a medical clinic tended by a jade-haired Kymeran
woman dressed in a shell-pink sleeveless robe. As Hexe
helped me approach the desk, she left her seat to greet us.

"The Daughters of Nana welcome you to her temple,"
she said with a warm smile. "My name is Miri. How long
have you been in labor?"

"About an hour, I guess," I replied.

As she drew closer, a look of surprise flickered across
Miri's face. "I'm terribly sorry, but I'm afraid the Daughters
of Nana only accept *Kymeran* mothers."

Hexe stepped forward, his golden eyes flashing in anger. "She carries *my* child—is that not Kymeran enough for you?"

The priestess lowered her head in ritual obeisance. "Forgive me, Serenity. I did not realize." She quickly turned back to the desk and spoke into an intercom that echoed throughout the temple. "Sister Tipi, please report to the reception desk. . . ."

Within seconds an older Kymeran woman with hair the color of sunflowers and dressed in salmon-colored robes appeared, seemingly from nowhere. "Welcome, Serenity, to our temple. I am Sister Tipi, midwife emeritus of the Daughters of Nana. I shall be the one tending the birth of your child."

Without warning, I suddenly found myself doubled over in pain. As I cried out, I was dimly aware of a splashing sound, followed by an abrupt dampness on my thighs, and for a brief second I was afraid I had wet myself.

"Her water has broken. Page Sister Zena and have her report to birthing chamber three fifteen," Tipi said, checking the clipboard she was carrying.

"Right away, my sister," the priestess replied.

Tipi led us to an old-fashioned birdcage elevator that took us to the third floor of the temple, which was lined with numbered doorways, like a hotel. I wasn't sure what to expect in a temple dedicated to a goddess of childbirth, but was pleasantly surprised to discover the birthing chamber contained a bed, rocking chair, and a bassinette, as well as a foldout chair that converted into a bed, and an oversized Roman bathtub.

"This is your birthing chamber," Sister Tipi said. "Please make yourself as comfortable as you can while I prepare the birthing pool."

"You want me to give birth in the water?"

"It is the Kymeran way," the midwife-priestess explained. "It is a ritual that ties us to the island that birthed our race, millennia ago. It also has the added benefit of greatly reducing your pain, supporting your weight, and taking the stress off your perineum during labor."

"Now you're talking," I grunted as I eased myself into the rocking chair. "Anything that keeps me from getting stitches is A-okay with me."

Just then another Daughter of Nana, this one with moss

green hair and dressed in candy pink robes, entered the room.

"Hello, my name is Zena," she said as she took my hand. "I'm going to be your Pain-Taker."

I frowned and looked at Tipi. "But I thought *you* were going to be my midwife?"

"Yes, I am," the priestess replied. "Sister Zena is here to alleviate your pain during labor."

"You mean she's an anesthesiologist?"

"Something like that." Zena smiled. "Save that we Daughters of Nana do not utilize drugs of any kind."

Before I could ask any more questions, I was hit by another contraction. And this time it was a doozy. It felt like everything below my breastbone was in a giant clamp that was being gradually, but mercilessly, cranked shut. I gripped the armrests of the chair I was sitting in so hard I was surprised they didn't splinter. Zena quickly stepped forward and knelt before me, so that she could look into my eyes, and placed her hands atop my own.

"Take a deep breath and then let it out, slowly," she instructed in a calm voice.

I did as I was told, focusing on Zena's scent, which smelled of almonds and violets. The priestess tilted back her head, and her eyelids fluttered like the wings of a butterfly. As I exhaled, she inhaled, and the pain I was experiencing abruptly diminished, as if someone had turned a dial.

"How do you feel?" Zena asked, her pale gray eyes seeming a little less focused than before.

"Much better," I said gratefully. "Thank you."

As Zena stepped away, Sister Tipi came forward and placed her hand on my stomach. "Premature birth is common with children such as yours," she said matter-of-factly. "But your baby's heartbeat is strong. All is going well."

The attending Daughters of Nana helped me change out of my street clothes into a lightweight linen gown, and for the next few hours I lay propped up in the bed, riding out the contractions with the help of Zena. That's not to say it was a walk in the park. Although the Pain-Taker was able to reduce my discomfort considerably, she did not erase it entirely. Hexe stayed with me the whole time, doing his best to try to make me comfortable by putting cold compresses on my forehead and coaching me on my breathing, or bring-

ing me tea or ice chips whenever I got thirsty. Whenever the
pain got to be too much, Zena would quickly step in and
"take" it from me by placing her hands on me.

Throughout all this, Tipi monitored the progress of the
delivery by her own laying on of hands. The light in the
room was kept subdued, and hidden speakers piped in natural ambient noise, like the sound of rain, wind chimes, and
birdsong. This, combined with the calm, self-assured manner of the attending priestesses and Hexe's presence, helped
prevent me from feeling stressed. Still, although I wasn't in
a lot of pain, I *was* exhausted by the start of my sixth hour
of labor, and eager to get the whole thing over with.

"You're dilated to six centimeters," Tipi announced in
her no-nonsense voice. "The child will be coming soon. It's
time to get in the water." She and Zena lifted me off the
bed, one to each arm, and guided me to the waiting tub,
which was large enough to accommodate three people. As
I eased into the warm water, I grasped the handholds
molded into the tub to anchor myself.

"You, too, Serenity," Tipi said, motioning to Hexe. "Your
job is to catch your child as he shoots free, and bring him to
the surface and . . ." Her voice trailed off as she stared at the
stump where Hexe's right hand should be.

"And do what?" Hexe prodded.

". . . hand him to his mother."

"Don't worry, Sister," Hexe said as he stripped down to
his boxers. "I might be missing a hand, but I still have both
arms. I'm perfectly capable of catching my son when he
makes his appearance."

As Hexe climbed into the water, Zena positioned herself
behind the head of the birthing tub, within easy reach of me,
while Tipi stood at its foot. The midwife-priestess held up
her arms, her palms open and turned outward, and began
chanting in Kymeran.

"What's she saying?" I asked.

"It's the Invocation of Nana," Hexe explained. "I'll
translate; it won't be exact, but it's close enough:

When racked with labor pangs, and sore distressed,
We, your Daughters, invoke thee as the soul's sure rest;
For thou, Nana, alone, canst give relief to pain,
Which the healer attempts to ease, but tries in vain.

Nana, Protector of the Child-Bed, venerable power;
Who bringest relief in labor's direst hour;
We beseech thee: Deliver this woman."

"What good is *that* supposed to do me—? *Ahhhhh!*" I cried out in agony and alarm as my entire body from the shoulders down suddenly *pushed* of its own accord. Zena leaned forward and placed her hands on my temples, pulling the pain from me as it crashed down like a wave from an angry sea. Tipi's chanting became louder and more urgent than before, and I became dimly aware that the cadence of her voice now matched the timing of my contractions.

"Nana's face is turned to you, now," Zena whispered, her lips pressed close to my ear. "You and your child are under her protection—now *push!*"

I gritted my teeth and bore down as hard as I could, struggling to jettison my precious cargo. I was so exhausted, I felt as if I were trapped in a Möbius strip—that I had, somehow, always *been* in labor, and would always *be* in labor; that there was no baby, no future, just the eternity of striving to push something that was and, yet, was not, of myself *from* myself. I looked in the direction of Tipi, who was still at the foot of the tub, invoking the name of her goddess, and saw standing behind her the shadowy outline of a woman. As I struggled to bring the figure into focus, her face changed from that of young woman, to matron, to crone, and back again. As different as each visage was, one from the other, each face bore the same smile and the same pair of golden eyes.

I heard Hexe excitedly call out, as if from an impossible distance, "I see the baby's head! I see his shoulder!" I took a deep breath and bore down a final time, forcing our baby out of my birth canal and into the arms of his father. "I've got him!" Hexe shouted, splashing about like a hillbilly trying to catch a catfish by hand.

As he brought our son to the surface, Tipi finally halted her chanting and stepped into the tub, using a ball syringe to suction the plugs of protective mucus from the baby's nostrils and mouth so he could breathe on his own. Only then did he begin to cry, giving voice to a lusty, insistent squall.

"Is he okay?" I rasped.

"He's more than okay, Tate—he's *perfect*," Hexe grinned as he placed our newborn son, still attached to his umbilical, onto my belly.

I had never been as exhausted and elated as I was at that moment. Esau, Boss Marz, the Maladanti, Hexe losing his hand, my parents disinheriting me—all those things lost their meaning as I gathered my child into my arms. I wept and laughed in equal measure, covering the top of his still-damp head with kisses as he waved his fists like a tiny boxer at the brave new world he now found himself in. I was so happy and relieved, I barely noticed the sorrowing look exchanged between Tipi and Zena as they noticed the number of fingers on my baby's hands.

Hexe climbed out of the water and put his clothes back on, allowing Sister Tipi room to deliver and dispose of the afterbirth, and then sever the umbilical cord. The priestess handed the baby over to Hexe, who proudly cradled him in his arms as she and Zena helped me out of the birthing tub and back onto the bed.

I propped myself against the headboard and reached out to take our son from Hexe, so I could breastfeed him. Suddenly Tipi and Zena gasped out loud in surprise and dropped to their knees.

"All Hail the Blood of Arum!" the priestesses proclaimed in unison. "All Hail the Heirs of Adon!"

It wasn't until I looked down into my newborn son's tiny, wrinkled face, and saw him looking up at me, that I understood the reason behind their adoration. For while my child might have his mother's hands—he had his father's eyes.

Chapter 30

"I can't believe we went through so much drama for something so *tiny*," I said in a hushed voice as I watched my new son nurse. "But it was worth every second."

Tipi and Zena, their jobs now done, had withdrawn from the birthing chamber to allow Hexe and me time to bond with our new child. Hexe was stretched alongside me on the bed, staring at his son in open awe. He chuckled as the baby wrapped his tiny hand around his left index finger.

"Now that he's here, what do you think we should call him?" he asked.

"I've been wondering that, myself," I admitted. "I thought we had a little more time to pick out a name. Boy, was I wrong about *that*."

Before we could discuss the topic any further, I heard what sounded like an all-too-familiar voice raised in argument just outside the door. A second later the door to the birthing chamber flew open and in came my mother, full steam ahead, trailing Sister Tipi in her wake.

"How *dare* you tell me I can't see my own daughter and grandchild?" my mother exclaimed, displaying her finest high dudgeon.

"Madam, *please*!" Tipi exhorted. "It is tradition that the first hour of the newborn's life be shared with the parents."

"What utter hogwash! Honestly, what kind of hospital *is* this?"

"It's all right, Sister," I said wearily.

The priestess gave me a dubious look, but withdrew from the room without further argument. I braced myself for the barrage of backhanded compliments and thinly veiled insults that were sure to follow. But to my surprise, my mother swooped down upon me, throwing her arms about my neck.

"I'm so sorry, Timmy, for everything I've said and how I've treated you! I love you more than you can ever know, sweetheart—I'm afraid I just don't know how to show it. I didn't really have anything to model myself on. My own parents didn't know how to deal with who *I* was, either, except to shun me for dreaming of a life outside the farm. And now I've become as narrow-minded and reactionary as they were! Please say you forgive me for being such a horrid bitch and making life so difficult for you all this time."

"Of *course* I forgive you, Mom," I said, returning her hug. I looked up at Hexe, who was staring, openmouthed, at my mother's unabashed display of affection. I was glad I wasn't the only one gobsmacked.

"If I had any idea you were so close to delivering, I *never* would have allowed you to leave!" she said as she started to fuss with my pillows. "I never *wanted* to drive you away, but that's what I always seem to end up doing. Your father and I dropped everything the moment Clarence gave us the call. We would have been here sooner but this . . . whatever you call it . . . isn't on any GPS."

"Mom, calm down and take a breath." I smiled. "And say hello to your grandson."

As I held up the baby for her to inspect, my mother gasped and covered her mouth with her hands. "Oh. My. God. Timmy—he's *beautiful!*" She sobbed, tears of joy filling her eyes. It was the happiest I had ever seen my mother in my life. "May I hold him?"

I smiled and nodded, adding my own tears to the mix. My mother carefully scooped him into her arms, cupping the back of his tiny little head in one hand as she beamed down at her first grandchild.

"Who's got the prettiest gold eyes?" she cooed. "*You* do. Yes, you *do*." The smile on her face faltered as she noticed Hexe watching her in approval. "I owe you an even bigger apology than I do my daughter. Can you possibly find it in your heart to forgive a foolish old woman who has said so many cruel and careless things to you? I have been unfair to you from the very start, accusing you of being a manipulative gold digger trying to magic your way to my daughter's inheritance, just like my in-laws treated me when Timothy and I fell in love. I refused to see just how much you love my daughter, and how deeply she loves you. And—dear Lord! What happened to your hand?"

"It was an . . . accident," Hexe replied evenly as he took the baby from my mother and placed him in the bassinette next to the bed. "And I accept your apology, Mrs. Eresby. Compared to what your daughter has had to deal with from *my* side of the family, I have nothing to complain about. I'm just glad that we can restart our relationship on new ground."

Suddenly the door to the birthing chamber flew open again, this time to allow a six-foot-tall teddy bear carrying a clutch of Mylar balloons printed with cartoon storks to lumber into the room. "Someone get the door, will you?" my father's voice said from somewhere behind the giant plush toy.

"*There* you are, Timothy!" my mother exclaimed. "What kept you?"

"Trying to squeeze this damned stuffed bear through the entrance of this place is like trying to—well, you know what it's like," my father grumbled as he dropped his burden onto the rocking chair. "Hello, Princess. Are you okay? What about the baby?"

"I'm fine, Dad," I assured him as he kissed my cheek. "As for the baby—you can see for yourself."

My father grinned as he peered into the bassinette. "He kind of looks like my grandfather."

"Timothy, *all* babies look like your grandfather: wrinkled and bald," my mother replied, rolling her eyes.

"Yes, but this one *definitely* has the Eresby nose," he grinned, tapping his own for emphasis. "Don't you, champ?"

"Oops! I think somebody's hungry," I said, reaching into the bassinette as the baby began to fuss. As I exposed my breast for a second feeding, my father blushed and quickly looked away.

"Maybe we should head out, Millie?" he suggested. "Let the new mom and her baby get some rest?"

"You're right, dear," my mother agreed. "There is so much that still needs to be bought: baby clothes, furniture, toys . . . not to mention baby-proofing the house!"

"Mom, I appreciate the concern—but I don't think he's going to be sticking his fingers into electrical sockets just yet," I pointed out.

"Well, better safe than sorry, I always say! Come along, Timothy—next stop Neiman-Marcus!"

As my mother turned to leave, she froze upon seeing Lady Syra and Captain Horn standing in the doorway. The two women stood at rigid attention, regarding one another for a long moment.

"Syra."

"Millicent."

To my surprise, my mother abruptly smiled and threw her arms around Lady Syra, kissing her on the cheek. "Isn't it *wonderful*? We're *grandmothers*!"

The moment the door closed behind my parents, I fixed Syra with a suspicious stare. "Okay—what did you do to her?"

"Honestly, my dear! Is it *really* so hard to believe that the birth of a grandchild might change your mother's mind?"

"There's a difference between a change of heart and a transplant," I replied. "What spell is she under?"

"It's called the 'Walls of Jericho.'" Lady Syra sighed, surrendering the charade. "It's designed to bring down the barricades around the heart of whoever drinks it. While I was waiting for you in the Grand Salon, I used the occasion to slip a small amount of the potion into her decanter. I didn't put *that* much in her bourbon—well, maybe a *little* bit more than usual. *You* know your mother. But the emotion she showed you today isn't fake or manufactured. I figured it was the least I could do, seeing how much of her animosity and fear of magic is related to me. Now—where's my grandbaby?"

As Lady Syra drew closer, her smile abruptly disappeared, to be replaced by a look of genuine shock. "I don't understand," she gasped. "The child has human hands ... but its eyes—! How can such a thing be possible?"

"They said the same thing when Hexe was born. Your family did not believe the child of a Servitor would breed true, either," Horn said proudly. "I still remember to this day the joy I felt when our son opened his eyes for the first time...."

Hexe looked at his father in surprise. "You were present at my birthing?"

"Of course I was," Captain Horn said with a sad smile. "It was the first, and last, time I held you as a baby. It broke my heart to surrender my rights as your father, but even as I did so, I was proud to know my son would, some day, be Witch King."

"Yes, but you, at least, are Kymeran," Lady Syra countered. "There's never been a half-human Heir Apparent in all our history, much less a Witch King."

"And yet he has been chosen," Hexe said. "Perhaps our child is a sign—a guidepost for the future of not only Golgotham, but the human race as well, proof that Kymerans and humans not only can coexist peacefully, but are capable of transcending the darkness that has plagued us for so many centuries."

"It is going to be difficult to coerce even the moderate members of the Aristocracy to accept a hybrid Heir Apparent," Lady Syra said worriedly. "And that doesn't even include the host of problems that will arise once news of your amputation spreads."

"The child has been born, my hand has been lost—these things cannot be changed, no more than we can alter the outcome of the Sufferance or undo the slaughter of the dragons," Hexe said firmly. "Golgotham is on the verge of great change—whether for good or bad depends on whether we embrace the future or fight to reclaim the past. I believe that is why Esau has returned, and why he has worked so hard to destroy me—and my son."

"I agree," Syra said. "But none of this will be easy. There are a number of aristos who would have no problem following your uncle into the bowels of hell over something like this."

As I listened to Hexe and his mother discuss the ramifications of our child's birth, I found my attention starting to drift and my eyes growing heavy. The next thing I knew my head was bobbing up and down like one of the CONGRATU-LATIONS! balloons tied to the giant teddy bear.

"All of this can wait, for the time being," Lady Syra said. "It's best your father and I leave, and allow Tate some time to rest. You must be exhausted, poor girl," she said, bending down to kiss my forehead. She then smiled at her grandson, curled in the crook of my arm. "And as for you, young man: Welcome to the Royal Family."

Once his parents left, Hexe took the baby from me and placed him back in the bassinette. "He's sound asleep," he whispered. "I'm going to step out for a few minutes and find something to eat. I'll be right back."

I looked over and smiled at the sight of my son, lying buttered-side up, oblivious to the chaos his arrival in the world would soon start. I placed a gentle hand on one of his feet, marveling at how tiny and perfectly formed it was. I must have dozed off at some point, because the next thing I knew the baby's foot was no longer in my hand and he was making a mewling sound like a kitten. I looked up to see one of the pink-robed Daughters of Nana lifting my son out of the bassinette.

"What are you doing with my child?" I asked.

"I'm just taking him to be bathed and change his diaper," the priestess replied, turning her cowled head in such a way that I did not have a clear view of her face. Although she did not appear to be either Zena or Tipi, there was something familiar about her voice.

"Why can't you do those things here in the room?" I asked suspiciously.

Instead of answering me, the priestess simply turned and fled to the door, clutching my son to her breast. As she ran, the cowl on the robe fell away, revealing slate-blue hair.

"Bring back my baby!" I screamed as I clambered out of bed, only to discover that my legs had been replaced by bundles of cooked noodles. I was able to take only five or six steps before stumbling and falling to the floor. *"Somebody, please, stop her! She stole my baby!"*

The next thing I knew Hexe was there, helping me back onto my feet. "Tate—what's happened? Are you all right?"

I frantically shook my head as I clung to Hexe. "It was her! I mean, it was him! Uncle Esau kidnapped our baby!"

Chapter 31

"I've got all available units scouring the streets in search of Erys," Captain Horn said, trying his best to sound confident and in charge as he watched his son pace furiously back and forth in the front parlor. "I've got my best dowsers on the case. They should be able to draw a bead on her general location. Then we'll cordon off the area and do a house-by-house search."

It was less than an hour after the kidnapping, and Hexe and I were already home. I had downed a panacea at the Temple of Nana in order to restore my stamina before leaving, and was now feeling back to normal, if somewhat sore. Hexe and I, along with his parents, were gathered in the front parlor, waiting to hear from the kidnapper.

"I wouldn't bet on your dowsers turning anything of use," Hexe said bitterly. "Esau's too good a wizard to be tracked that easily."

"Esau?" Horn frowned. "I thought you said it was Madam Erys who took the baby. And what could your uncle possibly have to do with all this? The man was murdered by Skua's useless punk of a son, Skal, over six months ago."

Hexe halted his pacing to scowl at his mother. "I thought you said you told him the truth about Esau and the Sons of Adam?"

Lady Syra shifted about uncomfortably, looking embarrassed. "No, I said was *going* to tell him. When the time was right."

"Tell me the truth about *what*?" Horn demanded, giving Syra a stern look.

Syra lowered her eyes, unable to meet his gaze. "Well . . . uhm . . ."

"That Esau grew the Sons of Adam in his alchemy workshop," I explained, "and, on top of that, he was secretly going around murdering people so they wouldn't figure it out. He was also the one who sent that demon to kill me, so he could start a race riot and become mayor and purge all the humans from Golgotham and try to start a new Unholy War. Oh, and *he* murdered Skal, not the other way around, and was going to do the same thing to me and Hexe, except I stole the junk jewelry he was using to control a demon, and ordered it to return to the Infernal Court—and take Esau with him."

"And why am I just *now* hearing this story?" Horn asked as he massaged his forehead.

"Because I was afraid of what might happen if it was discovered a member of the Royal Family had manipulated both Golgothamites *and* humans to generate racial unrest," Lady Syra admitted grudgingly. "Ever since Lord Bexe and General Vlad, the Royal Family has a tradition of taking personal responsibility for the rogues within its ranks. I deemed it best that Hexe and I kept Esau's involvement in creating and operating the Sons of Adam between ourselves—and Tate, of course."

"Heavens and hells, Syra! I realize you're the justicar, and accustomed to making rulings and judgment calls without having to defer to anyone else—but do you *always* have to be so chuffing secretive about it?"

"I'm sorry, my dear," she replied. "It's a family tradition—and not one of our finer ones."

"It turns out the old cack-hander has been behind everything from the start. As if trying to drive me mad and murder Tate wasn't enough, he's gone after our son as well!" Hexe fumed. "I'm going to make him wish he'd stayed in hell!"

"Now you're talking, boss!" Scratch growled from his perch on the mantelpiece.

Suddenly there came a tapping, as if someone was gently rapping, on the parlor window. I lifted back the curtain and was surprised to spy a raven on the windowsill, staring intently at me with a ruby-red eye, a piece of folded parchment held in its jet-black beak. Scratch arched his back, spreading his leathery wings to make himself even bigger and more imposing.

"That's Esau's familiar, Edgar!" he hissed. "I'd know that filthy feather duster anywhere!"

As Captain Horn opened the window, the raven flapped into the room, landing in the center of the floor. Scratch leapt from the mantelpiece, placing himself between the familiar and Hexe. The raven opened its beak and dropped the note it was carrying on the floor. Then, with an abrasive caw, it once more took wing, flapping its way out of the open window.

Hexe snatched up the parchment and unfolded it, reading it aloud for the benefit of the rest of us.

Greetings, Nephew:

Congratulations on you and your nump whore bringing forth an abomination whose very existence is an affront to our hallowed bloodline. It would please me beyond measure to rid the world of the ill-born freak you have spawned. However, seeing as we are family, I am prepared to be merciful. If you wish to ever see your brat again, you and your traitorous mother must formally abdicate as Heir Apparent and Witch Queen, respectively. If you do not agree to these terms, I will hand the infant over to the trolls living under the Brooklyn Bridge, to be raised—or feasted upon—as they deem fit. Write your answer, yea or nay, on the back of this parchment and set it afire, then await instructions.

Your loving uncle,
Esau

"He's out of his mind!" Horn snorted.

"No, he's far from insane," Lady Syra sighed. "My brother knows me all too well."

"You're not going to *agree* to this madness, are you?" Horn asked.

"If it means saving my grandson—I will do whatever he wants," she replied grimly. "My brother is more than capable of handing over a helpless infant to trolls." She turned to look at Hexe. "What about you? Are you willing to surrender the throne in order to reclaim your son?"

"I'd do it in a heartbeat, if I thought that was *all* Esau was after," Hexe replied. "But what good does our abdicating do him, if he's still trapped in the Infernal Region? If there's one thing I've learned about my uncle—nothing he does is as simple as it first seems. I'm certain he's got something up his sleeve—but what?"

"I think I know someone who might have some insider information," I suggested. "But it's not going to be easy to get it out of him."

"Are you *sure* you want to use that thing?" Hexe asked, eyeing the amulet. It was triangular in shape and fashioned from some unidentifiable metal and affixed to a golden chain. Both the front and back of the amulet were inscribed with symbols and words from a hodgepodge of languages, including Sanskrit, Greek, Kymeran, and Babel, the language of the Infernals.

"I'll summon a *hundred* Demon Knights if it means getting our son back," I replied—and I meant it. I have never wanted anything more in my life than to have my baby safe in my arms again. The ache of having him stolen from me was greater than any physical pain I had ever endured, and so unbearable it was all I could do to keep from screaming like a crazy woman.

"What is the demon's name, by the way?" Syra asked. "You can't summon an Infernal without first knowing its name—that's how you gain control over it."

"I don't know," I admitted. "We never really got to know each other, beyond him breaking my arm."

"Here it is, on the back of the amulet," Hexe said, pointing to an inscription that looked like it had been written by a chicken with a calligrapher's pen strapped to one foot. "He's called Mephitis."

"Well, it's going to take two hands to prepare the wards for such an evocation," Lady Syra said as she rolled back her sleeves. "Better leave this to me."

Ten minutes later, the rug in Hexe's office was rolled back and Lady Syra was putting the finishing touches on the pentagram she'd drawn on the bare floor with a piece of chalk the size of her fist.

"What do I do?" I asked as I slipped the amulet about my neck. "Do I just stand here and yell his name like I'm calling a dog?"

"As long as you wear that medallion, all you have to do is formally summon him—the amulet binds him to your will, just as it bound him to Esau," Hexe explained. "The pentagram is to make sure he doesn't escape or try to harm anyone."

I took a deep breath to steady my nerves. I told myself that the amulet and the pentagram would protect me, and that I had to be brave. I was doing this for my baby. As I thought about my child needing me, a resolute calmness came upon me, driving the fear and self-doubt from me. "Mephitis! Knight of the Infernal Court!" I shouted into the empty air. "I call you forth! Hear me, demon, and obey!"

Almost instantly the shadows in the corners of the room seemed to deepen, as if the light was being sucked inside them. Accompanying the rise of shadows was a sudden chill, and within seconds it was so cold I could see my breath hanging in the air. The flames of the candles anchoring the points of the pentagram began to gutter in unison, nearly snuffing themselves out, only to turn themselves into towers of roaring fire. The smell of brimstone abruptly filled the room, followed by the sound of a hog squealing in rage, as if being dragged by its trotters to the slaughter.

As the candle flames died back down, there stood revealed in the center of the pentagram a figure that put the hair on my head and arms on end, and not because the office was as cold as a meat locker. The demon Mephitis was humanoid in general shape, with the torso of a man and the legs and hooves of a goat. His face resembled that of a boar, complete with snout and tusks, save that there were three eyes instead of two, the third located in the middle of his forehead. Large batlike wings grew out of the demon's back, and ram's horns curled back from his temples. The very sight of the Infernal was enough to make my arm, long since healed, start to ache again.

The last time the Demon Knight had manifested in this world, he arrived bearing the wounds he won from battling Hexe's Right Hand magic, not to mention the business end of my acetylene torch. But now he appeared recovered from his injuries—no doubt the result of the restorative wonders of the sulfur baths of the Infernal Court.

"Mephitis hears your call, milady, and doth appear," the demon snarled, flexing his wings in an anxious manner.

"Do you remember me, Infernal?" I asked.

"Yes, milady," the Demon Knight replied, with a bow of his hideous head. "You blinded me in one eye. But I harbor no ill will, for it has since grown back. For what purpose have you called Mephitis forth?"

"I require information that only you can give. What has Esau been doing since you took him to your world?"

Mephitis made a snorting noise, like that of a pig at a trough. "It did not take the sorcerer long to become influential in the Infernal Court. He has gained the favor of high-ranked courtiers—not mere knights, such as I, but princes and marquises—by promising them a fresh hell to make their own."

"How can he make good on such a promise?" Hexe asked.

Mephitis snarled and shook his head, flashing his tusks in defiance. "I answer only to milady."

"Answer the question, demon," I said sternly.

"The sorcerer Esau is erecting a permanent portal in this dimension—one large enough to accommodate a legion of Infernals. Please, milady, I beg of you," the Infernal Knight pleaded, "do not make me speak more of this. I shall be sorely punished should they learn I spoke of it to you."

The thought of a punishment so extreme it would frighten a demon was nothing I wanted to dwell on. "Very well, Mephitis. Get the hell out of here."

"Thank you, milady!" the demon said with a bow, and then disappeared in a puff of sulfurous smoke. Within seconds of his departure, the room's temperature and lighting returned to normal.

"So *that's* his plan," Hexe said sourly. "I *knew* there had to be a hidden agenda somewhere."

"I was well aware Esau walked the Left Hand path," Lady Syra said in stunned disbelief. "But I still held out hope that there was *some* trace of the brother I used to know left within him. Now I realize the Esau I loved is long dead."

"It would seem that Esau has finally found his natural element—hell suits his temperament far more than Golgotham," Horn said grimly.

"I would have thought kidnapping your grandson and threatening to sell him to trolls might have been proof of that already," I remarked.

"You don't understand, Tate," Horn replied. "Portals are incredibly unstable. They can only stay open for a few minutes at a time. There is only *one* way to permanently open a portal between worlds large enough to accommodate troop movements: a blood sacrifice. But not just *any* blood. Only that of the Royal Family will do."

Just then, there was a knock on the office door, and Clarence poked his head into the room. "Excuse me, Miss Timmy . . ."

"Yes, Clarence—what is it?"

"I hate to interrupt, but there are some people here to see you and Master Hexe. Quite a few, in fact."

As Hexe and I returned to the front of the house, we were surprised to find the entire GoBOO council, at least all of those who could fit through the front door, standing in the parlor, along with several of our friends, including Bartho, Lukas, and Lafo.

Seamus O'Fae stepped forward, holding his Kelly green homburg in his hands as he spoke. "The news of the kidnappin' is all over Golgotham, Serenity. We have come here to offer our help."

"Centuries ago, our ancestors swore fealty to the Throne of Arum," Giles Gruff said solemnly. "That oath still binds us, by blood and honor, to aid the Royal Family in its time of need."

Lorelei Jones nodded her seaweed-green head in agreement. "When the humans' atomic tests drove us from our native waters in the South Pacific, your grandfather, Lord Eben, welcomed my people into Golgotham without a second's hesitation, giving us a new home *and* new hope. The merfolk owe his bloodline much."

"And I'm sure my son appreciates the council's show of support," Captain Horn said firmly. "But the PTU is already on the case. I've got my best officers out there looking for the woman responsible for the kidnapping. . . ."

"I don't mean any disrespect, Cap'n," the leprechaun countered. "But ye only have so many men. The way we see it, the more eyes ye got lookin', the more likely she'll be seen."

"Seamus is right," Hexe agreed. "We need as many boots on the ground as possible."

Skua, the querent for the GoBOO, stepped toward me.

Although I knew her to be unsympathetic toward humans, I saw none of her previous disdain in her deep green eyes. In her hands she held a multifaceted scrying crystal the size of an ostrich egg. "I know all too well what it is like to have a son disappear," she said sadly. "Picture the face of the woman who took your child and exhale onto the crystal."

As I closed my eyes, the face of Erys flashed across my mind and I quickly exhaled. When I reopened my eyes, the scrying crystal was filled with a swirling, multicolored mist. Within moments the image of Erys appeared, replicated within each individual facet, like the eye of a fly.

Skua placed the crystal on the coffee table and made a couple of passes with her hands, causing the crystal to disassemble into dozens of smaller shards, each holding the image of Erys at its heart.

"Take these with you," the querent said as she handed the crystals to the others. "This way you will be able to identify who you're looking for."

"Be careful—this woman is *very* dangerous," Captain Horn warned. "She is also wanted for questioning in the murder of Dr. Moot. If you see her, *don't* approach her or attempt to apprehend her! Instead, simply contact either me or Hexe or Tate, and let us know where you saw her and if she's travelling with anyone."

After Hexe and his father succeeded in eliciting a grudging agreement that no one would do anything stupid if they spotted Madam Erys, the assembled volunteers filed out of the house, each carrying the image of the kidnapper in their pockets. After the last one was safely out the door, Hexe turned to look at his father.

"I noticed you didn't tell them that Erys is, in fact, Esau."

"I decided your mother is right," Horn replied. "Revealing Esau's involvement in this isn't going to help. It'll only make matters worse."

"I'm sorry we didn't tell you sooner—you deserved to know," Hexe apologized.

"Damn straight I did," his father grunted. "But, what's done is done. To tell you the truth, I already suspected Esau was somehow connected to the SOA. It just seemed like an awfully big coincidence that the Sons of Adam disappeared the exact same time *he* did. I know your mother loved him—after all, he was her brother—but as far as I was concerned he was *always* a manipulative conniver, not to mention an elitist snob."

"It seems you don't have a great deal of fondness for my uncle," Hexe observed wryly.

"I loathe the man," Horn replied flatly. "And I've done so ever since he slapped my mother for not serving him a meal fast enough to suit him, when he was fifteen years old. Syra may have known a different Esau, but I never have."

Hexe frowned. "Your mother worked as a cook for the Royal Family—?"

Before Horn could reply, Hexe's cell phone ringtone began to play, alerting him that he'd received a text message.

"Who's it from?" I asked anxiously.

"It's from Bartho. He says, 'I think I found her!' There's a JPEG attached...."

Syra, Horn, and I crowded around as Hexe opened the file. Although the screen wasn't very big, I could make out what looked to be Erys, dressed in the traditional multicolored skirt and patchwork vest of a Kymeran witch-for-hire, standing in front of the Stronghold, the secured pier belonging to the Maladanti, and pointing at its locked gates. It took me a moment or two to realize that parts of her were transparent.

"Is that Erys?" I asked, frowning in confusion.

"No. It's Nina," Lady Syra replied. "And it looks like she's trying to tell us something."

Chapter 32

"Are you ready to do this?" Hexe asked his mother. Lady Syra nodded, her mouth set into a determined line. "Here goes, then." Taking up a pen, he flipped over the ransom note and wrote "We agree to your terms" on its back, and signed it. He then moved aside, allowing his mother to add her signature.

Lady Syra picked up a stick of sealing wax and snapped the fingers of her left hand, summoning a tongue of flame, which danced atop her index finger. Once the sealing wax was melted, she plunged her signet ring into the warm red puddle, leaving the mark of the Royal House of Arum: a pair of intertwined dragons.

Hexe took the parchment and placed it on the parlor grate. The tongue of flame flickering at the tip of Lady Syra's finger leapt into the fireplace, and within seconds the note was ablaze. The smoke from the parchment briefly took on the silhouette of a man, and then fled up the chimney with an unnatural speed and purpose.

"Well, that's that," Hexe sighed. "What's next?"

We didn't have long to wait, as there came a familiar tapping on the parlor window frame, signaling the return of Esau's familiar, Edgar. This time the raven flew in and perched on the mantelpiece. Beanie charged forward, stiff-legged, barking furiously at the feathered intruder, until Edgar cawed loudly and flapped his soot-black wings in consternation, sending Beanie scampering behind Scratch, who spread his own, leathery wings in challenge.

Edgar clattered his beak in what passed for laughter, and

then turned his beady, ruby-red eyes to Hexe. The voice that issued from the familiar was that of Madam Erys, but the intonation and inflection were unmistakably Esau's: "Midnight at The Lucky Fool. Come alone. No PTU. No familiars."

"Understood," Hexe said with a solemn nod of his head.

"We will be there," Lady Syra promised.

Having delivered his master's message, the familiar cawed a final time and flew back out the open window, but not before soiling the hearth on the way out.

"You know it's a trap," Horn said flatly. "He plans to kill you both—possibly even the baby—and paint the portal's lintel with your blood."

"Of course, but Esau isn't aware that we know about his plan," Hexe replied.

Horn glanced at me. "And you're good with letting them do this?"

"It's not just them. I'm going, too."

"But you've just had a baby!" Hexe protested in alarm.

"Yes, one that is being held for ransom by a murderer!" I reminded him. "And if you think I'm going to stay behind while you try to rescue him, you *really* haven't been paying attention over the last year. And for your information, Mr. 'You Just Had A Baby,' *you've* just had your *hand* cut off! So just *try* to keep me from being in on this!"

"She's got you there, son." His father chuckled.

"But—it's going to be dangerous!"

"If I have learned one thing about dealing with strong-willed women," Horn said as he slipped a paternal arm about Hexe's shoulders, "there's no point in arguing with them once their minds are made up."

"Your father's right, Hexe," Lady Syra nodded. "Believe me; he's learned the hard way."

"So what's this Lucky Fool?" I asked.

"It's a gambling house operated by the Maladanti—cards, Russian roulette, dice, that kind of thing," Captain Horn explained. "It's located down on the river. I'm not surprised Boss Marz is involved in this business."

"He's more a part of it than you realize," Hexe said dourly. "The reason I was wearing the Gauntlet of Nydd in the first place is because Marz kidnapped me the night of the Jubilee and smashed my right hand with one of the Witchfinder instruments stolen from the museum."

Lady Syra gasped so loudly I thought she was about to scream, while all the color drained from Captain Horn's face and his eyes narrowed into slits. When the PTU chief finally spoke, his words were as cold and hard as a lead pipe. "I'll kill him."

"Not if I get to him first," Lady Syra said, the deadly calm of her voice belaying the fury in her golden eyes.

"The time has finally come to bring down the Maladanti, once and for all," Horn said. "But it's going to take more than the PTU to take them out. We're going to need a small army."

"We already have one combing the streets," Hexe said, holding up his cell. "All you have to do is say the word. They've been waiting for an opportunity to strike back at Boss Marz and his croggies."

"In that case," I said, "we need to stop by the museum. There's something there that should come in handy."

The Lucky Fool was within smelling distance of the East River and looked like a run-of-the-mill gin joint. The only evidence of it being a casino was the neon sign above the door, which depicted the familiar image from the Tarot deck, bindle on his shoulder, blithely strolling off the edge of a cliff, eyes forever skyward.

A Maladanti croggy with magenta hair and a badly fitting tuxedo standing at the door stepped forward to greet Hexe, Lady Syra, and me as we approached. "We've been expecting you. Follow me, Your Majesty."

The interior of The Lucky Fool proved a little more upscale than its exterior, but not by much. A pall of cigarette smoke thick enough to part like a curtain covered the central room, which had the ugliest wall-to-wall carpeting I'd ever seen. The front of the house was full of loud slot machines and video poker, with craps, blackjack, and Pai Gow toward the back. There were plenty of gamblers, most of them human, wagering at the tables. None of them looked up from their bets as we were escorted to the back of the house.

"That's funny—I don't see a roulette wheel," I commented as I glanced at the games on display.

"Oh, we have roulette," the pit boss said with an unpleasant smile as he opened a door that said LUCKIEST FOOLS ONLY.

As loud and crowded as the gaming floor of the casino was, it was nothing compared to the back room. At each of the numerous tables were seated between two to six players, each and every one of them sweating through their clothes. It wasn't until I noticed the snub-nosed revolvers sitting on lazy Susans set into the middle of the felt that I realized what the plastic sheeting draped over the chairs and covering the floors was for. Each table was crowded by throngs of men, and some women, shouting and waving fistfuls of money like stock traders trying to corner the market on hog bellies. My stomach tightened as I remembered the crowds screaming for blood at the pit fights, and wondered how many of those same people were now wagering to see who would be the last to blow their brains out. As the pit boss opened yet another door, there came the sound of a single, muffled gunshot from somewhere behind me, immediately followed by a roar of excited voices. I did not turn around to look.

The second door opened onto the stairs that led down to the boiler room. Standing in front of yet another door was Marz's lieutenant, Gaza, and some nameless croggy.

"I'll take 'em from here," Gaza said with a smirk, eyeing where Hexe's right hand should have been. "Follow me, Your Highnesses."

The Maladanti opened the door behind him, revealing a low, brick-lined tunnel lit by a chain of witchfire, which cast an eerie blue glow. We walked single file for what seemed like at least two city blocks before reaching the end of the passageway, which led to a wooden stairwell. As we came to the top of the stairs, I recognized our surroundings as the same warehouselike building Hexe and I had been shanghaied to months ago.

"Welcome to the Stronghold, Your Majesties," Boss Marz's deep voice boomed out. The crime lord was standing in the middle of the warehouse, surrounded by several dozen of his minions. Next to Marz was an old-fashioned hanging cradle, and perched atop its peaked hood was the familiar, Bonzo, clutching a baby bottle. The sight of the hell-ape so close to my child filled me with a terror that made an attack by a demon seem like a ride on a roller coaster. "You do me great honor," the crime lord said.

"There is no honor in this place," Lady Syra retorted. "And I thought you said no familiars."

"The instructions were that *you* not bring familiars," Erys replied, stepping out from behind one of the pillars that supported the warehouse roof. "I said nothing about myself and my confederates."

"You are much changed since last I saw you, Esau."

"So you recognize me in this form?"

"Of course; who else would be walking around in your dead wife's body?"

Erys turned to Marz, speaking to him as she would a servant. "Make sure Her Majesty isn't wearing an ivory necklace or bracelet."

Marz nodded his understanding, motioning to one of his men to search Lady Syra. As the Maladanti reached out to frisk her, the Witch Queen drew herself up to her full height, peering down her nose at him with a glare sharp enough to cut glass. Cowed, the gangster had to satisfy himself with a visual inspection of her wrists and neck.

"She's clean, Boss."

Just then the baby started to cry, galvanizing every muscle in my body. I stepped forward, eager to answer his call, only to have Gaza block my way.

"Let me go to him!" I snapped, more command than plea.

Bonzo shrieked and hurled the baby bottle at me, and then began rocking the cradle faster and faster, causing my son's cries to grow more and more agitated.

"Get that thing away from my child!" I shouted.

"Now, now," Boss Marz said, clucking his tongue. "Is that any way to talk to your babysitter?"

"You'll get your brat back, soon enough," Erys replied, "but not before the abdication decree is signed." She pointed to the table that had served as a torture rack for Hexe, which now bore an old-fashioned inkstand and blotter, as well as an elaborately calligraphed document written on parchment.

Lady Syra stepped up to the table and took the quill pen from the inkstand and stabbed her forefinger with its sharp-

ened tip, using the blood for her signature, and then helped
Hexe by pricking his thumb with the same quill. Hexe's left
hand signature, while nowhere as neat as his old one, was at
least legible.

The moment Hexe finished signing his name, I headed
for the cradle. Bonzo refused to surrender his perch, and
bared his teeth at me. But I refused to back down.

"Get away from my baby, you stupid monkey!"

"Let her have it," Boss Marz sighed, waving the familiar
away with a beringed hand. "Maybe now the damned thing
will stop crying."

The baby was beet red in the face, his eyes screwed shut,
and his toothless mouth open wide as he voiced his fear and
displeasure to the world, but seemed otherwise unharmed.
As I lifted him from the cradle, his shrieks turned into
whimpers. It was all I could do to keep from crying along
with him as I cradled him in my arms. The terror I had felt
from the moment he was taken from me instantly disappeared, but the dread I felt for our lives was still there. I
hurried back to Hexe, who pulled us both into the circle of
his arms and held us fast.

"*Finally!*" Boss Marz exclaimed in relief. "I thought it
would *never* stop caterwauling."

"Place the Royal Seal upon it, and it shall be official,"
Erys said as she dripped black sealing wax onto the bottom
of the parchment.

As Lady Syra drove her signet ring into the wax, the ring
abruptly dropped from her finger, as if it had suddenly
grown too big to stay on. Erys quickly snatched up the piece
of jewelry, holding it up like a trophy.

"There. It is done," Syra said in a flat voice. "You've got
what you wanted. Now let me and my family go."

"I'm afraid I can't allow that, Syra," Erys replied with a
cold-blooded smile. "This piece of paper is meaningless, as
long as my corporeal form remains trapped in another dimension. But, thanks to you and your family, I won't be
there for much longer." She pointed to a huge, shrouded
object at the far end of the warehouse. With a snap of her
fingers, the canvas covering fell away, revealing a gigantic
stone portal, standing twelve feet high with a lintel fifteen
feet long, covered in occult petroglyphs.

"As you see, I have prepared a means of returning not

only my corporeal self to this dimension, but for bringing along a host of new friends in the bargain." Erys then turned and bowed in my direction. "As much as it pains me to do so, nump, I must thank you for consigning me to the Infernal Region. If not for you, I would never have found allies bold enough to embrace my vision of returning the Kymeran race to power by overthrowing humanity. They were even kind enough to teach me the finer points of possession!

"Manipulating homunculi was one thing—but to pierce the barrier between this world and the Infernal Realm by sheer force of will is another matter entirely. Luckily, I knew where to find the perfect vessel for my disembodied spirit—one that would not put up a fight when I moved in." Erys said, gesturing to her body as if it was nothing more than a suit of clothes. "Besides, it is only fitting that my beloved Nina's flesh should play a role in the destruction of the human society that robbed her of her future."

"So what is the Maladanti's reward for helping you bring this mad dream of yours to fruition?" Hexe asked dourly.

"We will be Golgotham's new police force, replacing the PTU," Boss Marz replied with a broad smile. "We will be a scourge to all who would defy the Witch King, regardless of how many fingers they possess."

"So, it was Esau's plan to smash my right hand with the witch-hammer."

"I wish I could claim such ingenuity!" Erys laughed. "Marz came up with that plan all on his own. But I must say, the idea of destroying the one thing you held in highest regard—your Right Hand magic—was absolute *genius*."

"Thank you, Lord Esau," Boss Marz said humbly. "That means a lot, coming from you."

"I believe in giving credit where credit is due. In fact, you inspired me to use my Infernal allies to locate the Gauntlet of Nydd. I knew Hexe would do whatever it took to regain his dexterity—his pride in his Right Hand magic was his weakness. I've studied General Vlad's spell books for decades, so it wasn't that difficult to weave one of my own into the existing enchantment and pass it off as the real thing. The chance to dance my fool of a nephew around like a puppet on a string was too good to pass up.

"I hoped to use the gauntlet to strip him of all he held

dear—his friendships, his reputation, and his family. He thinks he's so much *better* than the rest of us, blathering on about the Right Hand path and how Kymerans should stop bartering in curses. I wanted to bring him to such despair that he would finally recognize the Right Hand path for the foolishness it is—and then break him like a bundle of dry sticks across my knee."

"You did *all* that just to torment my son?" Syra scowled. "Your own flesh and blood?"

"Whatever kinship I felt for your half-caste bastard disappeared when he took up with that nump bitch," Erys snarled. "He's nothing more than a race-traitor—and now he has completed the disgrace to our bloodline by siring that five-fingered freak! The birth of such an abomination is sign that the time has come for a second Unholy War."

As if to illustrate her point, Erys aimed her left hand at the portal, contorting all six of her fingers at such angles that they looked as if they'd been broken and pulled out of joint. A lightning bolt of purplish-black energy leapt from her hand and struck the lintel stone, causing the inscribed sigils to glow with dark energy. A red mist began to form within the stone doorway as the membrane between this world and the Infernal Region thinned itself.

There were movements in the dim red fog that filled the portal's threshold, and vague shapes began to emerge, gradually becoming more distinct. I saw what looked like an army, lined up and girded for war. What little I was able to glimpse of the waiting hordes was so appalling I shuddered in revulsion and horror.

At the front of the Infernal legions stood four foot soldiers—if masses of human entrails given form and movement could be called such things—upon whose slimy shoulders a funeral bier was balanced. Although I could not see its occupant, I knew the body the frightful creatures carried was the corporeal form of Esau.

"If there is anything left of the brother I once knew and loved, I beg you to let Hexe and his family go," Lady Syra pleaded. "Whatever you have planned for me, I will not fight it, as long as they are granted safe passage."

"And have the hybrid bastard pop up twenty years later, looking to lay claim to my throne?" Erys sneered. "I'm sorry, Syra—but your son's blood is of more use to me as paint."

"That's exactly what I thought you'd say." Hexe said as he turned and looked at me. "Okay, Tate—give 'em the high sign."

I took a deep breath and reached out with my mind, seeking the invisible tether I knew to be there, channeling my will as Canterbury had taught me. Seconds later I was rewarded by a roar so loud it made the walls of the warehouse vibrate.

"Heavens and hells!" Boss Marz exclaimed in surprise. "What in the name of the Outer Dark was *that*?"

As if in answer, a young Maladanti came running into the warehouse, looking like the Infernal huntsmen were already on his heels. "Boss! The gates on the pier have been breached! We're under attack!"

"Is it the PTU?" Marz asked.

"It's not just them," the croggy said with a shake of his head. "There's leprechauns, centaurs, satyrs, huldrefolk, and a bunch of angry dames on motorcycles! And merfolk are climbing out of the river on the far end of the pier! They've got us surrounded! But that's not the worst part. They've got a *dragon*!"

Chapter 33

"A dragon—?" Boss Marz scoffed. "Don't be *ridiculous*!" Suddenly there was a second, even more thunderous bellow, which shook the entire warehouse like a maraca. Using the distraction, Syra hurled a bolt of lightning at Marz's head. Although the Maladanti was able to deflect the blow at the last moment, it still sent him flying across the floor.

"Hexe! Get Tate and the baby out of here!" Syra shouted, putting herself between her son and a livid Boss Marz, who was already back on his feet.

The Maladanti threw a ball of hellfire directly at Syra, which she was able to swat away with her right hand. The fireball flew wild, striking one of Marz's croggies and instantly setting him ablaze. The gang member screamed and slapped at the white-hot flames as they seared through his clothes, reducing his flesh to the consistency of burning marshmallow goo, but all that did was spread them even further.

Hexe and I made a dash for the loading dock; it was at the far end of the warehouse, and although the loading doors were down, it was the only visible means of escape.

"Don't let them get away, you idiot!" Erys shouted.

"Bonzo! Fetch!" Boss Marz commanded.

The organ-grinder's monkey squealed in delight as it disappeared in a puff of brimstone, only to reappear in its monstrous hell-ape form, blocking our way. Flashing canines the size of steak knives, the familiar yanked me away from Hexe.

"Get rid of the nump and her half-breed bastard!" Erys told Marz. "I'll use the others' blood!"

"You heard the man, Bonzo," Boss Marz commanded. "Kill the woman and the brat."

As the hell-ape opened his hideous multicolored snout, exposing his daggerlike teeth, I saw Syra out of the corner of my eye reach into her cleavage and pull out what looked like a white silken cord. As she hurled the white thing to the ground, Boss Marz threw another fistful of lightning in her direction. Caught off guard, Syra was able to deflect only a portion of the attack and was knocked to the ground and badly dazed.

What I had mistaken for a piece of rope instantly transformed into a twenty-five-foot-long albino king cobra as it hit the floor. Trinket reared up, hissing like a steam engine, and flared her hood, causing different heads, all belonging to various lethal snakes, to sprout from her milk-white torso.

Trinket lunged at Bonzo, but the hell-ape grabbed me about the waist and leapt out of the way. As Syra's familiar regathered for another strike, a vulturelike creature, larger than a condor, with the toothed bill and reptilian head of a pterodactyl, swooped down from the rafters of the warehouse, clawing at Trinket's ivory scales. I recognized it as Esau's own familiar, Edgar, in his demonic plumage.

Trinket's extra heads hissed and struck at Edgar, momentarily scaring him off, while her cobra head spit venom at Bonzo, striking the familiar square in the eyes. Bonzo shrieked and let go of me, clawing at his face. I took full advantage of my freedom and ran for cover behind a stack of palettes as the hellspawns continued their fight to the death.

As the blinded Bonzo staggered about, screaming like a monkey house, Trinket wrapped her two-story-long body around him faster than a thought. Once her enemy was caught within her limbless embrace, the hydra's heads struck as one, delivering a chorus of death bites. Bonzo screeched in agony as the venoms of the black mamba, krait, pit viper, puff adder, rattlesnake, and sea snake were pumped simultaneously into his body.

Boss Marz was standing over the prone figure of Lady Syra, his left hand aglow, ready to deliver the coup de grace, when he heard his familiar's death-scream. The crime lord's face turned pale as he saw Trinket slither away from the hell-ape twitching on the warehouse floor.

"Leave him alone, you monster!" Marz screamed. He turned his back on Syra and ran to his dying familiar. Dropping to his knees, he grabbed Bonzo's blood-smeared hand and pressed it gently to his cheek. "You can't die here," he told the hell-beast. "If you die in the mortal world, you die forever. Please, go home, Bonzo."

But it was too late. Perhaps Trinket's hydra venom had paralyzed the familiar, or maybe he needed eyes in order to travel between dimensions, but the hell-ape did not disincorporate the way it had when Scratch came close to killing him in battle. With a final, childlike whimper, Bonzo shuddered and went still.

Suddenly there was a huge thud, as if a battering ram had been slammed into the side of the building, and one of the loading dock bay doors abruptly gave way. The clockwork dragon, still dressed in the golden skin of the last battle-dragon, pushed its way past the twisted metal. As Boss Marz and his assembled Maladanti stared in disbelief at the creature before them, the clockwork dragon's hinged jaws fell open and issued a thunderous call to war.

PTU officers in riot gear, leprechauns armed with shillelaghs, Amazon archers, Valkyrie spear-maidens, centaurs in war-armor wielding maces and swords, merfolk equipped with tridents and nets, and unarmed satyrs, fauns, and huldrefolk came pouring through the breech. At the head of the charge was Captain Horn, dressed in his formal uniform, his hands empty save for their magic. *"For the Witch Queen!"* he shouted. *"For Golgotham!"*

Boss Marz quickly got to his feet, his dead familiar forgotten, to marshal his own troops. *"For the honor of the Maladanti!"*

And the battle was on.

The gang members surged forward to meet the invaders, hellfire and lightning leaping from their left hands. Some of their volleys found their marks, while others were dodged or batted away by PTU with strong right hands, sending the deadly missiles careening through the warehouse like errant pinballs. Within seconds the interior of the warehouse had become utter chaos.

A group of leprechauns, lead by Seamus O'Fae, swarmed a Maladanti like soldier ants, beating him mercilessly with their shillelaghs. As they took their much larger opponent to the ground, Little Big Man gave a war whoop and bashed in the gangster's skull. An Amazon archer put an arrow in the chest of a Maladanti spellslinger, only to be engulfed in hellfire. A Maladanti screamed in terror as he fell under the rending hands of a half-dozen maenads. Old Lord Chiron, accompanied by Kidron, Canterbury, and Lady Syra's chauffeur, Illuminata, charged through the madness, smashing their adversaries with flying maces and flailing hooves.

I saw Kidron gallop forward, snatching up Hexe and swinging him onto his back. Together the childhood friends stood their ground, the centaur swinging a battle-axe while Hexe bashed their attackers with a morning star.

Elmer, Lady Syra's former footman, charged one of the Maladanti, catching the gangster on his horns and sending him flying into the air with a single toss of his thickly muscled neck. The minotaur's bellow of triumph quickly became a scream of agony as he was fried by a shock of lightning and dropped to the floor like a side of beef. In turn, the Maladanti responsible for slaying the man bull did not have long to gloat before finding a Valkyrie's war-spear in his gut.

Giles Gruff, still wearing his monocle, used his shepherd's crook to pole vault himself into an enemy, smashing his cloven hooves into the gang member's startled face, while his fellow satyrs and fauns surrounded a couple of spellslingers, keeping them off balance and unable to defend themselves by butting them from every possible direction.

I heard the roaring of big cats and saw a pair of tigers and a mountain lion maul a Maladanti spellslinger. Once they were finished with him, Lukas, Meikei, and Dr. Mao set about looking for fresh prey. A half-naked huldra leapt upon one of the gang members, bearing him to the ground as she throttled him with her tail, only, in turn, to be set ablaze by yet another of Boss Marz's croggies. And in the middle of it all was the clockwork dragon, its golden hide immune to hellfire the same way a duck sheds water, lashing out at its attackers with its whiplike tail. I could feel the leash of energy between us, allowing me not to so much consciously control its actions, but guide them. The animating spark that I had placed within my creation made it both a part of me, and yet a thing of its own, not unlike, in its own way, the child I now cradled in my arms.

From my hiding place, away from the bloodshed of the battlefront, I could see that Erys had finished charging the portal that would serve as the doorway between worlds, the sigils and signs that covered the massive stones now glowing like they were radioactive. The red fog had all but disappeared, providing an all-too-clear view of what lay in wait beyond the threshold, not just for Golgotham, but the entire world as well.

"Bring me my sister!" Erys commanded. "With her blood, I can at least open the portal wide enough to allow the first wave through! Once my allies have a toehold in this world, there is nothing these fools can do that can stop them."

Marz turned to grab Lady Syra, who was lying on the floor, still dazed from his attack, only to find Trinket in his path. The familiar's multitude of heads hissed angrily at the Maladanti as she tried to defend her fallen mistress. But as the hydra advanced on the gangster, there was screeching noise and the hell-bird Edgar descended upon her yet again.

With a snap of his toothy beak, Esau's familiar succeeded in biting off one of Trinket's extra heads. Boss Marz summoned forth flame, scorching the flailing neck stump before it had a chance to regrow and multiply. The hell-bird snipped off another head, then another, and each time Marz cauterized the neck before it could regrow, until Trinket was left with just the one. The badly wounded familiar spat a streamer of venom at the Maladanti in a last ditch effort to protect itself, only to have it fall short of its mark. With an angry hiss, Trinket disincorporated in a puff of sulfurous smoke — fleeing back to whatever hell had spawned her to avoid meeting Bonzo's fate on the mortal plane.

"On your feet, woman," Marz growled as he dragged a semiconscious Syra to where Erys stood before the portal, ritual knife in hand. "The Witch King commands your presence." As he let go of her arm, Syra crumpled to the floor like a Japanese lantern at the feet of her brother's stolen body.

"Look at you," Erys sneered. "Your love has made you

grow old and soft before your time, little sister. I'm doing you a favor, really. But in memory of our childhood—I shall make it quick. I can not say the same for the others."

As Erys raised the ritual dagger above her head, the knife was abruptly wrenched from her grip, as if yanked by an unseen hand. The dagger hung suspended in midair, just beyond Erys' reach.

"Who dares?" Erys shouted, her face flushed crimson with rage.

"*I* dare, Esau," Captain Horn replied defiantly. He raised his right hand, levitating the knife farther from reach. Although his uniform hung in tatters and his face was bruised and smudged with soot and blood, a fierce determination blazed in his eyes. "You've done enough to your sister already—I'm not going to let you hurt her any more."

"You're in no position to stop me from doing anything," Erys sneered. "I am the Witch King—the blood of our gods courses through my veins. While you are nothing more than a servant, the son of a scullery maid and a bootblack!"

"You're wrong there, Esau," Horn replied. "I'm more than a Servitor. Even more than a Kymeran, or even a Golgothamite. I'm also an American and, by damn, a New Yorker, and I am not going to let you destroy this world simply because your father knew better than to trust you."

Erys' face abruptly lost its look of cool detachment and contorted itself into a mask of rage. "You want the knife so damn much?" she snarled. "You can *have* it!" With a flick of her left hand, the dagger flew at Captain Horn as if fired from a crossbow, striking him in the chest.

Upon seeing his father fall, Hexe leapt down from Kidron and ran to Horn's side. "Dad! Heavens and hells! Dad—are you all right?"

"I've—been better," Horn grunted.

"Lie still. Don't try to move," Hexe warned him. "The knife barely missed your heart—damn it, why are you smiling?"

"You called me 'Dad.'"

"How touching," Boss Marz said with a humorless laugh as he loomed over father and son. "I'm a big believer in closure." As the Maladanti's left hand filled with hellfire, Hexe lifted his own left hand in defense. "Lot of good *that's* going to do you," Marz smirked.

Although I knew the man I loved was about to be killed right before my eyes, I could not look away, if for no other reason than I owed it to our son, should we somehow survive this awful hour, to one day tell him how his father died. The fireball shot from the center of Marz's palm like a flaming tennis ball fired from a pitching machine. And, by all rights, it should have burned a hole through Hexe's face and exited out the back of his skull. Instead, it ricocheted back toward the Maladanti like a handball striking an unseen wall, scorching the left side of his face and boiling his left eye in its socket like a poached egg. With a dreadful shriek, Boss Marz fell to his knees in shock. Gaza came running to the fallen crime lord's aid, slinging a fistful of lightning at Hexe as he got to his feet. Hexe lifted his left hand to block the incoming spell, but wasn't fast enough to catch all of it and was sent flying into the side of a shipping container.

"Hey—you! Asshole!" I shouted as I stepped out from my hiding place, holding my child close to my breast. "That's *my* man you just sucker punched!"

Gaza turned to look at me and smirked. "What are *you* going to do about it, nump?"

There was a sharp snapping sound, like the crack of a bullwhip, only much, much louder, as a copper barb punched its way out through Gaza's chest and shirtfront, killing him instantly. The clockwork dragon gave its tail a little shake to free itself of the dead gangster, and then stepped forward and lowered its head so I could pat it on the snout.

"Good girl," I smiled. I hurried over to where Hexe was regathering himself from Gaza's attack. He seemed slightly dazed, but no worse for wear. "Are you hurt?" I asked.

"I'm going to be feeling this the next day—assuming there is one—but I'm okay," he said. "But we've got to get my father to Golgotham General."

Suddenly Illuminata and Canterbury were with us, their battle armor spattered in blood and their flanks covered in lather. Illuminata set aside her mace as she knelt to gather the wounded Horn into her pale arms. "Leave it to me," the centauride said. "I'll get him there. I used to be an ambulance driver before I was assigned to your mother." With that, she wheeled about and galloped off through the smoke and clash of battle in the direction of the exit.

Once he had seen his father safely away, Hexe turned

and pulled me to him, kissing me as if he might never kiss me again, and then delivered a far gentler kiss to the top of his son's head. As I looked into their golden depths and saw the resolve burning deep with them, I realized, no matter what anyone said, that Hexe truly had his father's eyes.

"Get 'em out of here, Canterbury."

Before I realized what was happening, the centaur had snatched me up in his arms and was galloping for daylight as if it was the final leg of the Kentucky Derby.

"Let me go!" I shouted. "Put me down right this minute!"

"Hexe is right," Canterbury replied. "It's too dangerous here for both you and the baby."

"But I don't want to leave him!" I wailed. "I *can't* leave him!"

"You don't have to," he reminded me. "Part of you is still on the battlefield."

Even as the centaur spoke the words, I opened my mind as far as it could go, reaching out to that fragment of myself that dwelt within my creation. As I felt something like a low-voltage shock run up my spine and lodge itself in the back of my head, I wondered, for a split second, if I did succeed in possessing the clockwork dragon, whether I'd be able to return to my body just as easily.

Before I could rethink my decision, I found myself staring out of a pair of unblinking eyes from an unaccustomed height. Although I could see and hear, my other senses did not seem to exist at all. It was as if I was drifting in a sensory deprivation tank, watching a video game through a virtual reality helmet wired for sound.

To my surprise, Boss Marz was still alive, although perhaps not for long. He had managed to crawl to Erys, who stared down at the Maladanti writhing at her feet with unalloyed disgust.

"You disappoint me, Marz," Erys said as she prestidigitated another dagger from thin air. "Honestly, I got better results from the homunculi than from you and your men. I guess it's true that if you want something done right, you better do it yourself." With that, she bent down and grabbed Syra by her hair, yanking her into a sitting position so that the blood from her severed jugular would squirt into a brass cuspidor. But as she put the knife edge to Syra's throat, she was rewarded by a shower of sparks, like those from an arc welder. Erys cursed and quickly let go of Syra in order to slap at the tiny mouths of fire clinging to her clothes.

"Leave my mother alone," Hexe said, placing himself between Syra and his uncle, his left hand held before him, fingers bent in the mirror-reverse of the traditional defensive pattern of Right Hand magic.

"How could you even *do* that?" Erys yelped. "You don't even *have* a right hand anymore!"

"But I still have my *left* one," Hexe replied. "Right hand, left hand—it doesn't matter whether I heal or harm, protect or destroy; the magic isn't in my hands. It's in my heart."

"Let's just see about that, shall we?" Erys snarled as she slung a fireball at Hexe's head.

Hexe returned the volley so fast, Erys had to lunge out of the way to avoid ending up like Boss Marz. The ball of hellfire struck the back wall of the warehouse, splashing like napalm, and instantly set it on fire.

As Hexe turned to check on his mother, Esau's familiar attacked from above, beating at him with a punishing fifteen foot wingspan and clawing at his head with a slashing beak and razor-sharp talons. Blood from lacerations to his scalp poured down into Hexe's eyes, momentarily blinding him. He dropped to his knees, trying his best to cover his head and the back of his neck from the vicious attack as Edgar repeatedly dive-bombed him, drawing blood from his exposed back with his talons.

Suddenly, with a mighty roar, Scratch, red of saber-tooth and claw, came zooming out of nowhere, striking Edgar in midair. The hell-bird and the hell-cat locked talons, twirling about like a living bolo, before crashing to the floor of the warehouse. Being a cat, Scratch landed on his feet—but Edgar was not as lucky. The demon squawked in panic as it tried to hop away from its foe, grounded by a broken wing. Just as Scratch pounced, the familiar disincorporated, surrendering the field in a cloud of brimstone.

"Yeah, that's right; you *better* run, chicken," Scratch sniffed.

Meanwhile, Hexe was doing his best to try to revive his mother and get her back on her feet. "Mom—Mom, snap out of it!" he pleaded.

Lady Syra's eyelids suddenly fluttered open, and she

smiled weakly upon seeing her son kneeling over her. "Tate and the baby—are they—?"

"Yes, they're safe," Hexe replied. "But we've got to get you out of here!"

"Hexe—watch out!" Syra cried, her eyes wide with alarm.

Before Hexe could react to the warning, Erys grabbed him from behind, jerking his head back by the hair to expose his jugular.

"Mom—run!" Hexe yelled, as he grappled with Erys. "Get out of here!"

But just as Erys pressed the blade of the dagger to Hexe's throat, a strange look crossed her borrowed face and she jerked her head first one way, then another, as if listening to someone calling her name.

"Who are you?" she snapped. "What are you doing?"

As if in reply, the knife fell from Erys' hand, allowing Hexe to quickly scuttle free of her grasp. Her face abruptly went slack and a hollow, distant voice issued from her gaping mouth. *"I've come to reclaim what's mine, my love."*

"No! Leave me be!" Erys said, her face returning to its usual, intense expression, like a rubber band snapping back into place.

"Enough is enough, husband."

"But I've done all this for you, Nina!" Erys protested, sounding more like a petulant child than a dark wizard bent on the destruction of mankind and the harrowing of worlds. *"This* is your revenge!"

"Do not place this abomination on me! My Esau would never do such things in the name of love! You are not the man I married—you are a demon in all but name!"

Erys' face began to contort, the muscles flexing like snakes locked in mortal combat. Then her features abruptly relaxed and Hexe found himself looking not at Erys, but Nina. Although the features were identical, there was now a kindness and warmth, mixed with a profound sadness, which had not been there before—or, rather, had not been there for a long, long time.

"Do it now, while I have control," Nina said urgently. "Do what only a strong Right Hand can do: exorcise him!"

Without hesitation, Hexe raised his left hand, chanting the

rite of purification as he moved his fingers into the mirror-reverse configurations used to drive forth demons. A burst of white light shot from his palm and into Nina's body, lighting her from within like a paper lantern, chasing out a cloud of wispy black smoke that buzzed like a nest of hornets.

"You've thrown him out," Nina said with a weary smile. "Now you must lock the door. Kill this body before he returns."

"No," Lady Syra said, pushing her son aside as she got up off the floor. "This falls to me. Just as it was up to Lord Bexe to end his brother's threat, Esau is mine to put down." And with that she drove the sacrificial dagger into her sister-in-law's heart.

Nina took a step back, wavering like a dandelion caught in a stiff breeze, crimson rapidly spreading from the knife sticking in her chest. "Thank you, Syra," she said with a beatific smile.

"I'm sorry, Nina," Lady Syra whispered tearfully.

"Why?" the ghost replied. "I've been dead for decades."

As Nina's truly lifeless body dropped to the floor, there was a horrific howling noise from the direction of the portal. Hexe and Syra turned to see Esau—once more unified with his corporeal form—standing atop the bier carried by his monstrous servants, his face contorted in fury. But as they watched, Esau's shriek of outrage became first a scream of protest, then anguish, as the legions of the damned that had, moments before, been eager to carry him to power, turned on him at once, dragging him down from his lofty perch, clutching and gouging at his flesh as if to tear him apart with their bare claws. And while in the Infernal Realm there is no unconsciousness, or sleep, or any means of alleviating pain, and neither is there death, there *are* consequences for making promises you cannot keep. Esau was still screaming as the portal closed.

Thanks to the reckless use of hellfire in an enclosed space, not only did the warehouse catch fire, so did the rest of the pier. While most of the Golgotham Army escaped the inferno, the same could not be said for the Maladanti, most of whom had either perished in the battle or simply refused to admit defeat and vacate the Stronghold.

Among the last to leave the burning building were Hexe and Lady Syra, who exited in style on the back of the clockwork dragon. As the Witch Queen and her Heir Apparent approached what remained of the gates to the pier on their mechanical mount, the crowd of onlookers who had been drawn from their nearby homes by the fire gasped in amazement. It was the first time in over a thousand years that members of the Royal Family had been seen astride anything that resembled a dragon.

I experienced a weird jolt as I saw myself through my creation's eyes, perched on Canterbury's back, my child still cradled in my arms. Then suddenly I was back in my own body. I quickly dismounted and hurried to greet Hexe as he and his mother climbed down from the clockwork dragon.

"Praise Arum you're safe!" Hexe said, throwing his arms about us. "What about my father?"

"Illuminata took him to Golgotham General," Seamus replied.

"Your father's been hurt?" Syra gasped.

"Not to hear *him* tell it!" Seamus said with a laugh. "You'd think takin' a knife to the chest was nothin'! He's a stubborn cuss, your da, but a brave one. He's just the kind of man I'll need, once I'm mayor."

"What about casualties?" Hexe asked.

"The ferrymen to the necropolis will be busy," Kidron replied solemnly. "But we gave better than we got. Luckily, once Marz and Gaza went down, most of the Maladanti broke rank and deserted the battlefield."

"Where's Scratch?" I asked, searching the crowd of exhausted warriors. "He's not still trapped in there, is he?"

"It'll take more than a burning building to slow *me* down," a voice said from above. I looked up and saw Scratch, still in his hell-cat aspect, coming in for a landing. "Sorry I took so long, but I wanted to bring you a present," the familiar said, spitting out Boss Marz's beringed left hand.

Chapter 34

"Stop fussing over me, woman. I'm fine," Horn grumbled as Lady Syra rearranged his pillows for the tenth time.

"You are *not* fine! You were stabbed in the chest!" she reminded him.

"That was a couple hours ago," he said with a dismissive shrug. "The psychic surgeons patched me up—they said I should be good to go come tomorrow morning."

"Go where?" Syra smiled as she leaned in to kiss him. "Your place or mine?"

"I'm glad to see you're both feeling better," Hexe said as we entered the room.

"How long were you two standing there?" Syra asked.

"Long enough," I replied with a laugh.

"I know you don't like having a lot of people hanging around while you're recovering, but we thought you might make an exception this time," Hexe smiled.

"You know I *always* make an exception for family, son," Horn replied.

"I'm glad to hear that," Hexe said, stepping aside to reveal Hana and Torn.

Horn's jaw dropped in amazement. "Mama? Papa?" he whispered.

"My boy! My brave, brave boy!" Hana wept as she hurried to throw her arms about her wounded son.

Torn moved to join his wife at their son's bedside. Although he was working hard to maintain his reserve, I could see tears shining in the old man's eyes. "Your son told us how you fought to protect Lady Syra and the Royal Family. You have done our ancestors proud."

Horn turned to look at Hexe. "How did you know—?"

"It's a long story," Hexe replied with a rueful smile. "And one I'm not too proud of. I'm just grateful they were willing to overlook my shortcomings as a host."

"You have nothing to be ashamed of, dear," Hana assured him. "Tate told us how that awful uncle of yours was controlling you the whole time."

"I never cared for Master Esau," Torn said sourly. "He was always such an imperious snot, even as a boy. No offense, Your Majesty."

"If that's the worst you can say about my brother, you're doing far better than I can right now," Syra said dryly.

Once visiting hours were over, Hexe and I returned Torn and Hana to their apartment in Fetlock Mews. As we bid them good night, Canterbury popped his head out of his shop next door. "Good—I was hoping I would catch you two," he said, motioning for us to come inside. "I take it your father is making a full recovery?"

"It's going to take more than a knife to the chest to slow him down," Hexe said with an admiring laugh.

"Glad to hear it. And how is our young friend, here?" the centaur asked, nodding to the baby dozing in the sling dangling from my shoulder.

"He seems no worse for the wear, now that he's been properly fed and changed," I replied.

"I'm even gladder to hear that," Canterbury said. "Well, the reason I wanted to catch you is that I have something I wish to give you. Call it a baby shower present, if you wish." The centaur clopped over to his workbench and picked up a long cardboard tube, the type used to store blueprints. "Here," he said, handing it to me, "I want you to have this. It contains schematics and blueprints for various clockwork limbs, including a right hand."

"Where did you get these?" I frowned. "They're not Esau's work, are they?"

"Those aren't his designs," Canterbury replied with a shake of his mane. "They were created by his mentor, Dr. Tork."

"The former Royal Surgeon?" Hexe raised an eyebrow in surprise. "How did you come by them?"

"Because Dr. Tork was my father," the centaur replied matter-of-factly.

"Canterbury, I can't accept these—!" I said, handing him back the tube. "These are heirlooms."

"No, I insist," he said firmly. "I am a mule, which means I must choose my own heirs, not make them. And I have chosen you, Tate, to inherit my father's work. Besides, with your talent, Hexe's knowledge as a healer, and my metal magic, I believe we could produce prostheses for both the human and Kymeran market that would make Esau's designs look like windup toys."

From where we sat inside the limo, it looked like just another middle-class suburban Long Island home. One of the next-door neighbors was mowing his lawn with a rider mower, occasionally butting up against the hedge that separated the properties.

I glanced over at Hexe, who was seated next to me in the backseat. The limo, along with the driver, belonged to my parents, who had lent both to us in exchange for an afternoon of spoiling the baby. "Are you nervous?" I asked.

"Just a little bit," he admitted as he pulled the purple kid glove over his gleaming metal right hand. "No point in putting this off any longer—it's showtime!"

The neighbor on the rider mower did a double take as we exited the limo, and plowed right into the hedge. Judging from his reaction, Kymerans on house calls were not a day-to-day event.

Hexe rang the doorbell, which was answered by a middle-aged man in dad pants. He raised his eyebrows upon seeing Hexe's purple hair and golden eyes, but did not close the door.

"Excuse me, Mr. Lattimer," Hexe asked politely. "Is Ashley home?"

"Come inside," Ashley's dad sighed, stepping aside so we could enter. "Sweetie!" he called out. "Someone's here to see you!"

As we stepped into the living room, I spotted a framed photo sitting on the mantelpiece that showed an attractive fifty-year-old woman, wearing a Homecoming Queen's tiara and corsage, standing next to a gawky seventeen-year-old boy in a rented tux. Both were smiling at the camera.

There was the sound of hurrying feet, and a second later the same fifty-year-old woman, dressed in Aéropostale jeans and a top from Forever 21, came running down the stairs from the second floor. "Who is it, Dad—is it Justin?" She froze upon seeing her visitors, then grinned ear to ear, revealing her braces. "Mr. and Mrs. Hexe!"

"Hello, Ashley," Hexe smiled as he took the brass clock from his coat pocket. "Are you ready to turn back time?"

"It looks like FAO Schwarz exploded in here," I said, staring in amazement at the nursery that had once been my bedroom. "Was he any trouble?"

"Oh, no. He was a perfect little angel. Weren't you, sweetheart?" my mother cooed. "By the way—what are you going to name him? You know, your father and I were hoping you would continue the Eresby family tradition. . . ."

"You want us to name him Timothy?" I frowned.

"Well, you've got to name him *something*—we can't keep calling him 'the baby.' That's going to sound funny once he starts school."

"Well, Hexe and I have been kicking around a few ideas," I admitted. "But his family has their own traditions, and they go back a *lot* farther than the Eresbies. . . ." I trailed off as I saw the look of dismay on my mother's face, and then sighed in resignation. "But we'll definitely take it into consideration."

Hexe and my father were talking over scotch and sodas in the Grand Salon. As I entered, I saw that Hexe was allowing him to examine his new right hand.

"There you are, Princess!" My father smiled. "Hexe was just showing off the prosthesis you crafted for him. I must say, I am extremely impressed! I have never seen anything like this before in my life! It's not just functional, but elegant as well. It's a true work of art."

"I guess my art degree wasn't such a waste of time, after all."

"I wouldn't go so far as to say *that*." My mother sniffed, reminding me, potion or no potion, some things never change.

"Mom, Dad," I said, clearing my throat. "I appreciate you reinstating my trust fund. I know that things have not been that great between us in the past—but I want to change that. You are right—I *have* been shirking my responsibilities to the family business. Well—I'm finally ready to take my place on the board of directors. In fact, I actually have a long-range real estate investment and development plan I would like to submit at the next meeting," I explained as I took a manila envelope out of my purse.

My father opened the envelope and studied its contents for a long moment, and then looked at me for another long moment, as if truly seeing me as an adult for the first time. "This is quite an ambitious undertaking. Are you sure you're ready to tackle something like this?"

"I've never been readier in my life," I assured him.

"Very well; I'm prepared to back you on this," he said, "but it's going to cost you."

"Just name it," I replied.

"Exactly." My father smiled.

"Okay, fellas!" I said into my smartphone. "Let 'er rip!"

"You're the landlady!" Octavia replied.

A couple of seconds later, the huge banner advertising Golgotham Vue was cut free from its moorings at the top of the apartment building and fluttered to the ground like a surrendered flag, allowing sunlight to strike the face of the building unimpeded for the first time in months.

As one of my ancestors was fond of saying, it takes money to fight money. And few people have as much money as the Eresbies. Not even Ronnie Chess, who, upon reading the latest poll numbers for Mayor Lash's reelection, decided to divest himself of his Golgotham properties. Oh, he made a tidy little profit on the deal, of course—his type always do—but nowhere near the killing he had hoped for.

The first order of business was changing the name of the building back to Machen Arms. The second was inviting back all the evicted residents, and reinstating their old leases. Octavia had already moved back in, but, as it turned out, Torn and Hana preferred living in Fetlock Mews, as it gave them the opportunity to serve as day care for their great-grandson while I was at work. Like Chess, I'm also interested in renting to humans looking to live in Golgotham—just not investment bankers, financial officers, and corporate lawyers. If the first wave of writers, visual artists, dancers, and musicians work out, then I'll convert another property I have an eye on into genuine artists' lofts, split equally between human and nonhuman creatives.

There's more than one way to have your world destroyed, and you certainly don't need to open a portal to the Infernal Region to create hell on earth. All it takes is for those who can make a difference to do nothing. And after all I and my family have gone through to protect these few city blocks, and all the blood that was shed to keep it and those who call it home safe, I'll be damned if I'm going to stand by and let a bunch of greedy real estate developers do what hordes of demons could not.

"Sorry I missed the big unveiling," Hexe said as he entered the courtyard. He was carrying our three-month-old son in a Snugli strapped to his chest and walking Beanie at the same time. "But someone needed a last-minute diaper change."

"There's my boys!" I laughed, kissing two and petting one. "So—is Operation: Date Night a go?"

"Ashley will be at the house by six o'clock to babysit," Hexe replied. "I thought we would start off with drinks at the Calf, then cab over to Lorelei's for dinner and a show, and then top it off by going dancing at the Golden Bough."

"Sounds positively delightful!" I smiled. "What do *you* think, Tymm?" My son and namesake laughed uproariously in response, because Beanie was licking his feet.

I keep thinking about what Mr. Manto said about it being the dawn of a new world. Sometimes I wish I could still turn to him for counsel, but he and Clarence live in Fiji now. Yeah, that's right. Clarence and Mr. Manto are shacked up. Talk about a September-February romance. Clarence hired Chorea's husband, Faro the Mover, to teleport them halfway around the world, so he didn't worry about travel sickness. At least Clarence can finally strut his Hawaiian shirts. I still believe Mr. Manto's prophecy was a true one. It's already a new era for Golgotham now that it's truly rid of the Maladanti once and for all and it's elected its first non-Kymeran mayor, not to mention the emergence of a new class of human artisan-wizards such as myself and Bartho. And then there's the small matter of the first half-human member of the Royal Family to take into account. Of course, change is never easy, and I don't doubt there will be plenty of opposition from both Kymeran and human society. But all that truly matters to me is that the Golgotham that emerges will be better, not worse, than the one I have come to love.

And as for my son, Tymm, he may never be able to work magic the way his ancestors did—but that doesn't matter to me or his father. That's because we're planning to raise him to be an artist, not a warlock.

My mother will be thrilled.

Golgotham Glossary

Abdabs: The frights/terrors; any number of creatures known for harassing/frightening humans. Used in Kymeran slang to connote annoyance, as in "Bloody abdabs!"

Ambi: Someone who practices both Right and Left Hand disciplines.

Artifex, pl. Artificēs: A type of Kymeran wizard, usually found within the Crafter class, who specialized in the domestication and "sculpting" of the amoebalike symbiotic organism known as living glass. Most artificēs died during the drowning of Kymera, along with the living glass they tended. The last known artifex was Lady Ursa, consort to Lord Arum, who managed to save the last sample of living glass in the world. There has not been another artifex born in ten thousand years.

Bastet: A shape-shifting race taking the form of different big cats, such as tiger, lion, and panther. Also known as the Children of Bast.

Berskir: A race of shape-shifters taking the form of various species of bear, such as grizzly, black bears, and polar bears.

Centauride: A female centaur; also known as a centauress.

Charmer: A wizard who creates charms for a living.

Chuff/Chuffing/Chuffed: Euphemism for sexual intercourse.

Come Hither: A spell that calls a man or woman against his or her will, often during sleep or in an altered state of consciousness. Because of this, the subjects of Come Hithers rarely have any memory of what happened to them once the spell is lifted. This spell is a favorite of date rapists and stalkers.

Client: Humans who pay to consult Kymeran witches and warlocks for any number of reasons.

Croggy: A subordinate or acolyte.

Crossed: Also known as cursed, afflicted, hexed, jinxed.

Dexter/Dexie: Someone who practices Right Hand magic, such as lifting curses and curing ailments. Right Hand magic is protective/defensive, as opposed to Left Hand magic, which is malicious/offensive.

Dowser: A psychic who specializes in finding lost things or locating fresh water.

Dunderwhelp: A stupid or unwanted child.

Dysmorphophilia: An inflicted preference for ugly sexual partners. A favorite curse among ex-wives whose former husbands have dumped them for a younger woman. Considered a nuisance curse.

Fecker: A contemptible person.

Glad Eye: The opposite of the Evil Eye. A charm that casts good fortune and success, especially in love and business.

Hamadryad: A shy, seldom-seen nature-spirit who lives inside one particular tree, such as an oak, birch, ash, or sycamore. Because of the urban nature of New York City, only a handful of hamadryads live in Golgotham.

Hamble: To cripple an animal, supernatural or not, by cutting out the balls of its feet for the purpose of fighting. This mutilation guarantees that the animal cannot physically back down from a fight because it lacks the ability to move backward without falling.

Hambler: One who specializes in crippling animals for the fighting pit.

Heavy Lifter: A well-regarded banisher; one who can lift malignant curses.

Hedger: Short for "hedgewitch" or "hedge doctor"; a wizard specializing in herbal treatments of various illnesses.

Huldra: Female member of the huldrefolk, one of the supernatural races living in Golgotham. They resemble beautiful young women, except for the cow tails growing from the base of their spines. The males of their kind, known as huldu, appear as handsome men, except for the tails of bulls growing from the base of their spines.

Inflicted: The state of having an illness or spate of misfortune supernatural in origin.

Inflictions: A number of spiteful/socially embarrassing medical illnesses and physical conditions that are the result of supernatural agents. These curses mimic genuine physical and mental illnesses, such as cancer or schizophrenia, and require a diagnosis by a Kymeran healer. If the illness is natural in origin, the client is referred to a doctor. Also referred to as afflictions.

Ipotane: One of the supernatural races found in Golgotham. Humans from the waist up, they are horses from the waist down. Unlike centaurs, they have only two legs. They are often mistaken for satyrs, much to their disgust.

Juggler: Someone who is known as a competent practitioner of both Right and Left Hand magic.

Lifter: A witch or warlock who specializes in lifting curses.

Ligature: Magical binding using knotted cords that prevents someone from physically doing something.

Maenads: One of the supernatural races living in Golgotham. Maenads are female followers of Dionysius, the Greek god of wine. They go into ecstatic frenzies during which they lose all self-control and engage in sexual orgies, ritualistically hunt down wild animals (and occasionally men and children), tear them to pieces, and devour the raw flesh.

Misanthrope: An antihuman bigot.

Norlock: A Kymeran incapable of magic due to being born with deformed hands or missing fingers. Norlocks are usually of mixed parentage, although some have been born to full-blooded Kymeran parents. It is viewed as a rare, but serious birth defect.

Munted: Extremely drunk or otherwise intoxicated.

Nump: A fool. A derogatory racial slur directed at humans.

Peddler: Short for "charm peddler"—a wizard who specializes in selling charmed objects for commercial gain.

PTU: Short for Paranormal Threat Unit, a separate branch of the NYPD in charge of policing Golgotham and responding to paranormal/supernatural events throughout the triborough area.

Pusher: Short for "potion pusher"—a wizard who specializes in selling love potions, untraceable poisons, etc., for commercial gain.

Satyr: One of the supernatural races living in Golgotham. Satyrs are humans from the waist up; goats from the waist down. They also sport horns on their heads. They are notorious for being prone to gambling, drinking, and kidnapping beautiful women. Female satyrs are called fauns.

Talent: A natural magic ability, applying both to humans and Kymerans.

Twunt: Slang for a paying customer who visits Golgotham's red-light district.

Widdershins: The direction in which a curse must be turned in order to undo it.

The Witchfinders: An elite medieval military group composed of both Christian and Islamic knights and soldiers during the Unholy War. Famous for severing the extra "magic" fingers of Kymerans.

R0172